A Desperate Journey

A Novel By

James E. Haynes
and
Andrew J. Haynes

A Desperate Journey

A Novel By

James E. Haynes
and
Andrew J. Haynes

INKWELL BOOKS
Writing - Publishing - Printing

ISBN: 978-1939625-71-7
Library of Congress Control Number: 2016023765

Published by Inkwell Books
10632 North Scottsdale Road, Unit 695
Scottsdale, AZ 85254

Tel. 480-315-3781
E-mail info@inkwellbooks.com
Website www.inkwellbooks.com

Printed in the United States of America

PROLOGUE

Cumberland Bay, Isla Mas a Tierra
March, 1915

The SMS Dresden, a cruiser of the Kaiserliche Marine, the German Navy, and the only functioning survivor of the South Atlantic Battle Group, lay anchored in the waters of the tiny island of Mas a Tierra, 373 miles west of Valparaiso, Chile. Chile was neutral in the war, and Mas a Tierra was Chilean territory. The Dresden had led the British Navy on a wild chase of epic proportions since it had slipped away when the naval battle at the Falklands Islands had become a British rout the previous December.

Taking the lead from his very bright young intelligence officer, the Dresden's captain had used stealth, deception and cunning to elude the British and slip around the tip of South America and up the west coast of Chile, seeking out that neutral haven. However, on the clear, bitterly cold morning of March 14, the British cruiser HMS Glasgow rounded a point and saw its nemesis sitting placidly in perfectly still waters, silhouetted nicely against the cliffs that rose behind it.

The Glasgow's captain, ignoring Chile's neutrality, ordered fire to be brought upon the Dresden. As he would later say, "We'll take care of business now and let the diplomats sort out the niceties later." The Dresden returned fire ineffectually, because being anchored in battle puts a ship at quite a serious disadvantage.

The Dresden's captain, recognizing the reality of the situation, quickly ceased fire and raised the parley flag. Even before the parley flag could be hoisted, a launch was being lowered with the ship's intelligence officer aboard. "Just buy us enough time, Willi," the captain hollered to him as the launch started down to the water.

In the end, young Willi's short and unproductive-appearing trip to the Glasgow proved indeed quite productive. It gave the Dresden's crew time to open ten sea cocks and to lay charges in its forward magazines. Meanwhile, an appeal to the Chilean authorities had resulted in an agreement to accept the German ship's crew for internment. As the crew motored away from the ship and toward the island, an enormous explosion rocked the Dresden and within minutes she sank. It was the policy of the Kaiserliche Marine never to surrender a ship and the Dresden's crew had adhered to that policy.

The internment of the Dresden's crew was an informal affair, in the sense that there was nothing like an internment camp to which the men were confined. Once transferred to the mainland by the Chilean authorities, they were housed in a series of hotels, private homes and other appropriate – in the eyes of the Chileans, if not the British – facilities. Young Willi, who had spent the entire three years following his 1911 graduation from the German Naval Academy with the Kaiserliche Marine in Latin America, was fluent in Spanish.

His best friend and the ship's signals officer, who was a year younger than Willi and whose name was Ernst, was adept at languages and was soon fluent in Spanish as well.

Within days, Willi and Ernst became acquainted with a Chilean of German descent named Krause, who used his connections with the local German ex-patriot community to arrange for money and false Chilean passports for the two young men.

Willi and Ernst set out on an improbable journey over the towering Andes toward Argentina, home of an even larger German ex-patriot population. Sometimes on horseback, but more often on foot, over the next eight months the two made their way into Argentina, arriving in Buenos Aires just before Christmas, exhausted and very hungry.

Word of their arrival spread expeditiously and a week later they were contacted by a wealthy, patriotic and influential German-Argentine named von Bulow, whose cousin was the German Ambassador in Rome. Von Bulow used his connections to arrange for new, and better, Chilean identities for the young men.

Several days later, two Chilean cousins named Reed and Raul Rosas – in reality Willi and Ernst – boarded the Dutch steamer Frisia, bound from Buenos Aires to Rotterdam via Plymouth, England. They were ostensibly returning to the Netherlands to take possession of some property left them by a deceased relative. Both men used the weeks at sea mostly with English passengers to study English language, idioms and customs.

Once the two disembarked in the Netherlands, which was neutral in the war, they used their Chilean passports to book a compartment on a train to Zurich. From there, they made their way across the border into Germany.

On their arrival in Berlin, they were received at naval headquarters as heroes, decorated and promoted.

CHAPTER 1

July, 1941
Near Kure, Japan

The little village – hardly big enough to have a name - was Rudolf von Althorp's favorite place in Japan. At least his favorite getaway place, a place to which he retired on those weekends when he could escape his duties as Commercial Attaché at the Embassy of the German Reich in Tokyo. That wasn't very often, so he savored every opportunity to drive there, to stay in the same shabby little hotel, to fish off the rocks or occasionally to hire an ancient little boat to take him out to deeper waters.

And to enjoy the company of one of the two geishas who had rooms almost adjacent to the hotel. He thought that calling themselves geishas was a bit of a stretch, considering the locale, but they were young and vastly different in so many ways from German women and he found the novelty of them quite satisfying.

Moreover, at a bit over six feet tall, with a trim, muscular body, startling blue eyes and wavy dark blonde hair, he was a man the geishas found quite satisfying, being so different in so many ways from Japanese men.

Von Althorp had been assigned to Tokyo for almost two years. This was longer than many such assignments. But with the signing of the Tripartite Pact that bound the Fatherland with Japan and Italy, Joachim von Ribbentrop, the Reich's Foreign Minister, had determined that the more seasoned the diplomats in the two allied countries, the better protected Germany would be. Von Ribbentrop, like every senior German official from the Führer on down – and for that matter, virtually every citizen of the Thousand-Year Reich – looked down on and distrusted the Japanese and Italians, in mostly that order.

The diplomatic assignment policy was actually, in some cases, the joint decision of von Ribbentrop and Admiral Wilhelm Canaris, director of the Abwehr, the largest and by far the most efficient intelligence agency on the planet. Canaris' involvement was necessary because the Abwehr had key spies – or spymasters – buried in every German embassy in the world, usually disguised as commercial or cultural attaches. Like Rudolf von Althorp.

Von Althorp, in fact, enjoyed a bond with Canaris that was available to almost nobody else in the Abwehr.

His Father, Ernst von Althorp, a tall and aristocratic-appearing man with dark brown hair and an easy smile, had been the signals officer on the cruiser KMS Dresden during the Great War. Canaris, in contrast, was short to the point of diminutive with very fair hair, and had been the ship's intelligence officer as a young lieutenant. The obvious need for an intelligence officer to rely on a signals officer to send and receive coded and very sensitive messages almost daily created between the two men a shared purpose and led to a strong friendship forged of mutual respect and absolute, unquestioning trust.

After the Dresden was cornered in Cumberland Bay and scuttled, the two set off on their daring and still-talked-about escape to Argentina, then England, the Netherlands, and finally back to Germany. This shared experience, remarkable as it was, forged a bond that could not be broken. Completely unalike physically, Wilhelm Canaris and Ernst von Althorp were almost like twins in their thinking.

At about the same time the two men were escaping and making their way back to Germany, an infantry corporal by the name of Adolf Hitler, who was originally from Austria before moving with his mother to Bavaria, was compiling an impressive record of accomplishment as a runner on the battlefields of France. He was known to most in his unit as someone so lacking in the most basic social skills that serving as a runner was the perfect – perhaps the only – appropriate assignment for him.

The elder von Althorp, putting his Spanish language skills to good use, was now out of the Navy and was the Reich's Ambassador to Mexico. Canaris had encouraged his appointment to that post, fearing that his Führer, megalomaniac that he was, would one day do something that would force the hand of the United States and bring it into the war. Canaris dreaded that eventuality and was determined to do what he could to see that it did not happen.

But if it did, Mexico – with its close proximity to the United States – would be an excellent place to have an ambassador who knew and understood the intelligence business. And someone whom Canaris trusted completely. Von Ribbentrop, who did not consider Mexico to be a particularly important post, readily agreed to Canaris' appeal and approved von Althorp's posting.

When Canaris and the senior von Althorp had arrived back in Germany in 1916, Canaris had immediately been invited to a long weekend at von Althorp's estate outside Karlsruhe, just northwest of Stuttgart. On a subsequent visit after the war in 1919, he met 7-year-old Rudi von Althorp.

Young Rudi, who worshiped his father, listened attentively and inquired insistently about the war in general, about Chile and Argentina and England, about naval tactics and about what a signals officer and an intelligence officer do on a ship of war. In encounters over the next several years, it became increasingly apparent to Canaris that young von Althorp had all the makings of a good intelligence officer – a bright, inquisitive mind, willing to ask questions - and when he became director of the Abwehr, he called the von Althorp estate to bring the young man into his organization.

Better to get him into the diplomatic service, he thought, than to wait and risk the Army drafting him. Young Rudi, then in his mid-20s, had not married. While it was clear to Canaris he was not one of those men who preferred the company of other men, he did not seem to be in any hurry to alter his marital status. That made him an even better prospect for the role Canaris had in mind for him.

When the signs began appearing that pointed to bringing Germany into alliance with Japan, Canaris immediately had Rudi pulled out of his posting at the Reich's Embassy in Washington, D.C. and sent to the Foreign Ministry's language school to learn Japanese, which Rudi accomplished in less than thirty days. Canaris considered the Japanese to be devious and bloodthirsty little devils who could be trusted not at all. Much like he privately thought of the Chancellor of the Thousand-Year Reich. Canaris regarded Hitler to be fatally-flawed as a man, as a national leader and especially as a military strategist.

Hitler, Canaris had long before concluded, lacked any sort of moral principle and the concept of battlefield honor was an alien concept to him. Men who thought like Canaris were not uncommon in the German High Command or in parts of the diplomatic corps. Ernst von Althorp was one of those.

Of course, those who shared such views did so very carefully and very privately. Almost everyone in their circles knew of fellow officers, diplomats or prominent citizens who had disappeared after voicing doubts about the wisdom of one or more of their Führer's many wise decisions. And they knew that such disappearances were almost certainly preceded by an arrest, a brief prison stay, a one-hour trial and a firing squad.

Thoughts of the ultimate fate of Germany swirled in the head of Rudi von Althorp that July day as he sat on a rock outcropping on the western shoreline of the little harbor south of Kure. It seemed against the laws of nature to think that a little country like Germany could conquer the world against the likes of England, France, now Russia and possibly, one day soon, the United States. Even with the help of two other small countries like Italy and Japan. All together, they possessed virtually no natural resources, produced little oil, and had to import most of the steel and other metals they needed. It seemed so illogical.

He knew his patron and boss, the Admiral, shared some, perhaps not all, of his skepticism. But he knew Canaris agreed completely, and adamantly, that the United States must never be provoked into entering the war. "The only thing that gives us any chance in a war," he had heard the Admiral say over more than one meal, "is that the United States is paralyzed by isolationism and mixed loyalties."

He also knew, after almost two years in the Reich's Embassy in Washington D.C., the industrial capacity of America. And while working there, he had become all too aware that most of the top-tier Nazis in Hitler's inner circle had never bothered to venture across the ocean to see anything for themselves, but preferred to hold to biased and derogatory opinions, which in most cases badly underestimated the giant democracy. And they systematically ignored reports from the Reich's Embassy that detailed the U.S. industrial capacity.

Canaris had told Rudi and his father that he thought Franklin D. Roosevelt, the U.S. President, badly wanted to enter the war alongside his friend, British Prime Minister Winston Churchill. But even Roosevelt was not powerful enough to overcome the isolationists and the large German-American population in the U.S.

The one thing that could change the stalemate that had Roosevelt boxed was an unprovoked attack by Germany. Now, with the Tripartite Pact, Rudi knew, that fear extended to an unprovoked attack by either Japan or Italy as well.

Suddenly, the peaceful early morning quiet was interrupted by the dull roar of the big piston engines of powerful airplanes. Lots of them. Soon they came into view, high and to his left. Probably twenty, perhaps more of them, silver with the red circle of the Rising Sun on their wings and on the sides of their fuselages. Two of them peeled away from the formation and dove for the water near the entrance to the little harbor, then another two and two more. Soon all of them were heading straight for the waters in front of him.

Rudi was transfixed. Are they coming for me, he wondered? Then, the lead pair banked to their left and the others followed suit in perfect formation, each pair spaced perhaps 100 meters apart. He recognized them, then. They were Nakajima B5N torpedo bombers and they looked like they were armed. But what the hell were torpedo bombers doing practicing in a little harbor like this? He knew from when he had fished from a boat here that the harbor was quite shallow. He could easily reel out enough fishing line to reach the bottom.

The stream of torpedo bombers screamed past where he sat and toward the rocky land mass that formed the closed south end of the little harbor. He could see the crewmen, a few of them seemingly staring right at him, especially some of the rear-facing gunners as they roared past his position. Now Rudi wished he had brought his Leica camera with him. He was immediately aware he was watching something he did not understand but which some instinct told him he needed to observe carefully.

When the formation closed on the rocky barrier, he noticed two large red stripes painted vertically on the rocks. The stripes were about 300 meters apart and the bombers appeared from his position to be flying toward a point halfway between the two stripes. Suddenly, the first two in the formation loosed their torpedoes and climbed steeply, banking sharply to their left, away from the harbor and out over the ocean.

Rudi now had his binoculars to his eyes and saw the line of bubbles that trailed the torpedoes on their path. The following torpedo bombers likewise dropped their missiles and climbed quickly. But there were no explosions, just trails of bubbles that ended at the base of the rocks. And then the Nakajimas were gone as quickly as they had arrived. He had counted 24 of them.

Rudi remained seated for a few minutes while he digested what he had seen. His first conclusion was that the Japanese were testing shallow-water torpedoes. He knew the British had them. They had famously used them at Taranto, a shallow harbor in Italy, but how reliable they were was still being debated in military circles. Next, he concluded that the torpedoes they were using were unarmed but otherwise operational. That made sense. Why call attention to what they were doing by blowing great chunks out of the south end of this harbor and frightening the civilian population?

But what did they need shallow-water torpedoes for? The Pacific Ocean is certainly not shallow. At length, he gathered his fishing gear and hurried back to the hotel to pack and check out. The geishas would have to wait. He needed to get back to his office and try to make sense of this. A niggling feeling told him there was something important about all this.

On the drive back to Tokyo, Rudi thought furiously about this puzzling matter. He had maps and charts of every naval facility in the Pacific, be they Japanese, British, Dutch, Russian, Australian or American. Everything from Dutch Harbor and Vladivostok in the north to Singapore and Sydney in the south; and from Tokyo Bay itself in the western Pacific to San Francisco and San Diego on the west coast of the United States.

Even though he knew that many of the charts – especially those of the distant South Pacific - were incomplete, and in some cases simply wrong, he needed to study them, to try to think through why a naval aviation commander would have his men practicing with shallow-water torpedoes.

Were these little fools actually insane enough to attack the United States or England?

He pressed down on the accelerator and concentrated on driving on the still-not-comfortable left side of the road.

CHAPTER 2

Tokyo
The Next Day

Commercial Attaché Rudi von Althorp stood at his desk in the Embassy of the German Reich in central Tokyo, maps and charts spread around. He started his study with the bases that were closest to Japan. His first thought was Vladivostok, home port of the Russian Pacific Fleet.

Actually, he knew it was now called the SOVIET Pacific Fleet, but he had never gotten used to thinking of them as anything but Russian. In any case, he thought, an attack on its Pacific Fleet would create a valuable diversion of Russian attention from its desperate efforts to throw the German invading armies back from its western front.

But after studying the charts for the port of Vladivostok, he could make no sense of the shallow-water torpedo strategy. Vladivostok was so deep the Japanese could almost send a squadron of submarines all the way into the harbor, if that was their intended target.

Later, Rudi concentrated on Dutch Harbor, a small American base in the Aleutian Islands of Alaska. But that made no sense either, because latest intelligence indicated no bases of sufficient size or other prizes in the Aleutian area to make such an attack on the United States worth the effort, other than as a possible diversion for a more serious attack on other targets more distant from Japan.

By the end of the third day of tedious studying of the maps and charts, he had dismissed Hong Kong, Singapore and all the ports in Australia and New Zealand for one reason or another. Now his focus narrowed to two ports and both were bad news for Germany, he thought.

Both were American bases: Cavite and Pearl Harbor. He studied the charts for both harbors.

The base at Cavite, on the southern edge of Manila Bay in the Philippines, had areas that were rather shallow but not, he thought, so shallow that special torpedoes would be required. But he could not be sure. It was the home port of the rather small and antiquated U.S. Asiatic Fleet, and that held some importance, he concluded, but would not be a primary target if he were the one planning to attack the United States.

Pearl Harbor, in the American Territory of Hawaii, was a different matter altogether. Now the home port of the U.S. Pacific Fleet, which had not too long before been moved from San Diego, he noted that the harbor was barely deep enough to allow the mighty battleships and aircraft carriers based there to enter and exit without running aground. A normal torpedo would bury itself in the mud of the harbor floor long before it had any chance of leveling off and reaching a target.

It must be Pearl Harbor! Rudi was as sure as he could be, but of course he was not an expert in naval and air operations as were many men the Herr Admiral Canaris could call upon. Indeed, the Admiral himself was a master of naval operations. He would alert the Admiral, share his own tentative conclusions, and let Canaris take it from there.

Three minutes later, after a brief bathroom break and a call to the signals section, he was writing out his message to Admiral Wilhelm Canaris in longhand. Once satisfied, he would take the paper down to the communications complex in the basement where it would be encoded and sent via the Abwehr's special Enigma G machine. In this embassy, as in most German embassies around the world, at least one of the senior signals officers was either Abwehr personnel or a man who had been thoroughly vetted by the Abwehr.

When he had called the signals section, von Althorp had ascertained that not only was his friend, Friedrich Pohl at his desk, but Pohl had assured him that he would remain there until his message was composed and ready to be sent. Then, he told his friend, Rudi owed him a few Asahi beers at their favorite bar two blocks away.

Forty minutes after ending his call to Pohl, von Althorp walked into the signals section and to Pohl's small office, closing and locking the door behind him. He handed his friend the handwritten page and said, "This must go immediately." He knew it was almost morning in Berlin and that Canaris would most likely be in his office within the hour, at least if he was in Berlin at the moment. Pohl took the paper, read it through to make sure he understood it, and started coding the message. Once coded, the message would transmit as a series of five-letter blocks.

```
EYES ONLY
THE DIRECTOR
ABWEHR HEADQUARTERS
TIRPITZUFER
BERLIN
PAST WEEKEND OBSERVED 24 NAKAJIMA
TORPEDO BOMBERS PRACTICING SHALLOW
WATER TORPEDO RUNS IN SMALL HARBOR
```

```
SOUTH OF KURE STOP TORPEDOS DROPPED AND
RAN TO QUOTE TARGET UNQUOTE BUT DID
NOT DETONATE STOP QUOTE TARGET UNQUOTE
WAS ROCK FORMATION SOUTH END OF HARBOR
STOP QUOTE TARGET UNQUOTE DEFINED BY
RED STRIPES ON ROCKS STOP SIGNIFICANCE
UNKNOWN BUT BELIEVE ONLY CREDIBLE
SHALLOW WATER TARGETS IN PACIFIC PEARL
HARBOR POSSIBLY CAVITE STOP
        R VON ALTHORP
        COMMERCIAL ATTACHE'
        EMBASSY OF THE GERMAN REICH
        TOKYO JAPAN
        END MESSAGE
```

Pohl took a sip of his first Asahi and asked his friend how the fishing had been last weekend. He would not, Rudi knew, ask anything at all about the message. He was a trusted communications man and a friend but he knew where his boundaries lay. He had already assured Rudi that he would decode and deliver Canaris' reply when it came in. He always personally handled communications between Abwehr headquarters and Rudi.

Friedrich Pohl liked his Tokyo posting and wanted to stay there as long as possible. Like Rudi, he enjoyed the company of geishas, or, more often, young Japanese women who desired to be geishas. He was barely over five feet, six inches tall and had found German girls were not, in general, attracted to short men. But the Japanese girls were used to short men, so his luck had improved markedly in Tokyo.

The Tirpitzufer was the informal name given to a large

granite five-story building in central Berlin, because its address was 76-78 Tirpitzufer. It was adjacent to the headquarters of the High Command of the German Armed Forces, the Oberkommando der Wehrmacht, or OKW. The building housed the headquarters of the Reich Admiralty, of which the Abwehr was nominally a part, given that it came into being as the intelligence arm of the Navy. Now, of course, it was the principle – but certainly not the only – intelligence service of the Thousand Year Reich. It specialized in human intelligence, sabotage and counterintelligence.

At one corner of the fifth floor was the spacious but spartanly-furnished office of Admiral Wilhelm Canaris. The desk was somewhat battered, the bookshelves metal. Along one wall was a Wehrmacht camp cot, which the Admiral used often to catch a nap when going home was out of the question.

Major General Hans Oster was nominally the director of the Abwehr's Section Z, its administrative arm. Oster was responsible for such seemingly-mundane matters as personnel, finance, legal issues and archives. In reality, he was much more: Admiral Canaris' closest friend and advisor in the agency, and one of his departments, ZB, was responsible for foreign reports evaluation. The seeming incongruity of the placement of this role in the Abwehr structure was attributable directly to Canaris' unquestioned trust in Oster. Department ZB was, in fact, a direct pipeline to the Director and could have just as easily been housed in the Director's office.

Oster was sitting in front of Canaris' desk, re-reading the signal from the Tokyo Embassy. A devout Christian and ardent anti-Nazi, Oster was even more convinced – if such were possible – than Canaris that Nazism and Hitler were to be the ruination of Germany if they were not checked soon.

After nearly two years of war in Europe, both men had

been involved in one way or the other in some of the plots among the mostly Prussian and Pomeranian officer corps and other German patriots to remove or overthrow Hitler and the murderous rabble with which he was surrounded. Few of the plots had gone past the talking stage, but even talk was often quite dangerous in Hitler's Germany.

Oster looked up when he had finished reading the signal through a third time. After his first read, he had put the signal in a leather folder and hurried to Canaris' office. "Those lunatic little bastards cannot be serious, Herr Admiral," he said urgently but softly. It was unusual for the religious man to use so strong a profanity.

"It would seem that they may be, Hans," Canaris replied. "As you are well aware, I know young von Althorp quite well and I think we would be wise to take this very seriously. Let us have a look at the maps of the Pacific."

The two men spent almost the entire day poring over very detailed maps of the entire Pacific and over charts of all harbors housing military installations, all the while bent over a well-lighted chart table Canaris kept in a corner of his office.

The Admiral knew that his personal attention being devoted to something as seemingly mundane as a cable from an agent in Japan would raise questions and start talk among the other sections in the Abwehr, but he liked to keep some things – actually many things – very close to the vest. This was clearly a matter that he and Hans Oster would handle privately.

Oster stood upright and massaged the small of his back. "It looks to me, Herr Admiral, like your young protégé has judged this matter quite well," he said. Although they were good friends and colleagues, and he referred to his friend as "Willi" when they were having schnapps or a private dinner, he was enough of a military man that he would not refer to his superior officer by other than his rank in the office or in the company of others.

Likewise, Canaris, who had known Rudolf von Althorp since he was a little boy and would call him "Rudi" in a private setting, would call him by his family name when referring to him in his Abwehr role. Proper military protocol was important – even mandatory - to both men.

Canaris stretched, too, but he was short enough that a prolonged session bent over the chart table bothered him not nearly so much as it did the taller man. "I think you are right, Hans," he replied after several seconds of thought. "I think now we must decide what to do about verifying this information."

"Herr Admiral, we must find a way to thwart this plan, if it is real," Oster said urgently but unnecessarily, for he knew that Canaris agreed. "If the Japanese attack the U.S. fleet, either at Pearl Harbor or in the Philippines, Roosevelt will have found his way to enter the war against all of the Axis nations, not just Japan. And he is not of the temperament to negotiate a fair peace with us, I do not think, with or without our beloved Bavarian corporal in power. Germany will certainly be doomed."

The Admiral nodded quietly, then asked, "But how, Hans? Who can stop it? To whom do we turn over this valuable information?"

Canaris and Oster spent the rest of the evening considering their alternatives. They knew that, for Rudi's suspicions to be taken seriously, it would be important to have at least one – ideally two or more – independent verifications. But they did not think they had much time to try to get them. While they thought about how to verify the suspicion, they settled on the obvious choice of to whom to get the information, hopefully after verification by another source: the Foreign Minister, Joachim von Ribbentrop.

His diplomatic corps could most quickly deal with the matter. Hitler himself would either dither or be completely disinterested. He was preoccupied with Russia and would think the flexing of Japanese muscle might well turn the Soviets' attention to the east and split their forces, now totally engaged against the Germans.

For two weeks, Canaris and Oster talked to or exchanged signals with every German and Italian asset they could think of who might have even vague suspicions about Japanese plans beyond Manchuria, China and French Indo-China. Canaris checked with several good friends in Spain, officially neutral but a country Canaris knew well from the days of German support of Generalissimo Francisco Franco's Nationalist revolution. He visited there often.

Nothing developed. Nobody seemed to have anything more than speculation about Japan's Pacific ambitions. Contacts, surreptitious and otherwise, were made with Japanese military attaches at embassies all over Europe, with Japanese businessmen who were in Europe buying or selling and with academics who had studied Japanese military history. Still, nothing concrete developed. The Japanese were extremely secretive, and it seemed there was no communication between its military and its diplomatic corps.

Finally, three full weeks after receiving Rudi von Althorp's signal, Canaris was sitting in front of von Ribbentrop' desk. The Foreign Minister read the signal through twice, then looked up with a blank expression.

"Is this all, Herr Admiral?" he asked.

"I am not sure I understand the Herr Foreign Minister's question," Canaris said.

"Has this been confirmed?" von Ribbentrop asked

sharply. "You know that we must have this verified by other sources. If the Japanese are planning such an attack, surely someone else has learned something about it."

"Herr Foreign Minister, my staff and I have evaluated all possible targets in the Pacific and have concluded that Herr von Althorp's conclusion is correct," Canaris stated with some force. "We must do whatever can be done to convince the Japanese that their intentions are ill-timed and misguided. We do not need the United States in the war, at least until the Soviets are brought to heel." He added the last so he would not appear defeatist, which in Nazi Germany was considered to be in roughly the same category as being a coward or an outright traitor.

Von Ribbentrop glowered at Canaris. He disliked being told what his foreign policy ought to be. At least, not by anyone other than the Führer. "My dear Admiral," he intoned as if he were attempting to explain a difficult mathematics problem to a slow student, "the Führer has made his position clear to me on a number of occasions. The Pacific is to be Japan's sphere of interest. The U.S. is the occupying force in Hawaii and in the Philippines. Those archipelagos are no more a part of the United States than India is a part of England. They are colonial conquests, no more. They are more naturally a part of a Japanese-East Asia economic unit than of the United States."

He got up from his desk and walked over to an antique liquor cabinet in the corner of his office and poured himself a drink. When he glanced back at Canaris with an inquiring look, the Admiral shook his head and mouthed a "no-thank-you." Von Ribbentrop continued as he returned to his desk, "The Führer does not wish to interfere with the Japanese in the Pacific. But I am sure he would agree that it is in our best interests to know as much as we can about Japanese intentions before the fact. I suggest that you signal your observant man in my Embassy to keep his eyes open and report any additional information he comes across at once. And keep trying to get independent verification."

He remained standing, signaling that the meeting had ended. Canaris, disgusted but not really surprised, got up, waved a half-hearted Nazi salute and muttered, "Heil Hitler." He turned and walked briskly out of the office.

At 4:00 that day, Canaris was back at his desk with Oster sitting in front of him. Oster was livid. "The idiots," he fumed. "They do not understand the first thing about the size and the industrial capacity of the United States. While Germany is being bled to death fighting a war on two fronts, the United States will have no such problem, especially with reliable allies like England and Australia. And they will have the Bolsheviks on their side as well. How much more damage do you think those barbarians will be able to do to us with the United States in this war and supplying them even more than they are now?"

Canaris grunted his agreement, but he was already thinking through his alternate options. If nobody in Germany would help him avert this disaster, he must look beyond her borders. England was out. Churchill would dance for joy on the floor of Parliament at the news that Japan was planning something that would bring the United States into the war. With one blow, they would accomplish what a powerful and popular President could not: overcome America's isolationism.

The answer had to be to go to the Americans directly. But how? He could not simply call the American Ambassador and tell him he had intelligence indicating a possible impending attack. The Ambassador would suspect a trap and he would want to know why the information had not come from the

Foreign Ministry. Von Ribbentrop would learn of it and would be furious, would go to Hitler with word of Canaris' duplicity, even after being told in no uncertain terms of the Führer's expressed wishes. Furthermore, it would totally unhinge the Tripartite Pact with Japan, which despite everything, did have some positive side effects. No, it was going to have to be subtler than that.

Abruptly, he stood, his eyes alight. "I think, Hans, that our best hope, and perhaps our only viable option, is to have Herr von Althorp travel to the United States on some unrelated pretense and look up his friend in the American Office of Naval Intelligence."

Oster nodded and smiled slightly, somewhat embarrassed that he had not thought of that connection but understanding immediately that he had work to do. He knew of the friendship von Althorp had developed with a young Naval Intelligence officer when he had been posted in Washington in the late 1930s.

By the next morning, the clever Oster had a plan to present to Canaris. Von Althorp's father would be asked to feign a medical emergency of some type – serious but not necessarily life-threatening, nor of such long-term seriousness that replacing him as the Reich's Ambassador to Mexico was called for.

A bowel blockage, perhaps, or a nasty ulcer. Great pain, in other words, possibly requiring surgery, something for which a visit from his beloved son would be both welcome to him and the humane thing for the Reich. Slipping into the U.S. for a visit after seeing to his father should be a piece of cake for young von Althorp. He had, after all, spent almost two years as a junior diplomat in Washington in 1938 and 1939 working as an Abwehr operative in the office of the German Naval Attaché, and had made several useful contacts and this one particularly interesting friendship.

Canaris liked the plan immediately and drafted an urgent signal to Ernst von Althorp in Mexico City, using the secure encryption code that was available only to those with whom the Abwehr headquarters communicated directly. Others got messages using the normal diplomatic code, or typed notes sent via the diplomatic pouch or by officer courier.

It was early morning in Mexico, but Ernst von Althorp had always ignored the Latin American practice of starting the day at 10:00 or later and ending it with dinner at 11:00 p.m. or midnight. He rose early, did so even when his diplomatic chores had required a late dinner the night before. And since his wife had died of pneumonia in Germany shortly before he was posted to Mexico City, he had no reason to linger at home.

Thus, he arrived in his office at just about the same time a man from his signals section delivered an URGENT-EYES ONLY from Canaris. In the message, Canaris had laid out the issue and Oster's plan. Von Althorp immediately drafted a return message in which he agreed, giving Canaris the name of a Mexican doctor who owned a very private and discrete clinic and who could be counted on for a variety of social and political reasons, and assuring him he would make the necessary arrangements immediately.

When Ernst von Althorp's message was received and delivered to Canaris by Oster, the two quickly drafted a message to Rudi. Oster had it hand-delivered it to the signals section by a trusted aide for encryption and transmission, most urgent.

```
MOST URGENT
R VON ALTHORP          ,
COMMERCIAL ATTACHE
EMBASSY OF THE GERMAN REICH
TOKYO
COPY AMBASSADOR
EMBASSY OF THE GERMAN REICH
TOKYO
REGRET TO INFORM YOU YOUR FATHER
HAS SERIOUS HEALTH ISSUE REQUIRING
SURGERY STOP NOT CONSIDERED LIFE
THREATENING STOP YOU ARE AUTHORIZED
IMMEDIATE HUMANITARIAN LEAVE AND
CLEARED HIGHEST PRIORITY BY NEXT
AVAILABLE TRANSPORT TOKYO TO MEXICO
CITY STOP GOOD LUCK
    CANARIS
    ABWEHR BERLIN
    END MESSAGE
```

Fredi Pohl knocked quickly, pushed open Rudi von Althorp's door and rushed to his desk with the signal he had just decoded. He had dropped a copy with the Ambassador's secretary on his way, as instructed. Rudi read the signal with a sense of shock mingled with a sense of disconnect. He was shocked at the news about his father, who had never had a medical problem in his life, apart from the near-starvation he had endured on the eight-month trek across the Andes in 1915.

The disconnect was attributable to the fact that this signal was not only unrelated to his signal of the month before but amazingly made no mention of it. Had it gone through or been lost or garbled in transmission? Fredi Pohl read his thoughts.

"Your signal went through last month, Rudi. It was acknowledged from Berlin. I'm sure Berlin just thought this was more urgent at this time. Perhaps they will signal you further, care of the Mexico City Embassy. If I get anything else for you here, I will forward it to you in Mexico City, private and eyes only." Rudi looked at his friend thankfully. The phone on his desk rang thirty minutes later.

"Herr von Althorp," the Reich's Ambassador to Japan said, "I am very sorry to hear about your father. I know you are very close. I know Ambassador von Althorp well and know how proud he is of you. I have called on a friend here in Tokyo and have you booked on a freighter of Panamanian registry leaving Tokyo Bay a week from today bound for Puerto Vallarta, Mexico. We were fortunate. It is a refrigerated ship that is inbound as we speak with fruits and vegetables from Mexico and will be returning with a cargo of North Pacific fish and crab. There are several guest cabins and I booked one for you. Please give your father my very best when you reach him."

Rudi thanked the Ambassador and assured him he would. It was August 30.

In the village of Bletchley, tucked into the Milton Keynes area of the countryside outside London, was a lovely estate called Bletchley Park. It had been commandeered by the British Secret Intelligence Service, or MI6, as the base for Ultra.

Ultra was one of the most critical operations in the war with Germany, a code-breaking operation whose technicians and cipher experts had found a way to decrypt messages sent by the Germans' Enigma machines, which were used for all military, diplomatic and intelligence traffic. While its denizens – and those who relied on the work product of the estate – referred to the place simply as "Bletchley Park," the official name of the operation housed in the estate was the Government Code and Cypher School.

It was far more than a school. And it was one of the most closely-guarded secrets of the war.

Even though the Abwehr had developed its own elaborate and technically masterful codes, along with its advanced Enigma G machine, the men and women of Bletchley Park had figured the Abwehr codes out too, as they had with all the others. The Germans continuously developed and modified their machines and codes, but in time Bletchley Park solved most of them. Still, the messages often took a few days, or even weeks, to decipher.

As Admiral Canaris and General Oster were trying to verify Rudi von Althorp's sightings and conclusions, a pair of analysts at Bletchley Park were poring over the message from Tokyo to Berlin, trying to deduce hidden meanings or subtle nuances. Finally, they concluded it was nothing more than it appeared to be, and if it was true the Japanese were conducting shallow-water torpedo tests, higher-ups in MI6 should know about it.

The analysts sent Rudi von Althorp's message to their section chief with a memorandum outlining the possible ramifications, as they saw them. The ramifications, in order of concern to England, they wrote, were: first, the Japanese had obtained the British plans for the torpedoes used at Taranto, which implied Japanese espionage and/or one or more British traitors; second, the new torpedoes were to be targeted at British or Commonwealth bases in Hong Kong, Singapore, Australia or New Zealand; third, they were to be targeted at Allied bases in French Indo-China or the Dutch East Indies; and fourth, they were indeed to be used in an attack on the United States in the Philippines or the Territory of Hawaii.

The message and analytical memorandum eventually made their way into Central London to the desk of Major General Sir Stewart Graham Menzies, the Chief of MI6 as well as of the Secret Intelligence Service. Menzies knew as soon as he read the message over that the fourth ramification pointed out in the memo, which would bring the United States into the war, would be the one of most immediate interest to Prime Minister Winston Churchill, with whom he met almost daily.

Seven days after receiving Canaris' message about his father, Rudi was on the dock and almost ready to board the freighter when he saw Fredi Pohl running toward him, gesturing frantically. Breathless, Fredi held out an envelope. "Thank God I caught you," he said. "This came in just 90 minutes ago, marked to be read only during transport. I didn't know if I had time to decode it and drive down here, but here you are." He held out his hand formally and wished Rudi a good trip and his father good luck.

Impulsively, Rudi embraced him. Embarrassed, he backed away from Fredi and with another wave, started up the gangplank to the ship.

Once in his cabin and unpacked and with the freighter starting to vibrate as it moved away from the dock and toward the mouth of Tokyo Bay, Rudi locked his cabin door and opened the envelope.

```
EYES ONLY - NO COPIES - TO BE OPENED
IN TRANSIT MEXICO
    R VON ALTHORP
    COMMERCIAL ATTACHE'
    EMBASSY OF THE GERMAN REICH
    TOKYO
```

```
FATHER FEELING WELL STOP IN
CLINICA BALLASTEROS MEXICO CITY UNDER
SUPERB CARE STOP SURGERY MAY NOT
BE REQUIRED STOP YOU ARE AUTHORIZED
HUMANITARIAN LEAVE OF DURATION YOU
FEEL APPROPRIATE STOP ON COMPLETION OF
HUMANITARIAN LEAVE YOU ARE AUTHORIZED
ONE MONTH VACATION LEAVE STOP SUGGEST
YOU VISIT WASHINGTON AND RENEW OLD
ACQUAINTANCES ESPECIALLY FROSCH STOP
CONTACT UNDERSIGNED FROM REICH EMBASSY
WASHINGTON AFTER CONTACT FROSCH STOP
NOTIFY UNDERSIGNED ON SCHEDULE FROM
REICH EMBASSY MEXICO STOP FATHER HAS
FURTHER INFORMATION FOR YOU STOP
    CANARIS
    ABWEHR BERLIN
    END MESSAGE
```

Rudi read the signal for a third time. Canaris was telling him something, he was sure. And with the certainty born of his intimate understanding of the brilliant little man in Berlin, he suddenly knew.

His father wasn't sick at all.

He was a willing participant in a scheme to get Rudi out of Tokyo and to Washington in a way that would raise no suspicions in the Tokyo Embassy nor in Berlin.

The key was the reference to Frosch, or Frog. Frog was the code name for his friend, an American naval officer, a young lieutenant (junior grade) in the Office of Naval Intelligence.

Frog's name was Alexander Jordan and the two had become friends in 1938 when Rudi had been posted to

Washington and Jordan was an Ensign, not long out of the United States Naval Academy. Jordan was from Fort Worth, Texas, and while he was attending the Naval Academy in Annapolis, Maryland, the football team from his home town school, Texas Christian University, had won the college football national championship in 1935, as it had again in 1938.

The TCU Horned Frogs had become an American phenomenon and Alex Jordan talked about them incessantly, reciting the exploits of quarterbacks Sammy Baugh – now a member of the Washington Redskins - and Davey O'Brien. It seemed he followed the Frogs of TCU even more than he followed the exploits of the Midshipmen of the United States Naval Academy. Thus, Jordan's code moniker, Frosch, German for frog.

Rudi was now quite certain that his mission to find Frog had to do with the signal he had sent the Admiral about the shallow-water torpedo practice by the Japanese Navy. He wondered why he had not thought of this course of action himself. He and Frog were the same age and he was genuinely fond of the man. It would be good to see him again, however this mission turned out.

At Bletchley Park, outside London, the same two analysts puzzled over the intercept of the latest Berlin-to-Tokyo message. For whatever reason, they had missed the Berlin-Mexico City signals, but of course were not aware they had missed anything. They finally suggested to their section chief that he signal MI6 in Washington and see if the name, Frosch, meant anything to them.

CHAPTER 3

Mexico City
September 12, 1941

Rudi walked into the room – really the suite – of Ernst von Althorp in Clinica Ballasteros on the outskirts of Mexico City. His father jumped from the easy chair in which he had been sitting and embraced him. Rudi was relieved, but perhaps not totally surprised, that there appeared to be nothing whatsoever wrong with the older man.

"How are you feeling, Papa?" Rudi asked in German as Ernst motioned him to a chair upholstered in plush red velvet.

"Never better, Rudi," the Ambassador replied in German. "Sit and I will tell you what this is all about." He offered Rudi coffee which Rudi accepted gratefully. The coffee on the ship had been awful, almost as bad as the coffee in Japan except, of course, for the coffee served in the Reich's Embassy.

"The Herr Admiral and General Oster were, it would appear, much impressed with your observations in Japan," Ernst resumed after pouring two cups of very strong Guatemalan coffee. "He briefed me on your signal. They have gone to some significant effort checking with other assets to try to get third-party verification, but have been so far unsuccessful. It seems you are one of the few – in Germany at least - who has his eyes open with regard to the Japanese."

Rudi took one of the cups of coffee and the two men sat. Ernst continued as he mixed a spoonful of sugar into his cup. "In any case, the Herr Admiral took your signal to Foreign Minister von Ribbentrop and got nowhere. I suspect that the Führer considers the Pacific to be Japan's area of influence, at least for the present time. I'm afraid the possibility also exists that Hitler would welcome further Japanese hostility in the Pacific as a diversion to the Soviets. The Admiral, and I believe many of the senior officers agree with him, sees it quite differently."

"It seems to me that in this case the Führer is at least partly correct, Papa. I doubt very much that Stalin would want to have to send more troops eastward while he is desperately trying to stop the Wehrmacht short of Moscow."

"No doubt, my son, but I believe the Admiral correctly sees this as the opening Roosevelt has been looking for to bring the United States into the war, not only against Japan but against the entire Axis."

Rudi started to reply, but his father held a hand up to let him finish. "Although we both know that a somewhat embarrassing armistice that could force Hitler from power would be a dream come true, a total war of annihilation against the German people and unconditional surrender is the more likely outcome and would make what we endured at Versailles in 1919 look like a child's spanking."

He paused for effect. "You must see the cumulative damage that could be inflicted on all of us if our Asian allies are allowed to pursue this path. That is why the Admiral wants your discovery to be brought to the attention of the proper people in the government of the United States. Perhaps they can somehow act to forestall an attack by Japan."

Rudi had been expecting something like that.

"But we must do so without the information being traceable to the Admiral or to the Abwehr?" Rudi asked, knowing the answer. Ernst nodded, his face grave.

"Therein lies the rub, as the English might say," he answered. For several minutes, both men sipped their coffee, lost in their own thoughts.

At length, Rudi spoke. "And I will then assume that that is where my friend, Alex, or should I say Frosch, comes in?" Again, Ernst simply nodded.

Rudi's mind was a jumble of thoughts. And questions.

For a full week, the von Althorps went through the motions necessary for public consumption, should anyone, especially anyone from the SS-SD, be paying attention. It was unlikely that anybody was, but in times like these, and in circumstances like these, discretionary measures must be taken. The SD, the Sicherheitsdienst, was the intelligence arm of the SS. It was staffed entirely by Nazi true believers or raw power mongers, many of them sadists. And although it was never overtly admitted, the SS-SD was the sworn enemy of the larger and more effective Abwehr. The head of the SD, Reinhard Heydrich, was once a protégé of Canaris but his thirst for power, meaning access to Adolf Hitler, had made him a rival, even an enemy.

So, for seven days, Rudi von Althorp rode in a car belonging to the Mexico City Embassy of the German Reich, from his hotel near the embassy to Clinica Ballasteros to visit with his father and consult with his father's doctor.

Each day, he would return to the Embassy and share with the Ambassador's secretary and senior staff the wonderful news that Herr Ambassador von Althorp was recovering rapidly and should be able to resume his duties soon. This news was invariably received with joy; the Herr Ambassador was a very popular man among the embassy staff, always respectful and solicitous of even the lowliest staff member.

No signals were forwarded to him from Tokyo.

Ernst von Althorp was ready to be "released" from Clinica Ballasteros. His friend, the doctor, had agreed gladly to their plan. He knew Ernst von Althorp to be a good man. He also knew him as a man who had called someone, or cabled someone, or otherwise somehow seen to it that his son, a student at Heidelberg University, was expeditiously granted an exit visa from Germany on November 11, 1938, two days after the Kristallnacht, the Night of Broken Glass, when Hitler had turned his goons loose all over Germany, murdering Jews and burning their businesses.

The good doctor and his family were Jewish, and for a German diplomat to take such a chance to help a Jew was an act of supreme honor. And if the act were discovered by the wrong people in Nazi Germany, it would most likely turn out to be an act of supreme sacrifice.

In fact, Ernst von Althorp, in the time he had been posted to Mexico City, had made a good many friends in the surprisingly-sizeable Jewish population of that city. He had rendered similar services for several others. Mexican Jews lived in a Catholic nation and understood prejudice.

That the German Ambassador, of all people, could be such a good friend to them secured for Ernst von Althorp a legion of admirers and supporters among the doctors, lawyers, skilled tradesmen and bankers who made up a large percentage of the Jewish population. In fact, he was so well regarded that it made him slightly uncomfortable, knowing that his reputation could be ultimately dangerous, to him and to his family.

Rudi was helping his father pack up when there was a

knock at the door. Ernst opened it and greeted the visitor in the Mexican way: a hearty embrace and loud slaps on each other's back. "Rudi, this is Ernesto Gutterman," he announced in English.

Rudi put out his hand to shake Gutterman's but got an embrace instead.

"So this is my companion on the journey," Gutterman said, also in English, and very good English at that. Rudi looked surprised. He and his father had talked at some length over the last several days about how best to get himself into the United States, once the subterfuge of the health scare had played itself out. His father had told him the day before that he thought he had an idea.

He had not elaborated.

Gutterman, one of his Jewish friends, was the Managing Director of Grupo Gutterman, S.A., Mexico's largest pharmaceutical company, with operations throughout Central America and northern South America. He was due to meet with procurement officials of the United States War Department in the next several days to arrange the sale of a large order of antibiotic powder he had developed for treatment of battlefield wounds until proper hospital care could be reached. Part of the order was to be retained by the U.S. for war preparedness purposes, but the lion's share of the order was destined for shipment to England and the Soviet Union.

He had booked two tickets on a 10-passenger Lockheed Electra operated by Aerolineas de Mexico from Mexico City to Miami, Florida, leaving September 21, two days hence. In Miami, after a one-night stop-over, they would board an Eastern Airlines flight to Washington, D.C.

Gutterman considered it an honor to accompany the son of a friend, who was on holiday and had many friends in

Washington he wished to see. They would arrive on a Monday afternoon, after which Rudi would be in a race to find Frosch.

The next day, in the Ambassador's residence, Ernst von Althorp gave his son a large leather suitcase containing a superbly disguised false bottom. It was the handiwork of another of the Ambassador's Jewish friends in Mexico City, a master saddle-maker and leather-worker. Hidden under the false bottom, at Canaris' directions, were $10,000 in United States currency and another $10,000 in gold coins, mostly Swiss francs. The coins were further secreted beneath a second false bottom, one underneath the U.S. $100 bills. Since the paper currency was all in $100 bills, it took up the entire false compartment above the coins. In fact, the suitcase had been designed to that specification. It was an enormous amount of money and Rudi was shocked.

However, as his father explained to him, Canaris realized that getting the information he possessed into the right hands might take some time, requiring commercial travel, extended hotel stays, perhaps even some bribes. Canaris always saw to it that Abwehr stations – especially those in critical capitals – were stocked with a clandestine hoard of currency: Reichsmarks, U.S. dollars, British pounds sterling, Swiss francs, gold coins, even Mexican pesos in this case.

The Abwehr's man in Mexico City was well aware of the Ambassador's relationship with the Admiral, and that the Admiral had personally ordered the cash be provided. He had supplied the Ambassador with the cash unquestioningly. Canaris, both von Althorps knew very well, devoutly believed that in the intelligence business, cash was king. And conversely, the lack of cash had cost many a king his crown. And in more than a few cases, his life.

The next morning, Ernst von Althorp accompanied his son, in the Embassy's Mercedes limousine, to the airport in Mexico City. Ernesto Gutterman was waiting for them at the ticket counter. Ernst stayed until the flight boarded. He knew it was quite likely - even probable - that he would not hear from his son again until his mission was over. And perhaps until the war was over. It even occurred to Ernst that he could be sending him to his death, and the thought chilled him.

It was now up to Rudi alone to make Canaris' plan work.

In the British Embassy in Washington, D.C., three men from MI6 pondered the meaning of the word, Frosch, and of the message containing it. Of course, they knew it was the German word for "Frog," but they could make no sense of it otherwise. The message made it sound like a person – a contact, probably – rather than an operational code.

After examining all their files on known or suspected German agents or sympathizers in the Washington area, they gave up and decided the thing to do was to ask their chief of station to have a discrete word with one or two of his American intelligence contacts. Perhaps they would know something.

What the bloody hell does "Frosch" really mean?

A Desperate Journey

CHAPTER 4

Washington, D.C
September 22, 1941

Rudolf von Althorp and Ernesto Gutterman both registered at the Hay-Adams Hotel, across the street from Lafayette Park and the White House.

Next door to the White House was the State, War and Navy Building, where Gutterman's meetings were to be held, and where Rudi would begin his search for Frosch. Gutterman would be flying back to Mexico in two days but would be very busy until then, so the two bade each other farewell when Gutterman stepped off the elevator one floor below the one to which Rudi had been assigned. Rudi was very grateful to the kindly man and hoped he would have a chance to see him again.

In his room, Rudi unpacked, hung up or put in drawers all his clothes, locked the suitcase and put it in the closet and went for a walk.

Washington was cooling down after its customary hot and very humid summer. He ducked into a small bar and ordered an American beer, a Budweiser. It was a bit weak compared to German beers, but it was served ice-cold, a taste he had acquired here in 1938 and 1939. The beer helped calm his nerves. He had grown more apprehensive during the flights from Mexico City and now it was as if every nerve ending in his body was protruding through his skin. He could be in grave danger. He'd never known that feeling.

At 4:00 p.m., he walked a few blocks to the German Embassy and presented his diplomatic passport and other identification papers at reception. He inquired whether Herr Helmut Ries might be available. They had worked together when he had been posted here previously. Ries was the Abwehr's station chief in Washington, and had taken great personal satisfaction in Rudi's elevation to station chief in Tokyo. Ries was a stocky 41-year-old with sandy hair.

"Rudi!" Ries cried when his secretary escorted von Althorp through the door to his office. "What brings you to Washington? And all the way from Tokyo?" Rudi told him about his father's medical emergency – thank God it had turned out well – and his 30-day holiday that went with his humanitarian leave to Mexico City.

"Well, that is wonderful news, and good timing, too," Ries exclaimed. "We must have dinner tonight."

"What is the 'good timing' all about, Helmut?" Rudi asked.

"I am leaving tomorrow at noon for a month in Germany," Ries explained. "I will be on holiday, too. Going to Düsseldorf to see my family." He paused. More softly, he muttered, "And Frieda." Frieda, Rudi knew, was Ries' girl, whom he intended to marry after so many years of bachelorhood. From things Helmut had said, and perhaps more importantly things he had not said two years before, Rudi wondered whether Frieda intended to marry him. Rudi knew he had been waiting several years for her. So perhaps Helmut was going on his holiday to find out once and for all whether he and Frieda had a future. Assuming anyone in Germany has a future, Rudi thought sourly to himself.

Helmut and Rudi went to a favorite German restaurant they had discovered in 1938. They had beer and schnapps and sausages and potato fritters and sauerkraut. They talked through it all, catching up on the last two years and speculating on how the war was going – and would go. It was all excellent, both the food and the conversation. Rudi told Helmut that he had been surprised to find that he recognized nobody else at the Embassy, yet he'd been gone just two years. He did not mention his mission.

Rudi paid the check and bid his friend bon voyage as he got out of the car when Helmut dropped him at the Hay-Adams.

Rudi liked Helmut. He hoped he would have a good and successful, visit to Düsseldorf. But his main mission in visiting the Embassy, and in talking with Helmut, had been accomplished: Helmut Ries, the Abwehr station chief in Washington, obviously knew nothing whatsoever of Rudi's mission. Nor of the information he had developed.

Helmut, of course, well knew Rudi was station chief in Tokyo and if he had known of Canaris' suspicions and fears, would have found a way to bring the subject up, even if he had no idea of Rudi's involvement, past or future. Rudi had told him he might need to use Helmut's office to send a signal to Canaris and Helmut assured him that he would alert his secretary, Meike, to help him with whatever he needed.

Rudi was on his own. Despite his nerves, he preferred it that way. And he knew the fewer people who were involved in this, the less chance for Canaris' involvement in it to come to light. It was his first real mission as an Abwehr operative "in the field" and he knew it could very likely set the tone for the balance of his career. Again assuming anyone in Germany has a chance at a real future, let alone a career.

In his room after leaving Helmut Ries, Rudi consulted his small, leather address book. He had no idea whether Alex Jordan was at the same telephone number he was in 1939, did not even know whether he was still in Washington. The two had exchanged a couple of letters in the two years since Rudi had moved to Tokyo, but none for the last several months. He could have been posted anywhere since then.

Yet the Admiral had been specific about him looking up Frosch when he got here. The Admiral must know he is still here, he thought. Or maybe he is just hoping.

"Lieutenant Jordan speaking, sir," the voice said in proper military fashion when the phone picked up, even though it was his home phone. The familiar vestige of a Texas drawl that Alex was trying to lose was clear to Rudi's ear.

"Are the Horned Frogs as bad as ever, Alex?" Rudi asked, grinning. Relieved.

A pause, rather a long one.

"I beg your pardon? Who is this, please?" Jordan asked warily. The voice was familiar. But it had been a long time.

"Alex, it's Rudi. Rudi von Althorp."

"Good God, Rudi. What a surprise! Where you at?" The Texas accent was back, as Rudi knew it tended to when Alex was relaxed and with friends.

"I'm in Washington, at the Hay-Adams," Rudi replied. "I know it's late, but I just got in and was hoping we could get together soon. Perhaps lunch, dinner." Rudi's English was virtually flawless, spoken almost too perfectly, as is often the case with someone who has learned it as a second language in a good school. He told Alex about his father's illness, his holiday leave. And added, "and I assume congratulations are in order for your promotion. The last time I saw you, you were

Lieutenant (junior grade) Jordan."

"Thanks for that, and hell, yes, Rudi. I'm in a damn meeting most of the day tomorrow, but it'll be over by 5:00 or 5:30. How 'bout dinner?"

"I would like that very much, Alex," Rudi said. "It has been too long."

"Good deal," Alex said. "I can't wait to hear about Tokyo. I'll call you at the Hay-Adams when I shake loose." Rudi had told Alex about his new posting before he had left Washington.

They said their good-byes and hung up. Rudi looked at his watch. It was 9:15. He was still tired from his journey, but he did not want to sit alone in his hotel room just yet. He splashed some water on his face, brushed his teeth and took the elevator down to the lobby.

After the call was disconnected, Alex Jordan sat staring at the phone for a long moment. He knew the war clouds were gathering and wondered if Rudi's appearance in Washington was really just a vacation.

The Hay-Adams bar was stately, all heavy leather furniture, dark mahogany bar and paneling. While not packed, it was still surprisingly busy for this hour. Rudi took a seat at one end of the bar. Again, he ordered a very cold Budweiser. With the American cigarettes – he especially liked Chesterfields – and the beautiful American women who seemed so comfortable in a place like this, even without escort, he could think of no better way of passing the evening.

Rudi could see out of the corner of his eye that two young women halfway down the bar appeared to be busy trying to make eye contact with him. He was not used to women sitting at the bar itself, with or without an escort, and he was reminded again how different American women were from those in Germany, and even more so from those in Japan. Japanese women would not have even been in the bar, let alone at the bar.

But his mind kept drifting back to why he was in Washington. The world seemed on the verge of exploding on all continents. Did he possess information that might keep some of that from happening? Perhaps more to the point, did he possess the skills and the means of getting his information in the hands of men who could use it to beneficial effect? And always: Am I going to live through this?

"Hello, Mr. von Althorp," a soft, feminine voice with only the hint of an accent breathed close to his ear as its owner slid onto the bar stool next to his. Startled, Rudi turned to see the smiling face of Meike Franzky, Helmut Ries' secretary. "Good evening," he responded with some hesitation. "I didn't expect to see you again so soon."

"Helmut called me at my apartment earlier tonight and told me you would require my assistance while you are in Washington and he is away." She told him that Helmut had told her that he was at the Hay-Adams and she had decided to see if he might be in the bar. To offer her assistance.

"That's very kind of you, Meike," he said, "but for now all I will need is your help sending a signal to Berlin at the appropriate time." He lowered his voice as he said the last because the bartender was making his way toward them to get Meike's drink order. She ordered a glass of chilled white wine.

They remained silent while the bartender fetched her wine. When he had departed for the other end of the bar, Rudi glanced around to make sure nobody else was in hearing distance. The two women who had been trying to make eye contact had abandoned their apparent quest and moved to a table soon after Meike arrived.

He thought he must be out of his mind. Or maybe he was smart enough – and mature enough – to put a very important mission ahead of the screaming of his hormones.

After he saw Meike safely to her taxi, Rudi returned to the bar rather than turning for the elevator. He liked the American beer and the Chesterfields and really had nothing to do tomorrow until Alex called late in the day. After three more beers and an interesting conversation in Spanish with a Chilean diplomat who happened to sit one stool away from Rudi, he retired to his room.

The Chilean diplomat had not responded in any useful way to Rudi's gentle probe about what Chile and Argentina were likely to do if the United States entered the war on Britain's behalf.

CHAPTER 5

Washington, D.C.
The Next Day

Rudi slept until 10:30 and would have slept past that had not the maid knocked on his door to inquire about cleaning his room. He cracked the door and asked her to return in 30 minutes and went into the bathroom to shave and shower.

Dressed in casual slacks and a long-sleeved casual shirt, Rudi went downstairs to have breakfast in the Hay-Adams dining room. He read two newspapers to catch up on the war news – and any hints of American feelings about a possible United States role in it - while he sipped his coffee and ate. Although he knew American coffee lacked the body of German coffee, it was better than tea, and the breakfast was satisfying. He did not care too much for American breakfast sausage but he loved American bacon, fried crisply. He had two orders of it with his soft-boiled eggs and toast.

At 12:30, he was out the door of the Hay-Adams on a mission of re-orienting himself to Washington, D.C. The weather was perfect. He considered Washington a beautiful city, with lots of parks and statues and grand buildings housing one government agency or another. But he well remembered how hot and humid it was in the middle of the summer and could not understand why the Americans had built their capital city in such a miserable swamp.

He walked by the White House and the State, War and Navy Building next door to it. Compared to most of the other government buildings, he thought the State, War and Navy Building to be an ugly monstrosity. In fact, it was ugly compared to any other building he had ever seen. He walked south toward the Capitol Mall, which instead of the large national park it was designed to be, was now home to dozens, perhaps hundreds, of ramshackle temporary wooden buildings housing offices needed for military and civilian workers unable to fit in the main buildings of their departments and agencies. It certainly appears that America is preparing for war.

He hoped that did not end up being the case, and knew that the effort to supply the English and Russians through lend-lease and outright aid required people. And he knew the American military was being expanded in case of war. The newspapers were full of stories about the military build-up. The draft had been re-authorized by Congress the year before. It was the prudent thing to do, he knew, and he would do the same were he in Roosevelt's position.

By 4:30, Rudi von Althorp had walked the length of the Capitol Mall to the steps of the Capitol building itself, taking time to stop frequently to take in the sights and sounds, then back to the Hay-Adams. He would need a shower before meeting Alex.

If he called.

Rudi was listening to war news on the radio in his room when the phone rang at 5:41. "Sorry I'm late," Alex said when Rudi picked up. "Just got out of the meeting. Are y'all ready for a drink?" Rudi assured him that he was and they agreed to meet at a small bar a few blocks away on K Street.

The two actually met on the way to the bar. Alex had been in the State, War and Navy Building and had about the same length and route of walk as Rudi. They settled onto two stools at the end of the bar farthest from the door. It was dark in the bar and darker still in the corner they chose. Most of the other patrons were standing or sitting at tables. This was obviously something of a neighborhood bar whose customers were largely regulars. Most were men. The few women in the place were with men, unlike the bar in the Hay-Adams.

Rudi again ordered a Budweiser and Alex said, "Make it two." The two men were quite similar in size and build and, while Alex's hair was a deep red – almost copper-colored – to von Althorp's dark blonde, it would be possible to conclude that the two men were related, if not brothers.

Rudi filled Alex in on the last couple of years and his posting to Tokyo. He elaborated on his father's "illness" and his 30-day leave, which he had described cryptically on the phone the night before. Since he was in Mexico City with his father, he told Alex, a visit to Washington, perhaps followed by a week or two in California seemed like a fine way to spend his leave. Certainly preferable to trying to get to Germany.

He asked Alex about his naval career over the past two years and the two talked quietly about the war and the chances of the United States getting into it. Both knew if the U.S. did get into it, it would be the end of their friendship, at least until it was over.

If they managed to survive it.

Alex told Rudi about the strength of the isolationists, especially the America First Committee, the most prominent spokesman for which was the enormously popular German-American aviator, Charles Lindbergh, who was first to fly solo across the Atlantic Ocean. Rudi was well aware of Lindbergh and his advocacy of neutrality in the European war.

They were on their third round of beers. Neither was in a hurry to get to dinner. Both were enjoying getting reacquainted.

After more small talk, some centered around how well Alex expected TCU to do in the current football season, Rudi lowered his voice still further and said, "Alex, there is actually one particular reason I wanted to come here to see you. It is very serious and very sensitive and will possibly be of interest to the Office of Naval Intelligence." Alex stared at his friend, trying to decide on an appropriate response. Finally, he simply nodded and said, "Go on."

Quickly deciding not to delay but simply get to the point, Rudi stated evenly and without emotion, "I think I have evidence that Japan is planning to attack the United States." After a short pause, he added, "most likely in either Hawaii or the Philippines, perhaps both."

Alex could only stare. So this really isn't a vacation!

He had wondered when they became friends in 1938 whether Rudi was Abwehr. He had been trained to assume diplomats – at least those below Ambassador rank – were in the intelligence business until proven otherwise. Rudi had never given any indication that he was, had never asked about anything remotely sensitive. If anything, in private conversations he had always seemed uncomfortable with the direction Germany was taking. Just before he had left Washington for his new Tokyo posting, Germany had invaded Poland, unleashing the new blitzkrieg tactic, and Rudi had expressed the view that no good would come from it.

Of course, Alex had been required by ONI protocols to report Rudi's name as a foreign national with whom he had contact. His superior officer at the time had confirmed that

ONI believed Rudolf von Althorp was connected with the Abwehr, that his father was the Reich's Ambassador to Mexico – a fact Rudi had volunteered without prompting – and that Ambassador von Althorp was known to be a former German naval officer, a shipmate and reportedly a close friend of Admiral Wilhelm Canaris, head of the Abwehr.

Alex had been encouraged to maintain his contact with von Althorp and to make note of questions asked or opinions offered by the German. Alex knew that was standard procedure but had still been a little uncomfortable with it because he had, over time, come to see Rudi von Althorp as a real friend and, like most people, disliked the idea of reporting on private conversations with a friend.

But he was a naval officer and had done his duty.

At the time, Rudi, of course, had also reported the name Alexander Jordan to Abwehr headquarters as a foreign national – naval intelligence at that – with which he had contact. And, of course, those at the Tirpitzufer had encouraged him to maintain contact, making note of questions asked and opinions offered by Ensign - later Lieutenant (junior grade) - Jordan.

In time – neither man could have specified exactly when nor how it came to be – the fact that they both were in the service of their country's intelligence services became an acknowledged fact, but their friendship continued, even flourished. Both knew the boundaries and they lived within them.

Now, Alex realized that Rudi's assertion that he may have evidence of an attack on the United States by another member of the Axis had moved those boundaries substantially.

"How?" Alex asked after a moment. "What kind of evidence?" At that time, three rather loud young men entered and sat on the barstools nearest them.

Instead of answering directly, Rudi said, "I think it is time for one more beer, and then we need to go find something to eat." Alex raised his bottle to the bartender, motioning with his fingers for two more.

When they had finished their beer and paid the bill, they slipped through the growing crowd and out the door. Once on the sidewalk, Rudi leaned close to his friend and said, "I think perhaps a room service dinner might be the best thing tonight." Alex thought that was a splendid idea.

They walked back toward the Hay-Adams.

Rudi described the little fishing harbor south of Kure and the Nakajima torpedo bombers, the target painted on the rocks at the closed end of the harbor farthest from the village, the operational but unarmed torpedoes and the depth he estimated the harbor to be. Alex listened without comment as Rudi went through it all, his brow furrowed and his mind racing. The first questions that entered his mind were, "Why is he telling me this?" and then, "If Japan attacks us, we'll be at war with the whole damn Axis, and Japan is a German ally, so is he committing treason, or close to it?"

There was a knock on the door and a voice called out, "Room service." Rudi stopped talking and went to the door. When the food was set out on the room's table and the waiter had departed, Rudi said, "That's about it."

Alex was not sure where to start. After a bite of his cheeseburger, he decided on the direct approach.

"Why bring this to me?" he asked. "I assume you've reported this to Berlin, to the Abwehr. What do they think of it?"

"You are correct, my friend," Rudi responded after some thought. "I am with the Abwehr and I reported this to them."

Alex nodded, his eyes squarely on Rudi's, but with a look of understanding, even respect for this clandestine side of his life.

"And what did headquarters say when you reported this to them?"

"They told me the Foreign Ministry has decided this is none of Germany's concern. Adolf Hitler apparently does not share Admiral Canaris' concern about forcing the United States into the war. Hitler feels the Pacific is Japan's sphere of interest, and I suspect he feels that Japan's major benefit to Germany is that it provides a Pacific Ocean diversion to the Russians and British." He paused. "And you know I agree with the Admiral."

He smiled sardonically, acknowledging the absurdity of talking about the Führer's opinions not being in line with those of a lowly Abwehr station chief, or even those of Admiral Canaris.

Alex chewed on another bite of cheeseburger. He noticed that Rudi had not touched his plate. Rudi went on. "Alex, I cannot stress enough how much I, personally and on behalf of my superiors, want to keep this attack – if I am correct in my assessment – from happening. But my information cannot – must not – be traceable to the Abwehr. I would be putting the head of Admiral Canaris, who is my father's closest friend, in a noose. If I must be identified to your superiors, it is better if they think of me as a rogue agent, so to speak."

Rudi paused, thinking that the Admiral would want him now to lay his cards face-up on the table. "I want to be completely honest with you, Alex. The story about my father's illness and my humanitarian leave to visit him was a subterfuge developed by the Admiral – with my father's cooperation, of course - to get me here. My father was never sick, but he communicates with the Admiral regularly and when he heard what I had seen, he invented his medical problem.

"The real purpose was to get me to Washington and to get this information to you. I don't know if the Admiral is aware of precisely what I am doing, but he ordered me to come to you with this. He, as well as my father, are men of conviction and they both feel it is important to try to avert this disaster if that is possible."

So there it was, Alex thought to himself. Rudi was an Abwehr agent who had a good friend who was with U.S. Naval Intelligence. My, God, he thought, Rudi von Althorp is committing treason by doing this and Admiral Wilhelm Canaris is committing treason by sending him here. And Rudi's father is committing treason because of his role in the subterfuge. He was quiet for quite a long time. Rudi just looked at him, still not touching his food.

Finally, Alex stood up and started circling the room, deep in thought. "So you're doin' somethin' that Hitler himself would not want you doin'? That he'd find treasonous. Not to mention that he'd find Canaris' sendin' you here treasonous on his part. Am I readin' this right?"

Alex was well aware that in Nazi Germany, the stakes for treason were even higher than they were in the States. In the States, at least, one usually got a trial.

In Germany, he knew, the price for crossing Hitler was an immediate firing squad – or a hangman's noose.

Rudi nodded. "I think that is quite an accurate way of putting it."

Alex stood still, quietly staring out the hotel room window, for several minutes. Is this some sort of trap? But why? Didn't Rudi have more to lose in this than he? Yes, without a doubt the real risk was Rudi's. His own risk would be limited to his career, if the bosses at ONI determined that he was a naïve idiot for believing such a story, if they dismissed it as idiocy simply because it was a German intelligence officer bringing the intel to them. Intel that was clearly disinformation.

On the other hand, if Rudi's estimation of the situation was right, if the Japs did hit the U.S. with a surprise attack at Pearl or Cavite – or both – and he had known and not done anything about it, how would he feel? Finally, he concluded that if Rudi were willing to take this risk, he was willing to take it with him.

"Well, by God, you make me feel damn good about my judge of character," Alex said in a voice both quiet and excited. "But not all of my superiors will agree. Some'll argue that what you're saying is so far-fetched that you must be here plantin' disinformation. Maybe tryin' to provoke the United States into a preemptive strike that would be downright unpopular to a lotta folks here. Underminin' popular support of the President, that sort of thing. The Abwehr is sorta admired around this town for its efficiency, and its role in disinformation is for damn sure something we've heard a lot about from the British."

"So you don't think your people will believe what I am saying?" Rudi asked.

"No, I believe some people won't believe it, but there are some damn good men in ONI and my boss is one of them. He'll figure out a way to get this shit in the right hands so it can be checked an' acted on. I'll get on it right away. But you'll need to give me a couple of days. First, I'll check all our intel and see if I can find any other information that connects with this."

Rudi smiled and finally took a bite of his prime rib. It was cold, now better suited for making roast beef sandwiches. He assured Alex he would remain in Washington for as long as he was needed.

Rudi's father had done a fine job providing a cover for him, Alex thought. What he left dangling was Canaris' role –

lead role, presumably – in providing that cover. And that alone was fascinating to ponder.

The next Monday morning, Alex was waiting outside the office door of the recently-promoted Lieutenant Commander Wallace Hammond, his superior and head of the ONI's Pacific region section. It was, Alex thought, an interesting coincidence that he worked in the Pacific section and his Abwehr friend was now stationed in Tokyo. It might give Rudi more credibility, or conversely it might make it easier for people to believe the disinformation angle. But Wally Hammond was a smart man and a fine officer and had shown great confidence in Alex Jordan on more than one occasion.

"What's up, Alex?" Hammond asked as he walked through the outer office toward his door. "You look troubled." Hammond was perhaps two inches shorter than Alex, but had broad shoulders and a confident – but not cocky – air about him.

"I need a few minutes of your time, Commander, if you can spare them for me," Alex replied rather more crisply than the tones in which they usually conversed.

Hammond noted the tone and his dark eyes stared at Alex. The last time he had heard that tone of voice from Alex, he was bringing him fresh intelligence that pointed to the Japanese invasion of French Indo-China in 1940. Intelligence that had proven impeccable, even though many in ONI considered it preposterous and delayed notifying their English and French counterparts, as they should have immediately. President Roosevelt, a former Assistant Secretary of the Navy, had reportedly chewed the ass of the Chief of Naval Operations when he got wind of the intel that was not shared with England and France.

Roosevelt was determined that, even if the isolationists in the Congress and the country were able in the long run to keep the U.S. out of the war, he was going to do everything in his power to help England and the Soviet Union in their fight against Hitler and the Axis. He privately had no faith in France, which was now a half-occupied shell, with the southern half of the country a puppet state, operating as Berlin's lapdog.

Hammond gestured to a chair and shut his door. Only then did Alex realize he had not thought about where to start. He decided on the very beginning.

"You know, sir, that I have a friend in German intelligence, a man I met in 1938 here in Washington. He's now posted to Tokyo."

Hammond nodded. Alex had always kept him up to date frequently on all his contacts, but he remembered this one especially clearly precisely because of his Tokyo posting. "You're referring to Mr. von Althorp, if I'm remembering correctly," he said. "As I recall, the two of you became something more than contacts for each other, that you became quite good friends."

"That's correct, sir. We did become good friends – are good friends - even though we both understand the possibility of the U.S. getting officially into this war and our being on opposite sides." He paused, feeling vaguely foolish because of his disclaimer, which he knew did not really need to be said.

He plunged ahead. "I think I've made it clear to you that Rudi – Rudolf von Althorp – is not, in my opinion, a Nazi and is really not supportive of the Nazi regime or of Hitler. He and I have had a lot of conversations along those lines, and I think he's been honest with me about that. It's also the feeling of several of our colleagues that the same could be said of Rudi's ultimate boss, Admiral Canaris, although on that point there are conflicting opinions."

"So what do you have for me?" Hammond asked. He had heard the questions about whether Canaris supported Hitler.

"Rudi is here in Washington," Alex said. He explained Ambassador von Althorp's faked illness, the Ambassador's and Rudi's relationship with Canaris, and Canaris' approving leave for Rudi. He told him Canaris had suggested that Rudi take some of his leave in Washington and that perhaps it would be productive to look up his friend. Finally, satisfied that the groundwork had been laid, he plunged into the story he had come here to tell.

"Rudi was on a weekend holiday at a little fishing village south of Kure – that's on Japan's east coast south of Tokyo – when he saw two dozen Nakajima torpedo bombers – Kates - practicing shallow-water torpedo strikes against a rock abutment with target lines painted on it." The U.S. military had the habit of naming enemy aircraft types and the Nakajima B5N was called a Kate.

"He wondered why they would engage in shallow-water practice," Alex continued, "since none of the military targets on the Asian mainland – Japan's main sphere of interest to this point – would really require shallow-water torpedoes. He studied charts for all the harbors in the Pacific, at least those which have any military significance. He looked at everything from Vladivostok to Sydney. He concluded that the only significant naval installations that might require shallow-water torpedoes are at Pearl Harbor and Cavite. Both of 'em our bases."

"Jesus Christ," Hammond breathed, understanding immediately the logic of that conclusion. "But why the hell would he bring this to you? To us?"

"That's the first question I asked," Alex responded. "He signaled Canaris with his intel, of course. According to Rudi,

Canaris privately believes the U.S. entering the war will doom Germany, so he went to Foreign Minister von Ribbentrop first in the hope that he would warn off the Japs using the diplomatic approach.

"Apparently, von Ribbentrop either knows or guesses that Hitler is not interested. Hitler may not care if we get into the war, as long as the Japs keep us busy until he can finish off the Russians and the British. I don't know. In any case, von Ribbentrop apparently basically told Canaris to keep Rudi's observations to himself, even to disregard it as unimportant."

Hammond felt in his gut that he was hearing something that was probably true and without a doubt important. "So if I'm hearing this right, Canaris – and by extension von Althorp – are told by the German Foreign Minister, presumably – or at least possibly - with the concurrence of Hitler, to sit on this and let the Japs go ahead and risk bringing the U.S. into the war. Yet von Althorp, possibly on his own, but probably at the direction of Canaris, comes here because he's got a friend in ONI and can get the intel in the hands of the Americans through the back door? Because he personally believes it's the right thing to do? That he's willfully disobeying what could be considered a direct order? Am I reading this right, Alex?"

"I believe you are reading it exactly right, sir. And I asked the same questions – almost word for word - of Rudi when he first told me the story. The problem I've got is that I spent most of last week checking with everyone I could think of and nobody can give me anything that might verify Rudi's observations, other than that some people think it's possible, even likely, that the Japs will attack us somewhere."

"Go on."

"That's just about it, sir. Rudi's dad, an old friend of Canaris, faked an illness so Rudi could plausibly be brought from Tokyo to Mexico City to be with him. Humanitarian leave, they call it. Then Canaris arranges for Rudi to be given vacation leave and 'suggests' that he use it to visit Washington to renew his friendship with Frog."

"Who the fuck is Frog," Hammond asked sharply.

"Frog is their code name for me, sir," Alex responded with a smile. "I'm from Fort Worth."

Hammond sat with a puzzled look on his face. Then he broke into a smile of his own. "Okay, I get it. TCU, right?"

Alex nodded. "I didn't know that was my code name until last night. Rudi quoted from memory the signal he received from Canaris and I asked the same thing. In German, the word is Frosch. But it makes a kind of sense, I suppose. I didn't realize I talk about TCU that much. Rudi told me sometimes I sound like a broken record."

He smiled sheepishly.

Hammond agreed that indeed it did make sense, and smiled too. "Okay. I believe you and I think I believe your buddy, Rudi. But I've got to tell you I'm not so sure Canaris is involved, except to do a favor for an old friend and approve leave for his son. I've heard too many stories about Canaris and the Abwehr to believe a man at his level is, in effect, committing treason. Besides, let's look at the other side for a second and say those rumors are true, and Canaris hates Hitler. Why would he want to stop us from coming into the war, something that any sane person would agree is bad for Hitler's war effort?" He leaned back in his chair momentarily, then asked, "Can you tell me that?"

Alex sat quietly thinking about it from that angle, when Hammond, apparently deciding that issue was unimportant, continued. "But, whatever Canaris' inner motivations might be, and whether or not he's actively involved, your friend is apparently sufficiently convinced of the need to keep the U.S. out of the war that he's willing to risk it. And the Kate is their first-line naval torpedo bomber. That, alone, tells me this intel probably has substance and needs to be kicked up the chain of command. I'll get on it. Can you get von Althorp for me if I need him to back me up?"

Alex assured him he could. It was interesting that Hammond had not even asked him where Rudi was. Maybe at this point he didn't want to know. It might be safer for a young Abwehr agent who was a friend of one of his officers if he didn't know where he was at this point.

Things moved fairly quickly after that. Lieutenant Commander Wallace Hammond was well-regarded at ONI – considered by many a rising star - and was a man known not to be prone to jumping to unfounded conclusions.

After he left Hammond's office, Alex went to his own office, called Rudi, and told him cryptically that the information was moving. He told him he would get back with him when he needed him, but to hang loose for the time being.

Two days later, Alex's phone rang.

"Wally Hammond, Alex. Meet me at the CNO's office at 0930 hours tomorrow morning." He did not ask him to bring Rudi along.

"Yes sir," Alex replied, feeling his stomach muscles tighten. For a young and very junior lieutenant to be summoned to a meeting at the office of the Chief of Naval Operations was, to say the least, unusual.

After receiving the call from Alex, Rudi had gone to the Embassy of the German Reich, asked Meike to take him to the signals section, and sent a message to Canaris.

```
EYES ONLY
THE DIRECTOR
ABWEHR HEADQUARTERS
TIRPITZUFER
BERLIN
PACKAGE HAS BEEN DELIVERED STOP
BELIEVE FROSCH LIKES GIFT STOP DETAILS
TO FOLLOW
     R. VON ALTHORP
     REICH EMBASSY
     WASHINGTON
     END MESSAGE
```

Alex Jordan entered the office suite of the Chief of Naval Operations ten minutes early. Lieutenant Commander Wally Hammond was already there. They knew the CNO, Admiral Harold Stark, was a stickler for promptness, at least on the part of everybody but himself. He was thought to enjoy keeping his subordinates cooling their heels for no good reason other than to appear more important than any man in the capital aside from the President and the Secretary of the Navy.

True to their suspicions, twenty minutes after the appointed time, an aide appeared and directed them to enter the Admiral's office. The Director of Naval Intelligence, Admiral Alan Kirk, was with the CNO and introduced Hammond and Alex to Stark. Stark waved impatiently for Hammond to begin. Clearly, Admiral Kirk had already provided Stark with the rough outlines of why he – Kirk – had asked for this meeting. That was a hopeful sign to Alex.

Hammond took Stark through the entire story, almost verbatim as Alex had told it three days before, and omitting the fact that the German source was currently in the country. The Director of Naval Intelligence nodded at various points through the telling, indicating to Alex that he had apparently bought the story. Stark scarcely moved a muscle and his face remained impassive, almost bored.

When Hammond had completed the story, he stopped, looking directly at Stark. Stark simply sat there. Finally, with a dismissive wave of his hand he asked, "Is that it?"

"Yes, sir," Hammond said. "That's all that we know at this point, sir."

Stark looked astonished. "Have you no verification?" he demanded, looking at the Director of Naval Intelligence.

"With respect, Admiral Stark," Kirk said tightly, "verify what, exactly? We received this information from a German intelligence officer. We don't see what motivation he would have to bring us something like this falsely. In fact, we think that he has put himself at some considerable personal risk to bring this to us."

"Bullshit," Stark roared so loudly that Alex thought his aides might come barging through the door at any moment to see what was wrong. "This is completely unfounded and unverified. A Nazi agent, who is neither a naval officer nor an aviator, I assume, thinks he saw some Japanese planes doing something he knows nothing about. Nobody is stupid enough to use torpedo bombers in either Pearl Harbor or in Cavite. They are too heavily defended. It would be a suicide mission. Most likely, the entire tale is a fabrication, and we know about the Nazis' talent for spreading false information."

He paused and looked back at Kirk, "But, just in case he is not on a disinformation mission, send a message to our naval attaché in Tokyo and tell him to keep his eyes open for anything that might corroborate this."

He stood up dismissively.

Kirk felt his blood starting to boil, but contained his temper. "Sir, with respect, even without the verification you seek, is this not something that should be brought to the attention of the President and General Marshall?" Army General George C. Marshall was the Chairman of the Joint Chiefs of Staff and Stark's nominal superior.

"Absolutely not, Admiral," Stark answered sharply. "I am trying to put this Navy onto wartime footing and I am not about to ruin my reputation by becoming an alarmist." He looked around the office. "Thank you, gentlemen. That will be all. Keep me advised if you receive any corroboration."

The three officers marched out of the office. When they were in the hallway, the DNI motioned for Wally and Alex to follow him. Once safely in his office with the door shut, he gestured for them to sit and said, "Commander, I believe you but the Admiral has always been a cautious man and I'm not completely surprised by his reaction. He got where he is because he does things by the book. And, between you and me, I've always seen him as more a politician than a naval officer. The only way he'll give Roosevelt any intelligence is if he knows for an absolute fact that it's true. And in this business, as you know, that just doesn't happen very often."

After thinking silently for a few moments, he added, "I think the story needs to be kicked up the chain of command, but it can't be to Marshall now, because Stark would hear about it immediately and the three of us would be on tugboats pushing garbage barges down the Mississippi by this time next week. Hell, between Stark and that asshole – pardon the French - Admiral Turner, they've made things so unworkable for me here that I've already requested transfer to a destroyer squadron." Admiral Richmond Turner was in charge of war plans for the Navy, but considered intelligence his domain and had become the de facto chief of naval intelligence, routinely overruling ONI plans.

Hammond shook his head in disgust that things operated that poorly this high up the chain of command. Kirk leaned back in his chair and pinched the bridge of his nose, then said while rubbing his eyes wearily, "Wally, I can't believe I'm saying this, but I think we need to find a way to get this intel to 'Wild Bill' Donovan."

William Donovan was the Coordinator of Information. That was both his title and the name for the small but growing spy agency Roosevelt had put together just a few months earlier. Donovan had been a Colonel in the Great War and had been awarded the Congressional Medal of Honor for battlefield heroism. He had gone on to be a very successful Wall Street lawyer and was an old friend of Roosevelt, despite being political opposites.

When the President had called on him to take this job just a few months before, he had immediately packed his bags and moved to Washington. After all, the agency had been created in large part at Donovan's urging. The British had also urged Roosevelt to try to centralize his intelligence branches. The Coordinator of Information's stated function, as the name implied, was to "coordinate" the activities of the various United States intelligence-gathering organizations, both military and civilian.

It was well known that the military intelligence community was not at all enamored of the idea of a new intelligence organization stumbling around on the same turf as the warriors, even though much of the Office of Naval Intelligence undercover staff had already been seconded to the COI.

For that matter, J. Edgar Hoover, the Director of the Federal Bureau of Investigation, who thought intelligence-gathering to be his own turf, was even less thrilled than the military with the emergence of the COI.

Somehow, Roosevelt managed to keep them all from killing each other and had found his own subtle and nefarious ways to use each of them for his own purposes, sometimes overtly competing against each other.

In reality, Admiral Kirk, as Director of Naval Intelligence, had developed a grudging admiration for Donovan's ability to get things done. Of course, his almost around-the-clock access to Franklin D. Roosevelt was a key factor in that ability. The DNI had formed a bit of a clandestine, back-door, relationship with Donovan that had been beneficial to the interests of the United States on a few occasions, although on the surface the ONI/COI relationship remained frosty at best.

The day after Kirk, Hammond and Alex met with Stark, William Donovan picked up his phone right away when his secretary announced the Director of Naval Intelligence was on the line.

He listened as Kirk explained that he had some intel he felt the COI would find interesting, and wondered if Colonel Donovan would be interested in talking, very privately and off the record, with two of his young officers? Donovan had responded that, of course, he was willing to talk with them, but upon consulting his calendar, was reminded he was to fly to Miami the next day for three days of talks on a number of South American issues that were both important and extremely sensitive, given that Hoover of the FBI considered South America part of his turf. Kirk agreed to have his men in Donovan's office at 10:00 on October 7, the day after his late-night return from Miami.

In the Tirpitzufer in Berlin, Major General Hans Oster was in the office of Admiral Wilhelm Canaris, with the latest message from Rudi von Althorp. Canaris was staring at it.

"I remember Herr von Althorp's reports from his last assignment in Washington," Canaris mused. "This would appear to confirm that his friendship with this ONI man is quite real."

"I agree, Herr Admiral," Oster replied in his usual formal way. "It is clear that young von Althorp is his father's son – smart, clever, resourceful."

"Yes, and I think it is time we had Ambassador von Althorp notify the Foreign Ministry that his illness does not seem to be clearing up as he would wish and that he requests that his son be temporarily detached from Tokyo duty to serve as his assistant until it does. And that means we should find someone to take the young von Althorp's place in Tokyo."

"I agree again, Herr Admiral, and as it happens I have been looking into an appropriate replacement."

"Of course you have, Hans. You are always a step ahead of me."

"I doubt anyone has ever been a step ahead of you, Herr Admiral," Oster replied with a chuckle acknowledging their running joke, "but we have worked together so long that I find myself anticipating your next tactical move."

"So who have you found for me to send to Tokyo?"

"I think Walther Annandale would be perfect, Herr Admiral." Oster paused and laughed again, this time at Canaris' shocked expression.

"That gentleman is an SS-SD plant inside the Abwehr and you want to send him to Tokyo?" Canaris sputtered.

"Who better, Herr Admiral? If the Japanese are serious

about starting a war with the United States, as we both believe they are, let Heydrich and his killers deal with them. Once they attack the U.S., there will be more intrigue and double-dealing in Tokyo than there is in Berlin, if that is possible. Putting Annandale in that slot keeps us insulated from the fallout and as a bonus we get one of Heydrich's vermin out of our hair."

"Hmm." Canaris still felt a level of paternalism toward, even affection for, Heydrich, yet it was increasingly apparent to him that his feelings were misplaced. He brooded over Oster's suggestion while he sipped his coffee.

Finally, he smiled at his friend and confidante. "Of course, as always, you are right, Hans. Make it happen, but only as a temporary assignment. We can send someone we trust to Tokyo in a few months, if need be. Also, send a signal to Ambassador von Althorp. He will need to arrange things so the Embassy staff in Mexico City feels the presence of Rudi von Althorp, even if they don't seem to see him around much."

"Immediately, Herr Admiral," Oster said and left Canaris' office.

In London, Stewart Menzies chafed at the lack of follow-up information from his men in Washington. Nobody had found anything connected to the name, Frosch. Yet Bletchley Park had supplied him with yet another intercept referring to the name. "Believe Frosch likes gift…" What the bloody hell does that mean? Who IS Frosch? He wanted more before he went to Churchill with this.

But maybe these intercepts would have to do. He put the file in the stack of files he would go over with the Prime Minister in two days when he next met with him. Maybe.

Then he sent another message to MI6 in Washington and told them, in effect, to get off their arses and get him something on Frosch.

At 9:45 on October 7, dressed in civilian clothing to better blend into the civilian surroundings at COI, Hammond and Alex appeared at Donovan's office in a non-descript building not far from the White House. Alex had lunch with Rudi the day before to let him know they were still on the job, brief him on the next step – so far – and to let him know he would see him at the Hay-Adams as soon as he could after the meeting with Donovan.

Meanwhile, the DNI had pulled Hammond aside and again given him orders to do what he needed to do to get the intel in the hands of Roosevelt, and that Donovan would be the best judge of how to do that – and probably of whether it would be done at all.

"Failing that," Admiral Kirk told Hammond, "do whatever you feel is reasonable and proper to get the information in the hands of CINCPAC. We at least owe him the warning. It will be his ass if he's attacked and is unprepared. If he chooses to ignore it, well, like I said, it's his ass. At least we will have done our duty and gotten the information in the proper hands. Just make sure he understands it's important he keep the info inside his command. Tell him he can't let Stark, Turner or Marshall know we've told him, or we're cooked."

CINCPAC was the acronym for Commander in Chief, US Pacific Fleet, a post held since earlier in the year by Admiral Husband E. Kimmel. The fleet was based at Pearl Harbor, the command having been transferred several months before from San Diego, California, theoretically as a deterrent against Japanese aggression in Asia. That transfer had been ordered personally by Roosevelt.

It had been strongly opposed by many in the U.S. Navy

leadership, including Kimmel's predecessor as CINCPAC, who felt Pearl Harbor was too vulnerable.

When they were ushered into Donovan's office, Hammond asked Alex to brief the Colonel on what they had and how they had gotten it. Alex started from the beginning and went through the whole story, again omitting that Rudi was in Washington. He felt he had told it a few hundred times at that point and earlier had jokingly suggested to Hammond they print a pamphlet to make it easier when they took it to yet another intelligence officer or bureaucrat.

When he was finished, Donovan sat for a full minute thinking. Alex had done such a thorough job telling the story that the COI could think of no questions for what seemed several minutes. After a few routine and largely mundane questions were answered, he said, "Thank you for bringing this to my attention. I'll look into it."

Alex's initial reaction was that they had hit another brick wall, but on second thought felt more optimistic. He did not know Donovan except by reputation, and had not seen anything in person to lead him to believe that he was not as sharp and efficient as everyone said he was. Donovan stood up and thanked them for coming to see him. "Stay close to your office," he told the Lieutenant Commander. "I'll be in touch." That seemed encouraging to Alex, too.

CHAPTER 6

Washington, D.C.
October 8, 1941

Alex met Rudi for breakfast at the Hay-Adams and filled him in – using general terms and not names – on his activities the day before. He was confident that one of the people they had talked with would get the warning to the President. He assured Rudi that his name had been kept out of it. As he left to walk over to his office, he told Rudi to stay close and he would be in touch.

At 10:00 a.m., Hammond buzzed Alex on the intercom and asked him to come to his office. It was only two doors away and Alex was there in less than a minute.

"I just had a call from Donovan," Hammond said tightly, without preamble. "He wanted to know the name and whereabouts of your contact." Alex froze. He did not want to have Rudi personally identified if he could help it. Hammond continued, "I told him I knew him only by our code name for him, Alpine, but did not even know if he was still in Washington. In fact, I told him I suspected he was on his way back to Mexico City and then back to Tokyo.

"Donovan told me it would be very helpful if his people – and the FBI - could talk with Alpine to help them determine if his information is valid. I expressed my surprise. I told him we left his office feeling he was quite sure it was valid. His response was that he thought it might be and should be taken seriously but it would have to be either verified or further analyzed before he could take it to Roosevelt. He also said he thought it would be helpful if the FBI looked at it as well, so he'd called Hoover. Donovan's trying to play nice with Hoover and he thinks Hoover's people may have contacts that could help with verification."

"Shit," Alex exclaimed. "What's with all these brass hats and their ass-coverin' verification? Don't they get that sometimes you have to take things on instinct?" And now we have not two, but three intelligence services involved in this, he thought to himself.

"He also asked me to provide him with your home address and phone number," Hammond said.

Alex felt himself go ice-cold. "What does he need that for?"

"He said in case any of his people might need to contact you after hours or on a weekend. He wanted my home contact information, too, for the same reason."

"Well, I suppose if he or the FBI really want to know where we are, they can get it on their own anyhow. Givin' it to them just makes us seem more cooperative." Alex scratched his chin while thinking aloud. "Did he tip his hand on how long this verification process or investigation or whatever he calls it is gonna take?" Alex felt at home with Wally and sometimes he reverted to his Texas pronunciations with him.

"He just said he wanted to take a few days to make sure he had looked at every angle."

"Shit," Alex muttered again. "I have the strangest feeling that we've been rollin' a snowball bigger 'n' bigger and it just may be getting' the momentum to roll on its own."

"Let's just try to stay out of its immediate path," Hammond

answered with an emotionless voice.

"Wally, if you don't object, can we agree to keep Rudi's identity an absolute secret? No Donovan, no Hoover, nobody, no way, no how?"

Hammond held up his right arm with the first three fingers raised and smiled slightly. "Scout's honor. But remember one thing: we told Donovan that Alpine is stationed in Tokyo – although not what his duties are there - and that his father is in Mexico City. With his – and Hoover's – resources, they can probably put two and two together if they really try. And failing that, he can get Roosevelt to order Stark to get him the information. Neither one of us can disregard a direct order from him." Not for the first time, Alex felt the chill of fear.

The following morning, a Friday, Alex walked over to Hammond's office to see if there was any further word from Donovan. It had been a frustrating two days waiting for word from the man. He was told by Hammond's very efficient secretary that he was not in yet, nor had he left word when he would be in. Alex thought that odd. Hammond was always punctual and took his job as chief of the Pacific section very seriously. The possibility that Donovan had called him at home and asked him to come immediately crossed his mind, but Alex knew better than to make that assumption and show up at the COI uninvited.

Back in his office, Alex thought about the events of the past several days. Stark's reaction didn't surprise him. He was, after all, generally considered a bit of a chickenshit when it came to taking risks. But Donovan's reaction – or more accurately, his non-reaction – did surprise him. And his wanting access to Alpine, not to mention wanting his and Hammond's home addresses and phone numbers, not only surprised him, it bothered him. Bothered the hell out of him. Donovan knew all he had to do was phone the office and they would both come running. There was something odd about his requests, but then again, Donovan was in the real espionage part of intelligence. Alex wasn't.

At 11:00, his phone rang. It was the office of the Director of Naval Intelligence. Admiral Kirk had left ONI for his destroyer command and a new Director had not yet been named. Thus a relatively junior aide – one who was administrative, not operational – had taken a call from the Washington, D.C. police.

They were inquiring about Lieutenant Commander Hammond and what he had been working on. The aide, new in his job, knew little except the Lieutenant Commander was in charge of the Pacific section and had been working a lot with Alex Jordan for the past several days. Thus he simply passed on the Washington police message, asking Lieutenant Jordan to get in touch with Inspector Roscoe Banyan right away, please.

Alex placed the call as soon as the aide hung up, a sense of deep dread spreading through his body like a fever. Banyan answered the phone before the first ring was complete. Alex could hear typewriters and voices in the background, and he imagined a newsroom rather than a police station. When he had identified himself, Banyan asked if he could come down to police headquarters right away, that it had to do with Lieutenant Commander Wallace Hammond.

Alex sat across the desk from Inspector Roscoe Banyan. His sense of dread had grown when, upon asking for the inspector by name, had been escorted by a young patrolman through a door on which was stenciled, "Homicide." Banyan was a big man with a deep voice and a no-nonsense look to him.

Once assured of Alex's position and working relationship with Hammond, Banyan got right to the point. "I'd like you to accompany me across the street to the morgue to attempt to identify a body we found very early this morning," he said. "But before we do that, I have a few questions about Mister, ah, Commander Hammond. Do you know where he lives? Anything you can tell me about his family?"

"The Lieutenant Commander is not married," Alex answered formally. "He has an apartment in Alexandria. I can get you the address. He's from Billings, Montana. He told me his parents still live in Billings. I've never met them and don't know anything more than that." Alex realized he'd been talking very fast, as if willing this all to be over. Attempt to identify a body? Shit!

Banyan scribbled in his notebook and rose to leave, beckoning Alex to follow. The building housing the police morgue was directly across the street from the building housing police headquarters.

In the morgue, Banyan motioned for the man from the coroner's office to open a drawer. When Banyan pulled down the sheet, exposing what once was a face and most of the torso, Alex nearly lost his breakfast. The skin was grey and wrinkled and the whole body had obviously been submerged in water for a while. There were abrasions on the body that looked to Alex's untrained eye like places where fish had nibbled. It was for sure he could not tell if it was Wally Hammond. The hair was right, what hair was left. Very dark and short-cropped. Alex, ashen from the shock, looked at Banyan and shrugged. The sheet was replaced and the drawer pushed gently shut. Banyan moved for the door and Alex followed.

"What happened to whoever that was?" he asked as they walked, his voice shaking. "And why do you think it was Wally?"

"The body was discovered, as I said, very early this morning, by a man out walking his dog down at the Tidal Basin. It was face-down in the water, floating just a few feet from the north shore of the basin. As you could see, the face was destroyed, and what you didn't see because I didn't pull the sheet down far enough, was that his lower body was pretty well cut up. Possibly got hit by a boat prop during the night. Anyhow, enough of his hands are gone that no fingerprints will be useable to us. It appears as if he put up his hands in a reflexive action to protect himself. But, of course, our hands are not gonna protect us from a shotgun blast. We'll wait for the autopsy, of course, but it appears he was shot with at least two rounds of 12-gauge double-aught buckshot."

"You still haven't told me why you think it's Wally," Alex said.

"We found his Navy identification and security clearance badges in his jacket pocket," Banyan said. "And his wallet was in his trousers, along with his keys. It doesn't look like a robbery."

"Why? What makes you say that?" In his gut, Alex knew that the chances that this didn't have something to do with Rudi's intelligence were nil, and the fact that he was the likely follow-up target made him feel even more nauseous.

"He had twenty-three dollars in his wallet. That's a lot of money for a robber to leave, especially after killing someone."

Banyan led Alex back outside and across the street, where he steered them toward a coffee shop rather than back into the police building. "Do you have any idea what he was working on that might be sensitive enough that it would get him killed? If it is as it appears at this time, it looks very much like the motive was murder, pure and simple."

Alex shook his head.

"No, I can't imagine why anything he was working on

would make someone want to kill him," he lied. "Mostly what we do in the Pacific section is to read and analyze signals about Japanese activities in China and Indochina."

Banyan asked him about girlfriends, any chance of a jealousy angle. Alex told him truthfully that he had never seen him with a woman, and that Hammond had talked a couple of times about a woman back in Billings that he thought he might marry one day, if he survived the war and if she didn't marry someone else in the meantime.

They finished their coffee and the inspector asked Alex for his contact information. Alex gave him only the office number, told him the office could reach him 24 hours a day. He did not know at that point who he could trust and decided his home address and phone number should be kept from as many people as possible. Of course, Banyan – or Donovan - could go to BUPERS, the Navy Bureau of Personnel, and if they knew the right strings to pull, get the information from them.

As they moved to the door of the coffee shop, something nagged at Alex's consciousness. Finally, it clicked. "Inspector, was Wally in uniform when he was found?"

"No, he was in casual civilian clothes. Loafers, casual pants, light jacket, or what was left of them. Why?"

Alex shook his head and muttered, "Nothing. Just wondered." He walked to the door, paused on the sidewalk to shake Banyan's hand and walked off. Banyan stood for a moment, watching him go.

Then he turned and walked back toward the police building.

Alex walked in the direction of his office. His mind was in overdrive. He knew without a doubt that if the body in the police morgue was indeed Hammond, then this was no random killing, that someone – Stark? Donovan? Hoover? The Germans? – may be trying to keep Rudi's information from spreading any further than it already had. Just like Rudi had said happened to Canaris when he tried to raise the alarm in Berlin.

Why the hell were so many people so anxious NOT to accept the possibility that Japan intended to attack the United States and bring it into the war?

Whatever the answer, that so many apparently did want to stop the spread of Rudi's sighting could put him and Rudi at risk, him more so because nobody knew where Rudi was. At least I hope they don't! Thinking about BUPERS had made him very uneasy. It was likely, even probable, that Donovan had the contacts in BUPERS to get any information he wanted, may even now have his home address. Obviously, they knew where he worked.

Whoever "they" were.

And if "they" were anxious enough about this to kill a very fine naval officer, they could find Rudi. He was, after all, registered in the Hay Adams under his own name. All they had to do was decide to canvas the city's hotels. He would be found. It was as simple as that. Alex knew he had to rectify that problem as soon as he could.

It had to be Donovan, he concluded. Stark was too much the consummate political officer, and probably too "Navy," to risk his ass by having a naval officer killed. He had no reason to, anyway. He had simply dismissed the intel, probably never to think of it again. But why Donovan? He was being paid $1 per year to develop information like this that would help the President call the right shots.

What could his motivation possibly be?

Then his thinking veered in another direction. What if

the Nazis had discovered Rudi's mission and had sent someone to take out Rudi and everyone he had been involved with? That was certainly possible. Alex quickened his steps and willed himself not to start checking over his shoulder with every step. He had to think clearly, but he felt like he was in a maze and his options were being closed off, one by one.

With the White House, the State, War and Navy Building and the Hay-Adams all in sight, Alex suddenly wondered where he should go. They knew where he worked. If they didn't already, they would soon know where he lived. And eventually they would find Rudi. He quickly analyzed his situation and came to the bizarre conclusion that with Wally Hammond possibly dead, the one person he could trust in the whole mess was Hitler's spy. Appreciating the irony, he laughed aloud to himself, turned and walked across the street to the Hay-Adams.

Rudi answered when Alex called him on the house phone from the lobby and told him to come on up.

"Rudi, we need to get you out of here," he said as soon as he was in the room and the door closed behind him. He told him about the body that might be Hammond and his own suspicion that Donovan was somehow behind it. He told him about the instructions Admiral Kirk – a man he respected deeply – had given to Lieutenant Commander Hammond – another man he respected deeply.

"Where should I go?" Rudi asked.

"It's more like where will we go," Alex replied. "I have to get to my apartment and get my clothes packed before the bastards find out where I live. Then we'll get out of here and take the train to Annapolis. I think for a while they'll be lookin' in Washington, so we should be safe there for a couple of days. I know the town from my time at the Academy. But we need to get to Hawaii and the Philippines if we're to carry out Admiral Kirk's order, and that's the only damn thing that makes sense or means anything to me now, aside from us keepin' ourselves alive."

Rudi started packing while Alex sat down at the table with the phone. He dialed a number from memory. "Lieutenant Price, sir," the man said when he answered the phone.

"Don, Alex Jordan," Alex said. "I need to talk to you as soon as I can. It's important." Lieutenant Donald Price was an Annapolis classmate of Alex's and owed him big time.

In their third year, Price had been on the verge of flunking a naval weapons course, which would have affected his career if not bounced him completely out of the Academy. Alex had helped him, even suggested to him several questions that would logically be on the final exam. This had been crucial to Price squeezing a passing grade out of the course, not to mention a possible violation of the very strict code of honor.

Price had made it clear when he had been assigned to BUPERS a few months after graduation that anytime Alex Jordan needed him, he would do anything he could to help him.

"Come on over right now, Alex," Price said. "And it's good to talk with you, too," he added with a dose of good-natured sarcasm.

"Can't right now, Don. How about tomorrow mornin'?"

"We're not normally open on weekends, Alex, but for you…" He let the sentence dangle.

"Thanks, Don. See you at 0830?"

"You got it, buddy. See you here." He hung up.

"Rudi, you sit tight while I grab a cab to my place. I'll meet you back here." He took off his uniform cap, jacket and tie and left them in Rudi's room.

Alex went down to the lobby, out the front door and into

the back seat of a waiting cab. He gave the cabbie an address a block and a half away from his apartment building. When he got out of the cab, he walked quickly to the side of the street opposite his building. As he approached, he noticed a blue Ford on his side of the street, across the street from his building and down half a block.

There were two men in the car, and they were not moving. He stopped in the doorway of a vegetable market and watched for a minute. Neither man moved, nor could he see any sign that they were talking. What they seemed to be doing was watching the entrance to his apartment building and the pedestrians walking by it. He decided that, while he may be suffering from acute paranoia, he was not going to take any chances.

He turned around and walked back in the other direction, away from the building and the car. At the next street, he crossed the street and walked a block, then back to his left and a block further he was at the rear of his building, in an alley.

He had heard that a resident of the building, a husband with wanderlust, had a long pole with a hook on the end of it stashed near the fire escape. The pole was used to pull down the ladder from the second-floor landing so the wandering husband could slip unnoticed into the building. Alex imitated the husband and was soon in the third-floor hallway and at his apartment door. He listened carefully, his ear to the door. Nothing.

In his apartment, which he was a little surprised to find empty of strange men, he grabbed a large suitcase – no navy duffel this time – and quickly tossed the things he could into it. Slacks, shirts, uniforms, underwear, socks, toiletries, a jacket. He pulled a trench coat on over his navy shirt and pants and felt less conspicuous. Fortunately, Washington was getting cool enough now that the coat would not be uncomfortable.

After locking up, it was back down the fire escape. The alley was quite narrow and in shadows, so a man in a trench coat with a suitcase slipping down a fire escape was not as obvious as it might have been. On the street behind his apartment building, he hailed a cab and rode back to the Hay-Adams.

When he walked into the lobby, on impulse he stopped at the front desk and inquired whether they had any rooms available. This would be a more convenient base than some place in Annapolis, and if Donovan – or whomever – tracked Rudi to the Hay-Adams and learned he had checked out, it seemed logical that the last place they would think to find him was in a different room at the same place. Told they did have a room available, he asked to speak with the manager.

When the manager appeared, Alex showed his ONI identification and explained that he had need of a room for a guest whose identity could not be revealed. The manager, used to such requests given the location of his hotel, smiled and said, "Of course, sir. I will personally take care of the forms. Will the guest in question be male or female?" Assured the guest was male, he said, "I will make a room available for Mr. Reginald Smith immediately, sir."

Momentarily, he reappeared from behind the counter with the key to room 210. Perfect, Alex thought. Second floor We can use the stairs and don't have to bother with the elevator.

"Thank you very much," he said. "I have my guest's suitcase with me and I'll just run up and put it in his room. He'll be along later this evening." The manager nodded, pleased that he was able to do his part for the war effort. Or whatever this was. A part of him doubted that the unnamed guest was male, however.

After putting the suitcase in room 210, Alex went to the elevator and rode up the fourth floor and knocked on Rudi's door. Rudi was packed and ready when he opened the door.

"Change of plans," Alex told him. "We're just moving down to room 210, which I've registered under a false name, Reginald Smith. Fortunately, it has twin beds, so we'll probably both stay in it. At least tonight." Then Alex told Rudi about the men he thought were watching his apartment building. He retrieved his cap, tie and uniform jacket and they headed for the staircase.

After Rudi dropped his luggage in 210, he went to the front desk and checked out, paying cash to settle the bill. He told the clerk he had sent his luggage ahead. When he got back to room 210, Alex left to go to his office, telling Rudi, "I won't be long. Stay in the room until I get back."

In his office, Alex gathered up his briefcase, stuffed the Alpine file in it, took the $500 in Navy cash he kept in his locked cabinet, and went to Marilyn Anderson's desk. She was – had been? – Hammond's secretary.

She had heard about the police call regarding her boss. Alex asked her to come into his office. With the door closed, he told her about his visit to the police, the police suspicion that the Lieutenant Commander may have met with foul play. A mature woman of 40+ years, she did not get hysterical, but she gasped, covered her mouth and tears flowed.

He told her he was going to take some time to try to work with the police to determine whether the body was Wally's, and if so, why he had been killed. She knew how close the two men were, or seemed to be, and she did not question him about it.

"Meanwhile, it's possible the body they found is not the Commander's, so please let me know right away if he calls or comes in." She nodded. "Thank you, Marilyn," he said and gave her the phone number of the Hay-Adams, asking her to call him in room 210 if she heard anything from Lieutenant Commander Hammond, and asking that she please tell nobody, Navy or otherwise, where he was staying. She had been in her job long enough not to ask why he was staying in the Hay-Adams and not his apartment.

Alex closed the door behind her when she left and called Inspector Banyan. Banyan had told him the autopsy would be performed right away and he was anxious to know if Banyan had learned anything more. The inspector answered his phone on the second ring.

"Nothing much we didn't already know, or suspect," he told Alex. "It was at least two shotgun blasts to the face. The wounds on the hands are consistent with the victim holding them up in front of his face in a defensive move. Stay in touch and I'll let you know if anything more develops."

Alex told him he had not come up with anything further that might link Hammond's work to his murder. He felt bad lying to a police homicide inspector who, he felt, was being honest with him.

The next morning, Alex was in Don Price's office at BUPERS at 8:25. The previous afternoon, after leaving his office, he had taken Rudi to a photographer he knew and had a photo taken of him, wearing Alex's Naval officer's coat, tie, and cap, but close enough for Alex's rank not to be visible in the photo.

Price was there when he arrived and the two old friends shook hands and made small talk for less than two minutes.

"What's on your mind, Alex?" Price asked.

"I have a mission and I need your help and I need it quick," Alex told him in a voice that conveyed the urgency of the situation. Price nodded, opened his hands in a gesture that conveyed his willingness.

"I'm makin' an inspection tour of the Philippines – leavin' as soon as possible - to look at our defenses at Cavite and talk with some of our ONI guys down there. I need travel orders cut, top priority, or as high as I can get."

"I can cut those orders right now," Price responded immediately. "And I could have yesterday, so why the Saturday morning stuff?"

"I've also got a new associate that I'm gonna take along, a guy who's just been transferred to ONI. The problem is that he hasn't yet gotten all the security clearances, but he's not a problem and if I had the time, getting those clearances would not be a problem. I've known him since we were in grammar school together. He didn't go to the Academy, got commissioned through the Corps of Cadets at Texas A&M. His name is Richard Barnhardt. Lieutenant (junior grade) Richard Barnhardt." He spelled the name, and Price wrote it down. "I've got his picture right here. I need an ONI ID card for him and travel orders just like mine. Any problem with that?"

"Jesus," Price muttered. "Travel orders are one thing, but an ONI ID card? Where is this guy? Can he come in so at least I can verify he exists and doesn't have horns?"

"I'd like to do that," Alex said, "but Dick is on a train tryin' his ass off to get back here from Texas so we can leave. Hopefully in a coupla days, if you can make it happen. I know this is way irregular, but I'll personally vouch for Dick. I really need you to do me this favor. We'll be even, Don."

"Well, I'll need to call in one of our clerks who knows how to make up an ID card." He paused, thinking. "Yeah, no problem, old buddy. I know the gal I can call. If I promise her a nice dinner and some flowers, she'll do anything for me. Give me three hours. Where will you be, the office?"

"In three hours, I'll be ready for lunch. Why don't we meet at Ernesto's? I'll get a booth. It'll be on me."

"Hell of a deal," Price exclaimed, "Free lunch at Ernesto's. I'll see you there at 1130 hours, give or take."

When Price walked into Ernesto's at 11:42, Alex was nervously sipping a beer in a booth near the back. Price slid into the booth and ordered a beer, too. When the waiter was gone, he slid a folder over to Alex.

"One ONI ID card, name and photograph of Lieutenant (junior grade) Richard Barnhardt, two AAAA travel priorities – the highest I could authorize without a General or Admiral's orders - Washington, D.C. to Manila, names of Lieutenant Alexander Jordan and Lieutenant (junior grade) Richard Barnhardt," Price said smugly. "The orders specify Manila but they'll be good for anywhere in the Southwest Pacific area, including Australia. I figured you'd maybe want to take in some other South Sea action while you're on vacation. Anything else I can do for you today?" He smiled and Alex had trouble covering the tremble in his hand as he took the folder.

The waiter delivered Price's beer and took their orders for lunch. When he left, Alex said, "Don, you're not just a friend, you're a magician. I really appreciate it. You let me know any time I can do anything for you."

CHAPTER 7

Washington, D.C.
October 11, 1941

Back in room 210 at the Hay-Adams, Alex proudly showed Rudi von Althorp his new identity. Rudi marveled at his friend's ability to make things happen that he thought only the bosses at ONI or in the Tirpitzufer could do. Alex then went back downstairs to use a pay phone in the lobby – he admitted to himself that he was consumed by paranoia -   and called Inspector Banyan. True to his word, Banyan was in his office on a Saturday.

"Still no definite ID on the body," Banyan said. "The mouth was so ruined that dental records are useless, but I guess you could see that for yourself. But we sure as hell haven't located even a trace of a live version of Lieutenant Commander Hammond. Have you?"

"No," Alex said. "His office still hasn't heard from him. What's your plan?"

"Even without a positive ID on the corpse, if we don't find anything else, I think he'll be declared legally dead by the end of the week. At least on the civilian side. I don't have any idea what the Navy will do."

Alex went over it all with Rudi after he got back to the

room. He explained his suspicions and went over the reasons Stark, Hoover and Donovan might or might not be motivated to stop Rudi's information from seeing the light of day. Then he asked Rudi point-blank what the chances were that the Abwehr had changed its mind – or had it changed for them – or that some other German agency had taken an interest in what they were doing.

"I cannot conceive of Admiral Canaris turning on me," Rudi said earnestly. "He simply would not do it. If for some reason he decided to abort my mission, he would simply signal me through the embassy here to shut it down and report back to Tokyo. And, of course I would do so if those were my orders from him. But I do think it is possible the SS-SD got wind of this somehow and they have taken it on themselves to stop us. Maybe the Embassy signals section is compromised. They really are ruthless bastards, the SS-SD."

He told Alex what he knew of Heydrich and of his more or less one-way rivalry with Canaris, of his thirst for power and his total lack of morality. He also vowed not to send any more signals from the Washington Embassy, just in case its signal section really was compromised.

"Well, maybe I jumped to conclusions about Donovan," Alex said after hearing the story, some of which he had heard before. "But for the time being, I think we have to plan on the basis that either a branch of your government or mine may be trying to stop us. At least I'm reasonably sure it's not the Japs, because they tend to stand out, if you get my meaning, and we would know if we've been shadowed."

The two men spent the next three quarters of an hour going back and forth, through every scenario either could imagine, for why someone would want Lieutenant Commander Wallace Hammond dead and why they would be staking out

Alex Jordan's apartment. They were unable to come up with anything that made sense and their paranoia was growing.

There was a knock at the door.

Alex and Rudi jumped like cats that had been rudely awakened from a nap. They looked at each other, alarm on both faces. Silent questions passed between them.

Who the hell could that be?

Did you order room service?

Did one of us send our laundry out?

I used a pay phone to call Banyan!

Alex went to the door and asked, without opening it, "Who is it?"

"Lieutenant Jordan, please open the door," came the unmistakable voice of Colonel William Donovan. With no place to go and trapped, Alex unfastened the dead bolt and opened the door. Donovan was alone, which was something of a relief. When he was inside and the door relocked, Donovan continued, "And I presume I am also in the company of Herr Rudolf von Althorp." Donovan put out his hand for Rudi and the two men shook hands. Donovan noted that Rudi was wide-eyed and his palm seemed as wet as a washcloth in a shower.

"How did you find us?" Alex asked lamely when they were seated. "And how did you get Rudi's name?"

"Alex, do you really think ONI is the only government agency with which our friend, the manager of this fine hotel, cooperates? Or that you are the only person in Washington who was aware of Mr. von Althorp when he was posted here previously?"

"The manager told you we were here?" Alex asked. "As far as he knew, Mr. von Althorp had checked out."

"A connection he did not make, Alex. May I call you Alex?" Alex simply nodded and Donovan continued. "He told me you registered someone whose name could not be used, but was apparently an ONI asset. And he told me he suspected from housekeeping reports that two gentlemen were sharing a room with twin beds. It was not difficult for me to make the connection, but he knew nothing of Rudi, other than as a former guest."

Donovan looked at Rudi and added, "Forgive me, Herr von Althorp. May I call you Rudi?" Rudi shrugged and nodded almost imperceptibly, fear and a hint of defiance mingling in his eyes.

"Why are you here, sir?" Alex asked, desperate to find out where this was heading. "Have you got any verification of Rudi's observations?"

"I'm here because I appreciate what you are trying to do – both of you. And I am concerned for you. And most of all because I fear I owe you both an apology."

"An apology?" Alex hadn't been expecting that. "Why?" Rudi was sitting, mute, just following the conversation like he might follow an extremely interesting tennis match.

"Because I fear my bringing Mr. Hoover in on this may have been a mistake. A grave one. I was trying to play nice with Edgar – as the President wishes me to - and keep the FBI in the loop and I thought they might have assets that could help us validate Rudi's observation. Instead, the G-men seem to have jumped to the immediate conclusion that Rudi is here for other purposes entirely. More dangerous purposes."

"What kind of dangerous purposes?"

"Well, it seems Hoover's men have been working some intel that suggests the Germans will try to infiltrate several teams into this country to sabotage military and industrial targets, thus harming our country's ability to supply the British and Russians, or to wage war ourselves if it comes to that.

They feel it's entirely plausible that Rudi is the leader of one of the teams, or perhaps even the overall mission commander. And they feel that even if that is not the case, they believe his mission is disinformation."

"And they think his intel is just a way to keep him 'safe' until his real mission starts?" Alex asked. Donovan nodded.

Alex was shocked initially but there was a certain logic to the FBI conclusions. IF those were the FBI's conclusions and not a Donovan ruse.

"I fear that may be it exactly, Alex." Donovan paused before going on. "I believe they're dismissing the sighting of shallow-water torpedo practice by the Nakajimas as simply a story to provide cover for his being here. I think they mean to find and capture Rudi and they will probably try to make you an accessory, unwitting or otherwise. As you may know, they are watching your apartment building."

Well, that explains the car with the two men, Alex thought to himself, more than a little relieved that that puzzle, at least, had been answered. Or has it? Is Donovan telling the truth or is this just another line of bullshit?

"So what do you suggest, sir?" Alex asked.

"You must leave – soon," Donovan responded quickly. "I'd like you to go to Pearl Harbor and do what you can to get this information in the hands of Admiral Kimmel's intelligence staff. I'll get you travel authorizations and clear it with ONI. After you leave, of course."

Because of his continuing doubts, Alex did not mention the travel priorities and new identity for Rudi that Don Price had provided. Nor did he mention that Admiral Kirk had also told him that he must get the intel to CINCPAC if all else fails.

Alex was puzzled. "If you haven't been able to verify Rudi's story, why are you sending us to Pearl Harbor?" he asked. "You don't know it's real any more than any of the others Wally and I talked to."

"A very strange thing happened a day or so after you were in my office," Donovan said in a flat voice. "I had a visit from the Washington station chief of MI6. He wanted to know if I knew any person who might be known as Frosch."

Alex and Rudi froze.

"I told him I didn't know what he was talking about and he told me the Brits had turned up some paperwork that referred to someone by that code name as a contact of an Abwehr agent who had information on a certain Japanese torpedo drill. I checked at ONI and Army Intelligence and ONI came up with information from Lieutenant Commander Hammond's files that identify your Abwehr code name as Frosch. I am making the assumption that the code name had to come from you, Rudi. Am I wrong?"

Rudi was jolted, but admitted that was the code name he had given his friend in 1938, when they first met. Alex agreed and added that so far as he knew, he had had no contact with anyone else connected to the Abwehr or any other Axis intelligence service. Privately, he was wondering how the ONI files had a reference to his German code name when he had only learned of it himself when Rudi told him about Canaris' message.

Donovan turned again to Rudi. "Rudi, I'm led to believe that Admiral Canaris often provides his people with alternative identities and passports. Is that so in your case?"

Rudi thought for a moment before replying, concluding he would be wise to go along with Donovan for now. "Yes, that is his practice. I have a Swiss passport in the name of Eugen Kraus." Rudi spelled the name and Donovan nodded before asking whether his alternative identity would be known to others in the Abwehr or in other departments of the German government.

"I believe that the Kraus identity is known only to Admiral Canaris and General Oster, the Admiral's deputy," Rudi answered truthfully. "It is their way of giving me an option should the SS-SD take a sudden interest in my activities." Donovan's nod indicated that he was aware of the friction between the Abwehr and the SS-SD. Aside from a difference in actions and tactics toward one another, it was not unlike the friction between COI and the FBI.

"In that case, I will have AA-1 travel authorities for Lieutenant Alexander Jordan and Herr Eugen Kraus, a Swiss national charged with a task of military importance to the United States, in your hands in two hours. Any higher travel priority might raise suspicions in the wrong quarters. You will be booked on a train departing Union Station tomorrow morning at 7:45. You will change trains in Philadelphia for Chicago and from there to another train to San Francisco. You will then be booked on a Matson liner to Honolulu.

"In Hawaii, you will have reservations at the Royal Hawaiian Hotel, and Governor Poindexter, the American governor of the territory, will be authorized to advance you more money, over and above what I provide you tonight, if you feel you need it. And as I said, your absence from ONI, Alex, will be covered. And speaking of cover, I will have the hotel watched tonight in case the FBI gets impatient. Once you leave and Rudi becomes Eugen Kraus, I am hoping the FBI loses the trail of Rudolf von Althorp, if they did not when Rudi 'checked out' of this hotel."

It was obvious to both Alex and Rudi that Donovan had planned this before coming to the Hay-Adams. But any suspicion either man might have had was overshadowed by an overpowering sense of relief in leaving Washington and being on their way to the Pacific. Perhaps both Hawaii and the Philippines.

When Donovan had left them, Rudi asked Alex why he had not told the man about the identity and travel authorities Price had provided.

"We may need them before this is over," he said simply. "I'm still not sure I know who the good guys and the bad guys are, although the Brits contacting him seems to have convinced him what you're really here for. And if I'd told him about the new identity, I would have run the risk of getting Don Price in some deep shit, especially if this is not all that it seems." Rudi nodded, smiling faintly.

At 4:45, there was another knock at the door. When Alex opened it cautiously, Donovan was standing there holding an expensive-looking briefcase. Inside the room, he handed a heavy envelope to Alex. "Your tickets and travel authorizations are in there. Along with $500 in cash. Take good care of it."

"I'm surprised, and maybe a little flattered, that you brought this yourself," Alex said as he took the envelope.

"Under the circumstances, I think the fewer people who know anything about this, the better," Donovan said. "Besides, I have a 5:00 appointment across the street." Alex knew that meant the White House and undoubtedly with Roosevelt personally. He wondered if he and Rudi were on the agenda.

After Donovan departed, Rudi began leafing through his pocket notebook.

"What are you looking for?" Alex asked.

"The number for the Embassy," Rudi replied. "I need to reach Meike Franzky before she leaves for the day." He had told Alex about Meike, including about her unabashed interest in him.

"What for?" Alex asked, a tone of alarm in his voice.

"I should signal the Admiral that I am leaving Washington," Rudi said simply. "And that we may have troubles with the SS-SD. He may have a way to sort that out."

"But what good will it do?" Alex protested. "Once we get on that train tomorrow morning, he won't be able to get a message to you. And what about what you said about the signals section maybe being compromised by the SS-SD?"

"We have a consulate in San Francisco," Rudi explained. "I don't know if it has an Abwehr man in it, but I would not be surprised if it did. And even if it doesn't, there may be a way for him to get a signal to me through the consulate. In any case, it is standard that when we are on a mission, we keep headquarters aware of our progress if we are able to without compromising the mission. And in case the signals section is compromised, I will not be specific about where we are going."

"Rudi, are you absolutely sure Canaris isn't running some kind of game, using you?"

"My friend, if I cannot trust Admiral Canaris, I have no hope of surviving this war anyway." Alex thought a few moments, concluded Rudi was right, and nodded. Rudi made the call. Meike was still at her desk, and Rudi left for the Embassy, dressed as inconspicuously as possible, with Alex following, as they had agreed, discretely watching for signs of a tail. There were none.

EYES ONLY
THE DIRECTOR
ABWEHR HEADQUARTERS
TIRPITZUFER
BERLIN

FROSCH LIKES PACKAGE STOP OTHERS
AT PARTY SKEPTICAL STOP FROSCH AND
UNDERSIGNED DEPART TOMORROW MORNING
TO POSSIBLE SITE FOR PARTY STOP PLAN
TO BE IN SAN FRANCISCO APPROXIMATELY
OCTOBER 20 STOP WILL STAY MARK HOPKINS
HOTEL STOP REQUEST ANY FURTHER GIFTS
BE DELIVERED THERE VIA CONSULATE STOP
DEPARTURE FOR POSSIBLE PARTY SITE
OCTOBER 21 STOP MAY HAVE ONE OF COUSIN
REINHARDS RELATIVES WITH ME STOP PLEASE
ADVISE OF ANY SPECIAL PREFERENCES ON
YOUR PART STOP
    R. VON ALTHORP
    REICH EMBASSY
    WASHINGTON DC
    END MESSAGE

CHAPTER 8

Union Station, Washington, D.C.
October 17, 1941

The platform was busy, as usual during the early hours of the morning, even on a Sunday. Rudi and Alex made their way through the crowd and found their train to Philadelphia. They were not in the first class car for the short part of the trip, although Alex had noted when he looked at the travel documents the night before that Donovan had booked them a first class sleeper compartment for two from Philadelphia to Chicago and from Chicago to San Francisco.

At 9:00 that morning, Henry Carter walked into a coffee shop not far from the building that housed the Coordinator of Information. Colonel William Donovan, who Carter knew by sight but not by name, was already seated at a table, the Washington Post spread out in front of him. There were very few others in the place.

Carter knew Donovan only as Oscar, the name he used when he called a special telephone number Donovan had given him. Because it was a Sunday, Donovan was dressed casually in gray wool slacks and an argyle-patterned cardigan sweater over a starched blue long-sleeved shirt with the collar open. Carter took a seat at the table.

While Donovan was not especially tall, he was always very well-groomed, his hair trimmed and face shaven. Carter was shorter by two inches, but quite stocky, with no distinguishing features, save for his expressionless eyes.

Donovan handed Carter a large manila envelope, which contained tickets on commercial aircraft from Washington to San Francisco, then on a Pan American Clipper flight to Honolulu. Both were round-trip tickets, with the return dates and flights left open. His high-priority travel voucher was also enclosed should any other travelers – usually military or national defense-related - attempt to bump him off of full flights.

Carter was not on the books as an employee of the Coordinator of Information. He was, one might say, an independent contractor, paid from a private fund controlled personally by Donovan. The funds themselves came from a private White House account that few in Congress knew anything about, the purpose of which was to give the President the ability to accomplish things "in the national interest" that might appear untoward were the press or political opponents to learn of it.

Many of the activities of the Coordinator of Information qualified for funding under that definition.

In fact, Carter's background, if exposed in the press, would be characterized as unsavory at best. Before making his services available to Donovan – at the suggestion of a New York Longshoremen's Union official and mob boss by the name of Salvatore Marinelli – he had worked for Marinelli and others in the New York underworld as a very discrete and not overly bright, but nonetheless effective, protection man, trailing, watching and guarding men whose enemies could be at once subtle, clever and extremely violent. And sometimes he was simply used to cause the disappearance of men who posed problems of various sorts for Marinelli and his people.

Because he was Anglo-Saxon and a Protestant – actually, agnostic would be a better term to describe his religious beliefs, because he never thought about the subject – he could never really have been a member of the organization for which he toiled. So when Donovan put out the word to his acquaintances in this subset of New York life that he had a need for a few people who could take care of important but unspecified assignments with precision and discretion, Carter's name had been one of the first suggested.

Donovan had little doubt that Henry Carter was not his real name. In fact, he very much hoped it was not. Anything could go wrong, and if it did, a man who did not exist would be easier to deny.

What Donovan did not know was that Marinelli had suggested Carter for his services as a convenient alternative to having him killed. Carter had committed the unpardonable sin of causing the young daughter of one of Marinelli's top capos to become pregnant. In the world in which such men lived, dallying with the bosses' daughters – or wives - was simply not done, and Henry Carter, non-Sicilian as he was, would never have been approved by the capo, or by Don Marinelli himself, as suitable marriage material for the young lady.

Thus, Carter had been exiled, as contrasted with loaned, to Donovan, while the young lady in question had been sent to visit relatives in Sicily until her "health problem" cleared up. The baby would be left with relatives to be raised in Sicily.

Before he had departed New York, Carter had been told by Marinelli that he fervently hoped he would die on one of his missions for the United States government, but that if he did not, his reappearance in New York would most certainly ensure his quick and violent death. This threat did not fall on deaf ears, and Carter had no intention of returning to New York.

Ever.

"Do you have everything you need for your trip?" Donovan asked after Carter had examined the envelope. It contained $7,000 in $20 and $50 bills, along with photos and physical descriptions of Alex Jordan and "Eugen Kraus," and confirmed reservations at the Moana Hotel for an unspecified period of time, to be billed directly to the office of the Territorial Governor of Hawaii. The money was intended to cover incidental expenses and Carter's stipend for this assignment.

It was a lot of money.

Carter liked working for this government man. Even though he had no idea who he was or exactly who he was working for, he paid much better than the Italians in New York.

"Yeah, I guess so," Carter mumbled. He was clearly a lot smarter than he acted and an excellent tracker of men, but verbal skills were not among Carter's strengths. Donovan handed him a second envelope, marked "OPEN ONLY WHEN INSTRUCTED."

"Let's make sure we are in agreement as to the nature of your assignment," Donovan said evenly. "You are to make visual contact with those men when they disembark in Honolulu on the date specified in your materials. They are on an important mission and I have reason to believe there are German agents who will try to follow them, and possibly try to intercept or even do them harm. I want you to keep them alive. Call me, collect, at this number when you make contact."

He handed Carter another envelope containing a letter of introduction to Governor Poindexter of Hawaii, who, in addition to covering his hotel bill, would be able to supply a telephone if there were problems with the public or hotel phones in Hawaii. Then he continued.

"Under no circumstances do I want anything to happen to either of these men." He pointed to the Kraus photo. "He is a person of extreme interest, and at the proper time I may want you to take him into what you might call protective custody, alive. If I decide to do so, I'll let you know very directly. Is that clear?"

"It's clear," Carter mumbled. "What about the other guy? Is he interesting, too?" Carter's thick New York "street" accent contrasted with Donovan's upper-class, cultured tones.

"Yes, but he's also a U.S. Naval officer. For the time being, just keep an eye on both of them." Carter nodded. He might have been tempted to puzzle some of the pieces together, but did not. The people he had worked for in New York were equally puzzling sometimes, the way they turned on former business partners, sometimes even on relatives or close friends. The why, in the end, was not his problem.

"You leave tomorrow," Donovan said, rising from the table. "Good luck." He offered his hand and Carter shook it limply. Social graces were not among his many talents either. Donovan paid for his coffee and left quickly, with the distinct feeling that he now needed a bath.

When the train pulled into Philadelphia's main station, passengers Alexander Jordan and Eugen Kraus grabbed their suitcases – they had two each – and climbed down to the platform. Both scanned the platform for watchers, although both knew it was most likely their watchers, if there were any, were on the train with them. They went into the terminal to find out from which track the Chicago train would depart. They discovered they had a two-hour wait and moved toward the coffee shop.

They recognized nobody from their Washington train.

Finally, after their fourth cup of coffee, the public address system in the station called for passengers on the Chicago train, leaving from Track 5. The two men found their car near the front of the train, and an extremely courteous, very black porter led them to their sleeper compartment. They politely declined his offer to unpack their suitcases for them, tipped him, and the porter disappeared in search of other passengers and other tips.

Alex and Rudi immediately bolted from the room, locking the door behind them and hurried to the restroom at the far end of the car to deposit their four cups of coffee before their bladders burst.

Back in the compartment with the door closed and locked, they unpacked only what they thought they would need for the two days they would be on this train and carefully relocked the suitcases. Rudi – Eugen – had not told Alex about the $20,000 he had secreted inside the false bottom – actually bottoms - of one of his suitcases. He did not distrust Alex.

He simply thought that if things started to get out of hand, especially if the SS-SD was involved, Alex was better off not knowing about the money. They had the $500 Donovan had given them, the $500 Alex had gotten from his office safe, and the $100-odd that Rudi had brought with him as yen and Reichsmarks from Tokyo and exchanged for dollars in Mexico City.

Twenty minutes later, they heard the conductor call "all aboard" several times as he walked the length of the train closing doors and the train lurched and began its journey to Chicago. It was 10:30. They were scheduled to arrive in Chicago a little over 28 hours later, then would stay the night in Chicago before boarding the San Francisco train at 8:00 the following morning.

They kicked off their shoes and decided to read a bit and relax until lunch was called at 12:30. Both were dozing on their narrow beds when the porter knocked on their door to announce lunch. The first class dining car was the car immediately in front of theirs and they were among the first to arrive.

A waiter wearing a short white jacket and white gloves that contrasted dramatically with his black skin directed them to a table on the right side and handed them menus. The choices were astounding and the prices very reasonable. Rudi ordered pork chops, Alex ordered a strip steak, and both ordered Falstaff beer, which, happily, came to the table very cold.

The train pulled into Chicago at 3:45 p.m. the next day, just one hour late. They had stopped at every village, it seemed, in the states of Pennsylvania, Ohio and Indiana. The next morning, the departure for San Francisco was exactly on time at 8:00.

They were shown to a sleeping compartment virtually identical to the one they had the day before in another car adjacent to the first class dining car. It was almost as if it were the same train. They still had not identified anyone, either on the train or on the platform, who showed the slightest bit of interest in them. That made both men even more nervous, and they were both resolved to a long and nerve-wracking journey.

They had eaten breakfast at the hotel, so they passed on the dining car breakfast when it was called shortly after departure. Alex was reading in their compartment, reclining on his bed. Rudi turned on the radio in the compartment, finding the signal surprisingly good. Between the radio and the noise of the wheels on the rails, he was satisfied that talking in the compartment could not be overheard outside the small space.

"Do you think we are being watched?" he asked Alex.

Alex shook his head. "At first, I figured we would be. Whoever killed Wally Hammond – if that really was Wally - has to be looking for us. If it was him, I'd bet my bottom dollar his murder is connected to the fact that he knew what we're tryin' to do, that he was tryin' to help. But it's been over two days and we haven't seen anyone, nobody's shown any interest in us. Hell, I haven't even seen that many faces on the train more than once. It sure seems like we got out of Washington without being followed. Donovan's got a reputation for making things work the way he wants them to. Maybe we had a tail and Donovan got rid of it for us. I just don't know, but it doesn't feel like we've got anyone with us."

Idly, Alex wondered to himself how Inspector Roscoe Banyan would react when he needed to talk again with Alex and discovered he had disappeared. But he could do nothing about that now, so dismissed the thought from his mind. Instead, he found some stationery emblazoned with the railroad's insignia and began writing a letter to his parents in Fort Worth. It might be some time before he would be able to write them again. And if things in Hawaii did not work out....

Rudi let Alex's words about the absence of watchers sink in. He was growing increasingly convinced in his own mind – primarily because he could make no sense of any other possibility - that the SS-SD had gotten wind of his report to Canaris and was trying to stop him, with or without the complicity of von Ribbentrop.

And he felt increasingly certain that they, rather than

one of American agencies, had most likely killed Hammond. He could not conceive of the Americans killing a U.S. Navy officer. But then, neither could he conceive of the Americans not wanting his information shared with all the Pacific military commanders.

And it would make sense that Donovan could have had SS-SD agents under surveillance, so delaying or diverting them – somehow throwing them off their tracks – would be relatively easy for Donovan's men.

The trip passed uneventfully. Both men remained on high alert, but neither noticed anything. Alex even walked the length of the train twice, looking for faces that did not fit or that seemed interested in him. It began to appear to both of them that they may have indeed, escaped Washington without anyone following. But they were also chafing with impatience as the trip dragged on. They were both convinced the Japanese were going to attack the U.S. and thrust America into the war, and they were equally determined to warn the people who could do something to head it off, or at least to minimize the slaughter. If they got to the Pacific in time.

Throughout, Alex remembered always to call his friend "Eugen."

CHAPTER 9

Oakland, California
October 20, 1941

The train pulled into the station in Oakland, just across the bay from San Francisco, virtually on time at 11:20 a.m. Alex and Rudi gathered their luggage and hailed a taxi to take them to the ferry terminal, less than a mile distant. The bay ferry deposited them at San Francisco's Ferry Building an hour later. Another taxi took them to the Mark Hopkins Hotel, directly up California Street from the Ferry Building. They could have ridden a cable car – one of San Francisco's most famous attractions - but chose not to because of their luggage.

Mindful of the need to be careful with their money, since they did not know how long this mission would take – and since Alex was unaware of the false bottoms in Rudi's suitcase and what was under them – they shared a room at the Mark Hopkins. Donovan's assurance that they could get more if they needed it from Governor Poindexter in Hawaii was all well and good, but that assumed they could trust Donovan. At the moment, neither man was in an especially trusting mood.

Alex toyed with the idea of going to the Pan American Airways terminal on Treasure Island to see if they could get on one of the Clipper flying boats to Honolulu. He had heard a lot about them, and the idea of five agonizingly-slow days at sea on the passenger ship held little appeal. The luxury of the cruise would not match the anxiety both men felt.

In the end, after talking about it with Rudi, they decided to stay with Donovan's arrangements. As Rudi had said, "If you trust Donovan half as much as I trust Admiral Canaris, he must have done what he thought best for us. We will be more anonymous on the ship than we could be on an airplane." They also knew the airplane was likely to be crawling with military travelers, all with very high travel priorities.

Alex also realized a Clipper trip might take all of the money they had. At least all the money he knew about.

They settled in to wait.

Late that afternoon, they rode the elevator to the lobby of the Mark Hopkins and went into the nicely-appointed bar. The bar was over half-full with what looked to be a combination of hotel guests and San Francisco businessmen. The Mark Hopkins was close to the financial district of the city, home to numerous banks, corporations and insurance companies and the accounting and law firms which lived off them like parasites off a whale.

They sat at the end of the bar farthest from the doors and surreptitiously studied everyone who was already there or who entered after them. Still nobody looked interested in them, aside from a very attentive and efficient bartender who was wearing black slacks and a starched white dress shirt with a black garter on each sleeve and a matching black bow tie.

After a very dry martini and two bottles of beer – each – Alex and Rudi ordered ham sandwiches, which they ate at the bar. Still no sign of anybody watching them. And no messages from the German Consulate appeared at the front desk of the Mark Hopkins.

At that same time, a man they had not noticed at the

Ferry Building earlier – he was having his shoes shined when they had passed - was sending a signal from the small German Consulate to the Tirpitzufer reporting that the package had arrived in San Francisco.

The next morning, two very anxious young men checked out of the Mark Hopkins shortly after daybreak and hopped in a taxi, directing the driver to the terminal of the Matson Navigation Company. Their ship, the SS Lurline, was available for boarding at 7:30 a.m., with departure set for 12:00 noon sharp. The cab driver was very familiar with the port facilities and dropped Alex and Rudi off at the end of the pier at 7:15. A short line had already begun to form. They were apparently not the only passengers who were anxious to begin this journey to Hawaii.

The line moved quickly when the gate was opened at 7:30, and soon Alex and Rudi reached the check-in station and handed over their tickets to a gate clerk who checked their names off the passenger manifest.

The tickets were in turn handed over to a uniformed steward who gathered their luggage on a dolly and showed them to their stateroom. It was much roomier than either man anticipated, with two single beds that were quite a bit larger than those on the trains. The beds folded up into the wall, turning the room into a sitting room when the beds were not in use. The restroom was also quite roomy compared to those on the train. They decided that this would be a very nice trip if not for their many nagging worries.

The steward handed them papers with lists of shipboard activities, locations of restaurants, bars and entertainment parlors and their assigned meal seating times and locations. He advised them the ship was almost full, so changes in meal times or seating would be difficult to obtain. Alex assured him they were fine with the meal times and thanked him with a $2 tip. He had checked the day before with the concierge at the Mark Hopkins and discovered that the accepted tip for the cabin steward on boarding was $2, with another $3 upon disembarkation.

The stateroom was an interior room, so they had no porthole. Thus, any orientation as to direction of the ship or of their surroundings would be available only when they ventured out to one of the decks.

Once they had unpacked and hung up their clothes, they went out to walk around and get themselves acquainted with the layout of the ship and the location of their assigned dining room seating. They decided it would also be an excellent idea to locate and check out the bars. After all, a shared taste for beer was one of the things that brought the two men together to begin with, back in 1938.

Passengers Jordan and Kraus were standing at the port railing on one of the uppermost decks looking down at the dock when the lines were cast off and two powerful tugboats began pulling the big ship away from the dock. The huge idling engines were soon engaged and the tugs, now one on either side of the ship's bow, nudged it toward the Golden Gate. Safely away from the waterfront, the ship was released by the tugs and made its way past Treasure Island, then by Alcatraz, an island prison from which nobody had ever successfully escaped. At least, that was what the authorities claimed.

Sailing under the relatively-new and very impressive Golden Gate Bridge and into the open sea, Alex and Rudi sat at a lanai bar high near the stern of the ship and sipped beer while the California coastline slowly slid behind them. It was, both men thought, a magnificent sight. After the very short time they had spent in their windowless stateroom three decks below, they had silently agreed that this bar was where they would be spending much of their time over the next five days.

The open side of the bar faced aft, protecting them from the wind and elements, if there were any. They decided to skip the lunch seating when they discovered they could instead order sandwiches here. The sandwiches came on china plates with French fries, coleslaw and a giant kosher dill pickle spear. They were also served with real silverware and cloth napkins.

This is the way to travel, Alex thought to himself, if it just didn't take so damn long to get there. On the trip, Alex passed much of the time studying the Navy hierarchy at Pearl Harbor. He had grabbed the relevant information from ONI when he was last in his office. He wanted to know as much as possible about the lay of the land, people-wise, as he could. He did not know how much time they would have once they got there.

If, for instance, someone was there who would do what he could to hamper their mission. At the same time, Rudi studied U.S. Navy insignia of rank.

During the entire voyage, they saw nobody who seemed to be paying them any undue attention whatsoever. They wondered constantly when the other shoe would drop.

In London, Sir Stewart Menzies had received word back from the MI6 Washington station. Menzies knew and respected Colonel William Donovan, even if he thought little of Donovan's organization, which he considered to be a bunch of bumbling fools, too quick to draw conclusions and too short on insight as to the possible implications of a particular piece of intelligence.

Washington station had reported to Menzies that Donovan had denied any knowledge of anyone named –

or code-named – Frosch, but that, curiously, he expressed great interest in what MI6 knew and how they had come upon such a name.

Menzies had also received word from Bletchley Park of another signal from the German Embassy in Washington to Berlin alluding to a trip and a party. He was still unsure of the implications and smart enough to admit it, but he thought it was time the Prime Minister was alerted, should anything else turn up in the next few days.

Winston Churchill had been a bit peeved when Menzies briefed him on the German signals and the possible Washington connection. His unhappiness was not based on the prospect of a Japanese attack on the United States, but on the fact that Menzies had not informed him earlier.

Churchill told Menzies to make solving this puzzle a matter of the highest priority and to come to him immediately with anything else that turned up, no matter the hour. He desperately wanted the United States in this war with him, but would not allow intelligence pointing to a Japanese attack on the United States fleet to go unreported to Washington.

He had once been First Lord of the Admiralty and his love of the Navy was well known. And with the American North Atlantic convoys literally sustaining the life of England, his love of the American Navy was almost as great as that he felt for the Royal Navy.

But most of all, he would not use any Ultra intercept on its own. Ultra was the most important British secret of the war – so far – and he would not do anything that might in any way alert the Germans that London was reading their Enigma traffic.

"Get me something with meat," he told Menzies, "and I shall personally present it to President Roosevelt. And you know, Sir Stewart, 'with meat' means that this information must be independently corroborated, by us or by someone other than an Ultra intercept." In a perfect world, Churchill thought, he would present the warning to Roosevelt just as the Japanese were readying their attack, but in time to thwart it, so there could be no mistaking, even to the American isolationists, what their intentions were.

"I shall bend all efforts toward that end, Prime Minister," Menzies intoned. "We shall find another source or, failing that, invent one."

When he returned to his office, Menzies ordered a signal to the lone MI6 man in Tokyo, where England still maintained an Embassy, although it had been gradually shrinking in manpower since the signing of the Tri-Partite Pact. The signal alerted the man to unconfirmed reports of shallow-water torpedo tests by the Japanese and urgently requested anything that might shed light on the veracity of the reports.

The MI6 man signaled his receipt of the message and assured London that he would get on it immediately.

CHAPTER 10

Honolulu, Territory of Hawaii
October 26, 1941

At last, the gangways were locked in place and the passengers began to disembark from the SS Lurline, now safely moored in Honolulu Harbor. Passengers Jordan and Kraus, leaving the porters to care for the more elderly passengers – which were most of them - carried their suitcases down the gangway and made their way to a line that had formed for taxis.

They scanned the faces outside the wire fence that separated the Matson Navigation Company's Honolulu terminal from the public area. They saw lots of faces, most intently searching for friends or relatives who were likely to be coming down one of the gangways. Neither noticed anyone who seemed to be looking at - or for - them.

Ten minutes later, their luggage stowed in the trunk, Alex and Rudi were settled in the back seat of a yellow 1936 Dodge bearing the markings of the Waikiki Cab Company. Twenty minutes after that, the cab, driven by a very polite older man of indeterminate Asian ancestry, pulled into the ornate semi-circular driveway of the Royal Hawaiian Hotel, where, according to Donovan's instructions, they were booked into two adjoining rooms paid for by the Coordinator of Information.

Across the street, Henry Carter was seated on a bus stop

bench and appeared to be reading a newspaper. He saw the two men climb out of the cab and walk into the hotel.

The reservation was for two weeks, Donovan having explained to Alex and Rudi that he thought that should give them plenty of time to accomplish their mission. If not, Donovan, as he had told them, would see to it that the office of the United States Territorial Governor of Hawaii, Joseph B. Poindexter, would keep paying for the rooms for as long as their mission required. Wild Bill Donovan, it seemed, was one of the very few in the U.S. government who never seemed to be bound by budget considerations.

After they had unpacked and hung up their clothes, stowing other possessions in drawers, and were sitting in Alex's room, Alex gave Rudi his U.S. Navy identity papers, under the name of Lieutenant (junior grade) Richard Barnhardt. He had also arranged for two sets of uniforms for a naval lieutenant (j.g.), complete with some innocuous but predictable service ribbons for his chest.

For this next step in their mission, Rudi's identity would be changed from Eugen Kraus to Lieutenant (junior grade) Richard Barnhardt – and maybe back again – depending on the circumstances and the situation. On the SS Lurline between San Francisco and Honolulu, Alex and Rudi had worked on the cover story they would use to provide background information on the Barnhardt identity.

Richard Barnhardt, it would be explained to anyone with whom that identity made more sense, such as at the headquarters of the Commander in Chief, Pacific Ocean Area (CINCPAC), was the son of an ex-patriot German naval officer who had sought refuge in the United States in 1930, when, in his opinion, Adolf Hitler's unaccountable rise in popularity foreshadowed doom for Germany.

The German ex-patriot's son, Richard, had been 18 years old when the family emigrated and had been accepted into the United States Navy after his father had proven his loyalty to his new homeland by furnishing a number of important pieces of information about the resurgent German Navy, or Kriegsmarine, to the U.S. Navy's Office of Naval Intelligence.

His information on submarine tactics had been especially useful, Alex would report, to the planners and defenders of the North Atlantic convoys.

Of course, young Barnhardt, now a lieutenant (junior grade), was soon assigned to ONI, due to his – and his father's – knowledge of the Kriegsmarine. This despite the fact that Barnhardt held a private pilot's license (which Rudi, in fact, did) and would have been useful as a Naval aviator. Once in ONI, despite his knowledge of the Kriegsmarine, Lieutenant (junior grade) Barnhardt had found himself, for those unexplainable reasons so common in military organizations, assigned to the ONI's Pacific section.

That story, Alex hoped, would explain away the very slight accent Rudi sometimes displayed – but only with a few words - if anybody noticed. Alex suggested that, since it was Sunday afternoon and there was little chance he could make contact with anyone in the Navy today, he and Lieutenant (junior grade) Richard Barnhardt should get acquainted with the sights of Waikiki Beach and environs.

Wearing Navy tropical worsted uniforms without jackets, the men strolled from the Royal Hawaiian toward Diamond Head and made it as far as the Moana Hotel, the other big Waikiki Beach hotel. It was an elegant building in the southern plantation style with an open-air bar in a courtyard - dominated by an enormous banyan tree - overlooking the beach and the blue Pacific beyond. The tables were largely occupied but there was nobody seated at the bar, so they seated themselves at one end, the one with the best view of the beach.

"I must try one of the tropical drinks I've heard so much about," Rudi, aka Dick, said to the bartender. "What do you recommend?" Alex noted with satisfaction that his accent was no more apparent than if he had been from Boston, for instance, or Brooklyn, or Mobile, Alabama.

Mai-tais in front of them, they scanned the many impressive sights on the beach as they puffed on cigarettes. The swimming apparel women in Hawaii favored seemed vastly more revealing than what one would find on the mainland, at least on the east coast. Moreover, some of these delightful creatures appeared to have discarded the breast supports with which most ladies' swimwear was equipped.

Unfortunately, those with the more revealing – and less supported – swimwear also appeared to be in the company of young men with close-cropped hair and the musculature that indicated regular physical training. In other words, military men. There were older men and women on the beach as well, but of course the eyes of the two men at the bar swept quickly past them.

When the bartender was at the other end of the bar making drinks for the table waiters and waitresses, Dick asked Alex in a low voice, "You mentioned you had a friend over here who may be able to help us."

"Curt Vinson," Alex answered, careful to keep track that nobody had intruded into hearing range. "He's a friend from my first days at ONI. Last I heard, he was on the CINCPAC intelligence staff." What he did not tell Rudi was that he had not noticed Curt's name on the CINCPAC personnel roster he had studied on the Lurline, and that he had no idea if that fact was significant. He knew personnel rosters were out of date the day they were printed.

"Was he at Annapolis with you?"

"Naw, he was in the Corps of Cadets at Texas A&M, like I told Don Price that 'Dick Barnhardt' was. I met him in Washington. We're both Texans so we spent some time together when he was in Washington. I'll try him first. If he can help us, he will. If he can't, he'll point us at someone who can." Alex said this with more confidence than he felt. He had no idea how intelligence really worked at the fleet level. Or if Curt Vinson was even still here at Pearl Harbor.

After their second mai tai, and feeling it, they left the bar and walked back toward the Royal Hawaiian. They crossed the street and explored the area north of the hotels. On a dingy side street off Kuhio Boulevard they spotted a local bar. The noise was subdued but steady.

Here, virtually all the customers were in their late 20s and early 30s, Alex judged, and were in Navy whites or Army or Marine khaki. Alex noted that all were officers, mostly of the junior variety. Army and Marine Lieutenants and Captains, Navy Ensigns, Lieutenants, that kind of thing. Enlisted men, Alex knew, had "their own" bars and preferred not to hang out with officers, and vice versa. In this bar, most were standing, and there were few women that they could see.

Those women who were there were seated at small tables, surrounded by Army, Navy and/or Marine officers. A few of the young officers were acting like a flock of peacocks strutting before the peahens, hoping their colors – that is to say their muscles, medals and insignia of rank – would cause one of the peahens to choose them over the other peacocks as their mate for the night. Alex noted that, as crowded at the place was, there were a few empty stools at the bar.

He headed toward the only two adjoining barstools that were vacant, Dick Barnhardt following.

As they sat, the young man to Alex's left turned and nodded a greeting. He was Army, a few years younger than Alex, had the gold bars of a Second Lieutenant on his shoulders and the winged propeller of an aviator on his collar. Alex knew that meant the odds were that he was stationed at Hickam Field, at the mouth of Pearl Harbor, or at Wheeler Field, up toward the middle of the island. He was seated with another Army Lieutenant, also an aviator, of about the same age.

"Howya doin'?" Alex nodded back at the aviator.

"Doin' good, gentlemen. How're things in the fleet today?"

Alex decided these two guys could give them some tips on Honolulu, perhaps without asking too many questions themselves. "We just got in town," he said. "I take it this is one of the places the officers hang out."

"It's popular," the young man said. "The prices are as cheap as you'll find in Honolulu and as you can tell from all the loudmouths back there, there are a few women who come in here."

The young man had turned and was now more or less facing Alex. He stuck out his hand. "I'm George Welch and this sorry-lookin' bastard is Ken Taylor."

"Nice to meet you," Alex replied, shaking George's hand. "Alex Jordan and this's Dick Barnhardt." He was immensely pleased with how easily he had rolled Rudi's assumed identity off his tongue.

"What do you swabbies do?" George asked.

Alex smiled at the good-natured inter-service jibe from the Army pilot. "Dick's a communications officer and I'm gunnery," Alex replied. "We're reportin' aboard the Arizona tomorrow." He knew the USS Arizona was the flagship of

Battleship Division One (BATDIVONE) and that specific duties beyond that would be off limits for either questions or answers.

"We're at Wheeler," George said, "Pursuit squadron."

Rudi's pilot past took over and he quickly asked, "What are you flying?"

"P-36s and P-40s. We're phasing out the old Hawks, but until more 40s arrive, we have both."

Rudi expressed surprise that officers from the various services - Army, Navy and Marines - were as comfortable as they seemed in the same bar.

"Hawaii is kind of unique," Ken put in. "Most places, it's either an Army town – or sometimes an Army Air Corps town – or a Navy town or a Marine town. This place has all three and all them are based pretty close together. So mostly we get along. A few fights for good measure, but usually nothin' serious."

The men chatted like that through two more rounds of beer.

"Shit," Ken announced suddenly after looking at his watch, "the last bus for Wheeler's in 15 minutes." Both aviators finished their beers and stood. "It's been good talking with you. Hope you get settled at Pearl okay. We usually come down here on Sundays. Maybe we'll see you next week." The men shook hands all around and the pilots departed.

Soon after, Alex and Rudi also left, both noting that the peacocks were still busily strutting before the peahens.

Once Alex and Rudi walked through the entry to the Royal Hawaiian, an Asian cab driver who had been parked on the street past the entry drive to the hotel flipped his "out of service" flag up and drove quickly to the Japanese Consulate.

Inside, he hurried to a small office which housed the only consular officer from Germany who was posted in the Territory of Hawaii. In a show of Axis solidarity, Japan had offered the accommodations to its ally.

Admiral Wilhelm Canaris, who had arranged for the posting earlier in the year, thought hiding his man in the Japanese Consulate was a delicious irony. His man was there as much to keep an eye on his ally as to watch American military units. And despite being housed at the Japanese Consulate, there was no sharing of intelligence between the Japanese staff and the sole German, nor did the German take the chance of using a radio in the consulate, instead using a small, portable unit to communicate with Berlin after driving to one of several isolated places he had discovered in the mountains above Honolulu.

The cab driver worked for neither the German nor the Japanese exclusively, but was called on by both for the occasional odd job. He was paid from three to ten dollars for each of these odd jobs, depending on how long they took.

The German acknowledged the cab driver, who said simply, in very broken English, "Your man and his friend are in the Royal Hawaiian, sir, and both are wearing U.S. Navy uniforms." English was the language through which they communicated because it was the only language both had in common. The German gave the cab driver a five-dollar bill and the cabbie left happy.

The German had no idea who the two men were, only that he had orders from the Tirpitzufer to confirm their arrival in Honolulu and to keep an eye on them while they were there. He was also told in no uncertain terms not to get caught tailing them. All he knew about the identities of the men was that one was on an Abwehr mission and the other was an American "asset" he was using. Probably from the German-American Bund, he figured. Now he assumed the man on the Abwehr mission was an operative of skill and resourcefulness, to have outfitted himself and his "asset" in U.S. Navy uniforms. That was impressive. And possibly quite dangerous.

But he did not need to know any more. He liked working for the Abwehr, especially in Hawaii, and was determined to follow orders and keep this job. It beat the shit out of a Wehrmacht uniform on the Russian front. He wrote out his message in German, encoded it, locked his office and drove into the mountains in search of a deserted spot where he could start the small generator that powered his radio. The message was soon in the hands of Hans Oster, who reported it to Admiral Canaris.

For a variety of atmospheric and technical reasons, the Ultra station in Bletchley Park, England, failed to intercept the message.

At 8:30 the next morning, Alex called the Office of Naval Intelligence at the Headquarters, United States Pacific Fleet, Pearl Harbor, Territory of Hawaii. An efficient-sounding male voice answered on the second ring, "Intelligence Section, Petty Officer Maltbie, sir."

"Mr. Maltbie, this is Lieutenant Alex Jordan of ONI in Washington. I'm looking for Lieutenant Commander Curtis Vinson." He supplied the Petty Officer with the appropriate information to assure his bona fides.

"Sir, it's Commander Vinson now, and he's not with CINCPAC any longer. He's the Intelligence Officer for BATDIVONE." Alex knew from his shipboard studies that BATDIVONE was commanded by Rear Admiral Isaac Campbell Kidd, a well-respected commander who flew his flag from BB-39, the USS Arizona.

"I'll be damned," Alex replied. "Do you happen to know whether the Arizona is in port at the moment?" He remembered, suddenly, that they had told the two Air Corps pilots at the bar the night before that they were reporting aboard the Arizona.

"It's in port, sir, but it's in dry dock. I don't know the details and I'm not sure whether the officers are being billeted ashore while she's laid up. If I can track Commander Vinson down, shall I have him call you?"

"I'd appreciate that very much, Mr. Maltbie. I'm here in Hawaii for a couple of weeks, at the Royal Hawaiian." Petty Officer Maltbie whistled softly, indicating he was impressed, and wrote that down, along with the number of the Royal Hawaiian, all the while wondering who this Lieutenant was – and what he was doing – that he got billeted at the Royal Hawaiian and not in Visiting Officer Quarters on the base. The VOQ must be full, he decided.

After breaking the connection, Alex briefed Rudi on what he had discovered and they headed down for breakfast on the scenic lanai of the Royal Hawaiian. After breakfast, they would walk around and familiarize themselves further with Honolulu. They decided that tropical casual uniforms would still be best.

Henry Carter was a solid 170 pounds and wore his brown hair short but not military-short. He was neither good-looking nor ugly.

In fact, if the average person were asked to describe Henry Carter after a casual encounter, he would have been hard-pressed to remember anything remarkable to describe. He had been in Honolulu for several days and was staying at the Moana. It was quite unlikely that, if asked, any of the efficient staff of the Moana could remember the Mr. Carter who was their guest in Room 312, even though they were well-trained to remember all their guests.

Henry Carter was dressed in casual grey slacks, loafers and a colorful Hawaiian print shirt. That is to say, he was dressed much like 90 percent of the civilian male population of Honolulu, at least those who were not wearing Bermuda shorts or swimwear. He had loved Hawaiian shirts from the time he tried the first one on. They were designed to be worn loose, not tucked into the trousers.

That made it very easy to carry his pistol in a concealed manner – an important consideration in a tropical climate where wearing a jacket would be both uncomfortably hot and would make him stand out like a sore thumb. And standing out was not something Henry Carter liked to do. Nor did he feel fully dressed without his pistol on his person.

Carter sipped his pineapple juice and gazed out at the Pacific from the lanai of the Moana. He had seen the two men he was here to watch over the afternoon before in the bar of the Moana. He had been sitting at a small table by himself, ostensibly reading a tourism map of the island. They had sat at the end of the bar and watched the women on the beach while they sucked down a couple of exotic concoctions. He had then followed them – unnoticed, he was sure – as they walked around until finding that loud goddamn bar on that shitty little street off Kuhio.

He had not gone in.

It was almost all military – officers at that - and he had been sure he would have stood out. After a couple of hours, he had seen them leave the bar and make their way back to the Royal Hawaiian. Once they went inside their hotel, he had turned and returned to his.

Henry Carter had been relieved, but not surprised, that neither man appeared overly concerned with being followed. Neither had made more than cursory attempts to check behind them, or for that matter, to look around the Moana bar when they had been sitting there. They were apparently not going to give him much of a challenge.

Carter had only been told to watch the men.

What he could not figure out was why the one "Oscar" had told him he was particularly interested in was wearing a Navy uniform. Oscar had said specifically that the other one was a Navy officer. Now they were dressed like they both were. What the fuck is going on here?

He would be notified if Oscar wished to change his orders. Still, he had been grateful they had decided to turn in early. That meant he was free to go to the teahouse.

Since arriving in Honolulu, Carter had become attracted to Asian women – one in particular. Asian women were a species he had scarcely noticed before in either New York or Washington. To him, they were mostly plain, flat-faced women with few curves who worked in laundries or Chinese restaurants.

But he had always loved Chinese food, so when he had asked an Asian cabbie on his second day in Honolulu where he could get some good Chinese food, the cabbie had told him that in Hawaii, the better choice was Japanese food. Carter did not know the difference, any more than he could have told the difference between a Japanese, a Chinese or a Korean woman, so he told the cabbie to take him where he would go if he were looking for good food.

The cabbie had driven into the foothills above Pearl Harbor and deposited him on Makanani Drive at a tea house, which the cabbie assured him served the finest Japanese food on the island.

What the cabbie had not told Carter was that, in the style of tea houses in Japan, this place was also well-stocked with pretty girls who acted sort of like geishas. Only the girls in this tea house offered a wider variety of entertainment options than the traditional geisha of Japanese history and culture. The cabbie had also failed to point out that he received a gratuity from the mama-san who ran the teahouse for every customer he deposited on her doorstep.

Carter would be worth an extra fifty cents to him.

When Carter had been seated – on an elaborately-colored mat on the floor in a sort of private room – a beautiful, pale Japanese woman in a very ornate full-length gown had gracefully sat down across the short table from him and asked him what she could get for him. Carter had been thunderstruck by her beauty, but had not known how to react, so he had said nothing, simply stared at the young woman, wondering how the hell she had been able to sit down like that wearing a full-length gown.

Shortly, an older Japanese woman – the mama-san - had appeared and asked Carter in heavily accented English if anything was wrong.

"I just came to get something to eat," he had said simply.

Patiently – she had done this many times before with first-time, non-Asian customers – the older woman had explained that the young woman was sort of a geisha, that her roles were to serve the gentleman the food and drink he wanted, but also to "keep him company" during his meal. At length, Carter thought he understood and nodded his head to the older woman that he did, although in truth he had only the vaguest idea what a geisha was. She had bowed elaborately and departed.

"I have never been here before," Carter had explained to the young goddess in front of him, "or any place like it. I just arrived in Hawaii yesterday." For Henry Carter, conversation did not come easily and that statement constituted a major speech for him.

The young lady had bowed her head, smiled and asked, "Would the gentleman like to try a cup of sake?" She explained that sake was the favored alcoholic beverage in Japan, that it was made from rice and was quite tasty when served warm. She did not mention that it also had a significant kick to it.

As he had sat sipping his first-ever cup of sake, Carter openly stared in fascination at the young sort-of geisha, at her beautiful almond-shaped eyes, her perfect white teeth, her silky black hair and the bright red lipstick she wore. She had talked with him as if they were old friends, but it had taken him some time before he thought he understood what she was saying.

She had great difficulty with the use of the letter "L" in English, so when she first told him her "American" name was Emily, it came out more like "Emory." In fact, he had called her "Emory" a couple of times until he noticed the hurt in her eyes and finally realized she thought he was making fun of her. When for the first time he worked out the problem and pronounced it, Emily, she had beamed. God, her smile was something, he thought, and had told her so. She had beamed even more brightly.

After he had eaten and the geisha had arranged through the mama-san to order him a taxi, he had asked Emily if he could see her the next night. She had assured him that she would be there and would be honored to serve the gentleman again. The mama-san also assured "Meestah Cautah" that Emily would be honored to be his geisha any time he visited the tea house.

Carter had followed that first visit with nightly cab rides to the tea house. On the third night, the mama-san had explained to Carter that if he wished for Emily to share a bed with him, that could be arranged for $5 for the night. The expense money Henry Carter's employer had provided him would easily handle that sum and he had readily agreed. Soon, they were what in New York or Washington would have been called a couple.

Emily had introduced Henry Carter to an astonishing variety of techniques Japanese women had developed over their long history to please their men. And for his part, Henry Carter felt that not only was he in love with Emily – whose last name she had tried to teach him but he simply could not pronounce – but that she was in love with him.

In his own mind – and he vaguely recognized that perhaps it was only wishful thinking – the $5 per night was only to compensate the mama-san for the loss of a waitress. The way she used her hands, her body and various implements of pleasure on him when they lay naked on her bed, she must be in love with him.

Henry Carter had been sexually involved with several women in his life – including, of course, the one who had gotten him banished from New York - but he could not remember any that he had thought were actually in love with him. Nor could he remember feeling anything like love – if, indeed, this was love – for anyone before. The unfortunate fact of the matter was that, at age 41, he simply had no idea what love was.

Still, knowing that a return to New York, or anywhere near it, was not an option once "Oscar" determined his services were no longer required, Carter had begun thinking increasingly that Hawaii might be quite a fine choice as a new place to live.

Carter had missed the tea house and Emily the night before. He was preparing for the Lurline's arrival and did not want to take the chance of having too much sake, or too much Emily, so he had not gone up the hill, as he thought of it.

But tonight, he was going. Earlier in the day, he had stopped at the office of the Territorial Governor, where he used the secure telephone line Donovan had arranged for him to have access to. There, he had called "Oscar" at the private number he had been given and reported that the two men were on the island and in the Royal Hawaiian. Donovan thanked him, reiterated the importance of the safety of the two men and asked Carter to keep him advised, at least once every three days. Carter had not mentioned the fact that both now dressed like U.S. naval officers. He simply did not care enough to make a big deal of it.

His focus right now was on the teahouse.

The next morning, Alex Jordan and Rudi von Althorp – in the persona of Dick Barnhardt - were having breakfast on the lanai of the Royal Hawaiian when a bellman came to their table.

"Excuse me, Lieutenant Jordan?" he inquired.

"I'm Lieutenant Jordan," Alex replied. He could see in the bellman's eyes that he had serious doubts that a man his age would actually be a Navy Lieutenant. He had seen all sorts of officers of all branches of the service in the Royal Hawaiian, and the bellman thought he was too young for a lieutenant. He did not realize that promotions were coming faster now that war was looming and the ranks of all the services were swelling – primarily as a result of the draft - than they had during the slow years since the Great War.

"There's a telephone call for you, sir," the bellman said.

Alex got to his feet and followed the bellman to the far end of the front desk of the hotel where a clerk handed him a house phone.

"Lieutenant Jordan, sir," he said when he had the phone to his ear.

"Alex, how are you? This is Curt Vinson," the voice on the phone said.

"I'm good, Curt. How about you?" Without waiting for an answer, and once he was satisfied nobody was close enough to him to overhear the conversation he continued. "And I understand congratulations are in order. Full Commander? At your age? Jesus, someone's got plans for you. And I hear you're with BATDIVONE."

"All correct, Alex, all except I don't know about anyone having plans for me. And how about you, already a lieutenant three years out of Annapolis? That's pretty impressive."

Alex ignored the compliment. "Listen, Curt, I'd like to talk with you when you can make the time. I've got a friend I want you to meet."

"Male or female?"

"Male, fellow officer. We've got something interesting we'd like to run by you."

"Well, I guess whoever you talked to at CINCPAC when you called told you the Arizona is in dry dock. A little collision at sea, thankfully nothing serious. We'll be here a few more days, and the repairs don't involve anything near my part of the ship, so some of us are still working aboard ship. Do you want to come out to the Arizona?"

"I'd like that, Curt. I've been to Pearl – once – but I've never been on a battleship and seein' one up close would be neat."

"Good. Why don't you come out tomorrow morning for breakfast? I'm up to my ass in staff meetings today."

"We'll be there at, what, 0700? 0600?"

"0700 will be perfect, Alex. I'm looking forward to it. And give me the other officer's name so I can leave it with the Officer of the Deck."

"Lieutenant (j. g.) Richard Barnhardt is his name. Thanks, Curt. It'll be good to see you again."

Curt Vinson rang off and Alex went back to the lanai to finish his breakfast, brief Rudi, and then they would go to their rooms and make sure their dress whites were freshly pressed for their visit to the Pearl Harbor Naval Base the next day.

CHAPTER 11

Pearl Harbor Naval Base
Dry Dock #1
October 29, 1941

Curt Vinson had sent a staff car – a blue 1939 Plymouth – to the main gate of the Pearl Harbor Naval Base to meet Lieutenant Jordan and his fellow officer. Once they had paid the cabbie and signed in – after careful scrutiny of their identification documents – the staff car drove them to Dry Dock #1. The Arizona loomed above them like a mountain range.

"My God, it's huge," Rudi breathed as they walked toward the boarding ramp. "I still find it hard, sometimes, to believe something that big can float." The intelligence agent side of Rudi made him instinctively admire the man-of-war, even though he knew that there were many more modern, and larger, ships of war in existence. Such as the recently-sunk German battleship Bismarck.

"It's amazing," was all Alex could muster. He had spent a little time on a destroyer after graduation, but the battlewagons were something from an entirely different world, he thought.

When they were at the foot of the boarding ramp, Alex called out to the OD – the Officer of the Deck – for permission to board.

An impossibly young-looking Ensign in starched khakis

looked down from the starboard quarterdeck. "State your business," he called to them.

"Lieutenant Jordan and Lieutenant (j.g.) Barnhardt to see Commander Vinson of BATDIVONE," Alex called back.

The Ensign consulted a paper attached to a clipboard and called back, "Permission granted."

Alex and Rudi climbed the boarding ramp. Once aboard, they came to attention and faced the colors, saluting. Alex had briefed Rudi on the drill one goes through when boarding an American man of war. Then, turning to the Ensign, who was saluting them, they saluted him back.

A young deck sailor in whites and a "Dixie Cup" cap, who had been standing behind the Ensign, stepped forward. Rudi noted the blue stripe around the right shoulder of his jumper, remembering it from his recent study of U.S. Navy insignia as that of an unrated seaman of the deck force. He was a good-looking, thin young man of medium height.

"Mr. Jordan, Seaman 1st Abercrombie, sir," he barked as he saluted.

After returning his salute, Alex replied, "Thank you, Mr. Abercrombie. This is Lieutenant (j.g.) Barnhardt. Are you here to take us to Commander Vinson?"

"Yes, sir. Mr. Vinson said you've never been on one of these overgrown gunboats and told me it would be a good idea for me to escort you to Officer Country. I know for a fact you can get lost onboard. I've done it myself, sir, more than once."

Alex smiled his approval. Abercrombie turned and said, "if you'll follow me, gentlemen?" and started walking. Halfway across the starboard quarterdeck, they came to a hatch leading down into the ship. Abercrombie said over his shoulder, "Y'all stay with me now, gentlemen. Some of the Chiefs say that there are probably a couple of dozen men who've got lost over the years still wandering around below decks. They say somebody's liable to find a whole mess of skeletons during the next major overhaul."

Alex could almost believe it. "What part of Texas are you from, kid?" he asked. He had picked up on Abercrombie's drawl immediately.

The young man beamed at him. "Leggett, sir. Down in East Texas. I reckon the accent is easy enough to pick up on. A lot of the guys rib me about it. Call me Tex, like I've never heard that before." He chuckled, then went on, carrying on conversationally the way few seamen dared converse with officers. "But how'd you know it was Texas, sir? Most folks can't tell a Texan from an Alabaman."

"I'm a son of the Lone Star State myself, young man," Alex said with pride. He liked the seaman with the engaging smile, the wavy jet-black hair and the gift of gab. "Fort Worth, to be exact."

"And never stops talking about TCU football," Rudi put in, chuckling.

By now, they were heading down a ladder just aft of the mainmast and into the ship. Rudi and Alex had some trouble seeing as their eyes tried adjusting to the darker conditions in the interior of the ship.

Abercrombie did not seem to have the same problem. "No kiddin'. Cowtown!" he exclaimed. He turned them aft and down a passageway before going on. "My sorta big sister lives up there in Fort Worth. Married a fella from up there a few years back. He's a copilot with American Airlines."

"Your 'sorta sister?'" Rudi asked, confusion on his face. Alex was not surprised that Rudi was baffled by the slang term. They were now walking by staterooms that looked, to Alex's more or less trained eye, to be for junior officers. Rudi's head swiveled, taking everything in.

Abercrombie, pegging Rudi for a Yankee, tried to explain.

"Yes, sir. My folks are dead and her folks kinda took my brother and me under their wings. Looked after us, like that. So even though the Malones – she's a Malone – aren't blood, I consider 'em family."

They ducked under a few low hatches and then the accommodations became noticeably nicer than the compartments they had just passed.

Abercrombie stopped in front of a closed wooden door that carried a placard reading "Wardroom" and turned to face the men. "Welcome to Officer Country, sirs." He knocked twice. A voice inside called out, "Enter."

Abercrombie turned the door handle, pushed open the door, and smiled at Alex and Rudi, gesturing with his hand to enter.

"Thank you very much, Mr. Abercrombie," Alex said, offering his hand. In the Navy, saluting indoors or below decks was not proper protocol. "We'd have never found our own way."

"My pleasure, sirs. Always nice to meet a fellow countryman," Abercrombie added to Alex smiling, and strode smartly back in the direction from which they had come.

Commander Curt Vinson was walking toward them as they entered the Wardroom, his hand extended. Alex shook Curt's hand, a smile on his face. Curt said, "It's been a long time, Alex."

"Too long, Curt. Good to see you again. I'd like you to meet Dick Barnhardt. We work together at ONI."

Rudi put out his hand to Vinson and said, "Commander Vinson."

Vinson shook hands with Rudi. "Very nice to meet

you, Lieutenant," he said. "And from now on we'll go by our Christian names, if that's okay by everybody." He gestured with his hand toward a table with three place settings set up on a very crisp white tablecloth.

"I thought we'd just eat here, rather than going to the open mess," Vinson said.

"That'd be fine," Alex said. "Not very busy this mornin'," he continued after they were seated. He had noted there were only five other officers at tables scattered around the large room.

"It's because we're on the beach," Vinson responded. "At sea, it would be full. Or maybe empty by now, because we'd have all had our breakfast by 0600. When we're in dry dock, a lot of the officers and most of the men take advantage of liberty. But Admiral Kidd is working on exercises and plans for BATDIVONE and most of the division staff are aboard."

A steward filled their coffee cups. Vinson asked Alex and Rudi what they wanted for breakfast. After giving the steward their orders – bacon and eggs sunny side up all around – Vinson and Alex brought each other up to date on their lives and careers since they had last seen each other, and Alex told Curt about Dick Barnhardt, his background and how he came to the ONI.

He did not tell him that "Dick" was a Texas A&M graduate, as he had told Don Price. That would have opened up the possibility of a conversation that Rudi may not have been able to deal with, such as specifics of the campus, big-name football players and senior military officers who were fellow Aggies, that sort of thing.

When Vinson asked how Texas A&M and TCU were doing in football this year – "damn little sports news gets out here" – Alex was reminded of the young seaman who led them where they needed to go. "That young seaman you sent up to escort us is from Texas," he said. "Leggett, I think he said."

"Seaman Abercrombie," Vinson furnished. "Yes, I know. He's a good kid, always around and willin' to help. Other than at battle stations, he doesn't have any specific set duties – like the radiomen or pharmacists mates and so forth - so I've found myself usin' him when I can. Otherwise he'd spend all his time moppin' decks or scrapin' paint. I met him, I guess you'd say, about a week after I'd been assigned to BATDIVONE. I still didn't know my way around the Arizona and I was as lost as I could get.

"Can't even remember now where I was trying to go, but this kid walks up to me and says, 'The Commander looks like he may need some help, sir. Is there anything I can do?' I told him I was lost and what I was looking for. He said, 'No problem, sir. If you'd just follow me, please?' And led me right to it, chattering away like we were a couple of guys walking down the street in Fort Worth or College Station. I was damn near at the other end of the ship from where I was supposed to be. Probably took 20 or 30 minutes. Most seamen would crap their pants at the thought of carryin' on a conversation with an officer. He's never disrespectful or anything like that, but he just thinks like we're a bunch of shipmates that happen to wear different patches or pins on our uniforms." Alex noticed that Curt tended to lapse into a mild Texas accent when in friendly conversation, as he knew he did himself.

"I noticed that," he said, chuckling. "I asked him what part of Texas he was from and the next thing we know he's tellin' us about a 'sorta sister' he's got in Fort Worth. Why don't you try to get him into OCS? With his gift of gab, if nothing else he'd make the best damn Chief of Staff any admiral ever had."

OCS was the acronym for Officer Candidate School.

"I hadn't really thought about that, but there'd be no

chance. He told me the first time I met him that his hitch is up – his words – in April and he's going back to Texas and become a preacher. Not much I can say to argue with that."

He paused and grinned before continuing. "You know what Abercrombie's Christian name is?" They shook their heads. "Adolphus. Can you believe a name like that? Of course, it probably wasn't so bad before Hitler came to power. But think about an East Texas preacher – maybe even a travelin' evangelist, the guys that do those tent revivals out in the boondocks – can you think of a better name than The Reverend Adolphus Abercrombie? Sounds like something out of a movie. I can see Errol Flynn, or maybe Ronald Reagan, playin' him."

They all chuckled. Alex said, "Well, his hair already reminds me of Reagan. But he seems like a good kid. Keep an eye out for him. I think he'd make a fine preacher and I hope he does."

When they had finished their breakfast, Alex lowered his voice and asked Vinson if there was somewhere they could go to talk privately. If, that is, the Commander could spare the time. Vinson nodded his head toward the door and made a follow me motion with his hand.

The three men were in the stateroom assigned to Commander Vinson in his role as Intelligence Officer of BATDIVONE. It was not a hotel suite, but spacious enough that three men could fit comfortably inside. Vinson sat in the desk chair and Alex and Rudi sat together on the single bed. Alex briefed Vinson on the Dick Barnhardt background they had agreed upon, that he had been born in Germany and emigrated with his family when he was in his early 20s, his assignment to ONI and so forth. Vinson nodded and smiled at the irony of a man so familiar with the Kriegsmarine ending up in the Pacific section at ONI.

"Curt," Alex said, "we've come up with some intelligence we think you should hear. Actually, Dick came up with it and I concur that it's important."

"We're all in the intel business," Curt said with a small smile. "I know what role gut feelings sometimes play. Go ahead."

Alex gestured for Rudi to begin. "In Washington," he began, "I became, ah, acquainted, I guess you could say, with a diplomat in the German Embassy. My family lived in the same town he is from in Germany before my father moved us to the U.S. Actually, his diplomatic role is cover for his posting for the Abwehr, I am quite certain. He told me that one of his associates, who I believe is probably the Abwehr agent in charge in Tokyo, personally observed Japanese torpedo bombers practicing shallow-water drops in an isolated fishing village. That was in July. My Washington contact researched all the harbors in the Pacific and concluded that the most likely targets where shallow-water torpedoes would be necessary are Cavite and Pearl Harbor. He asked me if that information might be useful to the United States Navy."

"Hold on! Why would he bring it to you?" Curt interrupted. "I thought the krauts and the Japs were on the same side. Or they're supposed to be."

He paused, immediately embarrassed. "Sorry about the kraut reference, Dick. Force of habit. Nothin' against you."

"No offense taken, Commander," Rudi said, smiling, then leaned forward in emphasis, "I don't know whether you've heard much about Admiral Canaris, the head of the Abwehr. In part because of my German background, I have studied him extensively. He is extremely bright and resourceful."

Rudi briefly described Canaris' escape from South America in the Great War before continuing. "There's a distinct possibility that he is not a Nazi and most information about him suggests he is not an admirer of Adolf Hitler. My contact believes this, and is almost certain he is not a Nazi.

"But most of all, my contact told me that Canaris believes it would spell doom for Germany, and the entire Axis, for that matter, if the United States becomes involved in this war as a declared belligerent. I do not really know, but I believe my contact has had enough contact with Canaris over his career to know such things about the man."

Alex picked it up from there. "Curt, if this dope on Canaris is true – and I've heard it from other sources, too – if I were in his place, I'd make sure my top agents in Tokyo, Rome and Washington are people in whom I have the utmost trust, people who I know well and people I can count on. And if his feelings about the U.S. being pulled into the war are as Dick's contact suggests, that means people who, among other things, are on the look-out for anything the Italians or the Japanese might do to force the hand of the U.S.

"Obviously, if I'm Canaris, I know two things: first, that of the Axis nations, Germany has the most to lose in an all-out war of survival; and second, the Japs are the likeliest to cause problems with us because of their interest in the Pacific, much of which overlaps U.S. interests. The Germans - at least Canaris - don't want to go through 1918 all over again, just as most people in this country don't want to get dragged into another war. I think it's quite possible, maybe even probable, that Canaris sent this guy to us."

"Do you trust this guy, Dick?" Vinson asked. "I mean, really trust him?"

"There's no question in my mind that the man is being honest with me, if that is what you're asking," Rudi said.

Curt Vinson stared at Rudi, then at Alex for a long time,

but his eyes seemed to be focused on a point on the bulkhead behind Alex's head. Alex could see that and said nothing more until Vinson spoke again.

"Okay," Vinson said in a very quiet voice. "So we have third-hand information that someone sees Jap planes practicin' shallow-water torpedo runs? The Pacific is full of harbors that might interest them. China, Russia, French Indo-China, the Dutch East Indies among others. What is it about this that makes you think it's anything out of the ordinary – not just trainin'? Something, more to the point, involving us?"

Rudi spoke. "Sir, I asked my contact the same thing. As I said, he studied the charts for every major port and harbor in the Pacific. The only two that have targets of any real strategic interest to Japan and that have harbors shallow enough to need these special torpedoes are Cavite and here at Pearl Harbor. I studied all of the charts, too, and he's right. Sir, based on all I know, and based on my gut feeling, I believe the Japanese are planning to attack the United States Navy at one or the other of those bases, and very possibly both." The earnest look on Rudi's face told Curt Vinson that he had, indeed, given the matter a great deal of thought.

After a long pause, "Why me?" Curt asked, spreading his hands in question. "Why come all the way out here with this when Washington is crawling with people who can probably analyze this more thoroughly than I can, and who can do more with it than I can?"

Alex jumped in. "Curt, we took this to my boss at ONI, Wally Hammond. Remember him?" Vinson nodded and Alex continued. "He took it up the chain from the CNI to the CNO and Admiral Stark as much as told Wally he was hallucinating. Then, at the suggestion of Admiral Kirk, before he left as CNI, Wally took it to Colonel Donovan at COI. We all talked with him and he told us he'd check it out with his people in Tokyo, et cetera, et cetera. I don't really think he's got much of a presence in Tokyo. In any case, he then sent us over here to get it in the hands of Admiral Kimmel or whoever, and even suggested we might want to go on to Manila and let MacArthur in on it.

"Honestly, Curt, the more I think about it, the more I think he was givin' us the run-around. Maybe hopin' that getting us out of town would put us on ice, since we aren't travelin' on specific orders to report to specific officers."

"Why would he be trying to put you on ice?" Curt asked.

Alex paused, thinking about how to frame his response. "Curt, if you want the honest-to-God truth, even though I don't think it's probable, I do think it's possible the President – and therefore Donovan – wants Japan to attack us so he has the excuse to declare war on the Nazis. The isolationists are giving him fits over Lend-Lease and all the other support he's giving England and Russia, not to mention the idea of getting into the war with them. An unprovoked attack on the United States would overcome all that." He paused again, then went on.

"And here's the kicker; right after we went to the CNO and the COI, Wally turned up dead. At least the police think an otherwise unidentifiable body that was found floating in the Tidal Basin is him. He's been missing since then, and the police seem to have given up on the case."

"No shit?" Curt exclaimed, then went on. "Of course! I heard he had been found dead. So you're here because Donovan made arrangements and sent you off with nobody specific to contact? And you called me because I'm the only one over here you know?"

"He gave us tickets and money and that's about it. And nobody other than the Washington police seems to give a shit about finding out who murdered Wally. Or if it was Wally that was found."

"Jesus," Curt muttered.

"So we've brought it to you. And you're right. It's because you're the only one over here I know. And I'm askin' you as a friend to keep Donovan's name out of it if and when you discuss this with others. Stark would have a hissy fit if he found out we'd taken this to Donovan. So where do we go from here, Commander?"

"How are you doing for money?" Curt asked in return.

"We're good. Donovan apparently has plenty of money to throw around, and he gave us enough to stay over here for a couple of weeks."

"Well, you're not living like enlisted men. I mean, the Royal Hawaiian is a nice billet. Stay close. I mean don't go sightseein' on the other islands or anything. I need to talk to Admiral Kidd about this. He can take it to Admiral Kimmel if he thinks that's warranted. Or maybe Admiral Layton." Rear Admiral Edwin T. Layton was Kimmel's Combat Intelligence Officer.

"And what about you, Curt? Do you agree with us?"

"I need to kick it around in my own head for awhile. Maybe take a peek for myself at the charts. But I'll say this; it sure sounds plausible. I'll call you at the hotel. I like the food there very much, by the way. I'll invite myself to dinner."

"Tonight?"

"No, I can't tonight. Admiral Kidd is at sea at the moment, on the Nevada. That's one of his BATDIVONE ships. She's due back in port in two, maybe three days. I'll talk to him then and get back to you."

Alex stood and put out his hand. "That's all I can ask, Curt. I trust you to do whatever's right." Curt shook his hand warmly, then turned and shook Rudi's.

"I'd better walk you up to the quarterdeck so you don't

get lost. I don't know where your pal Abercrombie is or I'd have him join us for the walk." On the way, Vinson asked Alex about Hammond's death – or his going missing, as the case may be - and who he thought was behind it. Alex told him he thought there were three possibilities: the German SS-SD, someone high in the U.S. government or – least likely – that it was an armed robbery gone badly. Curt Vinson stared in amazement at Alex. The second possibility sent chills down his spine.

The blue Plymouth staff car was waiting at the bottom of that ramp. The driver had been instructed to take them back to the Royal Hawaiian.

The next night, wanting to try something besides the Royal Hawaiian menu, Alex and Rudi had dinner at the Moana.

At the same time, Henry Carter was dining – among other things – with Emily at the tea house. While they were in the tea house's lounge, sipping sake after dinner and before getting around to "other things," a young Asian man sat at the next table, gazing intently out over Pearl Harbor. He was having obvious difficulty keeping his eyes off Emily. Henry Carter disliked that, and it showed on his face. Emily giggled, which caused the other man to look at Carter to see what she was giggling about, and saw that the white barbarian was glaring at him.

He didn't want, nor need, a confrontation, so he stood and bowed. "My name is Tadashi Morimura," he said. "I come here often and do not recall having the honor of making your acquaintance." His English was good, but with a strong accent.

Carter did not know what to do, but he stood and bowed slightly before putting out his hand. "My name is Henry, and the lady is Emily," he said. The two shook hands, neither with any enthusiasm.

"Are you from Hawaii, Mr. Henry?" Morimura asked, "or visiting?"

"On vacation," Carter grunted.

"Ah, very good place for vacation, is it not?" Morimura let the conversation die, and returned to his table. He finished his tea, took another long look at Pearl Harbor, then rose and bowed again. He turned and hurried to the door.

At about the same time, Alex and Rudi were sitting at the bar at the Moana, enjoying after-dinner drinks. Both were drinking Budweiser and smoking, Chesterfields for Rudi and Lucky Strikes for Alex. Both were aware of, but not paying undue attention to, a pair of young women sitting a few stools down the bar from them.

Suddenly one of the women was standing behind Rudi and tapping him on the shoulder.

"Hi," she said. "I wonder if you could spare a cigarette. I noticed you're smoking Chesterfields. They're my favorite and I'm out."

Rudi grabbed his pack and tapped out a cigarette. "My pleasure," he said. "Would you and your friend like to join us. We're just killing time after dinner." Alex thought it very clever of Rudi to make it plain to her that if they were looking for a free meal, we have already eaten. He also thought – not for the first time - that Rudi was a guy who didn't waste a lot of time when it came to women. Soon, the young women were sitting next to Rudi.

The one who liked Chesterfields made the introductions. "My name is Louise Wagner and this is my best friend, Ann Lassiter."

"I am Dick Barnhardt and this is Alex Jordan," Rudi

replied, rather formally. "Where are you ladies from?"

"We're from San Francisco," Louise said. "And no, we're not Navy nurses or anything like that. We're just on a vacation. We arrived on the Pan American Clipper flight this morning."

Alex and Rudi immediately had virtually the same thought: Pan Am Clipper? Money! Alex decided on the diplomatic approach.

"The Clipper? Damn, I wish I could afford to fly on one of them sometime. It's got to beat five or six days at sea on a ship."

"It's definitely the way to travel," Louise said. "And we just decided to do it right. It's a celebration for me. For Ann, it's a time to change scenery." Ann looked uncomfortable with her friend's statement, and Alex decided another question would be best left unasked. He just looked puzzled. Louise, as expected, elaborated.

"Ann just got a divorce. That's what I'm celebrating. He's a real asshole – pardon the French – and I've been telling her for two years to get rid of him while she's still young. He's not going to get any better. So anyway, here we are. Fortunately, Ann's ex-husband is loaded and so is my father. That's why we could manage the Clipper."

"Where are you staying?" Rudi asked.

"Here. The Moana," Louise said. "Two glorious weeks in paradise. How about you guys?"

"We're at the Royal Hawaiian."

"Vacation?"

"Navy," Alex interjected, wanting to make sure Rudi did not go too far afield trying to impress the women. Or more precisely, woman, singular. It was clear he was quite taken with Louise Wagner. And why not? The bold and outspoken young lady was quite attractive, as was the recent divorcee. Louise was a slim brunette who wore her hair in a pageboy. Ann was a little taller – maybe five-six or so – and wore her golden hair in a ponytail. Alex had always thought pony tails on a woman were vaguely erotic. He was not sure why.

He also noticed that Ann was being left out of the conversation, so he gathered up his beer and cigarettes and moved down to sit on the other side of her. Now, the Navy had the vacationing women bracketed, he thought.

Ann did not appear uncomfortable with the new arrangement.

Moreover, Louise looked visibly pleased at Alex's move and asked, "How do two Navy guys get to stay in the Royal Hawaiian? I thought they put you in barracks or whatever they call those little round buildings you see on the newsreels."

"Quonset huts," Alex furnished. "No, we're on TDY – that means temporary duty – and they don't have housing for us at Pearl Harbor so they've got us there for the time being. I'm sure the Navy gets a special rate."

"Well, I should think so," Louise said. "How long is 'temporary?'" She was looking now at Rudi.

"We're not sure," Rudi answered truthfully. "We think at least another couple of weeks. Maybe longer. Then we'll probably be going to the Philippines…" Alex made a subtle but clear chopping motion with his hand to stop Rudi. He disguised it by then raising his hand toward the bartender and with a circling motion indicated they wanted four more of the same. The women were drinking something unidentifiable with pineapple slices in them.

"Oh," Louise said, "That must be what they talk about when they say, 'join the Navy and see the world.'"

"We're not sure we'll need to go to the Philippines," Alex said quickly. "It's just a possibility, depending on what happens while we're here."

"What do you do in the Navy," Ann asked. Rudi looked at Alex expectantly, signaling that he expected him to answer the question for them.

"We're in War Plans," Alex said quietly, a signal that it was not appropriate to broadcast that fact to the entire bar area.

"We're assigned to Navy Department headquarters in Washington, and came over here to observe some of the maneuvers of the Pacific fleet."

"Oh, my, War Plans sounds ominous," Louise said. "Do you think we'll get pulled into the war in Europe?"

"I hope not," Alex answered, "and, in fact, no, I don't think we will, other than the supply operations we already have to England and Russia. But the Navy's policy, of course, is to be prepared for anything."

When Ann finished the drink Alex had bought, she picked up her small pocketbook and stood. "I think I've had enough to drink and I'm really tired. I guess the trip got to me. I can't sleep well on airplanes, not that I've had that much experience on them. But it's certainly been nice meeting both of you. I hope we see more of you while we're here. If your duties permit it, of course."

Alex jumped off his barstool, too. "May I walk you to your room?"

"That would be very nice. Thank you."

When Alex and Ann had walked off toward the elevators, Louise slid her hand over to rest it on Rudi's, while giving him a very deliberate look. Rudi gripped it with his hand, hoping he was properly interpreting what her look meant.

In the elevator lobby, Ann turned to Alex. "I can get to my room from here. Thank you, Alex. I'm pleased to have met you, and I was serious when I said I hope we see more of you."

"Unless something comes up tomorrow, we'll be back

here by 5:00 or 6:00," Alex said. "We could meet you again in the bar. Would that be okay?"

"I'll look forward to it," she said as she stepped onto the elevator.

Her smile seemed genuine. Is that wishful thinking? Alex asked himself.

When Alex got back to the bar, Rudi and Louise were nowhere to be found. Deciding he had had enough to drink, he picked up his cigarettes and Zippo lighter from the bar and headed for the Royal Hawaiian. Rudi had apparently taken care of the tab before he and Louise departed.

The next morning, when Rudi appeared at Alex's door, he looked like he had just finished the Olympic marathon. His eyes had dark circles under them and his complexion was flushed. Alex looked at him with a questioning expression.

"Good God," Rudi said. "What a woman." And he collapsed onto, rather than sat down on, the couch. "Now I should get some sleep."

The four got together the next night and the one following as well. Each night, Rudi stayed at the Moana with Louise. On the fourth night when Alex and Rudi saw Louise and Ann at the Moana bar, Ann was carrying a large handbag rather than the small pocketbook she'd had the nights previously.

Later, when Rudi walked Louise to the restroom, Ann made it clear to Alex that she would be agreeable to an invitation to the Royal Hawaiian when it was time to call it an evening. She was, as it turned out, carrying a change of underwear and her make-up in the large handbag.

"The things we do for our country," Alex muttered

under his breath with a smile, immediately grateful that Ann hadn't heard.

A frustrated Sir Stewart Menzies sat in his very nice office in London, fuming. He had just been told again, by his people in both Washington and Tokyo, that there was nothing new on the subject of Frosch, nor could anyone in his MI6 apparatus find anything that indicated any leak of the British plans for shallow-water torpedoes.

He decided to cast the net over a wider area.

The men responsible for the MI6 Asian, Southwest Pacific Area and Commonwealth desks were summoned. As usual, they hurried when they were called.

The Commonwealth man was told to immediately signal the intelligence chiefs of Canada, Australia, New Zealand, India and several other commonwealth countries that had a Pacific or Indian Ocean presence. The signals should brief these intelligence chiefs on the unconfirmed reports – again no mention of Ultra intercepts, of course - that the Japanese were testing shallow-water torpedoes and should tell them that the intent behind those tests, if true, was not known but that MI6 urgently requires any information any of them had that might shed any light on the reports.

The Asian and Southwest Pacific men were told to scour their sources in China, Hong Kong, Malaya, Singapore and any of the Pacific islands for information that might bear on the possible testing.

"And do it quickly, if you would be so kind," Menzies concluded with more than a slight touch of sarcasm as he concluded the meeting.

Menzies told none of the men the part about the test sighting coming from a German, presumably an Abwehr agent but definitely one with direct communication links to Abwehr headquarters. The less that was said about Ultra, even at these high levels, the better.

A part of Menzies despised Admiral Canaris for the brutally-efficient sabotage network he had organized. But he also harbored a genuine, if grudging, admiration for the man and the organization he had rebuilt when he took it over, and he had heard too much about Canaris' anti-Hitler and anti-Nazi feelings to discount the notion that the man could be an asset of significance to England as the war went on. He knew the Prime Minister shared that opinion.

But the overriding need to keep Ultra secret, regardless of other factors, would mean that Canaris and his role in this would be known only to Churchill and him.

CHAPTER 12

Royal Hawaiian Hotel, Honolulu
November 5, 1941

Commander Curt Vinson and Lieutenant Commander Samuel G. Fuqua walked into the ornate dining room of the Royal Hawaiian, there to meet Lieutenant Alex Jordan and Lieutenant (j.g.) Richard Barnhardt. When Curt Vinson had called Alex to schedule the dinner two days before, he had told Alex that Admiral Kidd was not back in port yet – in fact, he was not due until Friday, two days hence - so he had not had a chance to brief him on what Alex and Dick had told him. However, he would like to have dinner with them, and might bring a friend of his from the Arizona if that was agreeable.

The head waiter, once Commander Vinson had identified himself, escorted the two men to Lieutenant Jordan's table. Introductions were quickly made, handshakes exchanged, and drinks ordered. All four were wearing dress whites. A soft breeze was blowing through the many open doors on the beach side of the dining room, and the feeling was relaxed and peaceful, with a four-piece band playing Hawaiian music and big-band favorites and the sound of the waves coming through the doors when the band was silent.

"Sam is the Damage Control Officer on the Arizona," Vinson told Alex and Rudi by way of introduction to Fuqua.

"We only met when I was assigned to BATDIVONE. He's a sea-going sailor, unlike we unsavory intelligence types, but despite our differences in background we seem to get along."

"Sometimes even the most unlikely things happen," Fuqua added, chuckling.

"I've heard of stranger things, but not often," Alex said with a smile.

"Actually, this is my second tour aboard the Arizona," Fuqua said. He turned to Rudi. "Curt was telling me about you, Dick. Interesting that a former German national and expert on the Kriegsmarine finds himself in the Pacific section at ONI. Isn't that the Navy for you?" They all nodded and laughed.

During another very nice seafood dinner, Curt and Alex brought each other up to date on old acquaintances in ONI, Rudi talked – obliquely, to be sure - about what he knew of German naval strength in the Atlantic and England's chances against it, and Sam filled them in on what a Damage Control Officer does and where he fits on the ship's order of battle.

The next morning, Alex and Rudi went to the Moana for a fruit and coffee breakfast. Neither felt like eating a full breakfast after the dinner the night before. As they expected – hoped – Louise and Ann were already there, and they beckoned the men to their table.

"How was your dinner?" Louise asked, looking somewhat seductively at Rudi.

"It was very nice," he said.

"Wasn't better than being with us, was it?" she asked. She really was a saucy little thing, Alex thought to himself.

"Never," he answered truthfully. "But sometimes duty calls." Alex was impressed with Rudi's abilities with American sayings and slang.

"Does duty call today?" Ann interrupted.

Alex responded. "It would appear that at this point we're free today, and maybe tomorrow, too."

"Would you care to join us on the beach?" Ann asked. Alex realized suddenly that spending time with Ann was just about the best thing he could think of. That first night with her in his room had been a memorable experience, but it was more than that. She was bright and quite direct in her manner. She was not a game-player, and with all the other intrigue currently in his life, he found that especially appealing.

Ann had quickly overcome the innate shyness that was made more acute by the nagging feeling that she was acting like a cheap bimbo, inviting herself to a man's room three days after their first meeting and just weeks after her divorce.

But Alex had felt then like the two had connected in some real and significant way, and he thought now that Ann shared that feeling.

"Sure," he said, and then looked at Rudi with a questioning look on his face.

Rudi nodded. "Absolutely, although we have to at least acknowledge the possibility of false Eskimo sightings in tomorrow's newspaper, if you're really intent on running around the beach today with your shirt off." The girls laughed, and Alex good-naturedly laughed with them.

"Ha ha, laugh it up, but as an ethnic Scot, you should know that my feelings, as well as my fair skin, are sensitive," he teased back, with mock hurt on his face.

"Well then, due to your Highland heritage, I should think the proper application of spirits might patch your bruised feelings," Louise quipped.

"Touché, madame, touché." Alex responded with a wry smile.

After breakfast, they agreed to meet on the beach in front of the Moana in their swimwear at 10:00. They would, it was agreed, work their way down the beach from there toward Diamond Head.

At about noon, three hundred yards beyond the Moana by now, they paused in their stroll and sat down for the third time on the beach towels they were carrying. Rudi, then Alex, noticed a striking Asian woman walking with a rather non-descript occidental man of medium height in the surf. They were holding hands, and he was wearing shorts and an aloha shirt rather than swimwear. Neither Alex nor Rudi thought anything more of it and turned their attention back to the beautiful young women sitting with them.

Henry Carter kept walking, his hand holding Emily's. His attention had barely moved off the two men he was tasked with keeping an eye on. Later, he thought, he should to go by the Territorial Governor's office and call "Oscar" to check in and assure him that the two men were healthy and, it appeared, quite happy.

About 3:00, the sun having started to tire the four of them, they started back toward the hotels for showers and naps. Rudi and Louise turned off the beach into the Moana. Alex and Ann continued on to the Royal Hawaiian. It had become a bit of a routine, and each time it happened, Ann told Alex in an embarrassed tone of voice that she simply didn't jump at men this way. She could not imagine what had gotten into her. After all, her divorce had barely become final when they boarded the Clipper for Hawaii. Alex believed her and took it as a genuine compliment that she found in him someone with whom she wanted to spend time, both in and out of bed.

He knew she was more than a pair of hot pants out to

get laid in this vacation paradise. If he were completely honest with himself, in fact, he would have admitted that Ann was far more than an attractive woman who was a pleasure in bed. In addition to being bright, she was very witty and a great conversationalist. And he had connected with her, even if the timing was terrible.

And that was the source of his inner conflict. He was very taken with her and wanted to be with her as much as he could, even thinking that this could develop into something – marriage perhaps. But he was on a mission of some significant urgency, he knew, and he had come to the conclusion that, regardless of what he and Rudi did, the United States would be at war one day soon.

How fair was that to Ann?

Or to himself?

Because the Arizona was being readied to leave the dry dock on November 13, Vinson had to wait until the ship was at its moorings on Battleship Row before being able to get to Admiral Kidd for a half hour of his time, privately. They met the morning of November 14, a week after the Admiral had returned on the Nevada. As usual in Hawaii, it was bright and sunny, with a few scattered clouds hanging from the tops of the mountains in the center of the island.

Vinson entered the Admiral's stateroom, was offered coffee by the steward and when the steward had poured and departed, got right to the point. He still did not know how valid the intel from Jordan and Barnhardt was, and it had been a little over two weeks since he had first heard the story. However, he had not been idle. He had checked around, carefully, asking others in the Hawaii intelligence community what they were hearing.

He had checked with ships' intelligence officers from BATDIVONE, other naval units in Pearl, and several members of Admiral Layton's staff at CINCPAC. One of Layton's deputies, a captain whom he had come to trust, even though he did not know him well, told him there were all kinds of signals indicating that the Japanese were going to get more, rather than less, aggressive. They continued to gobble up huge chunks of Chinese and other Asian real estate. The stories of the atrocities Japanese soldiers were visiting upon the civilian population of China, in particular, were nightmarish, and they had designs on Thailand for its minerals and as a jumping-off point to interdict the Burma Road, the main Allied supply route into China.

The captain had then told him about reports CINCPAC was getting about escalating diplomatic tensions between the U.S. and Japan. There were now not one, but two Japanese Ambassadors to Washington, and the second – he was actually called a Special Envoy - was the same 'belligerent little shit,' according to the captain, who had signed the Tripartite Pact in Berlin which joined Japan in the Axis with Germany and Italy. And, really, what the hell does anyone need two ambassadors for, the captain had asked rhetorically, unless there was something in the wind? And that something was probably both big and bad news.

Finally, the captain had told Vinson that one of their colleagues at ONI in Washington, a guy he knew pretty well by the name of Lieutenant Commander Alvin Kramer, was working almost around the clock in a joint Army-Navy intelligence operation monitoring Japanese diplomatic radio traffic. Kramer had told him his Army counterpart, Colonel Rufus Bratton, was absolutely positive that a Japanese attack on the United States was going to take place somewhere – and soon. He had said that Kramer was now sounding more and more certain that Bratton was right.

Thus, Vinson felt on solid ground bringing the Jordan-Barnhardt story to Admiral Kidd. He had not just jumped when he had first heard it. He had spent two weeks checking and while he had found nothing to corroborate the details or to suggest that Pearl Harbor was likely to be a primary target, it was clear that war warnings were sounding. He did not feel he was out on a limb.

At least he hoped so.

But then again, Curt Vinson was not the kind of intelligence officer who worried about covering his ass before acting on intel that felt right to him. Admiral Kidd knew that to be true, and that is precisely why he valued Vinson as much as he did. It was why he had asked for him specifically, even though there were several other intelligence officers at CINCPAC who were senior to him and would have jumped at the BATDIVONE assignment.

Vinson explained to Admiral Kidd all that he had heard from Jordan and Barnhardt. He told him that his own research showed that if the shallow-water torpedoes were real and a key part of Japanese war plans, Jordan and Barnhardt were right. Cavite and Pearl Harbor were the most likely targets.

And the inattention and inaction in Washington when Jordan and Barnhardt had tried to raise the alarm was consistent with the absurd lack of specificity in the information the Army and Navy in Hawaii were getting from the War and Navy departments.

He concluded his briefing by summarizing his conclusions for the Admiral. "With respect, sir, as your intelligence officer, it is my conclusion that these signs, admittedly augmented by my gut feeling, point to an attack on U.S. Navy forces in the Pacific, and since Pearl Harbor is the key base, and the battleships are undoubtedly the key targets, I suggest you move this command to sea as soon as possible."

"Curt, I don't know about the shallow-water torpedoes," Admiral Kidd responded seriously after several moments' thinking. "I know the British sank those Italian battleships at Taranto in '40 in fairly shallow water, but it wasn't nearly as shallow as Pearl. And a part of me believes that Cavite would be the first target, not because it's more important to them but because I have no idea how the Japs could get close enough to Hawaii to hit us without being detected far in advance. Our search planes and all, and that new radar gizmo.

"But I also have no doubt they will attack us somewhere. Our Navy – the United States itself - is a threat to their expansion plans in Asia and the Pacific. So you give me good advice when you urge me to get out to sea as soon as I can. And I plan to do just that. We sure can't defend ourselves when we're tied up. But as you know, the decision is really Admiral Kimmel's."

Kidd paused, again thinking, clearly very serious. "I think the entire Battleship Battle Force needs to get out of here as soon as possible." There were three battleship divisions, or nine battleships, in the Battleship Battle Force, and in addition to being commander of BATDIVONE, Kidd was the Chief of Staff of the Battleship Battle Force. "I'll get our planning staff working on getting us fueled and provisioned and ready to go. So at least when the Admiral makes the call, we're ready."

Kidd stood, extending his hand to Vinson. "Good work, Curt. Keep your eyes open and keep me up to date on anything else you hear." Vinson shook hands with his boss and left the stateroom. As soon as he could, he called the Royal Hawaiian and asked for Alex Jordan. Alex, who of course had known that Vinson was scheduled to meet that morning with Admiral

Kidd, was waiting in his room when the phone rang. Vinson asked if he and Dick Barnhardt were free for lunch.

Naturally, they were.

At 12:30, Vinson arrived at the Royal Hawaiian and went directly to Alex's room. They ordered from room service. Once the room service waiter had laid out their lunches and departed, Vinson filled them in on his discussion with the Admiral, and the Admiral's response. "In short," he summarized, "your report seems credible to him, even if it hasn't been verified. I think I can safely say that while Admiral Kidd appreciates that good intelligence is based on solid facts, he also believes that great intelligence is often due to intuition and educated hunches."

The relief showed on the faces of both Alex and Rudi. Someone was finally going to pay attention to Rudi's intel. Vinson continued, "Dick, thanks for bein' dogged about this – and you, too, Alex. I know what it's like to have something you think is important and have the higher-ups payin' no attention – or worse, thinkin' you're nuts for even thinkin' it's relevant. But Admiral Kidd is takin' it seriously enough that he's going to push to get BATDIVONE, and hopefully all of our capital ships, out of Pearl as soon as he can. Stay close to a phone and I'll let you know anything that develops."

Alex spoke. "Some friends of ours are flying home tomorrow, on the Pan Am Clipper flight to San Francisco. We were gonna take them to Pearl City and see them off." The Pan Am seaplane base was on the north side of Pearl Harbor near Pearl City. "Other than that, we'll stay close to the phone."

Vinson stood to leave. "I really am glad you brought this to me, guys." He looked at Alex, then Rudi, and gave them a hopeful smile as he shook their hands.

Seated on the bench of the bus stop across the street from

the Royal Hawaiian, Henry Carter watched Vinson depart as he had watched him arrive. He marveled at how much Navy brass was coming and going from that hotel. He could not know, of course, whether they were coming to see his guys, but he suspected that some of them were. Why else would Oscar give a shit about them?

After Vinson's staff car pulled out of the driveway and turned in the direction of Pearl Harbor, Carter went back to daydreaming about Emily. He was going to the teahouse that night.

After Vinson departed, Alex and Rudi – both now in tropical uniform – went to meet Governor Poindexter at the Capitol building of the Territory of Hawaii. They had already been in Hawaii almost three weeks and they needed more time. That meant more money. They could not use any of Rudi's – which by then Alex knew about – without taking the risk of tipping off whomever was watching them that they were more than what Donovan had set them up to appear to be.

They had long since given up trying to identify followers in this land of anonymous faces, but they knew they must be there, probably both German and American. Maybe even Japanese. Once, Alex had even wondered whether Ann and Louise had been sent by someone to trap them in some way. The tension was constant.

Poindexter had obviously received his instructions from Donovan, probably backed up by Presidential authorization. He gave them $500 in cash and had his secretary call the Royal Hawaiian and inform the manager that the governor's office would be settling the bills of Lieutenant Jordan and Lieutenant (j.g.) Barnhardt when they checked out. In the meantime, the secretary informed the manager, it was necessary that their stay be extended for an unknown but indefinite period.

The manager of the Royal Hawaiian expressed his assurances to the Governor's secretary that the Royal Hawaiian was, as always, at the service of the Governor.

Back at the Royal Hawaiian and in civilian clothes, Alex and Rudi waited for their final dinner and evening in the delightful company of Ann Lassiter and Louise Wagner. Both men wished mightily that November 15 could be put off indefinitely like their own departure had been. A light rain fell, further dampening their spirits. The spirits of all four of them were raised later in the evening.

After a last lunch together at the Royal Hawaiian the next day, Alex hailed a cab and, because he had spotted one that was a wood-sided station wagon, managed to squeeze in all four of them in addition to the considerable luggage two adult women had brought for a two-week stay in Hawaii.

The drive to Pearl City took just under thirty minutes due to the fact it was a Saturday. On a work day, it would no doubt have taken much longer. A morning rain shower had left the streets damp but the skies were glorious. Neither Alex nor Rudi had been to Pearl City before. It was a working-class area catering to shipyard workers, longshoremen and other civilian employees of the Pearl Harbor Naval Base. It seemed very far removed from Waikiki.

At the Pan American Airways seaplane terminal, Alex and Rudi watched as Ann and Louise checked in for their flight. Take-off was scheduled for 6:00 p.m. so that most of the flight would take place during the hours of darkness. Ann told Alex that Pan Am had explained to them before their departure that the Hawaii flights were flown at night because it better facilitated celestial navigation on this long leg where there were no radio beacons until they got close to Hawaii, or on the return, to San Francisco.

In addition, she reminded him playfully, there were obviously no surface navigation aids, such as highways and railroads, like there were when flying over land. With this flight lasting between 12 and 13 hours, depending on the tailwinds, it would arrive at its Treasure Island base in San Francisco Bay at just after dawn the next morning.

Staring out at the Clipper seaplane, Rudi wondered aloud how such an enormous creation could possibly lift itself out of the water, let alone fly. Alex agreed.

The Boeing 314 was gigantic, with a wingspan half a football field across and a fuselage over 100 feet in length.

At 4:00, Pan American crews began loading the luggage aboard. At 5:00, passengers were called to the dock. Aside from Ann and Louise, Alex noted, most of the passengers were either wearing uniforms or expensive-looking business suits. The three other women they saw were dressed stylishly and, to Alex's eye, expensively. For the first time, he wondered how Ann and Louise had secured the travel priorities that must have been required to get them on this plane.

At that moment, a Pan American agent hurried up to Ann and Louise and, smiling broadly, told them that they were in luck. The plane was not quite full and "even with your priorities, we'll have no trouble accommodating you ladies this afternoon." Alex asked what that was about and Ann explained that they knew they had relatively low priorities and they had a back-up plan in the form of reservations on a Matson liner the next day. Alex wished they had been bumped so he could have one more night with Ann before they left. Selfish bastard that he was.

The farewells were brief but intensely felt. Ann and

Alex had exchanged addresses and telephone numbers and promised to write or call when they could. Alex had told her they would try to arrange to spend a day or two in San Francisco on their way back to Washington. He just didn't know when that would be.

Rudi told Louise the same thing, knowing that there was an excellent possibility he would not be returning to Washington at all. If this all blew up the wrong way, he might be shipped directly to Berlin (if he was lucky) or to a prison camp (if he was not). Or even killed (if he was very unlucky).

Alex and Rudi stood on the dock, watching as the boarding of the Boeing was completed and the four big engines, one by one, roared to life and settled into a loud hum as they warmed up. The engine roar intensified dramatically and the plane began taxiing toward the middle of the inlet where the take-off area was, turned and with a truly enormous roar, began its takeoff run.

After what seemed an eternity, the big airplane bounced lightly on the surface and lifted into the evening sky. Almost immediately, it whirled to the east as it climbed and grew smaller. Soon it was gone from sight, and the roar of its engines faded. Alex and Rudi walked glumly to the taxi stand in front of the terminal.

Two days later, Alex was awakened by the ringing of the telephone in his room. It was Ann, reporting they had made it home safely. They talked for just a few minutes, because trans-Pacific telephone calls were very expensive, even for someone whose ex-husband had not left her wanting for money. Just before she hung up, Ann said in a shaky voice, "Alex, I must be an idiot to say this, or even to think it. But I do believe I fell in love with you out there. Please don't hate me for saying that. I don't have any right to put any pressure on you, but I can't help how I feel. Take care of yourself, be safe, and write to me when you can." He was still formulating a reply when she disconnected.

Rudi didn't get a call from Louise.

Alex and Curt Vinson had talked by telephone several times since Ann and Louise had departed, Curt reporting on other signals Naval Intelligence had received pointing ominously at Japanese intentions and on what he was hearing about reports from Lieutenant Commander Kramer and Colonel Bratton in Washington. He had asked Alex for his take on most of the reports they discussed, and Alex almost always brought Rudi into these discussions.

They were now being treated as sort of ex-officio members of the Pearl Harbor intelligence community. But there was really nothing new, no confirmations nor any other reports related to shallow-water torpedoes. Curt urged Alex to stay in Hawaii a little longer.

When Curt Vinson called, just after noon on November 29, two weeks after the women's departure, and asked Alex if they could come and meet him right away, there was a noticeable strain in his voice. He could not leave the Arizona, he told them. Alex said they would be there as soon as they could get in their uniforms and get a cab. Vinson told him he would send a car and it would be there in 30 minutes. It was there in 25 minutes. Another blue Plymouth. Maybe the same one.

The car deposited them dockside where there was an Admiral's launch waiting to take them from shore to the Arizona, docked along Battleship Row off Ford Island. Curt Vinson was standing next to the launch. He had obviously been able to get off the Arizona but the ship was clearly in sight, so he really had not left it. They exchanged salutes and Curt gestured for them to board the launch. Aboard the Arizona, after saluting the colors and asking permission to come aboard, Commander Vinson led them hurriedly toward the bridge.

Both Alex and Rudi immediately noticed the difference in the atmosphere aboard the mighty ship compared to the day they had been aboard her in dry dock. Sailors were scurrying around, attending to countless details. It was obvious that the brass was aboard. Alex looked for but did not see Seaman First Class Abercrombie.

On the bridge level, Vinson paused in front of a doorway and knocked, then entered without awaiting a response. An imposing-looking man with the ornate gold braid on the shoulder boards and cuffs of his tunic that signified a Vice Admiral was at the desk in his sea cabin. "Admiral Kidd," Vinson said formally, "may I present Lieutenant Jordan and Lieutenant (j.g.) Barnhardt." Kidd rose from behind his desk, shaking the offered hands of Alex and Rudi.

"It's nice to meet you, gentlemen," Kidd said in a strong voice. He had the kind of commanding presence, mixed with the manners of a gentleman that caused enlisted men and officers alike to follow him. "Curt's told me a lot about you, Alex, is it? And you, too, Lieutenant." He was looking at Rudi when he added the last.

Curt spoke. "I've briefed the Admiral on our conversations, and he asked to meet you when you came aboard."

"This is very interesting, and distressing, information you have brought us," Kidd said. "I am also distressed at what Curt has told me of your reception in various offices in Washington when you tried to bring it to the attention of the appropriate people. I think Curt is one of the best intelligence officers around and I have complete confidence in him. If a commander of a Battleship Division needs an intelligence officer – and I think that he very much does – then he needs to put his confidence in him. Wouldn't you agree?"

"Yes, sir!" Alex barked, immediately embarrassed at how loudly he'd answered. Kidd smiled slightly, and nodded.

"Then I'll leave you intelligence types to sort out what's next." Kidd sat down and Curt opened the door. The three men departed. Curt led the way as they made for his wardroom in Officer Country.

"He's okay with all this," Curt said when they were seated, "although he still has a feeling the first strike is more likely to be Cavite because, as he said, how the hell could the Japs get close enough to Pearl to hit us without being exposed well in advance?"

Alex said, "So, what now?"

"Things are definitely heating up around here. I'm hearin' a lot rolling downhill from ONI in Washington, probably a lot of the stuff that Kramer and Bratton are working on. Admiral Kidd has talked to Admiral Kimmel and told him we have heard a credible – that's the word he used – story about Japanese Navy pilots practicing shallow-water torpedo runs. Kimmel believes him. The problem Kimmel's got, the poor bastard, is that he can't get a straight answer out of Washington. He's begging for intel and bein' told there isn't anything conclusive yet. I think he knows it's comin', just not when, where, or how."

"What about the Philippines?" Alex asked.

"I don't think it's worth your time to go there. MacArthur's got his own intelligence staff. A Colonel by the name of Willoughby is his G-2, and I hear he's a horse's ass of the first order. If he gets intel that comes from someplace other than one of his sources, he doesn't believe it, and he's able to convince MacArthur not to believe it. And one thing's for damn sure; if it comes from the Navy, no matter how solid, neither one of them is going to buy it. Sometimes I think MacArthur thinks the Navy is more the enemy than the Japs will ever be."

"So, what do you think we should do? Go back to Washington? Maybe try to get with Kramer and Bratton and see if they can link this to any of the dope they're gettin'?"

Curt paused. "I've been thinkin' a lot about that. I don't know what you've got for travel authority or what kind of resources you've got, but if it were strictly up to me, I'd have you go to Australia." He read Alex and Rudi's incredulous expressions and smiled. "Bear with me, guys. Go to the Aussies, and brief their Naval Intelligence folks. The Japs may actually be more interested in Java or Singapore or a thousand little islands down there than they are in Hawaii or the Philippines, at least at this time. I think they'll end up having to move on U.S. bases, but it's possible they have other targets higher on their immediate list."

"That's a little off-topic, don't you think, Curt?" Alex asked. "We're talkin' about a real threat to American ships full of American boys."

Vinson held his hand up to stop Alex, nodding. "I've met some of my Australian counterparts since I've been over here. They're cowboys. In a lot of ways, they're more willin' to think outside the box, so to speak, than our people are. And they're part of the British Empire, so they've already been in the war for a while. That gives them a little more inclination to listen than some of our people have so far. I think they'd love to hear your story. And they'd probably listen to it with an open mind."

"And if Australia pays attention to it, then they'll go through normal channels to the Brits, Dutch and the

Americans," Rudi connected the dots aloud. "It will force Washington to pay attention. They'll have to put the Army and Navy on full alert, or look totally incompetent." And it will keep Canaris and his role in this under wraps, and that's good!

"And Roosevelt would never risk that," Vinson added.

Alex was nodding. "Okay, sold. Well, we've got AAAA travel priorities if we need them, although I'd rather not," Alex offered. "And we've got money. I'm not sure if we have enough, but what the hell? How do we get there?" Curt picked up on the I'd rather not.

He said, "In the hope that you might agree that Australia should hear your story, I took the liberty of checking that out. It turns out there's a Clipper departing on 4 December" – he gave the date in the military manner – "for New Zealand. That's probably as close as you can get directly from here that doesn't involve two weeks or more on a ship, and it's just five days from now. There will be lots of ships between there and either Melbourne or Sydney, maybe even some air service. I haven't been able to check that out yet." He glanced around the mess of papers on his desk and looked at them with mock-sheepishness. "Been busy."

"Can we get on the flight?" Alex asked.

"I checked that, too," Curt said. "Pan Am told me that so far they only have twelve passengers booked, and it can hold 36 in its long-haul flight configuration, so there's plenty of room for you, and you won't even need to use your – shall we say 'questionable' - AAAA priorities."

Alex looked at Rudi, who nodded. "Let's get on with it, then," he said to Curt.

Alex stood. "We'd better get busy. Is there any way you can have the driver you sent for us take us over to the seaplane terminal at Pearl City after we stop at the hotel to get some cash? We should probably go ahead and buy our tickets so we're ready."

"Of course," Curt agreed, then stood and led them out the door and toward the boarding ramp. "Let me know when you're set with the flight, then let's stay in touch until you shove off," he said as he shook their hands.

Curt Vinson accompanied Alex and Rudi off the Arizona and onto the Admiral's launch. At the pier, he gave instructions to the driver of the awaiting blue Plymouth, then warmly shook both men's hands again as they debarked from the launch. They wished each other luck. It was not pro forma. Each of the men knew he would need a lot of luck in the coming days. And probably years.

At the Pan Am terminal, Alex and Rudi spent almost $1,000 for the two tickets. And that was one-way, but it was the Pan American military discount, so it could have been worse. They both knew commercial air travel was expensive, but were nonetheless staggered by the amount. They hoped they would have enough money left by the time they were finished in Australia to get back.

The phone in the room did not wake Alex up when it rang at 6:45 the next morning. He was already awake and thinking about the journey to Australia. When he answered, he heard Curt's strained voice telling him all hell was breaking loose. "Washington sent Kimmel and Short a war warning early this morning. Still no specifics, but the Admiral put the entire Pacific Fleet on full alert. General Short's done the same thing with the Army and Air Corps." Major General Walter Campbell Short was the Army Commander in Hawaii. "I'm sure as hell glad you got booked on the flight to New Zealand. I just hope you get out before anything gets really serious."

Alex assured him again that they had their Pan American tickets.

"Alex," Curt added after a pause, "I mean this, and I need to tell you now because I don't know whether I'll have another chance before you leave on the fourth. It was great to see you, and I can't tell you how much I admire the guts it took to come all the way here when nobody in Washington would listen. Not to mention the guts it takes to go off to Australia like this. Take care of yourself, my friend. And watch your back. It's very possible some people would not like the idea of you goin' to the Aussies with this."

Alex was surprised at the intensity of the man's voice. He assumed Curt was referring to Donovan, maybe even the President. Almost certainly Admiral Stark. He might even suspect that the German SS-SD and Hawaii-based Japanese agents might also be in the mix. But if this war warning was real, they might not need to go to Australia, not if war broke out in the next three or four days.

"I will," he said simply. "Take care of yourself, Curt." They rang off.

Alex and Rudi spent a very tense day waiting. They knew that Naval Intelligence was convinced the Japanese attack, if it came, would come on a Sunday. This was based on repeated analyses by the Army and Navy – and wholeheartedly concurred in by Lieutenant Commander Kramer and Colonel Bratton in Washington – that looked at the planning of an attack on Hawaii from the Japanese point of view, and always concluded the same thing: The Japanese would assume the American fleet would be at its most vulnerable on a Sunday, probably early on a Sunday morning.

This was because the fleet, unable to shake the habits –

and regulations, which unaccountably were still in effect - of a peacetime Navy, tended to be in port on weekends and sail out for training or maneuvers on Mondays. In addition, history showed that the Japanese always went to war on a Sunday. China and a lot of other countries could attest to that.

Alex hoped that Admiral Kidd was able to get the battleships out of Pearl Harbor and on the high seas before too many more Sundays came.

Nothing had happened on Sunday, November 30, or on December 1, and Admiral Kimmel and General Short had cancelled the alerts. Life in Hawaii had returned to normal, except for inside the Army and Navy high commands and their intelligence staffs. Curt Vinson called Alex in the late afternoon of December 1 to tell him the alert had been cancelled. He told Alex that he, Kidd and Kimmel all felt the war warning had been real enough. It just had not happened at that time.

And he said that Kidd was continuing to press to get the battleships fueled, provisioned and out of Pearl Harbor as soon as possible.

The days crawled by in nervous anticipation for Alex and Rudi.

CHAPTER 13

Pearl City, Territory of Hawaii
December 4, 1941

It was before daylight when Alex and Rudi stepped out of the taxi at the Pan American seaplane terminal at Pearl City. They were in their blue U.S. Navy uniforms. It was good that Alex had secured two uniforms – in addition to two sets of tropical casual uniforms - for Rudi before they left Washington. Indeed, Rudi could not have accompanied him on his visits to the Arizona without them. Alex had no reason to believe it would be any different in wartime Australia.

The past few days had gone by in a nervous blur with the preparations – both physical and mental - for the trip. They had even taken a bus to Pearl City the morning before to watch the giant Boeing 314 on which they would be flying touch down on its inbound trip from San Francisco by way of Los Angeles. They were both excited and apprehensive and wanted to make sure the aircraft was going to be there when they checked out of the Royal Hawaiian.

As it turned out, they need not have bothered. The plane's crew and the passengers from the mainland who were continuing on beyond Hawaii were bussed to the Royal Hawaiian for the night.

Now, they checked in at the Pan American departures

desk, staffed by two very perky, friendly and talkative young women.

Rudi had fretted about checking his luggage, especially the one with the false bottoms that still concealed over 18,000 dollars in cash and gold coins. In the end, Alex had been successful in convincing Rudi that this aircraft was not going anywhere they were not and that the luggage would be safely stowed.

One of the ticket agents explained that for the first leg of the trip they would go as far as Canton Island in the Phoenix Island group, where they would stay overnight in a hotel built and owned by Pan American. It was, as with all the Pan American facilities, quite nice, she assured them. The next day, they would fly from Canton Island to Suva, on Fiji, and again stay overnight. Then they would have a fairly short flight from Suva to Noumea, in New Caledonia. And finally, on December 8, they would complete their journey to Auckland, New Zealand. They would lose a day, she told them, because on the flight from Honolulu to Canton Island, they would cross the International Date Line.

She handed Alex and Rudi their boarding stubs, baggage checks and a brochure describing the features and specifications of the Boeing 314 Clipper – this one was called the California Clipper – and directed them to the departure lounge. She wished them a pleasant flight. "There are only 15 of you going on this flight, so you'll have plenty of room and I'm sure it will be especially comfortable," she said with a smile.

"I guess someone else decided to go to New Zealand at the last minute," Alex said to Rudi as they walked toward the lounge. "Curt told us there were twelve passengers booked last week." Rudi just nodded. Despite his experience as a pilot of small planes, he was clearly more nervous than Alex at the idea of getting into that monster and taking off from water, flying for hours over nothing but water and landing on water. Hopefully on the right patch of water. All in all, Rudi would have preferred a ship, except that ships were slow, and he had an unexplainable yet tangible feeling in his gut that time was running out.

At about 5:45, still before dawn, three young men began stowing the passengers' luggage aboard the California Clipper, which was sitting majestically at its berth at the end of a short pier. Soon after the luggage was stowed, Pan Am crew members began directing the passengers to board. Alex and Rudi were shown to their seats by an efficient steward in an immaculate uniform which looked strikingly like the U.S. Navy dress blue uniforms.

Inside, the cabin seemed even more enormous than they expected. Headroom was not an issue and all the passengers and personnel were able to walk around freely without worrying about hitting their heads. They also noted that, because the tail of the Clipper was more elevated than the front, there were single steps – up or down, depending on whether one was walking forward or aft - between passenger compartments.

Each compartment held four seats, which could be converted to berths on overnight flights. The berths would go unused on this flight because all of the legs were to be flown during daytime. Alex and Rudi sat in the two forward-facing seats in the compartment assigned to them. The rear-facing seats opposite were left unoccupied. The seats were leather, well-padded and very comfortable.

At 6:30, the cabin door was closed and latched. When the passengers were all seated and strapped in, the ground crew cast off the lines and a small launch towed the big aircraft out toward the peaceful waters of the Middle Loch of Pearl Harbor.

Through the window, Alex and Rudi watched as the launch left the Clipper and ran up the loch, checking for anything floating that might damage the plane on take-off, then, apparently finding nothing, it turned back toward the dock. Almost immediately, a low rumble followed by a cloud of white smoke, a high whine and a lot of cabin vibration told them the first engine had started. Alex was reading the brochure describing the airplane the ticket agent had given him.

In anticipation of the flight, he had avidly studied the aircraft specifications while they waited in the terminal, and now he mentally noted that the four engines – Wright Double Cyclone 14-cylinder monsters mounted on the wings – were each capable of generating 1,600 horsepower. Now that he was inside the beast, he could truly appreciate the rest of the sleek giant.

It was 106 feet long with a wingspan of 152 feet. It was rated at a gross weight of 82,500 pounds, would cruise at 13,400 feet at a cruising speed of 183 miles per hour. It had a maximum range of 3,500 miles, although they would not need to test that range for any of the legs on this journey, thank goodness. Alex had been reciting each of these statistics to Rudi, whose wide eyes betrayed his excitement – or fear. Alex could not tell which. It may have been both.

With all engines started and running smoothly, the Clipper began moving into its take-off position. Soon it was accelerating across the water. The vibration they felt both through their feet and through the well-padded seats beneath them seemed to be shaking the aircraft apart. After what seemed like a very long time, the vibrations lessened as the aircraft got light on the water.

Then, suddenly, the hard vibrations from the water ceased and the craft was airborne, still shaking slightly as the engines, at full take-off power, pulled the Clipper aloft over Pearl Harbor. Rudi noted as they climbed out that the harbor looked half empty, many of the great ships of the U.S. Pacific Fleet at sea on training exercises or maneuvers until next weekend. Astonishingly to Rudi, it was still a peacetime Navy and most of the ships would be back in Pearl Harbor by Friday so the sailors could enjoy another weekend liberty.

Next to him in the aisle seat, Alex again consulted his brochure and noted aloud that the fully-laden Boeing could climb at the incredible rate of 565 feet per minute. Rudi found that hard to believe too, and pulled his own brochure from the inside pocket of his uniform blouse. He was not yet breathing normally, but his nerves had settled somewhat following the take-off.

When they reached their cruising altitude, the two stewards began moving about the cabin, taking drink orders and answering questions. A man Alex had met in the Royal Hawaiian lobby the night before recognized him and introduced himself again.

"Steward Barney Sawicki, Lieutenant Jordan," he said to Alex, speaking very formally. "We met briefly last evening at the hotel. At the time, I didn't realize you'd be with us today, but it's nice to have you aboard, sir. And you must be Lieutenant Barnhardt." He nodded to Rudi. "My flight manifest shows you gentlemen traveling together. And did I recognize the insignia of rank correctly?"

"That's right, although Mr. Barnhardt is actually a Lieutenant (junior grade)," Alex replied in a friendly tone.

"And what may I get you gentlemen to drink this morning?" Sawicki asked. "It will be about three hours before our meal service begins." Sawicki was a small man who gave most people he met the impression of a friendly leprechaun. It was already apparent why Pan American had established a reputation for impeccable service.

Alex and Rudi both requested coffee and Sawicki told them he would be happy to serve them in the more comfortable lounge area between the second and third passenger compartments. Since Alex and Rudi were occupying the third compartment, that made the lounge especially convenient to them. Of course, everyone had been strapped in their own compartments for take-off.

Another steward was busy serving other passengers forward of where Alex and Rudi were sitting. They wasted no time moving to the lounge. It was situated almost directly beneath the enormous wing, and only about 20 feet behind the galley, which was forward of the first passenger compartment. Beyond the galley, in the nose of the plane, was the crew's rest compartment.

Because of the length of the typical flights flown by the Clippers, the flight deck crew was cross-trained in multiple disciplines and crew members rotated their shifts at the controls, the flight engineer's station and the navigation table.

Shortly after Sawicki had returned and placed their coffee, served in a silver service with cream and sugar bowls and china cups and saucers, on the low table in the lounge, another man walked into the same area and asked whether a chair opposite was taken. All the other tables were occupied. Alex gestured toward it in invitation with his hand and said, "Please, help yourself." Sawicki handed the man a glass of orange juice – freshly squeezed, it appeared.

"Alex Jordan," Alex said by way of introduction, "and this is Dick Barnhardt." The man shook each of their hands in turn before muttering, "Henry Carter," and sitting in the chair.

"What takes you to New Zealand, Mr. Carter?" Alex asked conversationally. "Or are you getting off at one of the other stops?" He knew that in the course of the next four days, there would be ample opportunity to get to know everyone else on the flight, so he might as well start now.

"I'm with a shipping company in Brooklyn," he said. "We build ships, and a cargo company in New Zealand is having trouble with a couple of ours. I'm on the technical side and they sent me to see if I could figure out what's the deal. I was already in Hawaii, on another deal, so the company figured I was the one to go."

It was arguably the longest speech Henry Carter had ever made, and he was quite glad that he had taken the time to rehearse it. Of course, "Oscar" had suggested the story when Carter had called Donovan to report that the two men he was watching had purchased tickets to New Zealand.

Carter had been lucky to learn of the destination, of course. He had watched them arrive at the Royal Hawaiian in the Navy staff car and run into the hotel while the car remained in the driveway. He wondered, of course, why it had not just driven off after depositing its passengers. When they ran back out minutes later and jumped back in the Navy car, Carter had figured something was up.

He had hailed a cab and followed the Navy car to the Pan American terminal in Pearl City. His subjects had rushed into the terminal and reappeared only a few minutes later holding envelopes in their hands. When they got in the Navy car and departed, Carter had decided it was likely they were simply going back to the hotel.

Carter was, in fact, quite good at reading and tracking people.

He had told the cabbie to wait and had copied their

mannerisms by rushing into the terminal, appearing out-of-breath and confused. He went to the ticket counter, where a lone woman was on duty. He breathlessly told her he had apparently missed his two colleagues – the two in Navy uniforms who had just driven away – and asked her if they had bought three tickets.

She remembered the two young officers, of course, and told their colleague that they had only purchased two tickets, for themselves. Carter feigned frustration and told her he was to travel with them and asked her to write down the details and the price and he would hurry back and get the cash or travel voucher to purchase his own ticket. She was more than happy to comply and assured the man that the flight had plenty of seats available.

Donovan had been startled by the news that the two men Carter was watching were going to New Zealand because he thought the two would be going to the Philippines from Hawaii if they went anywhere. He had hurriedly arranged for Governor Poindexter to get Carter on the same flight.

Henry Carter, Alex noted, had the rough voice and the accent associated with the East Coast, probably New York City, but he seemed to be much more a normal blue-collar worker than someone on the technical side.

"So what about you guys?" Carter asked, sounding a bit less than genuinely interested. It almost came out, "youse." "What's the Navy doing in New Zealand?"

"We're on a very long and boring trip to liaise with the New Zealand, and then the Australian, navies," Alex said, reciting the cover story the two had worked out at the Royal Hawaiian and tested on Curt Vinson, who agreed that it sounded appropriately boring and gave inquisitive busy bodies no really viable avenues for follow-up questions. Just liaise with them. Carter's face betrayed the fact that he was having trouble figuring out what the word meant.

Alex realized they had undoubtedly found the other last-minute passenger. He also realized that a conversation with this man would be, at best, tedious, so when they had finished their coffee, he and Rudi returned to their seats.

Soon, both men had books out and Alex retrieved a map of the Pacific from his briefcase and plotted their course to Canton Island. It was a tiny speck on the map and he marveled that the pilot could find that speck in the midst of all this water. Finding it from aboard a ship was one thing – a ship did not move that swiftly, after all, compared to this aircraft streaking through the sky – but there seemed no margin for error in an airplane.

He thought about the disappearance of the famous woman pilot, Amelia Earhart, somewhere in the South Pacific four years previously. One possible reason for her disappearance, so the speculation went, was that she missed the island she was looking for and crashed at sea. Her navigator, Fred Noonan, had been a Pan Am navigator. He immediately wished he had not thought of that story.

Alex and Rudi alternately read and dozed and the time passed. At 10:45, the second steward, a taller man than Sawicki who introduced himself as Verne Edwards, announced that luncheon would be served in the dining area, which had been set up in the lounge, in thirty minutes. They went forward to the surprisingly spacious men's room, where they washed their faces and brushed their teeth. Then they sat at the table Sawicki indicated and put their linen napkins in their laps. Real china and silverware were laid out in neat place settings around the tables and the other passengers were starting to converge on the lounge for their first meal of the journey.

Alex noticed the man he assumed – because of the four stripes on his epaulets - was the captain of the California Clipper coming down the stairway from the flight deck with a short, somewhat portly but distinguished-looking man sporting a white goatee. The captain turned the man over to Sawicki, admonishing him to "take care of Sir Harry." Alex wondered who the hell Sir Harry was.

Rudi was startled when he read the menu which sat atop his plate. They would be starting with their choice of an assortment of fine wines and other beverages, alcoholic and otherwise, followed by hearts of lettuce with asparagus tips and beef broth. The main course would be Swiss steak with new potatoes and cut string beans, followed by a dessert assortment that included sliced peaches, assorted cookies and crackers with cream cheese. He briefly wondered what two of his cousins had to eat at that very moment, stationed as they were with the Wehrmacht outside of Moscow.

"I take it they don't plan to starve us on this flight," he said to Alex. A middle-aged couple had just been seated across the table from them, and the man roared with laughter at Rudi's comment. He introduced himself and his wife. They were in the textile business in Tennessee and were traveling to New Zealand to try to work out how the wool he so prized from that country might continue to flow to his mills if war breaks out in the Pacific, as so many feared. Alex assumed the textile business must be quite lucrative, if this man could afford passage for himself and his wife for a trip like this.

"We've made this trip once before," the man said to Rudi, "and I can assure you that you will not be disappointed with Pan American's food." Alex and Rudi introduced themselves and repeated the mind-numbing story they had told Henry Carter. Rudi, Alex noted once again, had been well-trained by the Abwehr. He slid into his "Richard Barnhardt" persona effortlessly.

Later, as the dessert trays were being delivered to the tables, Sawicki announced that the pilot, whose name was Captain Robert Ford, had just notified him that they had crossed over the International Date Line and that it was now December 5. He also assured the passengers, one or two of whom looked a bit puzzled, that they would get that lost day back when they made their return flight.

A minute or two later, the Captain himself entered the lounge area and circulated around the space, introducing himself and welcoming them on behalf of Pan American. Then he walked to the forward-most compartment, the rest area for off-duty flight crew.

Later that afternoon, Sawicki and Edwards circulated among the passengers and told them they would begin their descent for Canton Island shortly and should be landing in about 30 minutes. Rudi looked at his watch, noting that it was 4:45, at least in Hawaii. He knew they would have to adjust their watches to whatever time it was on Canton Island.

It had already been a long flight, but entirely uneventful, save for the wonder of being on this magnificent aircraft. The big engines had hummed along uninterrupted, not nearly as loud at cruising speed as they had been during takeoff. There had been little of the weather-related turbulence he had expected and he was thankful for small favors. He knew Pacific storms could be quite vicious and wondered how this great aircraft would handle something like a typhoon, or even a really bad thunderstorm.

Sawicki, sensing what he was thinking, said, "This is the longest leg, Lieutenant. Eleven hours, roughly, depending on the winds and whether we have to dodge any storms, but luckily we haven't had to do that today." So with the aircraft's range, it simply dodges storms, Rudi concluded, relieved.

"Do we have a VIP aboard?" Alex asked Sawicki. "I noticed earlier the Captain asking you to take care of Sir something-or-other."

Sawicki smiled. "Yes, indeed we do," he said. "Sir Harry Luke is the British Governor-General of Fiji. He has been in Hawaii visiting with your naval command, as I understand it, and he's going home. We'll only have him as far as Suva."

Alex thanked Sawicki and smiled at Rudi.

They watched through their window as the Clipper lost altitude and the ocean seemed to rise to meet them. Soon, they heard Captain Ford – they assumed he was back at the controls - throttle back and the giant aircraft settled almost as lightly as a ballerina onto the calm waters off Canton Island. Ford taxied the craft expertly toward the dock, retarding the throttles to idle as they neared it, and the ground crew, working with a practiced efficiency, lashed the plane to a floating dock.

As the perky young ticket agent had told them at Pearl City, the Pan American hotel was quite nice, certainly the nicest building on the small island. The desk clerk, who was handing out room keys, told the passengers that Pan American had had the hotel built in the States and shipped here in sections for assembly. They would, he told them, stay in identical quarters on Fiji, but in Noumea the hotel was still under construction and he was not sure where they would be staying.

There was a restaurant in the hotel for the exclusive use of passengers, crew and staff, and Alex thought that was a very good thing, because there did not appear to be anything else in the way of a restaurant – or a hotel - on the island. The local fish that was offered for dinner was excellent and was complemented by a couple of glasses of very good white wine. A fine port was poured for dessert.

Sir Harry Luke was at Captain Ford's table with two of the other officers of the California Clipper and they appeared to be in a serious conversation throughout their meal. The dinner and wine provided Alex and Rudi the full bellies and light buzz that, combined with the long flight, made it easy to fall asleep, something they both did as soon as they hit the beds in their rooms. Their nerve endings were never far from the surface, but on this tiny island, they felt themselves relax.

The next morning, Rudi was walking the grounds of the hotel when he noticed a very tall tower standing apart from the hotel property. Sawicki walked by him, heading toward the seaplane dock, and noticed him staring up at it. "That's the directional beacon," he said. "Our radio operators just home in on the radio wave it sends out and that guides us right here. It's much more reliable than navigating by the stars, especially during the day. You see, Lieutenant, over water, we don't have the highways and railways to follow that we do over land." Rudi wondered if all the Pan American employees were given the same lines to recite to first-time passengers. He recalled hearing the same thing at the Pearl City base. Or was it from Louise or Ann?

Sawicki smiled to himself. He obviously loved his job, loved telling new people all the wonders of Clipper flight.

Rudi acted truly impressed and chuckled to himself as Sawicki walked on.

Once all were aboard the aircraft and it had been moved away from the dock, its engines started again. They did not seem as loud as they had the day before to either Alex or Rudi.

Maybe they were just getting used to it. Airborne, Sawicki and Edwards again circulated among the passengers offering coffee, tea and other options.

They briefed each passenger on the day's flight. It was scheduled to be just under nine hours, two hours shorter than the day before. The weather forecast was again good, and the Captain anticipated no delays. Alex was sure that the food would be good and just hoped the forecast was right and the weather cooperated as well.

Sir Harry Luke was hoping the same. When the California Clipper landed that afternoon, he would be home.

In the early morning two days later – December 8 - the passengers, as well as the crew, looked forward to the final leg of the flight. Sir Harry, of course, had deplaned at Suva, so the passenger count was down to fourteen. They had spent the night of the last stop-over at Noumea, situated at the southwestern tip of New Caledonia. They had stayed aboard a luxury yacht, the Southern Seas, which Pan American had leased as quarters until their ready-made hotel was completed. Alex thought the Southern Seas might have been a converted destroyer, as large as it was.

The crew had been augmented in Noumea as well. A man, introduced to Alex and Rudi as Eugene Leach, was a radio maintenance technician who Pan American was sending to Auckland to work on a radio problem there.

Now, a flight of less than seven hours was all that stood between them and Auckland. The crew would get a few days off before beginning the return flight, so they were anxious as well, but Sawicki and Edwards were, as usual, models of efficiency as they served drinks and prepared lunch.

The passengers had just been seated for lunch when, on

the flight deck above them, Chief Radio Officer Jack Poindexter heard the alert signaling a message about to be transmitted. He pulled his headset tight to his ears. The message was in Morse code, and he began jotting letters on the pad in front of him. The message was short and when he had finished copying it down, he stared at the pad in disbelief.

He tore the page from the pad and moved forward to the cockpit, where Captain Ford and First Officer John Henry Mack were chatting while their eyes scanned the gauges, alert for signs of anything out of the ordinary.

They were about to be presented with a message that was nothing if not out of the ordinary.

CHAPTER 14

Pearl Harbor Naval Base
Oahu, Territory of Hawaii
0600, Sunday, December 7, 1941

Seaman 1st Class Adolphus Abercrombie rubbed his eyes wearily and willed himself out of his bunk. He slipped on his deck shoes and made his way to the head, sailors' jargon for the toilet. He ached a little, but that was due to lack of sleep rather than from alcohol.

He was not a drinker, which meant that most of the time when he went on liberty with his shipmates, he spent his evenings reasoning with the authorities as to why it was better to let him take his drunken buddies back to the ship than it was to arrest them. And if successful, he then actually had to get them back to the ship in one cohesive group. Not an easy task, considering his buddies were normally too drunk to make it on their own, but not so drunk as to stop trying. Abercrombie thought it was probably something like herding cats.

Last night, fortunately, had not been typical. Although he left around five in the afternoon aboard one of Arizona's motor whaleboats with a score of shipmates, singly or in small groups they split off to head to various places, and Adolphus was on his own. He had made tentative plans to meet a friend to see a show, but when he had arrived, he had been informed that his friend had left on a date with a lady.

When the landlady at the friend's rooming house had told him he had been stood up, Abercrombie had to admit to himself that on an island that was currently very heavily male, he couldn't condemn his friend's decision. Deciding to simply take a stroll and see what there was to see, he came across a small bar that looked to be a Navy hangout. Dang, for some reason, he couldn't remember what the name of the joint was. He looked at himself in the mirror as if to say, "C'mon sailor, think!" After a couple of seconds, he acknowledged that it would probably bother him until he remembered, but oh well.

He splashed his razor in the sink of water in front of him, and continued shaving. Anyhow, wherever it had been, he had decided to have a beer – one beer only - there, and ended up spending four hours, mostly talking with those two marines, whose names he did remember! He chuckled to himself; he knew he remembered them because Marine Sergeant Morley and PFC Seamster were both from Texas. "And we do tend to stick together," he said softly to the mirror with his toothy grin.

After shaving and taking a quick shower, putting on fresh undress whites and tying his neckerchief, Abercrombie was ready for morning chow followed by Sunday church services, which he tried never to miss. Back home in Leggett, folks never missed church, mostly because Reverend Malone was a great preacher who put the fire of God into you, but also because it was the only big thing going on during most weeks in Leggett.

Either way, Adolphus embraced the preacher's words and tried to remember every sermon. He enjoyed it so much, in fact, that he had already made plans to try to go to seminary once he got out of the Navy. But all that would have to wait until the spring, when his enlistment was up.

A half-hour later, Abercrombie climbed a ladder onto

the boat deck, just between the two masts, and walked to the rail and looked out on the beautiful morning horizon. Dozens of ships were in his immediate view, each swaying gracefully at anchor. Just ahead, there were sailors coming to life, doing all the same things aboard West Virginia and Tennessee that were happening on his ship. A few were moving about the deck on the repair ship Vestal, which was tied up alongside, and dwarfed by, Arizona.

Normally, the ships would be completely full of wide-awake sailors and marines by this time, but being a Sunday, everyone was allowed to sleep longer. He sighed contentedly and prayed to himself aloud, "Lord above, this is one beautiful mornin'." Almost in answer, in the distance, over in Pearl City, he heard a church-bell tolling. Seven gongs. He looked at his watch, smiled and said to himself, "they're two minutes slow." He still had an hour before church and decided to wander.

At the same time that Abercrombie was enjoying the morning air, Commander Curt Vinson was feverishly poring over a table of charts, tables, and top secret intelligence files. He looked like hell, and he knew it. He had been up since 0110, when he startled himself awake. It had been a bad dream, full of fire, explosions, his childhood dog for some reason, and the constant droning of aircraft engine noise.

But it had shocked him wide-awake and motivated him to take another long hard look at his files. He was trying to put himself, for the millionth time, into the shoes of a Japanese naval officer, trying to figure out how he would attack Hawaii. He had been over all this before, but he calculated the distance between Japan and Honolulu, then re-checked the range of the primary front-line Japanese naval aircraft.

"And which direction would I come from?" he asked aloud. "We don't have nearly enough planes to search in all directions, and have to assume the Japs know that...." He rubbed the stubble on his face thoughtfully. "They have plenty of spies here, I'm sure. Easy enough for them to get in with ship and air service into the isla...." he stopped himself suddenly. He stood motionless for several seconds then excitedly pushed papers off the large chart at the bottom until he was gazing at the Hawaiian Islands and the sea areas just around it. He smiled tightly, and muttered, "Well, of course it's the northern route. Has to be."

Vinson quickly tied his black tie, using the small mirror in his stateroom in Officer Country. After one quick once-over to make sure he looked somewhat presentable, he grabbed his attaché case, stuffed his papers into it and was out the door. He turned aft and hurried for the radio room near the stern. Bursting inside, he startled Radioman 3rd Class Bernard "Bernie" Fields, who was lounged in front of several sets, feet propped on the table and headset over only one ear. The melodic waves of Hawaiian music floated softly on the air. God, this kid is in paradise, Vinson thought fleetingly. The sailor shot up and stood at attention with an embarrassed look on his face.

"Good morning, Commander! Please excuse me, I was...."

"Save it, kid." Vinson gestured to him to sit back down. "I just needed to check and see if you've heard anything unusual this morning? I mean anything."

The young sailor looked puzzled, and continued to stand. "Uh, I'm not sure I understand the Commander, sir."

"I just want to know if you've heard any strange messages. Anything that sounds cryptic?" The sailor shook his head. "Any unusual ship-to-shore, or plane-to-plane chatter?"

"No sir, everything has been quiet, and nothing out of the ordinary." He shrugged, "It's Sunday, sir." He paused, then added, "Oh, except for KGU Honolulu staying on the air all night." Vinson looked at the radio that was producing the Hawaiian music, the gears in his mind spinning wildly.

He looked at the sailor then back at the radio. "Yeah." He slapped the radioman on the shoulder and turned to rush out. "Thanks, kid!"

Abercrombie was standing along the starboard railing, just abeam Gun Turret Number 2, chatting with his friend Curt Haynes, a Quartermaster 2nd from Idaho. Another sailor walking nearby spotted them and came over to join the conversation. Haynes nodded a salutation.

"Morning' Lou," Abercrombie said amiably.

"Morning Tex," Quartermaster 3rd Class Louis A. 'Lou' Conter answered. "What kind of crap are you two salty bastards coming up with on this fine morning?" He smiled at them, then looked at his watch.

"Hey, what time ya got, Lou?" Haynes asked.

"Twenty 'til. What time you got the watch?"

"0900," Haynes answered.

Conter leaned over the side of the ship and looked aft at Nevada, tied to the mooring piers just behind them in Battleship Row. "A guy from the Black Gang on Nevada was topside a little while ago having a smoke and we yelled back 'n forth for a few. He told me they're doing something with their boilers today; tests or some such." He paused, grinning like a Cheshire cat. "So get this, poor bastards have to do a full duty schedule down in the damned engine room just like any other day. No Sunday for them this week." The other two sailors made groaning sounds, and Conter chuckled. "Yeah, I was trying not to laugh in his face, but I figured it'll be our turn next."

"Shoot, they missed out last weekend too, what with that alert we all got and all," Abercrombie offered with his grin, which always seemed to be in place. "Got everybody worked up and then nothin' doin'." The others nodded.

"Ain't that the Navy way?" Haynes offered.

They suddenly heard an authoritative voice call, "Gangway! Make a hole!" coming from one deck below, below the casement for the ship's starboard 5-inch secondary guns. They quickly noticed an officer in wrinkled khakis making his way at top speed, sailors backing out of his way. Abercrombie immediately recognized him.

"That's Commander Vinson, the Admiral's intel guy," he declared as he nodded toward the commotion.

"Whoever he is, he's in a rush about somethin'," Haynes said, matter-of-factly. "Better slow down or he'll tarnish his brass." Conter laughed again.

"Yeah, call me curious," Abercrombie said. "I'll catch up to y'all later on." He headed for the up-ladder to make his way in the direction Vinson had been going.

Curt Haynes and Lou Conter both answered, "See ya, Tex," and strolled aft.

Vinson reached the door to the Admiral's cabin and feverishly knocked on the door. Hearing "Enter" from inside, he opened it and stepped inside. Kidd was sitting in a small chair in the corner of the cabin, tying one of his shoes. He acknowledged Vinson with a nod. "Good morning, Curt. You look like hell."

"Yes, sir, sorry about that. I've had a hell of a morning." He was breathing heavily after his rush from the stern. He closed the door behind him. "Something came to mind and I wanted to mention it to you."

"Doesn't sound like it's just a passing thought, Curt. Spill it." Kidd was now standing and went to his small closet to get a clean khaki shirt.

"Well, Admiral, I was trying to shrink the brain of a Jap officer for the umpteenth time and it came to mind what that Air Corps officer told us a few weeks back about how short they are on long range patrol planes. Plus, we know that Kaneohe and Ford Island don't have nearly the number of PBYs to complete their patrol mission, either."

"We've known all that for weeks, so what's new?"

Vinson pulled his folded chart of the Hawaiian Islands out of his attaché case and laid it on the small table in front of Kidd. "Sir, ever since Pan American started the Auckland service, that puts commercial air routes out of the islands in every direction except north." He paused for effect. "So if I'm a Jap officer planning an air, or surface for that matter, attack on Hawaii, I would never risk approaching from any direction except north, because of the off chance of running into a low-flying Clipper as well as our military patrols. Sir, I'd bet that if the Japs are coming to Hawaii, they're coming from the north."

The Admiral looked at the chart, thinking to himself silently. He rubbed his chin, then replied, "Yeah, I agree with all that, but it's not a cracked code or something, that's just good common sense. I'm sure the boys in Washington came up with all that months ago. Don't you figure?"

Vinson nodded. "Yes, sir, I'm sure they did, and I think that the war warning last week was probably built on some pretty solid intel...."

"But?"

"But we were keeping good track of the Jap carriers until fairly recently, and then they disappeared. And if they had left Japanese waters heading for Honolulu, that would probably have lined up pretty good with the notion that they would hit us right at the end of November, just like the war warning suggested."

The admiral was deep in thought, his head nodding slowly. As Vinson was about to finish, Kidd cut him off. "But the longer northern route would take them another week at sea." Vinson nodded silently, and felt his blood running cold.

Abercrombie had passed by the closed door of the Admiral's cabin, then figured he would go to the bridge to see if one of his buddies was on watch. He was, and after asking quick permission to step just outside for a smoke, he went out to join Abercrombie. The lieutenant (junior grade) who had the con was a nice enough fellow, who understood that it was a quiet Sunday morning, and in the absence of more senior officers, didn't mind giving his guys short breaks.

"So she's talkin' to me, right? An den dis udduh guy, I'm pretty shuah he was a tin can schmuck... I heard 'is buddy say sump'm about da Monahans...." Abercrombie was grinning, amused just listening to his friend from Brooklyn. "An so de udduh guy gets all bent da wrong way because he thinks I'm tryin' to Shanghai his broad, see?" The New Yorker took a drag from his Lucky Strike, shaking his head. "I mean, how'm I s'posed to know she's spoken for?"

Abercrombie nodded. "So'd you just knock his lights out? Or were you feelin'...." He paused, obviously listening. "...generous?" He turned towards the noise. It was the sound of airplane engines. Lots of them. He looked off the port bow towards the submarine base and the mouth of the harbor, scanning the sky.

"Hey Ernie, why would the Army be practicing on a Sunday morning, without telling the Fleet?"

His buddy definitely heard the noise as well, and was looking for them too. "Dey wouldn't, 'less dey were lookin' ta get deir tails shot off."

The sound was getting really loud now, and then they saw them, flying right on the deck, coming from the southeast. Abercrombie pointed. "Will ya look at that?... What in blazes are they tryin' to do?" The first ones were now over the waters of the harbor, heading straight for the idle giants along Battleship Row. Small dots and what looked like matchsticks started falling from the planes into the waters of the main channel. A lump formed in his throat.

"Hey Ernie, I don't think those are Army boys...."

The flash of an explosion came from the port side of Oklahoma, the sound reaching them a second later. "Oh shit!" Ernie tossed his cigarette overboard and ran back into the bridge.

Abercrombie kept watching, and then there was a second explosion, also from Oklahoma. Then another, but he could clearly see that that one had hit West Virginia, which was close enough that he felt some of the shockwave. He couldn't help but just stand there and watch. Part of him was screaming to do something, but the panorama of increasing numbers of aircraft swarming towards them had him completely mesmerized.

"What the HELL is going on?" came from the bridge. Abercrombie saw that Captain Franklin Van Valkenburgh had just arrived on the bridge from his cabin and was already furious. It didn't take long before his ire was lifted from his sailors and redirected at the airplanes that were now swarming around the harbor. A keen officer, Van Valkenburgh immediately appreciated the situation and began barking orders into the cluster of telephones that led to different parts of his ship.

"Engine room? Yeah, this is the Captain. Light off all boilers. Make immediate preparation for getting under way. Report readiness in fifteen minutes." He slammed down that phone and turned to the lieutenant (j.g.) standing beside him. "Sound Battle Stations!"

Just then, Admiral Kidd and Commander Vinson came onto the bridge in a hurry, a rolled chart in one of Vinson's hands. "What's going on Frank?" Kidd asked.

"Looks like the Japs just made a big damn mistake, sir." Van Valkenburgh answered. "I've got the Black Gang firing up the burners, so as soon as we can, we'll get going, Admiral." He walked to the port side of the bridge and then saw Abercrombie standing there watching the planes. "Sailor, come here!" Abercrombie snapped out of his trance and hopped to.

"Aye, Captain!"

"Did you have duty this morning?"

"No sir! I was waiting for church, sir."

"Fine. I want you to be my runner. Understand?"

"Aye, Captain." Out came the toothy grin.

"Good man. First thing, Sailor," he pointed to the repair ship Vestal tied alongside. "Go tell those sonsabitches to get that goddamn boat outta my way!"

"Aye, Captain!" Abercrombie rushed aft.

Now the sounds of explosions were coming every few seconds.

Vinson was feeling completely helpless, standing on the bridge with no weapon, no orders, and no particular responsibility. As the Intelligence Officer for the Admiral, he had duties just about full-time. But not much of anything during actual combat. He was looking forward when another two explosions, followed by giant geysers of water shot up from the side of Oklahoma. She was already listing heavily to her port side, and even as he watched she was tipping farther and farther.

"Holy shit!" he exclaimed loudly.

Van Valkenburgh and Kidd stopped conferring and looked to see what Vinson had seen. Their jaws dropped simultaneously. All three officers watched in disbelief as U.S.S. Oklahoma kept listing farther to port, and then rolled completely over, her giant superstructure smashing into the harbor bottom, and her starboard screws sticking grotesquely out of the water. Vinson found himself looking at Admiral Kidd, looking for some reaction to the fact that one of his three battleships had just been destroyed in front of his eyes. Kidd just blinked and exhaled deeply.

"Curt, find out the readiness on Nevada." Kidd ordered softly.

"Yes, sir!" Vinson rushed off the bridge to signal the other surviving BATDIVONE vessel. Just then, the ship shuddered.

"Get me damage control, Sailor!" Van Valkenburgh barked. One of the deck sailors on the bridge picked up a phone. A few seconds later, he handed the phone to the Captain. The Captain barked into the handset, "What the hell was that, Sam?" Admiral Kidd and the others on the bridge waited while he listened to the report. A few seconds later he handed it back to the sailor.

"Fuqua says we took a bomb aft, near turret 3, but that it looks pretty superficial at this point. The turret is operational, and he's checking on the catapult." A Japanese Zero fighter zipped past the bridge windows, strafing the sailors in the water around West Virginia and Oklahoma as it went.

Several minutes later, Seaman 1st Abercrombie came back onto the bridge, panting. "Captain, some officer on the Vestal said they can be out of our way in twenty minutes. Apparently their engines are cold too, and that's the fastest they can move, unless we can get a tug to pull 'em out of our way."

Van Valkenburgh answered, "Thank you, son."

Another sailor rushed past Abercrombie hurriedly. "Sorry Captain, it's crazy out there!" Adolphus nodded a silent greeting to QM2 Curt Haynes, who returned the nod. He knew this was Haynes' battle-station and that he was apologizing for taking longer to get here than normal. Haynes continued, "Captain, when I was passing the anti-aircraft guns, I heard them say they couldn't get into the ammunition lockers."

"Of course not. Goddamn peacetime regulations." Van Valkenburgh picked up a phone and barked orders to open all ammunition lockers, then turned to Abercrombie. "Seaman, get down to the forward magazines and make sure they got the message. When we break outta here, I want to make sure our main and secondary armament is ready to go and not still waiting for ammo." He then gave similar orders for the aft magazines to another seaman.

Abercrombie nodded and immediately headed out the hatch. Passing Vinson, who was returning from signaling Nevada, he nodded and almost cheerily said, "Good mornin' Mr. Vinson." Vinson returned the strangely calm salutation and watched the young sailor as he rushed by, somehow amused by Abercrombie in spite of the fact that he was more scared than any time in his life.

Despite being right in the middle of the chaos and functioning in high gear, Curt Vinson's mind was racing through the past month, through all the intelligence he had analyzed, the intercepts that he had seen, dispatches from Washington, from Bratton and Kramer. He was thinking about everything that Alex and Dick had told him. They sure had it right, he reflected. There most definitely were torpedoes in the water. A hell of a lot of them.

All that effort to get the warnings to the right people, and in the end, they had all failed. He had failed. For a second he wondered where Alex and Dick were now.... New Zealand? Probably. Australia? Maybe. No, not yet. They couldn't be. Or maybe the Japs were already attacking down there too. "Devious sonsabitches. I wouldn't be surprised," he muttered aloud to himself.

Back on the bridge, he reported to Admiral Kidd that Nevada could be ready to move in twenty minutes at the earliest. Fortunately, they had had two of their boilers already lit because of the planned test, so they were more ready than any of the other battleships in the harbor, who maintained only one boiler on line, according to peacetime procedure.

Abercrombie arrived in the forward powder magazine a couple minutes after leaving the bridge and found the sailors there already making all preparations for full combat readiness. He found the young officer in charge frantically rushing this way and that while several older Chiefs calmly and methodically give instructions to their 'kids.'

"Sir, the Captain sent me to confirm that the forward magazines are ready, and that the ship will be able to commence fire with primary and secondary armament as soon as we are under way," Abercrombie said to the lieutenant (j.g) in charge.

"I don't know, we're going as fast as we can!" the young officer was flustered, obviously. "Those dirty, sneaky bastards!" He went forward through the next hatch. Abercrombie watched him go, and wasn't sure if that was an answer or not.

"Tell the Captain we'll be ready in all respects," a grizzled Senior Chief spoke up confidently and then headed over to help one of his sailors with a powder bag.

Abercrombie was turning to leave when a startling crash came from overhead. The impact was so strong that it knocked most of the men to a knee, if not down completely. One man screamed and several steel beams hit the deck, fresh water and steam escaping from severed pipes. He heard someone yell, "What the fuck was that?!"

The shock had thrown the Texan against the bulkhead, but he was still on his feet. He looked to his right, where the damage had occurred, and immediately went to see what had happened. In the corner of the powder room in which he was standing, amid the debris of steam, pipes, beams, and bags of black powder for Arizona's mighty 14-inch main guns lay an aerial armor-piercing bomb.

After a second he realized what he was looking at and Seaman 1st Class Adolphus Abercrombie gasped. "Oh dear Jesus...."

On the bridge, Curt Vinson was still hovering near his boss, and was watching the attack unfold very much as a spectator. Captain Van Valkenburgh had just rechecked with the engine rooms on their status, and had cursed that it was going to take another twenty minutes minimum before they would have the steam to move. Furthermore, the Vestal had made no visible progress in getting out of Arizona's way, leaving her blocked.

Vinson saw more fighters whiz past, and stepped just outside the bridge to watch when he spotted a formation of high-level bombers as they made a run on Battleship Row, and watched in fascination as they released their loads. One bomb in particular caught his eye, mainly because it seemed to be heading directly for him. Time seemed to be going unbelievably slowly as the bomb fell closer and closer to him. Then it passed over his head, but not by much. He spun around as it went by, seeing it strike the Number 2 gun turret just forward of the Bridge. It glanced off the side of the turret armor, and drove into the deck with a splintering sound. His heart leaped at the thought that it had failed to go off, and he rushed back onto the bridge to report what he'd seen.

"Captain, Admiral, we just took a bomb forward, off Turret Number 2, but it didn't deton...." In the middle of his sentence, Curt Vinson saw a flash just outside that seemed like thousands of giant camera flashbulbs going off, felt the ship start to raise up underneath him, and in a split second that seemed like an hour he saw Captain Franklin Van Valkenburgh and Rear Admiral Isaac Campbell Kidd looking at him, as if patiently waiting for him to finish his statement.

And then they were all gone.

CHAPTER 15

Auckland, New Zealand
December 8, 1941

The two hours that passed between the radio message about the Pearl Harbor attack and the landing in Auckland harbor were without any doubt the longest two hours of Captain Robert Ford's life to that point. When he had been shown the message by Poindexter, he had told him not to acknowledge the message and in fact to establish absolute radio silence.

The message had read, simply, "Pearl Harbor attacked by Japanese bombers. Implement Plan A." Like all Pan American captains, Ford had been given Plan A in a sealed envelope, which he carried in the left inside breast pocket of his uniform jacket. Like all Pan American captains, he had always fervently prayed he would never have to open one of these envelopes.

But now he had been ordered to do so.

The memo inside the envelope was addressed "To: Captain, PAA flight 6039 – SFO-LAX-HNL-CIS-SUV-NOU-AUK and return flight 6040." It was from the Division Manager, Pacific Division. It informed him that, in the event of hostilities between the United States and the Empire of Japan, Pan American would place its fleet of flying boats at the disposal of the military.

The memo also informed him of the obvious: that if he

had been instructed to open and read this memo, he could assume that hostilities had already occurred and that the aircraft "represents a strategic military resource which must be protected and secured from falling into enemy hands."

The memo listed various scenarios based on the leg of the flight in which the alert was issued. Under the section listing Noumea-Auckland, the instruction was to either return to Noumea or proceed to Auckland and await further orders. He was at that time closer to Auckland than to Noumea, not to mention that Auckland figured to be more secure, so his decision was easy and immediate.

They would continue on to New Zealand as fast as they could get there. Fortunately, the weather was continuing to cooperate, with nothing more than scattered clouds and mostly smooth air. Ford hoped that continued for a couple more hours.

Finally, Plan A ordered him to shut down all radios and maintain strict radio silence, and to consider all operational information of his flight was from that moment top secret. It warned him and his crew to talk with nobody except properly identified company or military personnel.

"Keep our transmitter off and you and Eugene just listen and see if you pick up any traffic," he told Poindexter, referring to Leach, the radio tech they had picked up at Noumea. Leach had been pressed into service backing up Poindexter. Ford also told him to ask the second officer and primary navigator, Rod Brown, who was currently in the crew rest compartment on break, to come to the cockpit immediately.

Brown, an intense and studious man of average height, was hunched over behind Ford almost before Poindexter finished delivering the summons. Brown noted Poindexter's tense demeanor and sensed something was up. Very probably, something quite bad. As usual, his instincts were correct.

"Rod," Ford said in an even voice as he continued to keep his eyes alternating between scanning the skies outside the cockpit windscreen and watching the gauges, "we just got a flash message that the Japs have bombed Pearl Harbor. There was nothing more in the message so I have no idea if they're up to anything else in the Pacific, but we're shutting down our radio until we get a visual on Auckland and I want you and Jim to alternate manning your blister to keep an eye out for any other aircraft."

The blister was the navigator's blister, a rather small glass dome behind the flight deck which was primarily used for getting a fix on the stars, especially during night flights. Jim was James G. Henricksen, who as third officer was the second navigator, behind Second Officer Roderick N. Brown. Both men also took their turns at the controls of the aircraft on the normal two-hour rotations the crew maintained.

Those rotations would be suspended for the balance of the flight into Auckland and all of the members of the flight deck crew who had been on break had returned to the flight deck as soon as Ford's summons of Brown had been received. The crew worked as a well-coordinated team and when the captain summoned the second officer the others on break knew instinctively that something was amiss.

The passengers were blissfully oblivious to what had transpired thousands of miles north of them. Alex noticed that, after Sawicki and Edwards had returned from taking coffee up to the flight deck, both had appeared a bit subdued. He attributed that to the weariness which, he assumed, went along with being on their feet almost constantly during the long hours of flight from San Francisco to Auckland and to the anticipation of their impending arrival.

In fact, Sawicki and Edwards had been briefed by Poindexter and informed of the captain's wishes that the passengers not be notified until they were on the water in Auckland, when Ford would address them. In the meantime, they were to go about their business as if nothing had happened. Of course, that proved not quite possible, but they did their best to act accordingly.

In reality, both realized that their route back to San Francisco had in all likelihood been blocked. Like the captain, the rest of the crew and the passengers, they simply had to await word on what to do next. The passengers, of course, were bound for New Zealand, so they would probably be able to just get off the aircraft and go about their business. New Zealand, after all, was a member of the British Commonwealth and thus already at war with the Axis. The country had a sizable number of troops serving under British overall command, mostly in North Africa.

The landing in Auckland harbor was as smooth as the calm waters. As the California Clipper was being tied up at the dock, Captain Ford came down into the passenger cabin and asked for attention. Ford was a man of medium stature, with a thin face and prominent ears, but had a commanding presence.

He had just been joined aboard the aircraft by Bill Mullahey, a tall, normally-jocular man who was Pan American's station manager in Auckland. He and Ford had known one another for many years, and had always enjoyed a good working relationship. Before the Auckland station had been opened, Mullahey had been responsible for building and opening the base on Wake Island, which was a stop-over on the Philippine and China routes.

When the fourteen faces were looking at him, Ford told the passengers about the attack and the resultant – and extreme – state of flux in which they all found themselves. He told them that thcy had reached their destination and were free to go about their business. If they were continuing on to another destination – by another air carrier or by ship – they could be taken, if they wished, to the Grand Hotel, which Pan American used for transient passengers and crew in Auckland.

He told them he would go the United States Embassy, where he and Mullahey would send a message to Pan American reporting their arrival and requesting further orders.

Five passengers – Alex and Rudi among them – chose the hotel provided by Pan American. Henry Carter was another of the five. That's curious, Alex thought to himself. He supposedly works for a ship-builder and is here to help fix two of his company's ships…or at least that's what he told Rudi and me.

Pan American, the only U.S. flag carrier operating in the Pacific – not to mention to Europe and South American - had long enjoyed a close and symbiotic relationship with the U.S. State Department. It was quite literally a matter of joint back scratching.

What was not generally known publicly was that Pan Am had relationships with a few foreign governments and more than a few foreign business and political leaders that were far closer than anything the State Department could claim. As a consequence, it was not unheard of for the United States State Department to call on Pan American to "assist" or "intervene" with some person or nation on behalf of the United States.

Thus, it was not uncommon for messages that Pan American, for one reason or another, did not wish to have broadcast on open radio channels to be routed in coded form through the communications centers of U.S. embassies. That would certainly be the case now, as the in-flight message had made clear.

Once the passengers and crew were safely deposited in the Grand Hotel, Captain Ford took his chief radioman, Poindexter, and with Mullahey hurried to the U.S. Embassy, which was just a little over a block away. It was Monday in New Zealand, so Ford knew the Embassy would be fully staffed. He also suspected it would be a chaotic place that day.

Over four hours had passed since the radio message and they knew that not only would the Embassy staff be in an uproar, but every American citizen, and a lot of New Zealanders with American relatives or American business interests would be mobbing the place, looking for answers. But they had a very valuable airplane, 14 passengers – maybe down to five now - and eleven other crew members that were Ford's responsibility, so he would deal with it.

Before leaving the hotel, Ford and Poindexter had changed into fresh uniforms, and since Pan American uniforms very closely resembled United States Navy officers' uniforms, they were counting on those uniforms to help get them to the front of the line that was sure to be formed in front of the Embassy gate. He hoped Mullahey's influence would help as well.

They were not disappointed.

There was, in fact, the predictable line of people waiting outside the front gate of the Embassy. However, when the Pan American contingent walked around the line and up to the gate, an Embassy employee who had seen Mullahey regularly and Pan Am crews often since the airline had begun its Auckland service on July 12, 1940, and who well understood the service Pan American rendered to the U.S. State Department, ushered them in and past the people clogging the reception area. He led them down to the radio room in the basement.

The two radio operators, one of whom had clearly been pressed into duty and was not as familiar with the equipment as the other, were, not unexpectedly, frazzled to the point of befuddlement. Messages were coming in at an amazing pace, from the State Department in Washington, from British Commonwealth military commands, from the U.S. Governor's Office in the Territory of Hawaii, even a few from the office of the U.S. Commander in Chief, Pacific region at Pearl Harbor and one from Army General Walter Short's headquarters at Fort Shafter on Oahu.

Another message had been received a short time before from General Douglas MacArthur's headquarters in Manila, announcing that the Japanese were attacking U.S. military installations at Cavite and at Clark Army Air Field on the main island of Luzon in the Philippines. But nothing further had been heard from Manila since that one message.

Poindexter knew the regular radioman, a rather young redheaded fellow whose first name was Dennis – Poindexter could not remember his last name – and he led Ford toward Dennis' desk. When it was apparent that Dennis was neither listening to nor transmitting a message, Poindexter asked him if he had received anything from Pan American.

Dennis told them he had nothing from Pan Am, but agreed to send a coded message to the company reporting that the California Clipper, tail number NC18602, was in Auckland safely and was awaiting instructions. After confirming that the crew and a few passengers were staying at the Grand, he told Mullahey, Poindexter and Ford that he would try to let them know as soon as he had anything from Pan American, but suggested they stop by at least once a day to check for themselves, because, as they could see, "things down here are pretty damn hectic." And, he added, he didn't see it getting any less so for a while.

Ford quickly wrote out his message and handed it to Dennis, who immediately started coding it. Satisfied they had accomplished all they could at the present time, the three Pan American men left Dennis to his work.

The five remaining passengers were milling about the hotel lobby, or in the case of Henry Carter, sitting in an easy chair looking faintly bored when Ford and Poindexter returned. Mullahey had returned to his office. Ford gathered the passengers in a corner and told them he had received no word from Pan American but that he had sent his message and expected to hear back soon – whatever that meant - and asked them to stay in or around the hotel.

In the middle of this, Alex could not help noticing again that the 15th passenger, the man Henry Carter, appeared detached and showed little concern. He simply sat watchfully, more curious than nervous or apprehensive.

The other two remaining passengers, a husband and wife from Salt Lake City, were trying to get to Australia, where their eldest son was a Mormon missionary living and working among the Aborigines. They told Captain Ford they would wait to find out what he was ordered to do before deciding on their best course of action.

After Ford finished his briefing, Alex spoke quietly to him. "Captain, was there any mention of the nature of the Japanese attack?" he asked. "I mean, do you know if they used torpedoes?"

"I haven't heard any more than what the message said," Ford answered, wondering about the question. "The message said, 'Pearl Harbor attacked by Japanese bombers.' That's all. I assume from that they used bombs, but I just don't know about torpedoes. Why?"

"No real reason," Alex said in a dismissive tone of voice that did not really work. "It's just that Dick and I have been involved in some war planning exercises and the question of whether torpedoes could be used effectively in Pearl Harbor has been a subject of discussion. Dick is one of those who has argued for some time that torpedoes could be developed that would work in shallow water. That's all. Just curious." He thanked Ford and went back to join Rudi.

At about that same time it was early in the morning in Berlin. In the Tirpitzufer, Major General Hans Oster was in the office of Admiral Wilhelm Canaris. They had seen the reports on the Pearl Harbor attack, as well as less specific reports on the ones on the Philippines. The Japanese had also been very active in Southeast Asia and Indonesia. After noting – with some level of pride despite what he saw as the beginning of the end for Germany – that Rudi's instincts about the Nakajimas practicing shallow-water torpedo runs was right on the money, Canaris asked Oster what they knew about von Althorp and his American friend.

"Herr Admiral," Oster replied, "The man I had watching young von Althorp and his friend reported that they boarded a flying boat three days ago in Pearl Harbor, one of the Pan American Airways Clippers. Huge thing, apparently. It was bound for New Zealand after three stops along the way. It should have been inbound to Auckland, New Zealand, when the attack occurred, according to the schedule he saw."

"And our man is certain they got on that airplane, Hans?"

"Quite certain, Herr Admiral. A detailed signal came in from him the night before last. As you know, we ordered our man to follow them 'loosely,' and not to be observed. He saw them depart their hotel quite early on December 4 and they took a taxi to the seaplane base in Pearl Harbor. Our man followed them in his car, watched them board the aircraft with the other passengers, and watched it take off. Then he went into the Pan American office and looked at the schedule of flights to find out where they were bound. As soon as he could, he drove into the mountains where he could set up his radio and send us a signal." Canaris nodded thoughtfully.

Oster went on, "Herr Admiral may remember that several days ago, our man followed them to the same seaplane base, saw them enter the office and waited until they reappeared. They were being driven in a U.S. Navy car. They were probably securing their tickets on that visit. I have already sent a signal to one of our men in New Zealand requesting that he watch the airplane and, if possible, determine where the aircraft goes from New Zealand. I am assuming it cannot return to Hawaii, since the Japanese are certain to invade, and there appear to be no acceptable routes to the U.S. mainland."

"Have we received an answer from our man in New Zealand?" Canaris asked.

"Not yet," Oster replied. "As the Herr Admiral well knows, he is operating in deep cover in a belligerent country and must be exceedingly careful. He has been there for several years and is well-established locally, so he will most likely hear or see something and when he does, he will get us a signal when he feels it is safe to do so. I feel, as he undoubtedly does as well, that an update on the whereabouts of von Althorp and his friend does not warrant undue risk on his part."

"Hans," Canaris said, putting his hand on his friend's shoulder, "As always, you are several steps ahead of me."

"I seriously doubt there will ever be anyone who is a single step ahead of you, Herr Admiral." It was the common refrain

- always jokingly delivered - between them. Oster smiled at Canaris and left his office.

In London, word of the Japanese attack had been received with both shock and joy. To be sure, nobody celebrated the loss of life among the unprepared soldiers and sailors in Hawaii, or the destruction of ships and airplanes, but it was seen by most of the British leadership as an act that would hopefully seal the fate of Germany and the Axis by bringing the full resources and manpower of the United States into the war.

Sir Stewart Menzies put the file with the Ultra intercepts relating to the sighting of shallow-water torpedo tests in a storage file and locked it. It was suddenly irrelevant.

Meanwhile, it was evening – after dinnertime – in Washington, D.C., and Colonel William J. Donovan, the Coordinator of Information, was reading a literal mountain of signals that had landed on his desk that day. The signals, almost all of which had arrived in code, were from all over the world. Some had been sent directly to him from COI operatives and in the case of many others, he had been included as a "copy to" recipient on a message to the President, the Secretary of State, the Secretaries of War or Navy, the Chairman of the Joint Chiefs of Staff, the FBI or others.

There was one message, which had not been sent in code because it was hand-written and hand-delivered, from President Franklin Delano Roosevelt, which requested his assessment "once he had been able to review all the information available."

Donovan knew that "all information available," in this case, meant a domestic political assessment as well as reports from his agents and from military dispatches he was receiving.

One of his staffers, a Navy lieutenant commander who had been assigned on temporary duty "until further notice" to COI from the Office of Naval Intelligence, knocked at his door and he called out, "Come."

The lieutenant commander entered and said, "Colonel, I'm sorry to bother you, but I've just gotten confirmation that Alex Jordan and 'Dick Barnhardt,' the name Rudi von Althorp is now traveling under, got on the Pan American Clipper from Honolulu to Auckland last Thursday. Pan American also confirms that the plane splashed down safely at Auckland harbor early this afternoon. I'll stay in touch with them. I made them aware that ONI has two officers on the plane and they've promised to let me know where they plan to send the airplane."

The lieutenant commander had figured out the Barnhardt cover by checking with the Royal Hawaiian and other sources in Hawaii and traced it back to Don Price at BUPERS and let Donovan know. Colonel Donovan had been impressed with the resourcefulness of Alex Jordan when he had heard it.

For his part in a clearly illegal forging of documents, Don Price was admonished to keep his mouth shut about it and not to do it again. At least not to do it again without authorization. The lieutenant commander knew that he would almost certainly have the need to call on BUPERS for confidential information during the next few years, and now had someone there who could be counted on to cooperate. He had one hell of a hammer poised over Don Price's head.

"God, I'd forgotten all about them," Donovan muttered, furious with himself. He seldom missed a detail, no matter how chaotic things became. "Thank you, Commander. Good thinking on letting the Pan American people know our men are on that aircraft. Do we know what Pan American's plans are?"

"No, sir, they're still working on that, but coming back to California doesn't seem like a viable option, at least until things settle down in Hawaii, if they ever do. They're working on it with the State, War and Navy departments. Once they have a plan, they'll let me know. I've asked them to let the Captain know that we'd appreciate it if they kept our men with the aircraft. I think that's their best bet to get back here before the Japs overrun the whole Pacific. And I don't think von Althorp getting back to Tokyo is much of an option, either."

Donovan nodded. "I agree," he said, then had another thought. "Oh, there's another matter in that regard. When I sent Jordan and 'Barnhardt' to Hawaii, I took the precaution of sending along another man to watch their backs. I thought that would be prudent since neither is a trained field agent and they are on a mission of some delicacy. Or I guess I should say they were on a mission. The events of the last day have made their mission a non-event, even though the intel they had turns out to have been quite accurate. In any case, the man's name is Carter. Henry Carter. Can you check with Pan American and make sure he got on that plane, too? I haven't heard from him since I got Poindexter to get him a ticket on the flight."

"Carter," the lieutenant commander repeated. "Yes, sir, I'll check. Do you want him to remain with the plane as well?"

"For now, I think that would probably be best. But in his case, just tell Pan American that he's with another U.S. government agency which asked us to pass along their request that they keep him aboard, too. If they ask which agency, tell them you're not at liberty to share that with them. They'll understand. Thank you, Commander. Keep me informed." He looked back down at his stack of signals and the lieutenant commander closed the door as he left the office.

In Auckland, the days dragged as Ford and Poindexter – and sometimes Mullahey as well - checked in at the U.S. Embassy only to learn that there had been no message from Pan American. The crew of the California Clipper, so unflappable when they were in their aircraft, were increasingly jittery as the lack of orders weighed heavily on them, all the more so when word came that Germany had declared war against the United States two days after the Japanese attacks.

How would they get home?

When would they get home?

Would they get home?

Alex and Rudi were jittery as well.

The Mormon couple from Salt Lake City, on the other hand, waited patiently for word. Carter seemed as serene as the Mormons, but Alex noticed that whenever he saw him, he always seemed to be watching him - and Rudi - from his habitual corner seat in the lobby of the Grand Hotel.

Finally, seven days after Pearl Harbor was attacked, Ford received his message. As he read it in the radio room, he could scarcely believe his eyes.

He was to try to make it back to the United States – to the east coast of the United States - by flying westbound, virtually around the world. But first, they were to strip all identifying insignia from the plane.

Then they were to go back to Noumea and pick up the Pan American station personnel and deliver them to Australia. From Australia, they were to make their way westbound by whatever route they could and deliver the California Clipper to the Marine Air Terminal at LaGuardia Field in New York City. And they were to do all of this while maintaining absolute radio silence.

The California Clipper is now a strategic military asset

and must not fall into enemy hands under any circumstances!

Ford's message informed him that passengers Jordan and Barnhardt were with the Office of Naval Intelligence and the Navy had requested they remain with the plane on its return. The government had also requested that passenger Carter be brought back to the United States with the plane.

Ford wondered about Carter, but he thought adding two Navy officers to his crew could be helpful. They might be familiar with territories and oceans that he and his crew were not. They were also clearly physically fit and could help with crew chores such as fueling the plane. He had a feeling he and his crew would be doing for themselves a lot of things that under other circumstances they had ground crews to do for them.

However, Carter, he thought, was something of a strange duck. He did not seem to interact with the crew or the other passengers. He wondered what the hell department or agency of the government he worked for.

Ford made the decision on his own to add the Mormons from Salt Lake City to his passenger manifest back to Noumea and then to Australia. They would be a step closer to seeing their son, and constituted no threat to his objective. Mullahey agreed with that decision, as he invariably did with any decision Captain Robert Ford made.

Ford then thought it prudent to have a word with the two naval officers who would be accompanying him and his crew on the journey. He quietly asked Alex and Rudi to join him in his room. When they arrived, he told them the Navy had asked that they accompany the California Clipper back, that they were to fly westbound to their final destination at LaGuardia Field in New York City. Good God! So someone in Washington does know who and where they are. Donovan?

Who in the Navy? Alex felt a chill run all the way up his back and prickle his scalp.

Rudi looked quickly toward Alex, who could not tell if his expression was more of fear or of surprise. He understood either way. The chances of their charade being continued once back on American soil were likely quite slim, he knew. Donovan would be hard pressed to protect Rudi - even if he was inclined to, which was far from certain – with the U.S. now at war with Germany and Japan.

It was more likely that he would be arrested and detained for the duration. There was no way Rudi would agree to turn on Germany and spy for the Allies. Perhaps as a credentialed diplomat, he would be exchanged for American diplomats who had gotten trapped in Germany or other now-belligerent countries.

But who really knew about that?

Ford asked for and received a full briefing from both men of all their Navy training and specialties, mentally storing the information for when he needed it during the upcoming journey. He told them the crew was getting the aircraft prepared for flight, including carrying out orders to strip all Pan American insignia – even the tail number - from the fuselage and wings. The aircraft was now considered a U.S. military asset and would be turned over to the government when they got to New York, he explained, and he was under orders not to let the aircraft fall into enemy hands under any circumstances.

They would depart the next night. He also told them about the government request that the other passenger, Henry Carter, also join them on the flight. No one knew what to make of that, but Alex was getting an increasingly uneasy feeling about the man. He chose not to voice his unease, but knew Rudi was thinking along the same lines. Obviously, his story about being "on the technical side" of a ship-builder was baloney. But was he in some way connected to the Navy? Is that why he had picked a ship-builder as his cover?

"We're very happy to be of whatever assistance we can," Alex said uneasily, for he was extremely skeptical that what Ford had been ordered to do was possible. "What's your planned route?"

"I don't have the foggiest idea," Ford said. "The first two legs are easy. We go back to Noumea tomorrow night, as I said, and I'll try to time it where we land at Noumea right at daybreak. Then we load the station people and take off as soon as we can for Gladstone. That's on the east coast of Australia north of Brisbane. Pan American has a small operation there. After that, we're on our own. Pan Am is building a base in Karachi and has a small operation in Bahrain, another in the Belgian Congo and a larger base in Brazil. But how we connect those dots is anybody's guess. And as you gentlemen are in intelligence, I'd appreciate any ideas you have along the way. In fact, Bill Mullahey is taking Rod Brown and me to the Auckland library this afternoon to look at their atlases, and I'd like you to join us."

"If there are no Pan American stations after we leave Gladstone, how do you intend to get fuel and supplies?" Alex asked.

"Again, no idea," Ford replied. "Beg, borrow or steal. Whatever it takes. My orders are to get the California Clipper back to the United States. I suspect that with us at war now, the Navy wants this ship even more than Pan American does. And I know they want to keep it out of the hands of the Japs and Germans. There's any number of things on board that I'm sure they'd love to see so they can copy them."

"Will you get any money to buy fuel?" Rudi interjected.

"All I've got is what I and the other crew members are carrying in our wallets. I'd guess that between us, we may have $100 or so dollars. And we'll take whatever cash is at the Noumea station with us, but I'm afraid that won't be much." Ford, an upbeat man by nature, looked a little dejected as he acknowledged his financial reality. "I'd like to think that our Allies will grant us some credit since we're on the same team now, but to be honest, we're going to be crossing a portion of the globe with which I have no experience and very little knowledge.

"We were given some expense money when we left Washington," Rudi said, glancing at Alex, who nodded. "It turned out the Governor of Hawaii covered our hotel rooms at the Royal Hawaiian, so we've probably got…what do you think, Alex?"

"I think we have a little under a thousand dollars left," Alex said. He did not want Ford or anyone else to know how much Admiral Canaris had provided to Rudi. We have no idea what Rudi's going to need to do, and he's likely to need money himself. Alex and Rudi had talked about it during the past week, and both had been trying to formulate a plan to get Rudi back to Germany.

He was not a Nazi, but he was a German and he was not a defector, nor a traitor. He believed in Canaris and agreed with his Admiral that the best hope for Germany was to work from within to get rid of Hitler. He had learned the depth of Canaris' true feelings from his father when he had stopped in Mexico en route to Washington. He had heard some of it before, to be sure, but his father had crystallized it for him.

"My God," Ford breathed. "A thousand bucks would have bought you a ticket on this flight even if the Navy hadn't asked Pan American to let you come along."

On impulse, Alex offered, "Captain, I think it would be best for all of us if we give you that money for your safekeeping, and we all agree to keep its source confidential. Maybe tell the others that Pan American had some money here or you got it from the U.S. Embassy." Rudi nodded his agreement.

Ford stood and offered his hand to them. "Very well. The crew and I are in your debt, even if the rest of them won't know it. We depart tomorrow night at 11:00, and Bill will pick us up for our trip to the library in 30 minutes."

Alex and Rudi left Ford's room with the assurance they would meet him in front of the hotel in a half hour, and Ford felt at least somewhat optimistic for the first time since receiving the action message from Pan American.

Three hours later, after poring over the atlases in the Auckland library with the other four men, Ford felt even better. At least, they had tentatively connected the Pan American dots and settled on the route he would try to follow to get to New York.

They would try to fly first from Gladstone to Darwin, on the northwest coast of Australia, then to Java, to Ceylon, just off the southeast coast of India, to Karachi – where Pan American was building a base – in British India, then to Bahrain – where there was another small company facility – in Arabia. From Bahrain they would go to Khartoum in the British protectorate of Sudan and on to Leopoldville, in the Belgian Congo, where Pan American had a small base.

From the Congo, a long trans-Atlantic leg would take them to one of Pan Am's South American bases in Natal, Brazil, on virtually the easternmost tip of South America.

From Natal they would head north to Trinidad, where the company had an active station, and finally to the LaGuardia Marine Terminal in New York City, which was reachable from

Trinidad. Ford reasoned that limiting the number of stops between established Pan American stations would greatly reduce the risk of unplanned expenses and/or complications with local officials.

Of course, all these plans were tentative and subject to change, based on what was happening in each of the areas they were targeting. Things like enemy activity, in particular, but including variables such as weather, fuel availability, mechanical issues with the aircraft and so forth.

Mullahey told Ford he would have three additional passengers, beyond those requested by the government. Mullahey had been instructed to send Verne White, one of his Auckland mechanics, to Karachi to help get that small operation up and running. In addition, Mullahey told Ford he had been asked by Pan Am to keep two of the Noumea mechanics with him rather than drop them in Australia and instead take them to Bahrain.

Pan American had also instructed Mullahey to get two new Wright Cyclone engines from the Auckland inventory, dismantle them and send them with Ford for use as spare parts. If they did not need to be used, they would be useful in New York. In addition, Ford was told there was a new engine, still in its crate, in Noumea that he was to drop off in Bahrain. With most of the passenger seats unused, and very little baggage, the weight of the three new engines should not pose a problem for the trip. Ford hoped not. It was going to be difficult enough without added complications.

Ford asked Mullahey if he could also "borrow" Eugene Leach and keep him aboard. Leach would give him an extra set of ears monitoring radio traffic and the mechanical know-how to fix any radio problems. Of course, with the radio silence order, all Leach would have to worry about was receiving, not transmitting.

Mullahey agreed, knowing that Ford would need Leach's talents more than his soon-to-be-inactive base would. Leach had also used the week in Auckland to fix the radio he had been sent to fix. Despite the hazardous voyage facing them, Leach readily agreed when approached by Ford and Mullahey. He had no desire to get stuck in Auckland for the duration of this war.

At 11:00 p.m. on December 16, 1941, Captain Ford applied power to the engines and the California Clipper started moving over the waters of Auckland harbor. The plane was completely blacked out – no running or interior cabin lights were to be used during any night-time operation, Ford had decided, and it was very dark in the cabin. Sawicki whispered knowingly that, of course, the navigational aids and engine gauges in the cockpit were lit, so it was perfectly safe. Alex and Rudi knew that to be true, but Henry Carter looked uncharacteristically nervous. The Mormon couple just sat together in their compartment forward of the lounge, holding hands and talking quietly. Alex wished he could be as serene as they seemed to be.

In addition to its blacked-out condition, the huge plane was devoid of all markings. Those who needed to know the identity of the aircraft was would hopefully recognize the Boeing 314 and to those without the need to know – Japanese fighter pilots, for instance - it would simply be an unidentified aircraft. Not ideal, by any means, but better than an aircraft which could be readily identified as American.

The five passengers and three mechanics on the California Clipper, with nothing else to do, soon drifted off into various levels of fitful sleep. The crew, not able to use the radio, navigated by the stars. It was not difficult. Most of them had flown the Auckland-Noumea route several times before and the heading, Ford knew, was almost due northwest. In addition, Navigator Rod Brown had hundreds, if not thousands, of hours of nighttime navigation in his log book.

The rest of the on-duty crew spent their time scanning the skies for any sign of aircraft, friendly or otherwise, and some of those who were supposed to be downstairs resting stayed on the flight deck. The adrenalin flow was high, even though all members of the crew were seasoned professionals.

As it turned out, the flight was uneventful and dawn was just breaking when Ford splashed the big Boeing into the water at Noumea. No company personnel were at the dock to help them tie up, for the very good reason that they were not expecting any inbound flights. They knew the United States was now at war with Japan and that they were in a precarious place, but they did not know whether, or when, they would be told what they were to do. Pan American, of course, had not alerted them, because risking radio interception might have resulted in a Japanese welcome for the California Clipper. It seemed that no one truly knew where the Japanese were, or were not.

Ford expertly maneuvered the plane as close to the dock as he could get it and the two Flight Engineers, Homans K. "Swede" Rothe and John B. "Jocko" Parrish, got up through the nose hatch and jumped to the dock. Then, with the onboard assistance of Sawicki and Edwards, they tied the California Clipper securely to the dock and opened the passenger door.

As soon as the plane was secure, Ford hurried off the aircraft and toward the Pan American station housing area. There, he roused Folger Athern, the station manager, and told him to round up all his personnel and get them to the dock within one hour, and to tell them they could take one suitcase – one suitcase only, no exceptions   with them. Anyone not at the dock on time would be left, he assured the stunned station manager, who dressed quickly and started rousing his people.

Then Ford went into the company store – a storeroom, actually – and collected Pan American uniforms of various sizes, along with underwear and socks. He was sure they would need them before this improbable journey was over, and he knew that he needed to get Jordan and Barnhardt something besides their Navy uniforms.

There was no telling who or what they might run into as they tried to make their way to New York, and it was entirely possible that some of the people they could run into would look quite unkindly on officers of the United States Navy. For example, the Japanese military, should they be unfortunate enough to fall into their hands. Ford had no intention of allowing the Clipper to be captured, but the lives of his crew were precious commodities, too.

Meanwhile, the crew was topping off the fuel tanks and muscling a 55-gallon barrel of engine oil aboard. The crated engine was loaded using a dockside crane which lowered it through the plane's topside cargo hatch.

Two hours after the California Clipper splashed down at Noumea it began its takeoff run and the flight south toward Australia. During the flight, the cabin was abuzz with frenzied conversation among the Pan American Noumea staff. One after another, they asked Sawicki and Edwards why they were going to Australia and where they would go from there.

Bud Washer and Ralph Hitchcock, the two mechanics who were to be taken on to Bahrain, were even more anxious but knew enough not to ask questions. They knew how close Bahrain was to Egypt, and they knew that part of Egypt, at least, was a war zone.

Ford had suggested to Alex and Rudi that they stay in the passenger cabin for the flight to Gladstone. They would be more comfortable there, he told them, and he would really need them after the Noumea folks and the Mormon couple had been off-loaded at Gladstone. During the flight, they were asked by most of the newcomers what they knew and they both truthfully admitted they had no idea. Carter sat alone, as usual, and nobody talked to him, scarcely even noticed him.

Late that afternoon, Ford saw the Australian coast appear on the horizon. Brown and Leach had gotten a radio fix on Gladstone by using their radio receivers for short periods of time to scan for commercial radio stations until they found one from Gladstone. They were on course, with no planes or ships in sight.

After a long, gradual, descent – Ford did not want to make any moves which might make a trigger-happy young Australian coastal anti-aircraft gunner nervous – the California Clipper splashed onto the surface of Gladstone harbor.

They were met by an efficient young man in uniform who was in an official boat and who led them to a large buoy, where they tied down. The young Aussie's name was Jeff Willoughby and he introduced himself as the Harbormaster. He had received a message from the U.S. Embassy in Canberra alerting him to the imminent arrival of the seaplane. He quickly took charge of the Noumea personnel – minus Washer and Hitchcock - and the Mormon couple.

Ford shook hands with all his departing charges and went out of his way to wish the Mormons luck, not only in visiting their son but for the rest of the war. How they would ever get out of Australia and back to Salt Lake City was anybody's guess, but they did not seem to be concerned about it. They had come to see their son. That was all that mattered now.

The crew set about readying the aircraft for its next leg. Ford had told them that the next leg was either all overland or a very long coastal route to Darwin, on the Australian northwest coast. Ford surprised Alex and Rudi by asking for their input again.

A flight along the coast, they all agreed, not only lengthened the flight substantially, but increased the chances of taking anti-aircraft fire from Japanese naval forces, or from jumpy Australian coast watchers, who had already made a name for themselves with their efficient and ruthless defense of their homeland.

Ford then pointed to the locker in the crew rest area holding the Pan American uniforms and extra underwear and suggested Alex and Rudi try to find something that fit. They agreed that it would be good to have a Pan American disguise for use in situations that may arise when being naval officers might be distinctly disadvantageous. Ford pointed over his shoulder with his thumb toward Carter and said he didn't think he needed one, since he was clearly dressed as a civilian.

Ford told the crew, the reassigned mechanics and their Navy guests that they would have to sleep aboard the aircraft. The Harbormaster had told him there were no suitable hotel accommodations ashore. Then he sent John Mack and Swede Rothe with the Harbormaster into town in search of aviation fuel.

Soon, the boat returned and Mack told Ford there was not a drop of aviation gas in the whole town. Ford knew they still had about one-third of their maximum fuel load in the tanks. It would get them to Darwin, but just barely, and he did not like flying without a fuel reserve. He had no choice, so did not dwell on what he would prefer. And that sealed the decision to fly the overland route. The coastal route would run them out of fuel far short of Darwin.

Alex asked Willoughby if there was an American consulate at Darwin. Told that there was not, Alex asked if he could impose on him to send a message to the U.S. Embassy in Canberra to be forwarded along to Washington. The young man said he would be happy to.

Alex had been thinking that letting Donovan know where they were might be a good idea, although the Navy's request that Pan American keep them on the aircraft meant that Donovan more than likely already knew where they were. Rudi wished he could let Admiral Canaris know where he was, but that was clearly out of the question. Furthermore, Rudi also figured that it was entirely possible that Herr Admiral already knew exactly where they were.

Alex encoded a message for Donovan, telling him that they were going next to Darwin, and would try by unknown routing to get back to La Guardia Field. The message also told Donovan that he thought that Ford was planning to try to get from Darwin to the Dutch East Indies, hoping they – or at least some of them – were still in friendly hands. They had received word that the Japanese had bottled U.S. forces up in the Philippines, captured Hong Kong, and were swarming down the Malaysian peninsula and wreaking havoc throughout the Dutch East Indies. Still, Alex was unsure enough about Donovan that he did not want to lay out the tentative route they had agreed on in Auckland.

The young man was not surprised that the message was encoded and was well enough trained not to ask any questions.

That day at the Tirpitzufer in Berlin, Major General Hans Oster marched smartly into Canaris' office, a slight smile on his face.

"Our man in New Zealand has been heard from, Herr Admiral," he announced. Canaris simply raised his eyebrows and nodded, his signal for Oster to continue. Oster simply handed him the message, which, of course, had arrived on Oster's desk in coded form.

```
EYES ONLY
DIRECTOR SECTION ZB
ABWEHR HEADQUARTERS
TIRPITZUFER
BERLIN
SUBJECTS ABOARD AIRCRAFT IN
QUESTION STOP SOURCE BELIEVED RELIABLE
BASED ON PAST SERVICES RENDERED STOP
INDICATES AIRCRAFT ORDERED TO NEW YORK
BY WESTERLY ROUTE STOP BELIEVE WILL
PICK UP CIVILIAN PERSONNEL NOUMEA AND
DELIVER TO AUSTRALIA STOP SPECIFIC
ROUTING BEYOND AUSTRALIA UNKNOWN AT
THIS TIME STOP WILL CONTINUE TO MONITOR
SITUATION AND ADVISE STOP
   JOHNSON
   NEW ZEALAND
   END MESSAGE
```

Canaris did not know Johnson nor did he have any idea who his source might be, and he did not wish to. He knew Johnson was a code name and he knew that Oster trusted the man. That was all he required.

"Well, Hans," he said after reading the message a second time, "it would appear that young von Althorp and his friend are not finished with their journey. But I think under the circumstances that his friend has arranged a good enough American identity for him that it serves our purposes as well as could be hoped."

"I agree, Herr Admiral," Oster replied. "If they are making their way westward, it will offer Herr von Althorp more options."

"What are you thinking, Hans?"

"I am thinking, Herr Admiral, that he cannot stay on the plane until it returns to New York. All the circumstances have changed. Our countries are officially at war. He and his friend know that as well as we do. But a westward journey offers several options for locations at which von Althorp might be able to disengage himself from the aircraft. If they get near enough to Europe, perhaps. But more likely in Africa or South America."

Canaris nodded, thinking. "Have our sources throughout the Indian Ocean area keep their eyes and ears open. That must be the next area they will have to traverse once they leave Australia." He was staring at his large globe.

"Of course, Herr Admiral. I will also alert our assets in Arabia and other areas as they move west."

"Thank you, Hans. Keep me advised."

CHAPTER 16

Darwin, Northern Territory, Australia
December 18, 1941

At first light the California Clipper lifted off from Gladstone harbor and turned northwest across the outback toward Darwin.

The flight was long and nerve-wracking. Once they had flown over the coastal jungles, what stretched before them, part of the famous Australian outback, was an enormous arid desert of yellow grass and sand. The great fear for all was that if anything went wrong with the airplane, there was nothing on which it could land. They would simply skid onto – crash onto - the desert floor and likely never be heard from again.

While Alex and Rudi, along with the crew, fretted over this, they could not help noticing again how detached from everything Henry Carter was. The afternoon before, Alex and Rudi had worked alongside the crew topping off the engine oil tanks and checking every square inch of the huge machine for cracks or other signs of possible trouble. Pilots call this the "walk-around," and with a seaplane it is a particularly difficult and time-consuming task. While they were doing this, Henry Carter had disappeared.

None of them could have realized that he had hitched a ride on the Harbormaster's boat, gone to a bank, one with a correspondent relationship with his bank in New York, and had told a helpful young bank officer that it was imperative he send a confidential telegram to the United States. He had the funds in his account to cover the cost, and a lot more for that matter. Henry Carter's previous "career" had been quite lucrative.

The young man had taken him to a telegraph office two doors away and instructed the attendant on duty to send Mr. Carter's telegram and to bill the bank. When he had returned to the California Clipper, Carter had simply sat on his ass in one of the comfortable passenger seats, dozing while the others worked. No help whatsoever. Not even an offer. By the time the crew had finished with the plane, every one of them heartily despised Henry Carter. Whoever the hell he was.

The telegram Henry Carter had dispatched from Gladstone arrived on the desk of Colonel William Donovan, who was not at all happy when he saw it. He had given Carter a "dead drop" address in case he needed to communicate by telegram from Hawaii, but he now realized that had been a mistake. It was bad enough that this idiot had sent a message in the clear – in other words not coded.

What made matters worse, it was a bold-faced threat. In so many not-very-well veiled references, Carter had claimed to have knowledge of President Roosevelt's complicity in a plot to hide good intelligence from the military chiefs in the Pacific, and to keep him happy – and quiet – he expected his fee to double, and that it should be deposited immediately into his New York account. He did not know when he would get back to the United States on what he inartfully referred to as "this flying boat."

Donovan knew as soon as he read the telegram for the second or third time that he had made the right decision to keep the man on the "flying boat." At least he was on ice until he could decide what to do about him.

Late in the afternoon, as the California Clipper closed in on Darwin, another menace presented itself in the form of an unbroken line of very black clouds that stretched completely across the horizon. Ford spent the last two hours of the flight trying to dodge around and between the worst of the clouds, and to avoid the almost constant flashes of lightning.

It was almost dark when they splashed down. Alex thought it was more of a controlled crash than a landing, and he knew that was not Ford's fault. Rain was pouring from the thunderheads in buckets, the waves were in swells of at least four feet and the wind was howling when they docked and deplaned.

They were met by a contingent of Australian soldiers assigned to coastal defense positions in the Darwin area. Those aboard the plane knew that Darwin, the northernmost city of any size in Australia, was the city closest to the actual fighting, and they assumed the coast watchers had been very nervous when this odd-looking aircraft appeared out of the heavy clouds and pouring rain. They could not have known that this detachment had been alerted to its arrival by another detachment in Gladstone.

Darwin was also very much a frontier town and reminded Rudi of some of the towns he had seen in American cowboy movies. He loved American cowboy movies. The Australian soldiers loaded Ford and his crew – including Alex, Rudi, the three mechanics and Henry Carter – aboard a rickety bus that might have been new during the Great War and drove them to a barracks that had been hastily made available to them. There were cots, showers and latrines. Nothing fancy, but nobody cared. It had been an exhausting day, more so emotionally than physically, and they were all anxious for a shower, some food and a night's sleep.

The Australians told Ford that they had aviation fuel available for them, but it was in a fuel dump of five-gallon jerry cans. That made it such a cumbersome and time-consuming job that Ford knew they would be lucky to get off the water the next day. That bothered him greatly. He was anxious to get out of there and get as far west as he could before the Japanese overran everyplace he could land.

Alex showed his ONI credentials to the leader of the Australians, a fairly young, very tall and rail-thin captain, who introduced himself simply as Richardson, and who then laid out for Ford and Alex everything he knew about Japanese activity in the region. When Ford asked him about the Dutch East Indies, Richardson told them that there were Japanese troops ashore on both Java and Sumatra, the two biggest islands in the archipelago.

He told them that he had better information on Java than on Sumatra, however, and that he would advise they make for Surabaya, which was situated on a large bay on the north side of the island in the Bali Sea. His information was that the Japanese had not reached that far east in the region and that in fact there was still a Dutch garrison in Surabaya. At least there was the last he had heard.

Ford looked at Alex and at Johnny Mack, both of whom nodded, and said, "Well, that's where we'll go, then." He knew from his maps that it would be close to an eight-hour flight over the Timor Sea, but almost anything beat the almost 11-hour nerve-wracking flight from Gladstone over the Queensland and Northern Territory desert.

Ford offered his hand to the captain and thanked him for

the use of the barracks.

"Right," Richardson replied with a bit of a grin curling his lips. "It used to be a whorehouse that serviced the poor army sods that got stuck up here. Now there's too many of us up here for one whorehouse to do any good, so the army reclaimed it." Alex laughed so hard his stomach hurt, and the general tension of the travelers lessened.

That evening, after a decent dinner prepared by Sawicki and Edwards from food they had stocked on the plane in Noumea, the crew set about fueling the California Clipper. Richardson brought along a contingent of his men to help, but it was still near midnight before they finished. The Australians hauled the jerry cans from the fuel dump on the beds of three very old stake trucks and dumped them on the dock and the crew had to man-handle each 40-pound load over the wing, where it could be dumped into the tanks of the California Clipper.

After a shower, Alex and Rudi were sitting on the porch outside the "whorehouse" smoking when Richardson walked up to them carrying a bottle of Australian beer, and for the first time they both noticed a slight limp in Richardson's step. Alex and Rudi were sipping from bottles of the same Australian beer – it was called Foster's lager – from the stock Richardson's men had left with them before dinner. Richardson lit a Dunhill cigarette with an American Zippo lighter.

"Hell of a way to go to war, eh, mates?" he asked as he sat down next to them.

"I had a different vision of what my first wartime assignment would be," Alex admitted with a small smile. "That Pan American crew has got a hell of a job in front of them, and even though we're Navy, I'm really not sure how much help we can be to them."

"It will be a hell of a journey," Richardson said, almost wistfully. "I wish I was going along instead of being stuck in the asshole of Australia with mostly under-trained men and a dozen ancient 25-pounders for artillery. I don't know what the fuck they think I can hit, much less destroy, with those goddamn popguns."

"How did you get stuck here?" Alex asked.

"Unlucky," Richardson answered simply. "I was a brand new infantry second lieutenant in North Africa early last year. I was havin' a lot of bloody fun, because we were mostly fightin' the goddamn Italians. You've never seen such totally horseshit soldiers, from the fuckin' generals on down. Complete clowns. But some asshole got lucky with his fucking artillery piece and his shell not only got close to us but actually went off. Most of them didn't, of course. But this one did and I caught a piece of it in my leg. Damn near got an artery and that would have been very, very bad, indeed. As it was, it was only pretty bad. Bad enough to get me a limp and out of the infantry and out of Africa and out here to the asshole of Australia with these fuckin' popguns."

"Sorry to hear that," Alex said.

Richardson sat staring into the distance for perhaps a minute before resuming. "So my hopes for a military career, at least one that involves real action and promotions – shit like that – are no doubt gone. Now all I want to do is beat the shit out of the Japs and the Germans and get on with my life." He had already dismissed the Italians.

"Do you really expect to see any Germans in the Pacific?" Rudi asked. Alex marveled at the straight face and inquisitive look Rudi maintained.

"I wouldn't be surprised," Richardson said. "Who the

fuck do you think planned the attacks? Think about it. The Japs attack Pearl Harbor." He raised one finger, then two more. "At the same time they attack Guam and Wake Island." A fourth finger went up. "That same day they attack the Philippines. Meanwhile, they invade Hong Kong and Malaya. All on the same fuckin' day. The goddamn Japs aren't smart enough to plan that by themselves."

Richardson paused, looking at the stunned looks on the faces of Alex and Rudi.

"Did I say somethin' wrong?" he asked.

It was Alex who answered. "You really think the Germans planned, or helped plan, the attacks?"

"It's all everyone's talkin' about," Richardson said solemnly. "I hear that everyone in Hawaii believes it. Not sure about Manila, but it makes sense, doesn't it? I mean, the fuckin' Germans have all these military brains, some of them geniuses, really, I've heard. You should see what that bastard Rommel is doin' in Africa. And who the fuck do the Japs have? A bunch of goddamn rice-eaters. Nobody can name a single Jap general or admiral except that prick, Yamamoto. Do you think that little bug-eyed bastard Tojo could have planned all that? I don't, but I sure as hell think that fucking Hitler could have, especially with all those generals and field marshals he's got around him."

Richardson, staring down at his nearly-empty bottle of beer, did not see Alex and Rudi exchange alarmed glances. Both knew instantly that, if German complicity in the Pearl Harbor attack was as commonly-assumed as Richardson said it was, the stakes involved in masking Rudi's true identity had risen enormously.

A sudden thought struck Alex. "Say, tell us what you've heard about the attack on Pearl Harbor. All we've heard is the message Captain Ford got, that Pearl had been attacked by Jap bombers. Have you heard whether they used torpedoes, too?"

"Fuckin' right they did," Richardson said. "Torpedoes sunk the Oklahoma. Rolled it over on its fuckin' side."

"No shit," Alex said. "We haven't even heard what ships were sunk or damaged. Our Navy has been debating for months about whether torpedoes would work in Pearl Harbor because it's so shallow. Do you happen to know what happened to the Arizona?"

"Oh, Jesus," Richardson breathed, and reached out for another beer. "That was the bad one. We heard it completely fuckin' blew up and sank. Supposed to have killed damn near everybody on board." Alex and Rudi both looked stricken and Richardson asked why.

"When we were in Hawaii, we were working closely with the intelligence officer on the Arizona," Alex said quietly. "He's an old friend of mine."

"Oh, shit," Richardson said, now quieter himself. "That's tough. We haven't heard names, of course, but all I know is it would have been bloody bad news to be on that ship."

Richardson drained his beer and stood. "I'll see you boys in the mornin'," he said and walked off, his slight limp barely noticeable.

Alex looked at Rudi and said, "Well, at least we know now your sighting and conclusions were accurate and we weren't wasting our time in Hawaii. I just hope to hell Curt's okay." And he thought about the young seaman, Abercrombie.

Rudi was too stunned by the news of the Arizona to think about how right he had been.

The rain had stopped during the night, and the next day the downpour was replaced by suffocating humidity. The most Carter had done the day before was to ask Richardson if he had a telephone with which he could make an important call to the United States. The captain had unsuccessfully attempted to suppress a laugh before telling him that he was, regretfully, without direct telephone communication with the United States.

The night before, after he returned from his talk with Alex and Rudi, Richardson had gotten a message, in code, from the headquarters of Australian Army Intelligence in Melbourne. In fact, the captain, whose coastal defense duties were real enough, also served as the area commander for Army Intelligence. He had, in response to an earlier inquiry, informed Army Intelligence that the next destination of the American seaplane would be Surabaya.

The latest message informed him that American intelligence – which branch of American intelligence was not spelled out – had asked that they keep an eye on a passenger on the plane by the name of Henry Carter. No reason was given and Richardson wondered what the hell that was all about. He was also requested to contact his man in Surabaya and ask him to watch Mr. Carter once the plane arrived there. And also to do what he could to assist the crew in the continuation of their journey.

The captain's man in Surabaya was a very tough Javanese with whom Richardson had become acquainted when the Javanese was working the docks at Darwin. They had met, naturally enough, in a bar and a friendship of sorts struck. As the Japanese had become more and more aggressive in the Southwest Pacific area, the Java man's hatred of them had become progressively more virulent.

He had been living in Australia for over ten years, having fled the poor treatment afforded Javanese natives by the ruling Dutch. In fact, he had married the abandoned bastard daughter of an Aborigine whore and an unknown Australian soldier. As he heard stories about Japanese atrocities visited on the civilian populations of China, Korea and other places, he had come to hate them even more than he hated the Dutch.

As a result, Richardson had recruited him – it had not been at all difficult – into his intelligence network. He had left his wife in their small house in Darwin and slipped back into Java. His wife, who worshipped him because he loved her when nobody else ever had, had accepted the separation without complaint.

Richardson relayed the order about Carter – he would be easy to identify because he would be the only one from the plane not in a Pan American uniform - and received confirmation of receipt from his man on Java.

Before daybreak the next morning – it was now December 19 and the United States had been at war for 12 days – the California Clipper cleared the water at Darwin and turned west, heading out across the Timor Sea on what those on board all knew was the next leg of an adventure into the terror of the unknown. Once Navigator Rod Brown had fixed the course, he sent for Alex and Rudi and with John Steers spent almost two hours studying what charts and maps they had liberated from the Auckland library – they had also secured a National Geographic map of Southwest Asia and much of the Indian ocean from Richardson – and discussing their best routing for the next leg, after their departure from Java.

If they made it that far.

CHAPTER 17

Surabaya, Java, Dutch East Indies
December 19, 1941

When the sun rose, the California Clipper was cruising steadily over a flat sea. There was nothing but ocean visible, but a Clipper crew was accustomed to that, and the "passengers," to varying degrees, had become accustomed to it as well. Finally, the easternmost islands of the Java archipelago came into view, and Captain Ford glanced over at Mack and smiled. Both men could feel an almost imperceptible level of relaxation. No matter how well trained, it was simply human nature to feel more secure when land is visible.

A little over seven hours after they had lifted off the water in Darwin, Mack pointed forward at two o'clock. There, far in the distance, Ford could make out a large bay. Soon, they could make out the city of Surabaya. It was, they both knew, the second-largest city on Java. Richardson had told them that the last he heard, there was still a Dutch garrison guarding the city – more the bay, really – and there was supposed to be a squadron of fighters based there.

Ford thought that made it probable that there would be aviation gas available and he hoped Richardson's information was still accurate. But the fragmentary reports he had heard in Gladstone and Darwin also indicated the Japs were storming all over the south Pacific. And, most importantly to him, they were in the Dutch East Indies. But nobody seemed to know how far south and east in the East Indies they had pressed.

When Ford estimated he was about 30 minutes out from Surabaya, he saw a fighter – or was it a small bomber? - rising up on a course to intercept them. Actually, it was Swede Rothe who spotted it first from his window at the engineering desk on the right side of the flight deck. Ford's hands tensed on the controls, but alarm turned to relief when Rothe reported he could see of the Dutch Air Force insignia on the airplane's wing-tips and fuselage.

On the passenger deck, Alex and Rudi were blissfully unaware of the drama until they heard Carter, who was seated in his usual compartment in the rear the cabin and was staring out his window, exclaim, "What the fuck?" His New York accent always irritated Alex and the expression he used sounded especially vulgar when uttered in that accent. Alex scrambled to the seat facing Rudi so he could see out the window, too. They could both see a small fighter-type airplane with Dutch markings level off at the Clipper's altitude and even with its cockpit.

Alex recognized the aircraft. It was an old Brewster, which had been designed primarily as a night fighter and was reputed to feel not at all at home during daylight hours. Nonetheless, there it was.

Almost as soon as Alex – and above him, Ford and his crew – had accepted that the Brewster was there to escort them safely to Surabaya, they noticed several more of the same type were coming up rapidly to join him.

Ford's earphones suddenly came to life. The receiver was on.

"Unidentified aircraft over the Bali Sea, identify yourself and say your intentions," a voice said in accented English over the prescribed channel. "I say again, identify yourself and state your destination."

But Ford was flying under orders to maintain radio silence.

"I repeat, unidentified aircraft, this is the Dutch Air Force aircraft off your starboard wing. Identify yourself and state your destination."

The one-way conversation went on for a few minutes more as the fighters moved closer to the Clipper. By that time, Alex had run up the stairs to the flight deck and was kneeling behind Ford and Mack. "Captain, these guys have probably never seen this type of aircraft before," he said. "They don't have anything like this in Europe that I know of. But they undoubtedly know the Japs have large seaplanes, and they use them as bombers as well as transports."

Ford nodded his understanding, silently cursing Pan American's orders to strip the company markings from the plane and maintain radio silence. He was gesturing to the first Brewster, which he assumed was the flight leader, pointing down and in the direction of Surabaya, hoping his gesture would be interpreted as an indication of his hoped-for destination. He even held his uniform cap up to Mack's window, but knew it was next to impossible the Dutch pilot would be able to recognize it with the late afternoon sun reflecting off the windows.

Ford and his crew listened in horror to the conversation that ensued between the fighters and between the flight leader and their air controller. They were discussing their options, which were elegant in their simplicity: let them land or blow them out of the sky. Alex and Rudi had rushed to the flight deck when they saw the rest of the fighters approaching. Ford considered breaking radio silence and decided he would have to if the Dutch started shooting, but he was a man who followed orders.

Suddenly, Alex had an idea. Pan American usually kept small U.S. flags on their flying boats that were used when they were on the water, while idling up to docks in foreign lands, mostly for public relations purposes. He asked Jocko Parrish, the number two flight engineer, where a flag was. Parrish pointed to a cubby under the navigator's chart table. Alex quickly grabbed one and declared with a tight smile, "C'mon Ol' Glory, I've got a job for you."

Finally, a new voice came over Ford's headset. "Unidentified seaplane approaching Surabaya," the accented voice of another man said, "This is Surabaya air control. If landing at Surabaya is your intention, please tip your wings three times." Ford rocked the plane as ordered and they heard the flight leader report this to the controller.

At just the same moment, the flight leader saw the copilot's window on the unknown airplane open, and the Stars and Stripes popped into sight, whipping violently in the slipstream. Alex knew it was a very good thing that Ford had already throttled back significantly in his landing approach, or he would have never been able to hold onto the flag. As it was, he had lots of trouble holding it.

What seemed an eternity later, the radio crackled again. "Unidentified aircraft," the controller said, "We understand you wish to land at Surabaya. You are cleared to descend immediately. Be advised that any sign of hostile action will result in my flight leader being authorized to open fire on you immediately."

Ford immediately pushed the control yoke forward, starting a descent far more steep than he would have with passengers aboard. "Nice work, Lieutenant," he said to Alex. Immediately, the crew got about the business of preparing to land. Alex handed the flag back to Parrish and went back down to the passenger cabin so he would not be in anybody's way.

Now, with the nose down slightly, Ford and Mack got a better look at the harbor. It was jammed with warships and merchantmen flying an astonishing variety of flags. Mack said, "Not much room to put it down in there." Ford had been thinking the same thing. He had also decided that heading in the general direction of a warship could very well meet the controller's definition of "hostile action," and he asked Mack what he thought of putting the Clipper down just outside the harbor.

"It sure looks smooth enough," Mack said in a calm voice. "That's what I'd suggest, too."

And Ford did just that, settling the California Clipper onto the water smoothly. He did not get on the radio to report he was down, as was normal procedure. He was certain the flight of Brewsters – and probably the controller himself – had seen their landing perfectly well.

As the big plane slowed, Ford turned it toward the harbor entrance. Looking to his left, he noticed a launch that had apparently been dispatched to meet them, and he steered toward it. Strangely, though, the launch did not seem to approach them any farther than the mouth of the harbor. It lay stationary, and Mack, who was now looking through his binoculars, reported that a crewman was standing on the launch and waving the Clipper in toward them.

"Christ Almighty!" Alex – now back on the passenger deck - shouted, erupting from his seat and heading for the stairs to the flight deck on the run. Just outside his window, which was not far above the waterline, he had seen a strange metal apparition with what looked like large spikes sticking out from it.

Rushing to the cockpit, Alex said, much louder than he

intended, "We just passed a goddamn mine, Captain." Almost immediately, Brown and Poindexter confirmed Alex's sighting, and it was soon obvious to all aboard that they had not "just passed a mine," they had in fact landed in a minefield. There were spiked metal spheres everywhere they looked. It seemed like nobody was breathing. The only sound was the roar – even at just above idle - of the huge Wright Cyclone engines. Ford decided that it would be pointless to stop. The danger of one of the mines simply drifting into an idle aircraft was at least as strong as trying to navigate through them.

Three excruciating minutes later – it had seemed like at least three hours, maybe three days – the Clipper passed the launch, which then sped up and led them to a buoy, where the crew tied the seaplane securely.

A group of Dutch soldiers, led by a Colonel, met Ford when he arrived after the California Clipper had been lashed to the buoy and the launch had taken Ford ashore. The Colonel was quite anxious to talk with Ford and find out what the hell this aircraft was, and more to the point, what the hell it was doing here in Java.

He and his men led Ford to a truck, which transported them to his headquarters for a full debriefing, further action to be determined.

In the headquarters, Ford started at the beginning – Auckland – and filled the Colonel in on the orders to get himself, his crew and his aircraft back to the United States by heading westbound. He told him Surabaya had seemed the logical next stop after Darwin and he would be grateful for any thoughts the Colonel might have about where they should try to go next, and what areas they should avoid. He also mentioned casually that he would need aviation gasoline and that he had the cash to pay for it, if necessary.

The Colonel announced that, regrettably, the stores of aviation fuel on Java were severely limited and, of course, restricted to the use of the military. Both the British and the Dutch had aircraft which needed it quite badly, he told them, and in quantities that far exceeded current supplies. And with the damned Japs running all over hell and gone around here, he added sadly, there was little real hope of replenishing their supplies soon. Japanese submarines were blowing tankers out of the water almost at will all over the Pacific. And then there was the matter of the minefield just outside the harbor.

The good news, the Colonel told Ford, was that the island was awash in automobile gasoline. In fact, they could take as much of that as they wanted, and he would not even bother charging them for it. Ford was jolted by the news. He knew that automobile gasoline was ten or more points lower in octane rating than the 100-octane aviation fuel the Clipper required. He made a note to tell Swede Rothe and Jocko Parrish to work out a way to make the lower octane fuel work, then turned to the Colonel and asked him for his advice on their routing to Ceylon.

"The problem there is the damnable Japs are so unpredictable," the Colonel said and added nothing more.

He then recommended a hotel near the harbor, the Orange, but told Ford he already knew that there were no rooms available that night. He assured Ford that the aircraft would be safe where it was, "unless, of course, the damnable Japs decide to bomb the harbor before you depart, in which case I cannot guarantee anything."

Ford thanked him and told him they would sleep aboard the aircraft and depart first thing in the morning.

"That is quite out of the question," the Colonel told him.

"Where you are going, you and your men must have inoculations against typhus, dysentery and cholera. I cannot allow you to leave Dutch protection without those inoculations. My doctor will provide them tomorrow afternoon." Ford realized with a jolt that he would not be leaving tomorrow, so he asked the Colonel if his men could be accommodated in the Orange the next night. The Colonel assured him that should not be a problem. There was a group of Royal Navy personnel who would be leaving the next day.

Then the Colonel and his entourage bade the skipper of the California Clipper farewell. Ford was taken back to the dock in the same truck that had taken him to the Colonel's headquarters.

The next day, after getting settled in the Orange Hotel and while the crew of the California Clipper set about pouring the inferior fuel into the plane's wing tanks – Rothe and Parrish had transferred the remaining aviation fuel to the fuselage tanks – Ford asked Alex, Rudi and Carter to go into the city. There, Richardson had told them in Darwin, they would find a marketplace to rival any they had ever seen.

Ford told them to concentrate on fruits and vegetables, but if they found any meat that looked decent, go ahead and get some of that, too. Provided the meat was identifiable. He reminded them to be back by 3:00, when they would be picked up and taken to the Dutch infirmary to get their shots. Carter protested that he didn't know shit about fruits, vegetables or meats.

"Then you can damn well help carry what Mr. Jordan and Mr. Barnhardt find for us," Ford snapped. He was sick of Carter and fervently wished he had never agreed to let the lazy bastard come along with him, government big-shot or not. The son of a bitch was useless and was going to end up creating a big morale problem for him. And with the journey they were facing, it was important for the crew to pull together.

At least Jordan and Barnhardt are trying to be helpful, he thought as he turned away from Carter disgustedly.

"C'mon, let's get moving," Alex said. Rudi had about $40 in his pockets and Alex had almost that, so they were more than set as far as food shopping was concerned.

They had no trouble at all finding the huge, open-air marketplace. It was just a block from the harbor and perhaps 50 yards from the hotel they would stay in that evening. They found oranges, limes and mangoes in abundance. Not surprisingly, wherever Alex and Rudi were, Henry Carter was someplace else.

When Alex and Rudi started down an aisle lined with stalls selling fresh and dried fish, large strips of sheep jerky and other meats which were not so readily identifiable, an attractive young Javanese woman approached Carter and asked him, in whispered and heavily accented English, if he would care to sample a different kind of meat while his friends were busy looking at dead fish. He looked at her greedily – she was quite attractive - and followed her wordlessly as she led him down a narrow passageway and into a ramshackle building.

As soon as the door closed behind them, Carter felt a sudden, searing pain on his left side, just under the rib cage. He had been punched in the kidney with what felt like a sledge hammer by a Javanese man who had been waiting inside the door. As Carter writhed on the floor, the Javanese woman expertly frisked him, relieving him of all the cash he was carrying – $735 – and was about to take his passport when another Javanese man, who was married to an Aborigine/Australian bastard now living in Darwin, walked through the door and, with a menacing gesture with a long stiletto, told her to leave the passport. The newcomer suggested she and her accomplice take the money and be satisfied.

Further encouragement proved unnecessary. It was enough money to feed a family for two or three years. They left.

The man with the stiletto decided that he need not worry about watching his man any longer. Playing the Good Samaritan, he helped Henry Carter to his feet, asked him where he lived, and helped him to the hotel, got him into a room and eased him into the bed. He had seen the blow Carter had taken and knew he would not be leaving his room that night. Later, he signaled Richardson with a synopsis of what had happened and Richardson relayed the message to Australian Army Intelligence.

Just after 2:00, when Alex and Rudi had finished their shopping – it had become quite a haul at very attractive prices – they looked around and were not surprised that they were unable to spot Henry Carter. After looking for ten minutes, they assumed he had simply stolen away and headed for the hotel to rest up from his difficult labors and get ready for his shots. They found a young boy with a cart and for a few pennies he agreed to haul their purchases to the hotel.

Carter, of course, was indeed back at the hotel, lying on his bed and waiting for the agonizing pain to abate. He was fortunate the native had come along when he did and helped him back. He was certain he would not have been able to walk.

The next afternoon, when Alex, Rudi and the crew – each carrying a portion of the previous day's purchases, and each nauseous to varying degrees from the required inoculations - were leaving the hotel for the dock and the next leg of their trip, Carter was nowhere to be found. To be truthful, none of the crew cared if they left him in Surabaya or not. He had not appeared for his shot and nobody cared whether he came down with one of the diseases. Ford had successfully masked the fact that one of his people was missing when they had reported to the doctor.

Ford said, "The hell with him. If he's at the dock when we're ready to go, fine. But I'm not waiting one minute for him otherwise. We've got a hell of a trip in front of us today." That was, of course, an understatement. Not only were they going to torture the engines with inferior gasoline, but they were facing a trip of almost 2,800 miles. After discussing their options with the Dutch colonel and among themselves, Ford and Brown had reconfirmed Trincomalee, on Ceylon, as their next stop. They had asked Alex and Rudi what they thought, and both agreed it seemed as sensible as any of the alternatives. In truth, there were not that many alternatives.

There was no sign of Henry Carter on the dock when the Dutch Army truck deposited them there. Then, just after the launch had started to pull away from the dock, Mack spotted Carter struggling toward the dock, almost dragging his suitcase. Ford swore and called to the helmsman to wait.

Carter, with some difficulty, got onto the launch and sagged into the nearest seat. Then, with more difficulty, he got aboard the aircraft and sagged into the nearest passenger seat. Sawicki took his suitcase for storage and asked if he was all right.

"Fucking native jumped me at that goddamn fruit stand yesterday. Had a bitch working with him. Took my money," Carter said, clearly still in pain. Sawicki, like all Pan American stewards, was trained in first aid and ministered to him as Ford fired up the engines and started taxiing. Then all of them needed to be strapped in for takeoff.

CHAPTER 18

Surabaya, Java
December 21, 1941

The plan Rothe and Parrish had worked out, with the agreement of Ford and Mack, was for the California Clipper to take off on the 100-octane aviation fuel they had in the fuselage tanks, then switch in flight to the automobile gas.

It was late in the afternoon when Ford eased the throttles forward and big ship began to move through the water. Even with just six passengers, it was quite heavy because of the three spare engines and all the gasoline they had aboard to make a flight of this distance. Rod Brown had calculated that they faced a flight of over 19 hours to reach Trincomalee, on the northeast shore of Ceylon. They had worked out a take-off path inside the harbor, or course, because of the minefield outside of it.

Alex and Rudi, with Ford's encouragement, had assumed the roles of part-time crew members, Rudi primarily working with Rod Brown, the chief navigator, because of his flying experience, and Alex working primarily with Ford, Mack and Poindexter on strategy and communications matters.

Carter had no apparent skills, nor did he have the inclination to be helpful, so Ford had told Sawicki and Edwards to keep him down in the passenger cabin with the three mechanics. For take-off, Alex and Rudi sat strapped into passenger seats, along with Carter and the mechanics, and out of the way of the crew, which would be especially busy, given the load and the bad gas.

The Clipper lumbered through the water and just when Rudi looked at Alex with a questioning expression – it meant, "are we going to make it?" – both felt the sudden rush of speed as the aircraft cleared the water. When it was obvious they were climbing, both jumped from their seats and rushed up to the flight deck to do what they could to help.

When the California Clipper passed through one thousand feet, Ford pulled back on the throttles. Noticing Alex had sat down on a small jump seat behind the cockpit, Ford told him, "We're throttling back to cool the engines down as much as possible before we switch over to the other gas."

After seeing the engine temperature gauges drop to where he wanted them and getting a nod from Rothe when he glanced back at him, Ford announced, "Switching to wing tanks." There was a barely-perceptible pause as nothing happened, then the Clipper was hit with a massive vibration. Rothe called out to Ford that the manifold pressure and cylinder head temperatures were going up and he and Parrish quickly disappeared into catwalks that were on the inside of the leading edges of the wings. They were there to allow the crew access to the engines during flight.

The vibrations seemed to decrease in intensity as the engines appeared to settle down a bit after the first shock of the inferior fuel. Rothe and Parrish popped out of the catwalks almost simultaneously, nodded to each other, and Rothe walked to Ford and said, "They seem to be handling it okay. Nothing's leaking – yet. We'll keep a watch on them." Rothe sent Rudi downstairs to fetch the three mechanics so they could help keep an eye on the engines.

Ford nodded, staring ahead as he steered the big plane northwest along the north coast of Java before turning southwest through the Sunda Straight, which separated Java from Sumatra. He would like to have run a more northerly course, over Singapore and Malaysia, but Japanese activity in Malaysia made that impossible, or at least foolhardy. So he planned instead to fly northwest parallel to the southern coast of Sumatra before setting out on the long journey over the Indian Ocean.

The Dutch colonel in Surabaya had told Ford he would try to contact the British garrison on Ceylon to alert them of the Clipper's plans, but nobody had a lot of faith that he would be able to get through. This part of the world was in such chaos and disarray, who knew what communications facilities still existed? And with absolute radio silence, there was no way Ford could check.

Armed with the latitude and longitude of Trincomalee, Brown had plotted their course from the western tip of Sumatra. Rothe and Parrish seemed to spend as much time in the catwalks or conferring with the mechanics about the engines as they did at their engineering desk. The engines were running hotter than normal because of the lower octane rating of the gasoline, but otherwise appeared to be working reasonably well. That fact did little to alleviate the anxiety felt by every man on the flight deck. This would be a very long and dangerous flight under the best of circumstances, but the automobile gas made it more so.

The Indian Ocean seemed endless, and, with Mack flying the plane and Third Officer James G. Henricksen in the right seat as co-pilot, Ford checked once more with Brown to make sure of their course. He knew that if they missed the island, they would be doomed.

Then he went down to the passenger cabin and angrily instructed Carter to stay where he belonged when they were ashore, that he would not hold a launch or otherwise wait for him in the future. And especially, Ford told him, stay the hell away from whores or any other local women – or men, for that matter. Then he went to the crew rest compartment in the nose section and laid down for a nap.

Just after Brown, with Rudi by his side, announced that by their calculations, they should be about an hour from Ceylon, Ford, who was now back in his customary left cockpit seat, saw a cloud bank ahead. He took the controls from Fourth Officer John Steers, who had been flying from the right seat, and began a gradual descent. As he told Alex and Steers, "We can't risk missing that island, so we need to stay under the clouds."

They had to descend to just 300 feet off the water to get below the cloud cover, at about the same time as the sun was beginning to lighten the horizon behind them. Ford, Mack – who had now taken over from Steers in the right seat - and Alex, almost simultaneously, pointed forward, their eyes widening in shock. A submarine, its colors not yet visible in the semi-darkness, was surfacing.

As they got closer, Alex, who was using Ford's binoculars through the windscreen, faintly saw the Japanese colors unfurl and crewmen rushing toward the deck gun, some of them pointing back toward the Clipper. When he started to say something to Ford, the Captain nodded that he had seen them as well.

Ford called "full throttles" to Rothe and both jammed the throttles full forward while Ford pulled back on the yoke. On the Boeing 314, the pilot's throttle levers were on his left, and the co-pilot's on his right, because between their stations was the passage to the anchor and mooring hatch in the nose of the plane. The flight engineer had a redundant set of throttle controls, which were always used on take-offs and landings, and sometimes – such as this – in case of emergency power applications.

As tracers started to come up toward them from the sub's gun, the California Clipper disappeared into the relative safety of the cloud bank, and the men on the flight deck began to breathe again. Below them on the passenger deck, Carter was snoring loudly, blissfully unaware of the encounter. He is a pig, Sawicki thought as he listened to Carter's snoring, in human skin.

On the flight deck, Ford chuckled. "I'll bet that Jap skipper was as startled to see us as we were to see him." His heart was beating rapidly, despite his outward calm.

He asked Alex and Rudi if they knew anything about Japanese submarine tactics. He wanted to know if they ran in packs like the German U-boats were known to do, and he wanted to know if it was safe to get below the clouds again so he didn't miss Ceylon.

Rudi came up behind him and said, "Captain, I studied Japanese naval tactics for almost two years, and even spent a little time in Tokyo observing them." He glanced at Alex, who nodded and gestured with his hand as if so say, "go on."

"The Japanese like to use their submarines as marauders, almost always acting alone. They are sent to an area and told to watch for anything – merchantmen or warships – and like I said they're usually on their own. The Germans, I have been told, think they're idiots when they do that, but the last I heard that was still their main submarine doctrine."

"So that one's not likely to have a buddy down there?" Ford asked as he nosed the Clipper downward to get beneath the clouds.

"Not very likely," Rudi replied. Alex hoped he was right. So did every other member of the crew.

The last 30 minutes of the flight was passed with all hands on full alert, looking not only for the island but for other signs of the Imperial Japanese Navy.

Finally, having seen no other ships – of any flag – Captain Ford splashed the Clipper down in the still waters of Trincomalee harbor. A tender boat raced out to meet them and led them to a seaplane buoy, where Steers and Parrish, manning the lines from the forward hatch, tied the California Clipper down. The tender pilot then pulled alongside the port sea wing, and the crew climbed aboard. Mack and Parrish stayed on the plane as the security watch. Pan American regulations required that at least two crew members stay aboard the plane at all times when in a harbor that is not a Pan American base of operations. Ford rotated the men so assigned.

As at Surabaya, despite the early hour they were met by a small contingent of military men, but here it was the Royal Air Force, rather than the Dutch army. A signal had been received the day before from the British consulate in Surabaya, and once the aircraft and the crew had been identified to the satisfaction of the RAF contingent, the leader of the group, an impossibly young flight lieutenant, informed Captain Ford that they were extremely interested in any news he had on activities to the east and Ford told him he had a very interesting piece of information for the local commander, something they had seen on the inbound flight.

The flight lieutenant led the way.

After a short ride in several cars from the dock to the airfield, the crew was introduced to an extremely arrogant Wing Commander, a man who somewhat reminded them physically of Sir Harry Luke of Fiji. He was squat, perhaps 25 pounds overweight and sported a reddish mustache that seemed to stand straight out from his lip. In the fashion of many British officers, he focused his attention entirely on Captain Ford, ignoring any of the rest of the crew, as if they were not actually people but various devices used by the captain for this or that.

"Welcome to Ceylon, Captain!" he extended his hand and smiled broadly. "Bloody fine job finding your way all the way from Surabaya."

Ford was very tired from days of little sleep and lots of stress, but he managed a smile and a "thank you," while the RAF officer blathered on about something or other regarding the "jewel of southeast India." During a momentary break in his monologue, his subordinate recognized the chance to jump in.

"Sir, Captain Ford told me they saw something coming in that you would find quite interesting."

The Wing Commander's eyebrows perked a bit. "Oh? Do tell, Captain!"

Ford took the cue and told him about the Japanese submarine that they had passed directly over, and handed him a small piece of paper that Rod Brown had given him after the encounter with the sub, which had the navigational coordinates written on it.

The Wing Commander didn't look convinced, much less concerned. "Thank you very much, Captain, but I really doubt very much that the Japs have snuck a submarine that close to Trincomalee without my patrols knowing about it. It was more likely a small fishing smack and your crew was simply confused."

"I'm pretty sure it was a sub shooting at us," Brown blurted incredulously.

Ford gave him a withering look, and he took the hint and

shut up.

The RAF commander never even glanced at Brown, but answered to Ford, "No shame in it, Captain, but it's common to be mistaken if you're not a military man. It's quite easy to take a sampan for a destroyer and such."

Swede Rothe felt a muscle in his arm twitch, and he broke a grim smile, knowing that it was because his instinct was to break this guy's nose. Alex saw the smile, and nodded imperceptibly to Rothe that he was in total agreement. Then they both smiled their best PR smile at the pompous Brit.

Ford had already decided that he didn't have the energy or the inclination to argue about it. "Well, we passed no more than 300 feet over, directly over, the son of a bitch and it had a rising sun painted on the side of the sail, as well as the Japanese flag flying over it. That's a fact. Now what you do with the information is up to you, Wing Commander."

He immediately regretted using crass language, and looked at his crew who had unconsciously moved into a semi-circle behind and around him, as if taking sides in a schoolyard fight. That amused him, and it helped him relax a little. "In any event, did anyone from Surabaya or anywhere else contact you guys about our needs?"

The younger RAF officer was clearly glad to be on another topic, and quickly answered, "No specific instructions were received from our consulate, Captain. Only that you'd be on your way through, and to give whatever assistance we could." Feeling suddenly aware that he had answered without deferring to his superior, he stepped back slightly and turned towards the Wing Commander. "If I understood the message correctly, sir!"

The portly officer nodded. "You did indeed, Flight Lieutenant." He pronounced it 'Lef-tenant', a Britishism that always amused Ford when he heard it.

"Excellent. Well, we're going to need 100 octane aviation fuel first and foremost. Secondly, we could really use some aviation charts for the trip as far as Leopoldville, if possible, but at least as far as Karachi. Do you have any here?"

The Wing Commander nodded and replied, "I think we can manage your petrol needs, Captain. As far as the charts go, the answer is yes, but with one small rub. Whatever we have available isn't here, but at our main headquarters in Colombo." Noticing immediately that the Pan American crew had little idea where that was, he added, "It's on the other side of the island. About a three-hour ride by car from here."

Ford's shoulders slumped very slightly, revealing his true feelings, but his face remained stony. "Fine, how do I get there?"

"I'd be glad to have a car and driver take you, Captain. When would you like to leave? This afternoon too soon?"

"No, that's fine. I'll take my Second Officer with me, while my First Officer stays with the ship." His mind suddenly envisioned more military officers like this guy at the main headquarters, and added, "And I think Mr. Barnhardt as well." He looked at Rudi inquisitively, who in turn glanced at Alex. Alex made a go-ahead gesture, and Rudi answered that he would be glad to come with them. After all, he had been working with Brown on navigation, and he felt flattered to be invited.

Ford seemed satisfied with that. "Oh, and what about some accommodations for my crew while we're here? Is there a local hotel where we can stay?"

The Wing Commander answered that in the "spirit of full cooperation between their allied countries," space would be made available in the RAF transient officers' quarters for the entire crew, less the two who would remain aboard the California Clipper.

Rudi asked Ford if he could go out to the Clipper and grab a couple of things out of his luggage before they departed for Colombo. Ford - who had ordered the luggage left aboard the plane until housing arrangements, if any, were made - in turn asked the flight lieutenant if they could use the tender again to bring ashore all the luggage the crew would need for their overnight in the transient officers' quarters, and the friendly young Brit immediately ordered it. The crew piled aboard to ride out to the plane and get what they needed. As usually, Alex, Rudi and Carter let the crew members go first.

After all, it was their plane. When all the Pan Am people had retrieved the luggage they would need, Alex and Rudi scrambled up the aft hatch to the luggage compartment. Carter loitered behind them unnoticed. Rudi unlocked the suitcase containing the false bottoms and rummaged under clothing until he found what he was looking for: his Swiss passport.

He did not know what might happen at British headquarters in Colombo, but he thought it might be prudent to have a fallback if, for whatever reason, his ONI cover came unraveled.

Watching from the aft hatch, his eyes barely above the level of the floor, Henry Carter saw Rudi pick up a different-colored passport, slip it into his left rear trousers pocket and button the pocket flap. What the fuck does he need two passports for? Carter wondered. He backed quickly and quietly down the stairs to the main deck. Mack and Parrish were in the crew rest compartment in the nose of the plane and did not notice him.

Then, Alex and Rudi backed down the stairs, each carrying one of their suitcases. The others would remain aboard, secure under 24-hour watch. Alex nodded to Carter, indicating he should get up there and retrieve his bag.

Carter hurried up the stairs, his left hand retrieving a

small leather packet from his trouser pocket as he climbed. He went directly to Rudi's suitcase, the one "Barnhardt" had rummaged through to find that funny-looking passport. In seconds, he had the locks picked, a skill he had perfected and used often in his previous life in New York.

Glancing behind him to make sure nobody had come back up the stairs, he unsnapped the lock. He quickly flipped through the clothes in the case and found nothing, then ran his fingers deftly around the sides and bottom.

His right hand stopped when one of his fingers brushed a small leather tab. He tugged on it and the false bottom gave a bit. Using both hands, he quickly pried the false bottom up and saw the hoard of cash. Jesus Christ! he exclaimed under his breath. It had almost come out as a shout, so shocked was he. He instinctively moved to begin scooping the money up and into his pockets. Suddenly, the angry voice of Alex Jordan boomed out from below.

"Hey, Carter," the voice demanded, "get a move on. It's hot as hell down here." Carter heard – or felt, maybe – a foot on the bottom stair below him. He grabbed his suitcase and snapped it open, the instinct to take the money driving him toward piling the cash into his suitcase before that asshole, Jordan, made it up the stairs. He had to move, and fast!

But something inside of the seemingly-slow but very larcenous mind of Henry Carter told him that taking the money now was not smart. Rudi would discover the missing money soon enough and would raise the alarm. Everyone's luggage – and pockets - would be searched, and the bastards would either have him arrested or, worse, just abandon him in one of these God-forsaken shitholes at which they were stopping.

No, Henry Carter was smarter than that. He would wait until the time was right and have a quiet talk with the phony bastard, whatever his real name is. He quickly assessed the size of the stash, thinking it had to be over five thousand dollars, re-secured the false bottom and closed the suitcase, swiftly and quietly relocking it with his tools. He never suspected a second false bottom, so he missed the gold coins.

Carter grabbed his own suitcase, slammed it closed and hurried down the stairs, where Alex, who had descended back downward when he heard Carter moving toward the hatch, and Rudi were waiting impatiently for him. They were anxious to board the tender, which had already made a run to shore to drop off the rest of the crew and their luggage and returned. When Alex stepped out on the sea wing after Rudi and Carter had done so, he called to Mack and Parrish that they were leaving, and closed the passenger door behind him. Parrish moved to the door and locked it, securing the California Clipper. Then he and Mack hurried up to the flight deck, where they could open windows and the loading hatch and get some breeze to relieve the stifling humidity a little.

At 2:00 that afternoon, the car arrived to take Ford, Brown and Rudi to Colombo, and they settled into the monotony of bumpy roads across the island of Ceylon. Ford and Brown were asleep in the back seat within a few minutes of leaving Trincomalee, while Rudi stayed awake only by maintaining a conversation with the Indian RAF corporal who was driving. He soon concluded that the front seat was a fortuitous choice because he could turn the wind wings all the way out and force a blast of air directly on his face and torso. Combined with his sweat, it provided a degree of relief from the torturous heat and humidity.

As dusk was settling, the car pulled up to the British headquarters in Colombo, and the three men began their search for suitable navigational charts. After a fairly brief encounter with a very helpful but sometimes hard-to-understand sergeant from Edinburgh, they had what they needed and returned to the car, where the Indian corporal awaited them, seemingly oblivious to the heat and humidity.

Rudi had just opened the back door of the sedan for Ford when a young British Army officer came hurrying out of the building. "Captain Ford! Captain Ford!"

"I'm Captain Ford." He looked as if he was expecting the young man to snatch the charts back from him, now that he had finally gotten what they needed.

"Captain, I've been sent to convey an invitation to dinner at the Commander's local residence this evening."

A look of relief passed over all three of their faces, and Ford quickly answered, "That's very kind, but we really need to be heading back to our plane to get some rest. Furthermore, I doubt anyone wants to have us to dinner right now, since we haven't bathed in a couple of days, nor changed our clothes." Rod Brown quickly and discreetly sniffed at his armpits, and gave a slightly sour expression. Rudi saw the gesture and stifled a laugh.

"Not to worry, Captain. The Commander anticipated as much, and I'm happy to say that I can escort you chaps to rooms at our transient officers' quarters for a shower and a short nap while I have your uniforms cleaned and pressed." Ford looked at Rudi and Rod with a look of surprise, and they all found themselves nodding in agreement with such a fortuitous turn of events.

"Well, I don't think we can refuse that. Lead the way."

After being awakened after just an hour of sleep, they felt barely rested. But the baths had been amazingly welcome, and the feel of freshly-cleaned uniforms was a God-send. They were driven to the residence of what they thought was the British commander on the island, whose identity was still unknown to them, even after inquiring, presumably for security reasons. As they entered the foyer of a stately, colonial-style home, they were greeted by a handsome, middle-aged woman in very fine evening wear. All three of them were momentarily stunned at the sight of a well turned-out female, after what seemed such a long journey through a world of men.

The woman gracefully extended a hand to Ford, and greeted him with a wide smile. "Welcome to Ceylon, Captain Ford. You'll forgive us taking up your valuable time but we've so very much been looking forward to meeting you. Ever since we heard about your journey."

He shook her hand and nodded. "Not at all, madame. It's I who must thank you for having us. But I'm afraid you have us at a disadvantage."

"Oh, forgive me, Captain!" she gasped. "I was certain the Lieutenant had informed you. I am Lady Wavell. My husband is General Sir Archibald Percival Wavell, commander-in-chief in this theatre of operations." Rudi almost choked.

"The General has been called away at the last minute on some pressing matters," Lady Wavell told them, "so I am afraid I will be your hostess this evening solo. Her smile and demeanor remained cordial and genuine throughout, and it was clear to all that the status of her husband had not given her an inflated sense of importance.

Even after the nap, Ford was so fatigued that he dozed in the midst of various conversations over dinner several times, each time nudged awake by Brown. Rod and Rudi tried to answer whatever questions the other dinner guests - mostly high-ranking British officers - had for them.

Primarily, they were all curious about the dangerous journey from Surabaya, but the army and navy men also wanted to know about the military situation they had witnessed in the Dutch East Indies, while the handful of RAF officers were more interested in the magnificent Boeing Clipper itself. Throughout, Rudi tried to remain completely calm, and in fact he actually enjoyed the irony that he was dining with some of his highest-ranking enemies.

It was close to eleven in the evening by the time the dinner party wound down, and they were able to graciously thank Lady Wavell and excuse themselves. The car took them back to their temporary quarters on the British base and their welcoming beds. They would wait until morning to return to their comrades at Trincomalee.

By early the next afternoon, Ford, Brown, and Rudi were back in Trincomalee. For the crew it was a rest day, and everyone had taken the welcome opportunity to bathe and catch up on sleep. The California Clipper was full of 100 octane aviation fuel again, much to everyone's relief. Freshly-showered and dressed in civilian clothing, Alex and Rudi walked from the transient officers' quarters down toward the harbor and into a small English-style pub they had seen British enlisted airmen come out of the night before. They sat down at the bar and ordered pints of a British lager which was surprisingly chilled, if not actually cold.

"Those poor bastards," Alex said quietly to Rudi, motioning with his head toward a table where four Brits were resting their drinks while they engaged in a spirited game of darts. "I wonder how long you have to be in a place like this before you get used to this awful humidity."

"Depends. I suppose they have."

"I don't see how you could ever get used to it," Alex said. "There were days in Washington when I thought the humidity was as bad as it could get and be survivable, but my God! In this place I feel like I need to chew the air before I can breathe it."

One of the British airmen came over to the bar to order another round for his mates. Alex said to him, "Let us get those for you, friend. We appreciate what the Royal Air Force has done for us." Rudi's mind suddenly recalled the face of one of his schoolmates from Karlsruhe, whose remains were now on the bottom of the Atlantic inside the broken hull of a rusting U-Boat that had most likely been the victim of an RAF air patrol. Sorry, Günther. But these probably weren't the ones who got you.

The young man smiled and said, "Bloody good of you. Cheers, mate." He nodded at them, nimbly picked up all four full pint glasses and marched them to the table. It was clear that he had accomplished that maneuver more than a few times in the past. His three chums waved their thanks to Alex and Rudi when he told them this round had been covered by the two Yanks.

The airman who had ordered and carried the beer came back to the bar, slipped up beside Alex, who was closer to the table than Rudi. Alex could tell from the smell of him, that it certainly was not his first pint of beer. "Have you blokes seen any sign of any Jerry ships or planes since you left Australia?" he asked.

"We've mostly been too high to identify any ship, except for the Jap sub we saw on our way in here," Alex said. "Mostly, it's looked like empty ocean since we got clear of Java."

"Any Germans in Java?" the young man persisted.

"We saw nobody in Java except natives, some British and Dutch soldiers and the Dutch Air Force. They said the Japs were further west on Java but haven't got close to Surabaya yet. What's with the Germans? Aren't the Japs the ones you're concerned about in this part of the world?"

"Not bloody likely, mate. The fookin' Hun planned all that shit in the Pacific and everybody knows it."

"We heard something about that in Darwin," Alex said in a careful voice, now concerned about the direction of the conversation. "We didn't hear anything about it from the army or air force guys on Java, and your RAF Wing Commander didn't say anything about it last night."

The Brit leaned closer, conspiratorially. "That fat fook wouldn't know a kraut from a bloody Jap," he said. "But two of us" – he waved an arm toward the table – "have lost family in the London bombings, and I can tell you we'd love to find some Germans to kill, we would. Me, if I ever come across a fooking kraut, I'll slit his throat from one fooking ear to th' other. Bombing civilians like that, what a bunch of treacherous bastards."

Alex almost winced, thinking about what must be going through his friend's mind right now. He said, "Well, the Japs aren't all that discerning themselves. I'm sure there were a lot of civilian casualties in Hawaii and the Philippines, not to mention what they've done in China for the last few years. And before this is over, we're going to have to beat both of them, so you'll likely get your chance."

"Yeah, both of them is right. But for me and my mate over there, the fooking krauts are personal." He slapped Alex on the shoulder and, with a final "thanks for the beer," headed on semi-unsteady legs back to rejoin the darts game.

Just then, Henry Carter walked into the pub and walked past Alex and Rudi with nothing more than a curt nod in greeting. Carter headed for the far end of the bar, close to where the barkeep was polishing glasses, removed a bill from his wallet and ordered a beer. Alex noted that Carter stared at them in a strangely smug way as he sipped his beer and wondered again about the man.

Rudi had drained his beer and signaled the barkeep for another round. "I've been thinking about what I should do," he said quietly after the man had delivered their beer, collected enough change to pay for them and departed to the far end of the bar where his radio was playing softly. "I don't see how I'll be able to join up with any of 'my people,' at least unless we get to Khartoum." He looked around to make sure nobody had loomed into earshot, and saw that Carter now seemed to be paying attention to the radio. "At least I assume Khartoum would be an easier place to make contact than Bahrain."

"So, what do you think your options are?" Alex asked for perhaps the tenth time since they had left Auckland. "Going to New York probably means Donovan's people will grab you as soon as we get off the plane, and I don't think he could do anything else but keep you under lock and key until the end of the war, or until you get sent home in some kind of diplomatic exchange. Worse, he and Roosevelt may conclude that your whole mission was a ruse to get you to Hawaii where you could help coordinate the attack. You might be shot if that happened."

Rudi's sour look told Alex that he had concluded much the same thing. "I think my best bet is to disappear when – if – we get to Brazil," he said at last. "I think Bahrain or even Khartoum would be too risky, and I know we have people in South America."

Both men stood in silence, thinking and sipping their beer. Alex signaled the barkeep for one more round. Then they would get back to the hotel and rest for the trip to Karachi.

"As I've told you," Rudi continued, "my boss spent time in Argentina in the last war and in the years since, and is supposed to still have a lot of contacts there. And I know for a fact that there is a big European population there."

He was talking as obliquely as he could in case anyone might overhear any part of their conversation. He glanced again toward the other end of the bar, and found Henry Carter fixing him again with a curious stare. The man was rattling him, no doubt about it. He felt sweat trickle down his spine.

Alex nodded. "Sounds like the best plan to me," he muttered and they turned their attention to the news coming softly over the radio as they sipped their beer and smoked. Both noticed that Henry Carter continued to glance in their direction regularly, occasionally turning his attention back to the radio. "That guy gives me the creeps," Alex declared to himself under his breath. Rudi could not have agreed more.

They drained their beer and headed for the transient officers' quarters, leaving Carter to his beer and the radio.

Early the next morning – Christmas Eve - Captain Robert Ford advanced the throttles of NC18602 – minus the markings so identifying it - to full take-off power and pointed it to the northwest as it struggled to gain speed and altitude in the incredibly heavy, humid air. The men on the California Clipper had been soaked with sweat before they had gotten to the airplane, and inside the fuselage it was like a steam bath. It reminded Alex of Washington, D.C., in the summer, only worse. Perhaps ten times worse, he thought, although that was hard to conceive, even to him.

The Clipper fought the air, shuddering and bucking as if they were flying through a thunderhead. The members of the crew, seasoned aviators as they were, seemed to be taking it all in stride, but Rudi shot Alex worried glances every time the big plane bucked. He had several hundred hours as a small plane pilot but he had never flown in this kind of air and he marveled that Boeing could build something strong enough to take this kind of abuse. They made their way up to the flight deck on unsteady legs.

Even Henry Carter was looking alarmed. His naps were less frequent, the longer this journey went on, and he seemed to be casting worried glances out the window more often. Clearly, the intercept by the Brewsters going into Surabaya had spooked the enigmatic man.

Just as Rod Brown called out to let Ford know he was on a direct course to Karachi, a loud explosion erupted in the plane. Ford looked to his left and John Mack, in the right seat, looked to his right, both desperate to find the source of the explosion. The plane was still flying, but Ford saw the airspeed bleeding off. Alex and Rudi were white as ghosts.

"Number three's losing oil fast," Mack reported in what, to Alex and Rudi seemed an amazingly calm voice.

Engineering officer Swede Rothe, who had ducked into the catwalk leading into the starboard wing within seconds of the sound of the explosion, quickly reported his suspicion that number three had blown a cylinder. Ford had quickly moved to shut the ruined engine down, even before Rothe's pronouncement. Brown, businesslike as always, quickly calculated their best option and immediately called out a heading that would take them back to Trincomalee. Ford repeated the heading aloud and pitched the California Clipper into a 180 degree turn.

The three in-transit mechanics had raced to the flight deck when they heard the explosion and all concurred with taking the plane back to Trincomalee.

Ford slipped the Clipper onto the still-smooth waters of Trincomalee harbor 57 minutes after he had lifted off. When their tender got to the dock, the arrogant Colonel and several British officers and sailors were there to meet them, their curiosity overwhelmed by the sudden return. Once they noticed the oil streaked behind the number three engine of the big plane bobbing at the seaplane buoy, combined with the fact that number three was not turning as the aircraft had approached the buoy, they deduced the cause of the abrupt return.

Two British sailors caught the tender's ropes and tied it up to the buoy.

Swede Rothe and Jocko Parrish, the engineering officers, had jumped onto the top of the wing as soon as the Clipper was secured to the buoy, and when they jumped down to the tender had confirmed to Ford that the offending engine had indeed 'thrown a jug.' Soon Ford was on the dock negotiating with the Colonel for some oil and a top-off of the fuel tanks. He had no illusions that much oil remained in the engine and he wanted to maintain the 55-gallon barrel they had brought with them from Noumea as a reserve for when they might need it and had no other source of supply.

An hour later, after returning to the plane for further diagnostics, Rothe, Parrish and the three mechanics, greasy and sweaty, motored back to the dock and reported again to Ford. "Looks like one of the cylinders let go and the vibration jumped the engine off one of its mounts," Rothe said. It sounded catastrophic to Alex, but Rothe was smiling.

Ford translated for Alex, Rudi and even Carter, who was standing nearby looking alarmed. "It's easily repairable," he said. "But it'll take time. Probably two days, but luckily we've got the parts, thanks to the spare engines we brought. And there's nothing that any of you can do for us here, so why don't you work with our British friends here to see if we can get rooms back at the transient quarters, tonight for sure and maybe tomorrow?" He pointed an angry finger at Carter and said, "And you behave yourself. I want no more trouble from you." He had lowered his voice to avoid being overheard by any of the Brits.

They spent Christmas Day in Trincomalee.

CHAPTER 19

December 26, 1941
Trincomalee, Ceylon

Just after daybreak, Captain Ford again lifted the California Clipper off the waters of Trincomalee, and again the plane struggled and clawed its way through the dense air. All aboard held their collective breath until Rothe, who had made a quick inspection of number three from the catwalk, pronounced the repair - which, as expected, had taken most of two days - to be a success. Mack confirmed that the gauges were all indicating in the normal range.

Alex and Rudi had spent much of the time on their "second trip to Trincomalee," as they were calling it, in their quarters but had returned to the dock twice to see if they could be helpful in any way. Both times, they had found the crew busy with various tasks, albeit while looking more like vagabonds than uniformed aviators, sporting undershirts and with the legs of their pants rolled up.

The engine repair crew, they had seen, had been on the airplane, and Sawicki and Edwards had been on the launch, passing water or Coca-Cola bottles to those who were working on the engine. The two dutiful stewards had also made sandwiches, which had been wrapped in waxed paper as protection from the humidity and set out on a platter on the rearmost seat of the tender. Most of the work on the engine had been done by Rothe and Parrish, with the assistance of Verne White, Bud Washer and Ralph Hitchcock, the in-transit mechanics they had picked up in Auckland and Noumea.

It had been far too hot and humid to spend any unnecessary time inside the aircraft, so onboard chores, such as cleaning, had not been bothered with. Back at the transient officers' quarters, Ford had arranged for a table to be set up in the fan-cooled lounge area.

Ford, Mack and Brown sat at the table, looking at what maps they had, and those that Brown had drawn by hand from memory. Alex and Rudi sat in chairs to the side in the lounge, and were consulted by Ford and the others from time to time. When Ford, Mack and Brown finished their work, Alex and Rudi went to their rooms.

They had made an afternoon stop in the British pub they had discovered the day after they arrived in Ceylon, and neither had been surprised to see Carter standing in the same place at the far end of the bar. Seated at a table far from Carter, Alex and Rudi had talked again about Rudi's options. Argentina still seemed the best idea, but Ford would never fly that far south, and they did not know whether Pan American had a base at Buenos Aires and they certainly could not inquire about that.

In any case, the main consideration was that the distance across the Atlantic to Argentina was simply too great for the Clipper. Ford would, they were certain, make for Brazil, as he had planned in Auckland and where the airline had at the base at Natal.

So, logically, the next questions that occurred to them had been how to get Rudi off the plane in Brazil and how to get him from Brazil to Argentina. The third question, of course, had been what story Alex could use to explain Rudi's disappearance to Ford and his crew. Then, perhaps more critically, he would need to consider what he would say to Colonel William J. Donovan, if and when they made it to New York.

There was little doubt in Alex's mind that Donovan had been behind the Navy's request that Pan American order Ford to keep them on the plane for its return trip, and would therefore send for them when – if – the Clipper made it to New York. Alex wondered who had issued the order on behalf of Henry Carter. Could that have been Donovan's work as well?

As the California Clipper droned across the Indian sub-continent, bouncing through the humid air, the crew remained strapped in at their stations and Ford encouraged Alex, Rudi, the mechanics and the two stewards to remain on the passenger level where they could be safely strapped in as well. Nobody had to tell Carter to remain in his seat. He spent most of the time in the air now staring out the window like a lookout. Sawicki and Edwards sat toward the front, near the galley. Alex and Rudi took seats near a window midway in the same compartment they were assigned in Honolulu, close enough to the under-wing area that the turbulence was least severe. And where they could talk, far from Carter, who was seated, as usual, in the rearmost compartment.

"Brazil is an ally of the U.S.," Alex said quietly as he sipped from a bottle of Coca-Cola. "I think I can get Ford to buy off on you gettin' orders to get off in Brazil to work with the Brazilian Navy for a couple of months. Somethin' about that was to be your next duty assignment anyway. That would make it logical that, rather than goin' all the way to New York and then goin' back, you simply 'jump ship' in Brazil."

Rudi thought, nodded in agreement. "That makes sense," he said. "But what will you tell Donovan?"

"I think what we talked a little about yesterday makes the most sense," Alex said. "The more I think about it the better it sounds. And I think Donovan will buy it."

"Which one of the things we talked about?"

"That you're a German but not a Nazi, that you're of the opinion that Canaris is anti-Hitler. I'll tell him I believe that working inside Canaris' organization you'll be more valuable to us – the U.S. – than if we had you locked up somewhere."

"I'll still be a German, Alex, and that puts me on the other side. And that may mean you will be in a lot of trouble for letting me get off the aircraft."

Alex gazed out the window, thinking. The landscape which seemed to be moving along beneath them was the deepest green Alex had ever seen. And dense. The plane continued to vibrate gently in the heavy air, but it was not as bad as when they were still climbing out from Ceylon. Most importantly, the number three engine continued to hum along.

"I think Colonel Donovan understands that there are gradations to the definition of 'the other side,'" he said, then stopped and put his hand on Rudi's arm as he noticed Barney Sawicki moving toward them down the aisle, carefully balancing a tray with sandwiches on it. The tray also held two fresh bottles of Coca-Cola. Alex motioned to Rudi and they got out of their seats and made their way forward to the lounge, where Sawicki put the tray down carefully on a table.

"Anything else I can get you gentlemen?" Sawicki asked.

"Nothing at all, Barney," Alex said. "And under the circumstances you don't need to keep servin' us like we're regular passengers on a regular flight. Let us know when you've got food out and we can go forward and help ourselves."

Sawicki nodded and shrugged at the same time, indicating it was no big deal but that he understood what Alex was saying.

Alex asked him if there was anything new.

"Captain Ford said we should put down at Karachi somewhere around four this afternoon," Sawicki said. "No problem with number three or with anything else as far as I know."

"Why don't you join us?" Alex asked. "You and Verne both. You've got to eat, too, don't you?" The four had shared meals like that several times since leaving Australia, and each time it had started with Alex reminding one of the stewards that they had to eat, too. It had become a bit of a running joke among them. However, the two proud stewards would have none of the ONI men's offers to help them serve the flight deck crew.

The three Pan Am mechanics, exhausted from the heat and humidity they had to endure while fixing the ruined cylinder, were sprawled out, asleep. Alex wondered how Rothe and Parrish, who had done as much of the work as the mechanics, could simply shake off the exhaustion and concentrate on their flight duties. They are all remarkable men, these Pan American people.

"Thank you," Sawicki said. "We will as soon as we finish getting the boys upstairs fed." He nodded toward the stairs leading to the flight deck. Five minutes later, Sawicki and Edwards were seated across from Alex and Rudi. Edwards had taken a sandwich and Coke back to Carter, too. The four of them spent a companionable half hour talking about where they had been and guessing at what was to come. Ever the efficient – and discreet - Pan American stewards, Sawicki and Edwards never tried to probe into what Alex and Rudi did for ONI.

After they had finished their lunch and helped Sawicki and Edwards carry the tray, dishes and empty Coca-Cola bottles to the galley, Alex and Rudi went up to the flight deck to see what they could do to be useful to Captain Ford and the crew.

When he saw Alex walking toward the cockpit, Ford, who was standing behind the flight deck while Mack and Steers flew the plane, asked him – for the second time – what he knew of Japanese or German activity in the Karachi area. "I don't want to land on another Jap submarine," he said. Alex repeated what he had told him the first time he had answered that question: that he was unaware of any enemy activity in that area of the sub-continent.

"I think that we're safe in this area, since the Allies, with Pan American's help, are building a forward base in the area," he said, knowing the definition of safe was subject to interpretation. The forward base under construction was to receive the crated spare engine and the loan of Verne White from Pan American. Still, the problem with the number three engine two days before had imprinted in his mind once again the fact that enemy gunfire was not the only danger they faced.

"Dick and I went over this together, and neither of us has heard of anything other than Allied activity around Karachi to this point. We think we're more likely to run into enemy shipping or aircraft when we get closer to Arabia and North Africa. We know the Germans and Italians are in that general area."

Ford nodded, his eyes still alternately scanning the horizon and looking out side windows at the surface of the Indian Ocean below them. They had just cleared the west coast of India and were now over water.

"I just have a hard time getting comfortable in an area I'm completely unfamiliar with, especially when we're at war," Ford said. "Pan American has never thoroughly surveyed this region and it's a part of the world that I don't think anybody but the Brits knows a hell of a lot about." Alex assured him he completely understood – and shared - his concern.

In truth, Alex would have thought much less of Ford if the pilot was not uncomfortable. Mack appeared equally uncomfortable. His eyes roamed the skies ahead and the ocean below. The man, like Ford and the rest of the crew, was very controlled.

At 3:30 that afternoon, Ford, now back at the controls, retarded the throttles slightly and eased the yoke forward an inch or two, starting his slow descent toward another land mass that appeared in front of them. This one was not as green as that they had flown over that morning. It had brown in it as well, and mountains beyond. Some of them looked quite high.

As the plane descended through 5,000 feet, the straining eyes peering from inside the airplane began to pick out surface ships dotted randomly on the sea. None appeared to anyone to be a warship. As they descended, it became apparent that most of the ships were coastal steamers hauling cargo along the southern coast of Southwest Asia. There were no submarines visible.

Which, in reality, only meant they were not on or near the surface.

Ford made a low pass over the harbor to get his bearings and to check the flags on the ships that were berthed there. There was a British destroyer and what looked like a smaller British patrol craft. The rest of the ships looked like more coastal steamers. All looked to be either anchored or tied up at docks, so Ford banked and started his landing approach.

By the time the California Clipper had settled on the water, taxied to an unoccupied dock that appeared to be for smaller boats – thus was closer to the water – and tied up, a small crowd had gathered. Clearly, airplanes that landed on the water were not a normal sight in Karachi. Neither, most likely, were airplanes the size of the Clipper, whether or not they landed on water. A youthful Royal Navy officer who was just over six feet tall and was wearing shorts against the heat and humidity was the first to jump down on the dock and stride out to meet the crew of this unusual aircraft.

He waited for Captain Ford to emerge from the airplane and introduced himself as Lieutenant Trevor Heath, the Executive Officer on the British destroyer anchored in the harbor. He explained that his Captain was abed in a local hospital with what the doctors feared was a mild form of malaria, as if there were such a thing as a mild form of malaria.

Ford shook hands and explained who they were, where they were coming from and where they were headed next. He also asked for the officer's help by telling him what he knew about enemy forces to the west. Lieutenant Heath, obviously quite taken with the plight of this civilian airline crew, agreed to meet with Captain Ford over dinner at the Carlton Hotel, where he recommended they stay. It was two blocks from the dock to which they were tied. That would give the crew a chance to fuel and service the Clipper so it would be ready to go at first light.

Heath told Ford the Royal Navy patrolled the harbor all night, so their aircraft would be safe from unwanted intrusion. Even so, Ford left two men onboard, as per Pan American policy.

They agreed on dinner at six o'clock, shook hands again, and Ford turned back to his crew, gesturing with his hands to get started with inspection, maintenance – as required – and fueling. Also, the crated engine needed to be off-loaded and

Verne White, who would leave the California Clipper here, supervised that operation once the Pan American liaison man in Karachi appeared and identified himself.

The Royal Navy had a supply of aviation gas and, happily, was willing to share it.

Lieutenant Heath was seated at a table in the hotel dining room when Captain Ford entered, trailed by Alex, Rudi and Mack. All were wearing short-sleeved shirts and their uniform pants. All wished they had shorts, a wish they had shared since landing in Surabaya. Heath looked a bit startled to see Mack, Alex and Rudi, but quickly returned his face to a neutral expression as he rose to greet them.

"My First Officer, John Mack, Lieutenant Heath," Ford said by way of introduction, "And these gentlemen started this journey as passengers, not as members of my crew. Alex Jordan and Dick Barnhardt." They shook hands again with Heath. They had done so on the dock, but names had run together and Ford knew Heath had no hope of remembering them.

"Pleasure, gentlemen," Heath said, and glanced at Ford with a look on his face that clearly asked why they were there.

"Between us, Lieutenant," Ford said, "Alex and Dick are with the United States Office of Naval Intelligence and I was asked to keep them with me rather than disembark them in New Zealand or Australia. I must say they have been a great help to me. As I told you this afternoon, I am in the unenviable position of having to travel a great distance over land and water with which I am completely unfamiliar. Their naval training has been a great help. And, of course, First Officer Mack is the number two man on my crew."

"Well, it's a greater pleasure, gentlemen," Heath said, now smiling broadly, directing his attention to Alex and Rudi. "Very nice to meet allies from our sister service." He gestured grandly for them to sit down. Signaling for the waiter, a short, very dark Indian, he asked, "What can I offer you to drink?"

"It's we who would like to buy you a drink, Lieutenant," Alex said. "We're in your debt for the fuel, and we have some money. Dick and I were on our way to Australia when the attacks occurred, and we were advanced expense money for a month or so in Australia, so we would appreciate being able to host you tonight."

Heath inclined his head in the British manner, indicating acceptance. "Quite gracious of you, gentlemen," he said. To the waiter, he said, "Make mine a Beefeater martini, quite dry, if you would, please." Alex and Rudi ordered beers and Ford and Mack, who would be flying early the next morning, ordered Coca-Cola.

The drinks arrived quickly and Heath launched into his briefing on the Indian Ocean area from Karachi to Arabia. Ford mentioned that they had been planning on Bahrain as their next stop and Heath smiled broadly.

"You're right on it there, Captain," he said. "Bahrain has had a British alliance since it broke away from Iran, and five years or so ago – I think it was 1935, to be exact – it became home to the Royal Navy's Middle Eastern Command. So our presence there will provide as much security as you could hope to find anywhere else in your range. And they're more used to foreigners in Bahrain than they are in Arabia." He paused.

"In fact," he went on in a conspiratorial whisper, "there have been some bloody frightening stories out of Arabia of what the damned natives have done to British pilots who have been forced down there. They're mostly Bedouins, nomads." He paused, a smirk on his face, watching for any indication any of the Americans were familiar with Bedouins.

Rudi said, "They're the ones that run camel caravans around North Africa?" He had heard some stories regarding Bedouins coming from the German Afrika Korps, and immediately wished he had not said anything.

"You make it sound like a bunch of international traders," Heath said, laughing. "They're more like international bandits, as the bloody Krauts are finding out in their little adventure in North Africa."

Rudi's face reddened slightly at the pejorative but he took a sip of beer and gestured to Heath to continue. Alex studiously avoided looking at Rudi.

Heath went on. "They move from oasis to oasis, robbing anyone they come across, herding their goddamn goats and their wives, eating shit and never bathing. They've got the morals of their goats. The world, for them, ends at the horizon. They don't have any loyalty except to their own tribe, sometimes just their own caravan or family. Countries don't mean anything to them." He paused, a bit embarrassed now at the vehemence of his own words.

"No, Captain, I don't think you want any part of those bastards. Take my advice and go to Bahrain, and when you leave it, try to avoid any part of Arabia." He paused again, considering, then went on.

"I'll signal our chaps in Bahrain, tell them to expect you, and ask them to give some thought on how best to proceed from there. Would that be acceptable?"

Ford, raising his Coke bottle in salute, said, "We would appreciate that very much, Lieutenant. That would be a great help." Mack joined in the salute.

Dinner was lamb that was quite good, potatoes roasted in the English style and a local vegetable that none of the men found offensive, even if they all found it lacking in taste. After dinner, they went off to bed. Ford planned to take off at 6:30 or so the next morning, and Commander Heath promised to be there for the send-off.

At the Tirpitzufer early the morning of December 27, Major General Hans Oster knocked and entered the office of Admiral Wilhelm Canaris. The white-haired admiral was hunched at his desk, working his way through a tall stack of correspondence and reports from field agents, deep-cover assets and what he referred to very privately as "those fools in Hitler's cabal." Most of the material from the latter he considered more propaganda and outright bullshit than anything that might be useful to the Abwehr.

When Oster came through his door, Canaris had been having difficulty going through a lengthy memorandum from Reichsführer Heinrich Himmler, whom Canaris felt was one of the worst of Hitler's inner circle, a man who, having been unsuccessful as a chicken farmer, had moved quickly up the ranks of the true believers and been installed in a position of immense power by Hitler.

As the man who, among other duties, oversaw the Gestapo, or Secret State Police, he wreaked havoc and terror throughout Germany, its occupied countries and its armed forces. To Canaris, his frequent missives were as rambling, nonsensical and lacking in logic as those from Hitler himself. Thus, Canaris was doubly pleased at the interruption of his friend and confidante.

"Ah, Hans," he said. "What do you have for me that will take my mind off this latest nonsense from the chicken farmer?" He could always be brutally honest with Oster, knowing Oster would die before any thought of betraying his boss and friend.

"Herr Admiral," Oster began formally, as always when they

were in the Tirpitzufer. "Our Signals Section has intercepted a Royal Navy radio transmission, one that I think will be of particular interest to you." Canaris nodded for him to go on. "It was not in their highest-security code, so it was relatively easy to decipher. It was from a destroyer in British India to the headquarters of the Royal Navy Middle Eastern Command in Bahrain, alerting them that an American civilian flying boat was to depart this morning from Karachi to Bahrain, and requesting Royal Navy assistance while in Bahrain and advice on the best route for the aircraft to follow to get to the Atlantic."

"Well, Hans, it would appear that our Herr von Althorp and his friend have made progress." He paused for a full minute, thinking. "This makes sense, Hans," he continued, "especially with an American Naval Intelligence officer aboard, the British Navy would be more than willing to help them. What we must do now is try to anticipate the course of the aircraft."

"As Herr Admiral knows, we have a man in Bahrain," Oster said. "Perhaps we can ask him to try to make contact with young von Althorp. It would make sense, would it not, that he and his friend have by now discussed where he should try to get off the plane before it crosses the Atlantic? Perhaps they already have a plan in place – that is, if they have a good idea where the plane will attempt its crossing. Based on the performance and range information I have been able to learn about this type of aircraft, an Atlantic crossing would be a bit of a stretch unless they attempt it at one of the narrowest points, which would be either north on the Azores-England-Iceland-Greenland route or from the westernmost coast of Africa across to Brazil."

Canaris glanced at the large globe in the corner of his office to the left of his desk and nodded his agreement. He asked, "Where is our man in Bahrain, Hans?"

"He is in the capitol, Manama. That is undoubtedly where the plane will go. Not only is the Royal Navy command based there, but it has a large protected bay."

"Is he one of ours or a local?" Canaris, who despite a head for details, could simply not keep track of his assets in places like Bahrain.

"He's a local, Herr Admiral. I checked before I came to see you. Actually he's from Arabia. He's been quite good about advising our people on the movements of the Royal Navy in the region."

"How did we recruit him?" Canaris asked, a sour edge to his voice. He did not like nor trust Arabians, or almost anyone else from the Middle East region of the world, for that matter.

"He came to us, Herr Admiral. The Arabians, at least those who are literate at all, tend to be very devout Mohammadans and this man is actually an Imam. That's a Muslim cleric, as the Herr Admiral knows. I regret to say the man is apparently more motivated by his support of the German policy regarding the Jews than he is by support of Germany itself. Nevertheless, our men who watch that part of the world tell me he has given us no reason to question his dependability."

Canaris' shoulders slumped imperceptibly. "My God, Hans, what have we become? We have people from neutral countries offering their services to Germany simply because they hate Jews and admire what Hitler and his thugs are doing to them?"

"The thought makes me feel unclean, too, and if it is the Herr Admiral's wish, I will have our people cease to deal with this Imam."

Canaris got up, walked to his window, and stared out in silence for what seemed to Oster to be a very long time. Finally, Canaris turned and said, "No, let us use this despicable creature to try to help us extract young von Althorp, if we can, Hans. Then, at least, he might unwittingly accomplish something noble in his pitiable life."

"In that case, I will have our Middle East desk send him a signal to watch for the aircraft, see if he can make contact with von Althorp, try to ascertain where the plane will be heading, and report what he learns. Does the Herr Admiral have any thoughts on what we should have him use as a recognition signal? I would imagine young von Althorp is on edge these days and this man will definitely not strike him as an Abwehr colleague."

"If he can get close enough to von Althorp to talk with him – or perhaps to call him in his room, if he can find out where they will stay – tell him he carries with him a message from Mexico City, and greetings from his Uncle William. When he was a boy, he called me 'Onkle Willi.' I think he will recognize that as being a reference to his father and to me."

"Very good. If that will be all, Herr Admiral?" A smile creased Oster's face at the thought of this great man being referred to as Onkle Willi.

"I have nothing further. Thank you, Hans. Please inform me when we hear back from him, no matter the hour."

Oster nodded his understanding and left Canaris to his paperwork.

CHAPTER 20

Karachi, British India
December 27, 1941

When Ford and the crew arrived at the dock for the flight to Bahrain, Swede Rothe, who was already there, approached Ford.

"Jocko and I were doing our routine pre-flight check," he said, "and we found a stuck pitch control piston on number three. I don't think it's related to the problem we had with the cylinder, but we need to fix it."

The pitch control pistons made it possible for the pilot to vary the pitch of the propellers, and were used regularly, especially during take-offs and landings. The pistons also allow the props to be feathered, as Ford had done when the cylinder had blown on number three just after leaving Trincomalee.

Ford sighed, knowing there was nothing he could do but hunker down in Karachi for another day and wait for Rothe, Parrish, Washer and Hitchcock to fix it. He told the crew, and they returned to the Carlton Hotel, leaving the flight engineers and mechanics with the plane.

The next morning, with a farewell to Lieutenant Heath, who was on the dock – again - to see them off, Ford and his crew boarded the California Clipper and began the next leg of their journey, refreshed by the rest and a bit more relaxed than they had been because of the assistance of the Royal Navy.

Alex hoped he would someday meet up again with Heath. The man was his definition of a colleague and fellow naval officer, even if from a different navy.

Supplied with additional charts of the Indian Ocean area between Karachi and Bahrain by Heath, the flight was less stressful than most of the previous legs. Rod Brown had no trouble calling out headings and course corrections to whomever was piloting at the time, and the plane settled into the waters off Bahrain in the middle of the afternoon, after a bit over eight hours in the air. Even without any particular drama on this leg, the crew – including Alex and Rudi – were clearly getting tired of the mind-numbing monotony and of listening constantly to the four big Wright Cyclone engines, hoping not to hear an explosion like they had at Trincomalee.

They were hoping not to hear a sound from them, in fact, except their steady roar. Carter seemed increasingly concerned, and had almost never been seen asleep aboard the Clipper since Trincomalee.

Lieutenant Commander Allan Throckmorton of the Royal Navy stepped forward when the Clipper was tied to the dock in Manama harbor and the crew started to climb out. He introduced himself to Captain Ford and told him he had been asked to give whatever assistance he could to him. Unfortunately, Throckmorton told them, the tanker they had been expecting had not arrived so he did not have any stores of aviation gas, but could supply automobile gas, as much as they needed.

Ford groaned.

But the flight from Karachi had used only about half their fuel load, so perhaps with just half their tanks filled with the lower-octane gas, the engine temperatures could be managed better than they had on their flight from Surabaya to Trincomalee. Ford and the crew bid farewell to Washer and Hitchcock, who went off to their new assignments in the company of another Royal Navy officer.

Ninety minutes later, after fueling the Clipper, the crew was in a western-style hotel just over a mile from the harbor and five of them – Ford, Mack, Brown, Alex and Rudi – were sitting with Throckmorton at a large table in the empty dining room, looking at charts and maps. Nobody had noticed the dark-complexioned man wearing a neatly-trimmed beard and a shabby western suit who got out of an aged Jaguar sedan behind the bus on which the Royal Navy had transported the crew.

Ford told Throckmorton that he wanted to get to Khartoum, then to the Belgian Congo, which had a small Pan American base under construction and from which he thought he would have the best chance of getting across the Atlantic. He had no desire, he said, to fly over the Sahara Desert, where a mechanical problem would mean crashing the airplane and where their chances of survival would have been non-existent.

As he studied a map of Africa, he decided he wanted to stay as close to the Nile River as possible for as long as possible, then his finger traced a route across the African land mass toward the Congo River, which ultimately ran through Leopoldville.

Throckmorton confirmed Ford's notion that Leopoldville was a large city which had air service and would thus have a supply of aviation gas. Also, as a Belgian colony, it would be an ally and they would be unlikely to run into any enemy. Thus, all agreed that for the next leg, Khartoum, which was near the confluence of the White and Blue Niles, was indeed the best choice. It provided plenty of wide water on which to land. It also had a detachment of the Royal Air Force.

Ford looked at Mack and Brown, his eyebrows raised in question. Brown was studying the maps, too, and traced his finger across the Arabian Peninsula over to the Red Sea and the eastern seaboard of Africa. He nodded. "That should work just fine, Captain," he said and Mack agreed.

Throckmorton then told them, rather forcefully, that they should make no attempt to fly over Arabia, repeating what Heath had told them about the Arabs and their treatment of outsiders. In addition, apparently unknown to Heath, Arabia had recently imposed a ban on flights – military or civilian - over the areas on the western side of the peninsula in which Islam's most holy shrines were located. He told them they would need to fly north and skirt around the northern end of the Arabian Peninsula before turning west and south.

Ford frowned. That routing would extend their air time significantly and nobody on the plane wanted to spend any more time in the air than was absolutely required. Especially with their fuel tanks half filled with automobile gasoline. Still, he saw the logic in Throckmorton's words and told Brown to plan accordingly. Ford glanced at the others, and they all nodded, indicating acceptance of the plan. They all got out of their seats and Throckmorton bid them farewell, like Heath assuring them he would be at their dock in the morning to see them off.

The British are very civilized, Alex thought. Or maybe they feel they owe the United States a lot for all the food and military supplies we've been sending them for the last several years.

While Throckmorton disappeared outside through the hotel doors, the others all turned for the elevator, or lift, as it was called here in the British fashion. Again, nobody noticed the bearded man in the shabby western suit who was sitting in the lobby with his face buried in a newspaper.

Rudi had started to take off his clothes in preparation for a badly-needed bath when the telephone on the bedside stand rang. It was an ancient instrument and he assumed it was Alex wanting to talk about dinner. He picked up the receiver and was startled by the unfamiliar sound of the voice he heard. The voice was speaking in heavily-accented English.

"I bring greetings from Mexico City and from your Uncle William," the voice said. Rudi's mind raced and he fought the urge to slam down the receiver. Then the connection struck him - Mexico City and Uncle William. He's talking about my father and the Admiral. What the hell? The Admiral HAS been tracking us on this flight! But this guy sounds like an Arab!

"Are you there?" the voice asked.

"Who are you?" Rudi responded.

"I sometimes work for your Uncle William and he asked me to try to meet with you. I am here in Bahrain," the voice said.

Rudi knew he could not meet with this man in the hotel. The crew were all staying on the same floor. But he also knew he did not want to meet in some alley. Who knew if he was what he said he was?

"Give me 15 minutes to get a bath," Rudi said. "Where can I meet you? Is there a place to get coffee somewhere close? Not at the hotel?"

"If you turn to the left when you come out of the hotel, you will walk across the side street and there will be a small coffeehouse on the next, ah, block. I will be there. I will be waiting. I will have a table where we can talk."

Rudi's stomach churned while he jumped quickly in and out of the bathtub. He was put off by the contact, especially the man's accent, which he was convinced was Arabic. He knew the Admiral, like all spymasters, used local assets, but he thought Canaris considered Arabs to be among the most untrustworthy and bloodthirsty savages on the planet, and Heath's tales of the Bedouins and nomads the day before had reinforced that profile.

Still, the man had clearly mentioned "Uncle William," English for Wilhelm, and he had also mentioned Mexico City, an unmistakable reference to his father. At least he hoped so. His instincts told him that it was a recognition code that had very likely come directly from Canaris. Few others knew he had referred to him, as a child, as Onkle Willi.

And he badly needed to know what Canaris wanted him to do.

He liked and respected Alex, and had come to feel the same about Ford and his crew. But, as he had told Alex so many times, he was a German and he could not be a traitor. Despite any personal feelings about Hitler and the Nazis, his duty, and his loyalty, must be to Germany. He did not call Alex.

So he hurriedly dressed and slipped out of his room without talking to Alex. He was relieved when the elevator came without Alex or any of the crew coming out of their rooms. Neither did he see any of them in the lobby, so he hurried across and out the door. He turned left and crossed the street on the side of the hotel.

As he had been told, there was a coffeehouse in the next block and he entered, trying not to look nervous. The place was empty except for a small, dark man sitting alone at a table against the far wall, well away from the windows. The man nodded but did not smile when Rudi made eye contact with him. Despite his worn western-style suit, the man was definitely Middle Eastern.

Henry Carter, who had been standing unseen in the rear of the hotel lobby when Rudi hurried out, and who had followed him, now watched Rudi through a darkened window on the side wall of the coffeehouse. The bastard is definitely more than he seems! he muttered to himself.

Rudi sat down at the end of the table to the man's left, where he could keep an eye on the door. He could not see Carter through the dirty window to his right.

"Your Uncle William sends his regards," the man said in accented English. He did not offer to shake hands, nor did Rudi.

"Who are you, if I may inquire?" Rudi asked.

"My name is not important," the man said, "and in any case if I gave you a name it would not be my own, nor, I suspect would you give me your true name if I inquired." He paused when a waiter, who was most likely the proprietor as well, appeared with a battered tin pitcher of coffee and a cup and saucer, both heavily chipped, for Rudi. The waiter was wearing filthy clothes that looked to Rudi to be a combination of western and Middle Eastern in style. I wonder if the coffee is as dirty as he is.

"I have been working with your uncle for some time, more than one year," the man went on by way of further introduction. "He asked me to try to find out, if I can where you and your airplane will be going. My instructions say that he is quite anxious to arrange a reunion – is that the correct word? – with you. That is all. I have no instructions beyond that."

"And when you find out where we are going, what are you to do?" Rudi asked. He did not want to prolong this meeting, and it was clear from the man's furtive glances around the coffeehouse and his fidgeting in his chair that he was anxious to be on his way as well. The odor emanating from the man made Rudi even more anxious to get away from him.

"I am only to supply whatever information you give me to my contact, who I believe will relay them you your uncle, who I do not know. As I said, I have no other instructions regarding you." Rudi saw that the man was as nervous as he, and he could sense little harm in telling him what he knew. Perhaps, assuming his instincts were right and the man was what he claimed to be, the Admiral would use the information to plan how and where he should leave the California Clipper. He already thought he knew the where. He just needed help with the how.

He liked the plan he and Alex had worked out – leaving the plane in Brazil and making his way to Argentina – but perhaps the Admiral could find a better alternative.

Or, perhaps if Canaris came to the same conclusion as he and Alex had, he would work out a plan to get him from Brazil to Argentina. Of course he would! He and Alex had not yet thought of a way to do that. But he realized now that he and Alex did not have to worry about how to get him from Brazil to Argentina. "Uncle William" would do that for him. *Why didn't I think of that before?*

"The captain of the aircraft plans to fly from here to Khartoum." The man nodded. He did not make any notes, which meant he was comfortable trusting his memory. Perhaps the man's memory was not as shabby as his clothing. "From Khartoum, we will proceed to Leopoldville, in the Belgian Congo, and from there we will fly across the Atlantic to Brazil. A place called Natal, near the eastern tip of Brazil. Pan American Airways has a base there.

"Once we leave Brazil, I assume we will fly up the east coast of South America. Pan American Airways has a base in Trinidad, in the south of the Caribbean. But I have not heard specific plans being discussed beyond Natal."

Rudi sat back in his chair, sipped the last of his coffee, signifying that he was finished.

"I will tell my contact what you say," the man said. He paused, then went on. "It is a very strange airplane, is it not? It flies like an airplane but it lands on the water like a boat. A very strange airplane." Obviously, the little man had been watching when the California Clipper had landed in the bay.

Rudi did not want to spend any more time with the man and he guessed he would not understand what he was saying if he tried to describe its workings to him. He stood and said, "Thank you for passing along the message, and please have your contact tell Uncle William I hope he is well."

"I will do so. Tonight. May Allah go with you." Rudi felt his stomach lurch, but nodded, turned and walked out, turning right and back in the direction of the hotel. It was twilight and the air was cooling quickly. He glanced back as he approached the hotel and saw the man hurrying in the other direction, toward an aged Jaguar sitting forlornly at the side of the street just beyond the coffee house. He had also caught movement to his left as he looked back, like someone had darted into a doorway. He stood still and stared for a full minute, but saw no other signs of movement, so he turned and hurried to the hotel.

As he entered the hotel, he ran into – literally – Alex, who was hurrying toward the door. There was nobody else in the lobby except a bemused front desk clerk who made an almost-successful attempt at not noticing the collision.

"Jesus Christ," Alex blurted when they had regained their

balance. "I called your room, then knocked on the door. Where the hell were you?"

"I just took a short walk," Rudi said. "The weather is cooling and it felt so good compared to where we've been that I just wanted to stretch my legs."

Alex looked a bit chagrined, but led Rudi back out the door where they could not be overheard by the desk clerk. "It's just not a good idea for you – probably for either of us – to be out walking around by ourselves. But it does feel nice out here, doesn't it?" Rudi felt relief when Alex motioned to the right and said, "If you feel like walking a little more, let's go together." Carter kept them in sight, trailing them by most of a block and staying very close to the buildings.

Rudi wrestled with the question of whether to tell Alex about his contact as they walked. Finally, knowing they had come too far together to risk the fractured relationship that might be the result of Alex finding out in some other way, Rudi decided to brief his friend on the contact.

"Alex," he began cautiously, "I was not just walking. I got a call from one of the Admiral's people just after I got to the room. I think he is a local who works for the Admiral. He told me the Admiral wants to know where we're going from here. I went to meet him – back there in a coffeehouse - and told him what I know, up to the point of Brazil. Do you think that was a mistake?"

Alex thought, a troubled look on his face as he walked. "I wish to hell you'd have talked with me about it before you went to meet with him. At least I could have watched your back."

"He was a Middle Easterner, probably an Arab. I don't know, but the Admiral uses locals in some countries, and I think they are well checked out. But I didn't want to meet him after dark and he seemed anxious to get it over with, too. I thought it was better that way. Plus, if I were him and expecting to meet someone, and two showed up, I would fade into the shadows and disappear. I'm very sorry."

He knew Alex was upset and on edge, but there was nothing he could do to relieve his mind except to tell the truth. He told him about the recognition signal the man had used, how it was a clear reference to his father as well as to the Admiral.

"That was probably a smart move," Alex conceded at last. "In this business, you can't risk scarin' off a valuable contact, but I could have covered you from outside." He paused, thinking again. "So what'd the guy say?"

"He told me his instructions were to find out from me where we will go and that he would pass that information to 'my uncle' tonight."

"Well, maybe 'your uncle' can come up with a better idea than we've had so far. In fact, maybe this solves our problem. He'll figure a way to get you from Brazil to Argentina, or to Germany, if that's what he wants to do. Is that what you're thinkin'?" Alex looked behind them to make sure nobody was in hearing range of them. They paused and lit cigarettes, and Alex motioned behind them. He had seen Carter, he was sure, just before the man had ducked into a doorway. They stayed where they were, smoking, certain they were out of earshot of Carter.

"I think 'my uncle' will come to the same conclusion we have," Rudi said quietly. "It would be hard to get me from Khartoum or Leopoldville to Germany. It would be easier for him to do it from Buenos Aires. Germany and Argentina still trade freely, as far as I know, so there must be German shipping in and out of Buenos Aires regularly. The problem is getting from Brazil to Buenos Aires. I think that he will come up with a way to do that."

Alex nodded his agreement, then nodded his head back toward where he had seen Carter.

He broke into a run, sprinted 30 yards and confronted Carter in the doorway of a closed shop that appeared to sell curios to tourists when it was open.

"What the hell is this, Carter?" he demanded angrily. "Why the hell are you followin' us?"

"I was gonna take a walk and just saw you guys and wondered where you were goin'. And I saw this one before, meeting with some little rag head," Carter said defiantly, jerking his thumb in Rudi's direction defiantly. "You guys are always going off on your own and I was curious."

"It's none of your goddamn business what we do or where we go or who we talk to," Alex snapped.

His temper was rising with each word and he realized he was close to taking a swing at the man.

"So maybe you're spies or some fucking thing," Carter spat back. "Just because you got them fancy Navy IDs don't mean shit to me. They could be fakes."

"Yeah, right, we're spies. Listen, you stupid asshole. Stay away from us." Alex pushed Carter backwards and pointed toward the hotel. "Now get the hell out of here." Carter seemed to consider his options for a minute, then turned and walked slowly toward the hotel. A confrontation, despite all that was in his history, did not make a lot of sense at this point in the journey, he thought to himself. Plenty of time later for that. And he had business to talk with Barnhardt. Or whatever the hell his name was.

Carter had been tempted at first to pull his pistol and blow this smart-mouth Navy bastard away. In the same situation in his New York days, he would have, in a heartbeat. But this was a different situation. As dumb and lazy as Henry Carter appeared to others, in truth he was neither. He was not brilliant by any means, but he was cunning and he had a very strong feeling these two clowns were going to be worth money to him. Or at least one of them was.

One way or the other. He knew they had money – a lot of it, actually - with them, and even if he didn't get it and instead discovered they were up to no good, "Oscar" might reward him.

Carter was going to be trouble, one way or the other, Alex and Rudi both realized as he walked slowly back in the direction of the hotel.

Alex and Rudi then stopped in a small café and had dinner. The café had no beer. It was owned by Muslim fundamentalists, apparently, and did not serve alcohol. They did not want to drink water of unknown origins and settled for their old standby, Coca-Cola.

They had both put their minds at ease over the issue of Rudi's contact. They had convinced themselves that it was for the best and were mostly relaxed as they ate.

CHAPTER 21

Manama, Bahrain
December 29, 1941

The skies were solid gray with overcast and a chilly mist hung in the air the next morning as Captain Ford and the crew boarded the California Clipper. It felt wonderful after Surabaya, Trincomalee and Karachi.

Ford was still chafing at the idea of flying north before heading west and a little south en route – hopefully – to Khartoum, in an area originally called North Sudan. He knew that since the turn of the century it had been a part of Egypt, which, in turn, was de facto operated as a British colony.

Despite his unhappiness over the circuitous routing, once airborne, Ford pointed the Clipper's nose north and climbed into the clouds. As they passed through 8,000 feet, they broke through the clouds into blinding sunshine. Scrambling for their sunglasses, Ford and Mack could see nothing below them except the top of the cloud cover.

Ford switched over to the automobile gas, and again the engines bucked and jumped but continued running. He wanted to burn through the automobile gas so they could be filled completely with aviation gas in Khartoum. As they droned north, Ford noticed that to the west he could see nothing but an unbroken cloud cover all the way to the horizon.

He called Brown to the cockpit and told him he was going to turn west. Brown returned to his table to re-plot their course, and Ford put the plane into a banking turn to the left, then turned the controls over to Mack, with Steers moving into the co-pilot's seat. Ford went downstairs to rest. At this stage of the journey, he was beginning to wonder whether he would ever feel fully rested again.

Just over three hours later, with Ford back in the left seat, a break in the clouds appeared suddenly. Ford looked down and exclaimed, "Hey, guys, look down there."

He was pointing at about the ten o'clock angle.

"What's that?" Steers asked as the others crowded against windows to get a look. There was a large building with what looked like several hundred people pouring out.

Brown looked at the British charts he'd reviewed in the last few days. Ford said, "If I had to bet, I'd say that's the mosque at Mecca. Where else would that many people be in one building in this part of the world."

"If my map is right, that's exactly what it is," Brown pronounced.

"The engine noise must have interrupted their prayers," Alex offered.

Ford nodded, then said, "And some of them are shooting at us – at least those light flickers look like muzzle flashes to me." Fortunately, they were high enough to be out of range of rifle fire, and all the men on the California Clipper silently thanked God that the Arabs did not have anti-aircraft weapons. Ford turned a little to the north, putting a bit more distance between his plane and the men with rifles.

Soon they were past Mecca and the tedium of flight resumed. Just to be sure about the effects of the rifle fire, Sawicki and Edwards climbed down to the passenger deck and conducted an inspection, looking for bullet holes. Rothe and Parrish disappeared into the wing catwalks and checked the wings and engines. The inspection teams reported no damage that could be seen and the never-ending westward trek continued.

Carter had been oblivious to the action on the ground and wondered what the two stewards were looking for as the made their way around the passenger cabin. He was still sitting in the rearmost compartment of the plane, trying to stay as far away as possible from Alex and Rudi. Until the time was right. He had decided that he wanted to get to South America, however, before making his move.

He had heard enough talk about the planned route and he was aware the captain planned to go to Brazil after he left Africa.

No way I'm getting off this damn thing until we're on the right side of the Atlantic Ocean.

A part of him was still trying to figure out how he could get back to Hawaii – and Emily – but he thought that might not be until after the war was over.

Less than two hours later, Brown announced that they should be approaching the Red Sea. Mack pointed straight ahead, squinting in the hot sun that was now streaming directly into the cockpit windows. Ten minutes after that, they passed the coastline of the Red Sea and were soon over Africa.

Nobody aboard was sad to leave Arabia behind. Still, the land now below them was nothing but sand dunes interrupted by the occasional rock formation jutting upward and they knew that their lives remained in the hands of four big Wright Cyclone engines and a very sturdy Boeing 314.

From time to time, they spotted a hut, a collection of makeshift tents or a tiny green spot that indicated an oasis.

Once, they saw a small group of men tending some sort of animals – Alex assumed they were goats or camels, but they were too high to make them out – which seemed suddenly agitated as the plane passed overhead.

"They've probably never seen an airplane or heard anything as noisy as this," Ford muttered, glad that the men were not shooting at them, unlike the religious gentlemen of Mecca.

At 3:30, the Nile River appeared on the horizon and the apprehension on the plane lessened greatly. When they approached the great river, Ford banked the California Clipper to the south and flew above it, allowing the river's path to guide him to his destination. He started descending as the plane approached Khartoum, knowing from the charts and maps he had studied that his "runway" was just south of the city, at the confluence of the White and Blue Niles.

Before much longer, Ford slipped the plane onto the water perfectly and taxied to a buoy. As the crew was tying up to the buoy, a delegation from the Royal Air Force approached in a dingy and, after all the introductions were made, the Brits displayed the same hospitality as their counterparts had in Bahrain and Karachi.

Ford and his crew, along with Alex, Rudi and Carter, were set up in another British-style hotel a few miles from where the California Clipper was tied up and after it had been refueled. Like the one in which they had stayed for a week in Auckland, it was called the Grand.

The Royal Air Force had produced an aged bus with the driver's seat on the right side to transport them, and Ford quietly asked Rudi, who was seated across from him on the bus, if he and Alex were okay with him taking from their cash to pay for the rooms and was assured again that was not a problem.

The hotel prices in the places they had been staying could best be described as modest.

Alex and Rudi received rooms on the first floor. In the British style, that meant the floor immediately above the ground floor, so they used the stairs to get to their rooms, leaving the lift for those on higher floors. Rudi had noted at the reception counter that Carter was given a room on the fifth – or top – floor.

On the stairway and out of earshot of the others, Rudi asked Alex if he had noticed the man who had gotten out of a small Austin on the other side of the road and who had seemed quite interested in the crew's arrival. Alex had not. Being in enemy territory had obviously sharpened Rudi's powers of observation. Or maybe I'm just showing how tired I am, Alex thought to himself.

The two tossed their bags in the rooms and hurried back down the stairs. None of the crew, nor Carter, was in the lobby and they went out through the front door, scanning the street for the watcher. Rudi could not spot him. They talked briefly and decided it was definitely possible someone was shadowing the airplane and its crew, but that it was more likely he was watching one – or both – of them.

They decided to split up briefly, Rudi going to the left and Alex to the right. They would go one block each way, checking the side streets, and return to the hotel entrance.

Four minutes later, both were back at the hotel. Neither had seen anybody suspicious, and they went back to their rooms, knowing Ford intended to start at first light in the morning to give them enough time for a long flight and enough remaining daylight to land on the Congo River in Leopoldville. Sandwiches from room service would serve as dinner tonight.

Alex closed his door behind him and froze. Something in his peripheral vision had caught his eye - something about the room that did not register. He turned slowly and froze again. There was a man sitting in the one chair in the room, an ancient wingback with threadbare tweed upholstering. He was holding a small pistol, aimed at Alex.

Alex stared at the man, raising his hands to show he was unarmed.

"Colonel Donovan sent me," the man said softly, so as not to chance being overheard in adjacent rooms. Alex breathed again, not realizing he had stopped doing so when he had first sensed something amiss. "Why don't you see if Dick would like to join us?" he continued, referring, of course, to Rudi. He lowered the small pistol, laying it on the cushion next to him.

"How did you find us?" Alex asked when his breathing had returned to normal. "We've been observing radio silence since Auckland."

"We've got people all over the world," the man said, "and the colonel has ways of finding things out. He actually enjoys quite a close relationship with the British. I got a message yesterday that you'd be in Khartoum today – God willing – and here I am."

"And you are?" Alex asked a bit more belligerently than he intended.

"Oh, sorry." He put his gun in a shoulder holster and stood up, his right hand outstretched. Alex shook it. "Name's Cyrus Philpott. I'm with COI, of course. I cover Northeast Africa and some of the Middle East out of Cairo. Naturally, I work a lot with our British cousins and the military attaché at their Cairo Embassy has kept me up to date on your travels – discretely, of course."

Alex nodded warily. "Let me call Dick."

Two minutes after Alex put the phone down, Rudi appeared at the door of Alex's room, trying very hard not to look as apprehensive as he felt. Philpott unknowingly put him at ease by offering his hand to him and saying, "I'm Cyrus Philpott, Lieutenant Barnhardt. Colonel Donovan asked me to try to meet with you both and see what you know of the Pan American captain's intentions from here."

"To what purpose?" Alex asked. "We're with ONI."

"I was only told that the colonel sent you – with the blessings of ONI, I might add – on a mission that has turned problematical for you and he'd like to do what he can to assist in your safe passage home."

"Does that mean he would like us to get off the Clipper and return with you?" Rudi asked.

"Not at all, although that is a very reasonable question. So let me answer you this way: First, I am based in Cairo and we have no other staff there. And second, getting back home from Cairo would probably be at least as hazardous an undertaking as staying with your Pan American friends."

He spoke with a New England accent that had the feel of aristocracy. Alex remembered hearing somewhere that Donovan liked to recruit from the upper crust of society and from Ivy League schools – people whose patriotism, the colonel thought, was above reproach. And who, incidentally, were people with whom the colonel was most personally comfortable.

Alex answered. "Our understanding is that Captain Ford, who I hope you will tell the Colonel is one of the bravest men and most skilled aviators we could entrust our lives to, plans to fly tomorrow to Leopoldville, in the Belgian Congo."

"I'm familiar with the location of Leopoldville," Philpott remarked dryly.

"Anyway," Alex went on as if he hadn't been interrupted, "from the Congo, Captain Ford will make the Atlantic crossing to Brazil. A place called Natal, on the easternmost point of Brazil. Pan American has a base there. We haven't talked a lot about anything beyond that, but I would assume from there, we'll move up the South American coast to the Caribbean, where Pan American has stations, and back to the States. The captain told us his orders are to deliver the aircraft to the Marine Terminal at LaGuardia Airport. That's in New York City." He added the last as a return jab at Philpott for his Leopoldville jab. He also realized he had been speaking without his North Texas accent, as if Philpott were military brass.

Philpott inclined his head, smiling as if to say, "point made." Instead, he said, "That sounds quite sensible. I spent some time on the way down here looking over maps of the Southern Hemisphere and I believe your Captain Ford has planned well."

"Did the colonel have any instructions – or advice – for us?" Alex asked.

"No instructions or advice, I'm afraid. He did indicate in his message that if I was successful in finding you and making contact, he would let your colleagues at ONI know you are safe and on your way." He paused, then asked, "How are you doing for money? I expect the colonel supplied you with some at the beginning of your mission, but I would also assume the mission has gone on rather longer than it was intended, much longer, in fact. Am I correct in that?"

Alex was surprised at the question but did not want to raise any suspicions that might point to Rudi's stash of Abwehr cash.

"It's very nice of you to ask," he said. "Our resources have been taxed on this trip. We've had to pay for hotels at some stops and food at almost all, and Captain Ford and his crew did not expect to need any money so they didn't have much. Fortunately, we haven't had to buy any fuel, thanks mostly to the British, or we wouldn't have been able to buy sufficient food and we would probably have spent some nights – like this one – sleeping in the airplane rather than in a hotel."

"Would $200 help? That's all I've got with me," Philpott said, handing over a stack of $20 bills.

"That will help a lot," Alex said, taking the money. "And I'll return any that we haven't spent when we get back to Washington." Rudi understood Alex's reasoning and played along accordingly.

"One other question, if I may, gentlemen?" Philpott said and when Alex motioned for him to continue, went on. "It is my understanding that there is another passenger, as it were, on the flight with you. A man named Carter, I believe?"

"What about him?" Alex asked a bit more sharply than he intended. "Is he one of the colonel's men, too?"

Philpott looked startled, but recovered quickly and said, lying through his teeth, "No, not at all. But the colonel learned – I assume from Pan American or the State Department – that a man called Carter was on the plane. What is your take on him, if I may ask?"

"He's a sneaky, lazy son of a bitch," Alex spat. "We caught him following us on Bahrain, but most of the time he just sits on his ass or sleeps. He's never offered to help with fueling or any of the other things the crew's had to do. He got robbed and beaten in Surabaya chasing what he thought was a whore but turned out to be a bandit. What's his story?"

"I've no idea, but according to the colonel's message to me, someone in our government asked Pan American to bring him back from New Zealand. I assume the colonel is curious about that and instructed me to ask for your take on the man."

"Like I said, we have no idea who he is, but I pity anybody who has to work with the son of a bitch. And he acts more like a common thug than he does a representative of the United States government."

"Well, then, that covers everything I was asked to talk with you about so I'll be on my way and I will send my report to the colonel as soon as I get back to Cairo," Philpott said, rising from the old chair. He was a short man with a beak nose and perfectly-trimmed hair, and Alex could picture him reporting to a Boston bank's Board of Directors rather than to Colonel "Wild Bill" Donovan.

They shook hands all around, then Philpott departed after Alex had poked his head out the door to make sure nobody else was in the hallway.

Alex and Rudi sat looking at each other for a long moment, then Alex said, "I think I could use a beer and something to eat, and the room does not appeal to me anymore. What do you say?" Rudi nodded and they made their way down to the hotel dining room. Khartoum was largely Muslim and they figured the one sure place to find a beer would be in an English-style hotel. They were right.

Ford and most of the crew – less the two who remained on the plane that night – were in the dining room at a scattering of tables when Alex and Rudi arrived. Ford waved them to his table, which had two empty seats. The others all looked very unhappy, for some reason.

"I've just been filling the crew in on the surprise I received this afternoon," Ford said. Alex and Rudi nodded expectantly, and he continued. "The commander of the RAF detachment here came to see me bearing an armful of charts covering the area between here and Leopoldville."

"That's great," Alex blurted, then realized Ford, too, looked unhappy.

"The charts came at a price," Ford went on. "He also told me that the British Command Headquarters in Cairo has ordered him to hold us here to await a VIP passenger who is to be transported to Leopoldville. He told me it was an order."

"Oh, for God's sake," Alex said, and the looks around the table confirmed that he had given voice to the opinion of all. "How long do we have to wait?"

"They said 'a day or two,' but I don't think they really know," Ford said unhappily. "This VIP is coming in on BOAC from Cairo. I have no idea how reliable BOAC's service is between here and Cairo and I gather than the RAF folks can't predict it, either." BOAC was the British Overseas Airways Corporation, the British state-owned international airline.

"So we just have to sit on our asses and wait!" Rod Brown exclaimed bitterly, not for the first time.

"That's about it," Ford said. "At least the Brits feel bad enough about it that they've arranged for us to stay here in the hotel – at their expense – until the VIP shows up. And I don't know about the rest of you, but I intend to eat very well while we're being hosted here."

Despite their unhappiness, they all knew – and appreciated - that this journey would have been significantly more difficult if not for the cooperation of the various British garrisons they had encountered along the way.

Two days later – New Year's Eve – Ford got a message that the VIP had arrived and they could depart the next morning. It would be about a ten-and-a-half-hour flight, he had calculated, and he wanted to leave early in the morning so he had enough light for a Congo River landing.

On the first morning of 1942, the weary passengers and crew of the California Clipper climbed aboard the Royal Air Force bus before daylight and made their way to the dock. Once there, they saw an RAF sedan with the detachment commander standing next to it, talking with a somewhat striking woman.

She was introduced as the wife of a British supply officer in Cairo who had urgent business in Leopoldville. Ford, who had difficulty containing his fury, nodded in her direction, spun on his heel and marched toward the plane.

What the hell could be so important about her going to Leopoldville that my crew and I have been forced to cool our heels for two days?

Alex leaned toward Ford as they walked and said, "It's the same in every branch of every military I know of. The supply officers – even the supply sergeants – always have ways of getting what they want. They trade supplies for favors. But I agree with you. This is complete bullshit."

Ford, refusing to further acknowledge the woman, angrily waved to Sawicki and Edwards to get her aboard and made for the cockpit.

CHAPTER 22

Khartoum, Egypt
January 1, 1942

The sun had just begun to peek over the eastern horizon when Captain Ford applied power to the Wright Cyclones and the California Clipper accelerated across the water, lifted off and climbed into the sky.

All aboard knew that this was going to be a long day, almost all over land and thus more tense. Suddenly, a loud bang could be heard from the left, followed by a continuous rattling sound. It did not sound as bad as the near-disaster leaving Trincomalee for the first time, but it did not sound good. From downstairs, they could hear the VIP passenger scream and begin wailing.

Rothe jumped quickly up to the observation dome and immediately saw what had happened. "We've blown the exhaust stack off number one, Captain," he told Ford when he got to the cockpit. Ford and Mack checked the gauges and Rothe looked them over quickly as well. Everything seemed normal, and Ford decided they would have to live with the racket. He knew the exhaust stack was mostly a noise-deflection device, and the more he thought about it, the more he thought it would make little difference in the plane's performance.

Rothe and Mack agreed. Ford maintained his heading,

speed and altitude, and asked Alex to run downstairs and ask Sawicki if he could find a way to "muzzle that bitch." Her wailing was getting on his nerves, and his nerve endings did not have that much left to them after this journey.

Brown hunched over his desk, furiously poring over his maps. The headings he gave Ford now would mean the difference between arriving at Leopoldville and crashing on land – not a happy consideration at all.

The landscape below them was just a dingy brown for the first hours of the flight, then the hills turned to green, with occasional rocky outcroppings. Mack was fascinated by his first exposure to Africa and his eyes scanned the changing scenery below them as they sped across the Dark Continent. The scattered villages of what looked like no more than a few thatched huts got more scattered and vast expanses of grasslands appeared.

Mack pointed to a herd of wildebeest – at least that was what he thought they were - which had panicked at the sound of the Wright Cyclones and was in full stampede. It seemed to Mack and Ford that there must be thousands – perhaps hundreds of thousands – of the animals. Then other herds of various animals appeared and one by one they panicked and stampeded as well.

"They're like those Arabs at the mosque," Ford said, grinning. "They've never heard a sound like this and have no idea where it's coming from or what it is, the poor devils. But at least they're not shooting at us." Several members of the crew were now pressed against windows, watching the show. It was a nice diversion from the constant anxiety of the flight over unknown territory.

"Sure are a hell of a lot of animals down there, though," Rothe observed laconically as he gazed out the window above his desk.

As the California Clipper roared onward, the grasslands gradually turned to jungle and the men aboard could see little on the ground beneath the dense canopy. Brown was now taking a turn in the left seat and Henricksen - who was in the co-pilot's seat while Ford and Mack got some rest – was trying to reference small rivers that they flew over with Brown's maps. But some were clearly too small to have been mapped, at least accurately. Still, Henricksen was sure that the heading they flew was correct. The sun had gradually crept overhead and was slightly in front of them, but not enough to cause a vision-robbing glare.

Mack returned from his rest and took over the controls from Brown, with Henricksen continuing to scan the horizon constantly. Henricksen pointed, and a large river – much larger than those they had been trying to identify - suddenly appeared several miles ahead.

"That must be the Congo River, Johnny," Brown announced from behind the cockpit, the relief in his voice evident. "It's right about where the map says it should be."

A few minutes later, Brown confirmed it was the Congo when they saw a medium-sized town which the map identified as Bumba. "Now we just follow the Congo, and it will take us right to Leopoldville," Brown said.

The relaxation on the flight deck was palpable, as all of them now realized that the Congo offered them a safe haven in case of mechanical trouble. The hours of droning over the scrublands and jungles of Africa were behind them. Brown also announced that they still had 500 miles to go, meaning another three hours. That didn't dampen their spirits because the men knew three hours over a wide river was preferable to one hour over the terrain they had just traversed.

As the time approached 4:30, the city of Leopoldville appeared on the horizon. After a low pass to orient himself to the dock area, Ford, now back in his left seat, circled back and approached the city from the east, setting the big plane down with the current. The landing, as usual for Ford, was flawless, but he soon sensed the strength of the river flow. It pushed the big machine ahead as if it were a small water toy in a child's bathtub.

He taxied toward the empty Pan American dock with much more engine power than normal, fighting the flow. Finally, the crew got the California Clipper tied down. Ford shut down the engines and the crew stepped out onto the dock.

Any among them who thought the humidity of Trincomalee was the worst they would ever experience were soon disabused of that silly notion. The air was so heavy and thick that it felt like a hot towel had been dropped over their entire bodies, and they were all pouring out sweat before they had stepped from the airplane onto the dock.

The men, who still faced the task of fueling the airplane, now wondered where they would find the store of energy to complete that job. Already exhausted by their long flight from Khartoum, the Congolese heat and humidity were combining to drain what energy remained. A British Embassy official appeared and took the "VIP" passenger off their hands. Again, Ford bit off the parting shot with which he would like to have sent her away, but noted with substantial satisfaction that she was sweating as badly as were the men. And, from the grim look on her face, not enjoying the sensation one bit.

Another surprise awaited them on the dock. A Pan American station manager and a radio operator strode toward them with broad smiles.

The station manager, an American who introduced himself

as Bolton, looked vaguely familiar to Ford. Bolton quickly filled them in. The Pan American service in Leopoldville – and other parts of Africa - was still in the planning stages while the station was being completed, although they all realized the war might derail those plans indefinitely.

Bolton, who was almost giddy with excitement as he inspected the Clipper, proved very helpful in securing a Congolese fueling team, saving Ford's men the exertion they did not know whether they could make, and in arranging accommodations in a nice hotel, one that Pan American would be using for its overnighting crews and passengers once service began. And he had beer.

He was immediately accepted by all as a true hero. The hotel turned out to be another one called the Grand. It was a popular name for hotels, Ford decided. Auckland, Khartoum and now Leopoldville.

Bolton reminded Ford that they had met briefly a few years before when he had been a junior operations man at the Pan American base in San Francisco, which explained why he had looked vaguely familiar. They were soon joined by a man in the uniform of a United States Army captain, who introduced himself as the Military Attaché in the U.S. Embassy in Leopoldville.

He told them that he – like a few of his military counterparts who were in on the story – had been following the odyssey of the California Clipper with great interest, although he acknowledged that they did so knowing that the flight of the great aircraft was classified top secret. If the Congolese public had known of the aircraft and its journey, he told them, there would have been thousands of people lining the Congo River when Ford landed.

The captain asked who the navigator was and when

Brown stepped forward, he shook his hand and presented him with a set of military charts of the west coast of Africa, the South Atlantic, eastern South America and the Caribbean. They were quite detailed and Brown was as proud as if he had been presented with the Congressional Medal of Honor. He immediately took them back into the plane and stowed them at his navigation table. They would be very handy for the longest leg of this journey.

Once he had his charges deposited in the hotel and the Army captain had departed, Bolton dispatched his radioman, a short, skinny young Belgian named Fougere, to the office to send a coded message to Pan American's headquarters announcing the safe arrival of the California Clipper.

Bolton also told him to include in his message that they were supplying Ford with a full fuel load and four extra 55-gallon drums of fuel, which Rothe calculated would give them an extra safety margin for the trans-Atlantic flight the next day. They would allow for detours which weather may dictate or for course miscalculations, which in reality Rothe did not expect to happen, given Brown's skills as a navigator and his new military charts. But anything was possible.

The engineering officer was seldom off by much in his fuel calculations, but his safety margins always allowed for stronger headwinds – or weaker tailwinds, as the case may be – than were actually expected. The 220 extra gallons Bolton would supply simply added to the safety margin.

Bolton briefed Ford and the crew on what he knew about conditions affecting the take-off from the Congo River. They could expect winds from the west, especially in the morning, so he would need to take off with the current, which Bolton said flowed at about six miles per hour. That was not surprising to Ford after fighting to the dock after landing earlier. But for takeoff, the current would help Ford pick up speed.

Then Bolton stressed to Ford that he "must" get airborne before passing the downstream end of Leopoldville. The reason, he suggested almost nonchalantly, was that just beyond the city, the river turned into a series of rapids, with large boulders and rock outcroppings "waiting to ruin your day." And the swift current that would help Ford pick up speed would also have the effect of shortening his "runway."

Ford looked at Mack, who said, "Damn glad to hear about that now instead of learning about it tomorrow morning on our takeoff run." Ford raised his beer bottle in a toast indicating his agreement. Ford had agreed to one beer after Alex, Rudi and several of the crewmen had remarked after their first taste what really good beer this Congolese brand was.

Alex asked Ford whether he expected any new instructions from Pan American in response to Fougere's message. Ford told him that, given the time difference between Leopoldville and the U.S. East Coast, it was unlikely there would be any response before noon the next day, which is when Ford intended to depart. Ford wanted his men to be well-rested for the next leg of their journey.

After a dinner of bison steak and gossip about the war, Ford and his men retired to rest up for the long day coming.

With profuse thanks ringing in his ears, Bolton left them with the promise that he would see them off in the morning.

The war news they got had been disheartening. The Japanese were roaming the Pacific seemingly at will and the Germans controlled Western Europe and North Africa. Since Belgium had fallen, Bolton had told them that many in the

Congo wondered what that would mean for this colony. And that he was worried about what it would mean for the future of the Pan American base.

CHAPTER 23

Leopoldville, Belgian Congo
January 2, 1942

Just after noon, the somewhat-rested but still-weary men of the California Clipper climbed aboard and prepared to cast off. Even though it was marginally cooler than it had been when they arrived, the humidity had not abated a bit. Bolton, whose Pan American uniform had a Bermuda shorts option in the British style, shook each man's hand as they climbed aboard.

Bolton was still marveling at the passenger comforts of the Clipper, not to mention those monstrous engines. Fougere was back on the dock, too, anxious to take in the show, but he watched from a distance. He had stopped at the office on his way and there was nothing from Pan American in reply to his message.

As soon as Ford started taxiing upstream, he could feel the weight of the plane, with the topped-off tanks, the four extra drums of fuel and the drum of engine oil they had loaded aboard all the way back in Noumea. That seemed years ago. The plane felt like it was waddling in the river rather than sailing. Ford knew the heat and humidity would also be working against them this morning, sapping the plane of lift as it had sapped the men of energy.

When he got to the last bend in the river upstream and

with the engine gauges all in the normal range, Ford turned the Clipper around and applied full take-off power. The plane shuddered as it fought the force of the water against its hull, and with the help of the current began to pick up speed.

The sights on the shores of the Congo River started to pass faster, but the weight worked against Ford and he fought to get it "up on the step." The step referred to the time in the take-off run when the Clipper got up to a point where only the boat-like hull on the bottom of the plane was in the water and it was almost ready to fly.

Alarm grew among the men as Ford used the ailerons on his wings to rock the plane, trying to free it up to the step. The downstream end of the city was nearing quickly and all aboard were aware of what lay beyond.

Finally, they could feel the plane get up on the step and just after the rapids came into sight, the slapping of water against the hull ceased. They were flying, but just barely. Ford knew he was going to have to fight and claw for elevation in these conditions. Suddenly, his eyes scanning what was ahead of them, he realized that they were far from home free. Just beyond the start of the rapids was a steep gorge and they would not have the altitude to clear it. Why didn't Bolton mention that? Ford thought to himself. Maybe he doesn't know about it, or he thought we'd just fly over it.

His only choice was to fly through the gorge. As they began to gain altitude, an inch at a time, the men stared out at the walls of the gorge, perilously close to the wingtips of the Clipper, which were bowed under the weight they were trying to lift.

"Captain, engine temps up," Rothe called out and Ford muttered a curse, looking at his own gauges. He had been too busy watching the walls of the gorge to focus on his instruments.

He knew the engines had been at full take-off power now for over five minutes. They were not designed to do that, and the temperatures were all above their red lines and still climbing.

Finally, still struggling, the Clipper rose just above the rock walls into the clear and Ford retarded the throttles to climb power.

The temperature gauges slowly moved back toward the normal zone.

Once satisfied that the engines were not going to blow out of their mounts, Ford turned the plane due west, toward the Atlantic Ocean, and, perspiration from nervous energy and the stress of the close call he had just avoided coating his face, turned the left seat over to Mack. Steers took the right seat. Brown would relieve Mack in another hour. On this extraordinarily long leg, there would be plenty of crew rotations.

The crew was at once relieved over the perils just avoided and gripped by anxiety over the Atlantic crossing they would soon begin. It would really be no different than an overland journey. Out there, they all knew, mechanical trouble meant almost-certain death. As it would be during the California-to-Hawaii crossing.

The difference in this case was that their engines had not had the attention they would have received before a scheduled crossing, such as California to Hawaii, and God knew they had been tortured and not thoroughly-enough maintained since leaving Auckland.

Thank God, Rothe thought to himself, the automobile gas had burned through the system and they were now flying on undiluted 100-octane aviation fuel.

An hour later, the California Clipper crossed the West African coastline and they were alone with the vastness of the sea and the long hours ahead. The regular two-hour rotation for all crew members was worked out carefully and strictly enforced so that all could get the rest they would need.

Now that there was nothing to see and nothing they could do to help the crew, Alex and Rudi returned to the passenger deck and the two stewards went to their galley to start preparing a late lunch.

Carter was still sitting in the last compartment, so Alex and Rudi sat in their usual compartment behind the lounge, facing one another.

Alex could tell Rudi was growing more concerned now that they were on what they presumed to be the final leg – for him - of this long trip. "Worried?" he asked Rudi as they stretched out in the comfortable seats.

"A little," Rudi responded after a pause. "I just don't know what to expect. I don't know who will meet me, if anybody, and that worries me." Alex just nodded his understanding. "And," Rudi went on, "to tell you the truth, I will miss being with you on this great journey. It is frightening, to be sure, but who do you know who has had an adventure to match this?"

"If we survive it – and the war – this will definitely be somethin' to tell our grandchildren," Alex said.

Suddenly, Carter slipped into a seat next to Alex and across from Rudi.

"So you are a Kraut," he said. "I figured there was something up with you guys."

"You don't know what you're talking about," Alex said forcefully, leaning forward in his seat so he could speak quietly to Carter.

"No? So why would this one" – he jerked his thumb toward Rudi – "be worried about who would meet him after he gets off the plane in Brazil?"

Alex and Rudi stared at Carter, their eyes wide as both

recognized in that instant that Carter had somehow slipped up close enough to them to overhear their conversation.

Carter went on. "Are you a Kraut spy, too?" he asked, looking sideways toward Alex.

"No, of course not, and neither is Dick," Alex replied, but much of the heat had left his voice. He suggested with a hand gesture that they move to the rear of the plane, where the stewards would not be able to overhear them.

"Well, don't look so spooked," Carter said when they were seated. "I don't give a fuck who you work for. When that bastard in Washington asked me to trail you in Hawaii, I figured sump'n wasn't kosher. And he told me one of you was a Kraut sympathizer or some such. As soon as we get to South America, I'm off this fuckin' airplane. I don't want no part of going back to the states and gettin' drafted."

"Okay," Alex said, "you're full of shit, but what do you want?"

"What else? Money. Cash, to be exact. I figured I'd have a bunch of money left over from what the guy gave me in Washington, but that fucking whore stole some of it."

"We've got a little," Alex said.

"Bullshit," Carter said, looking instead at Rudi. "I seen your stash under the fake bottom of that suitcase of yours. You're loaded." How does he know about that money? Alex and Rudi wondered to themselves at the same time.

"We've spent most of it." Alex was doing all the talking for them. Rudi was stunned, almost paralyzed with fear.

He was prepared to take risks or he would not have taken the job with the Admiral. But the thought of this thug turning him in to be tried as a spy or thrown in a jail for the duration of the war scared him to death.

He was praying desperately as Alex and Carter went back

and forth.

Carter threw them a wolfish grin as he pulled his pistol from a holster in the small of his back. "Bullshit. I looked. It was only a couple of stops back. Ceylon, I'm pretty sure it was. After I saw you get that other passport out of your suitcase, I took a look, and there it looked like more than five grand in it. You ain't spent that much since then." He pointed with the pistol at Rudi. "I know Adolf gave you a pot full of cash before he sent you over to the states and it's my duty as an American to liberate it. Ain't that what they call it? Liberating it?"

Alex remembered he and Rudi waiting in the stifling heat on the passenger level as Carter took his time in the luggage compartment. *That explains what took the son of a bitch so long.*

"Adolf didn't send him, you witless asshole," Alex said, getting hot all over again. "He's working with me on a matter of national security."

"Well, you guys did a hell of a job, didn't you? Or did I hear it wrong? The Japs didn't really bomb Pearl Harbor? We're really not in this fuckin' war?" He paused. "I want all of it. And I don't want no bargainin'. That will give me enough to get settled in South America. I hear it's cheap to live down there, and nobody can draft my ass if I'm down there, right?" He slipped his gun back in the holster, satisfied that it had had its desired effect.

Alex asked Carter to sit tight while he and Rudi talked privately. Carter said again he wasn't prepared to bargain. He would get it, Alex finally assured him, and Carter suggested that he and Rudi go right that minute up to the storage area and make the transfer. Alex knew that would not be the end of it, but it would buy them time, so he nodded for Rudi to go up with him.

Carter looked as smug as a cat with a bird in its mouth. In truth, he had a nice bankroll tucked away in that bank in New York, and Brazil would have banks that had correspondent relationships with it, like the one in Australia. But with an extra five grand or more in cash, in addition to the three grand or so he still had left from "Oscar," he would not have to touch the bank account for years.

As it turned out, when Rudi and Carter got to Rudi's suitcase and counted the money, there was still almost $6,700 in U.S currency. Carter had said nothing about the gold coins, so fortunately he had not seen the second false bottom. Rudi gathered the currency and Carter recounted it as he shoved it, a stack at a time, into his own suitcase. By the time the cash was transferred, Carter was quite pleased. He locked his suitcase elaborately and wound a full roll of black electricians' tape around it before carrying it down to his compartment. Rudi knew that it would stay with him for the remainder of the flight.

Rudi also knew the gold would be easier for him to use in South America, although he and Alex had both marveled during the trip how everybody in the world seemed willing, even anxious, to take U.S. dollars in payment for hotel rooms, food and such. But gold Swiss francs would probably be better for him than United States currency anyway.

"If you open your mouth to anyone about this, just know that I will find you," Alex hissed at Carter when Rudi and Carter came back down the stairs. "There's no place on earth you'll be able to hide."

"You keep runnin' your fuckin' mouth and I'll raise the price," Carter snarled. "I bet you can get more sent to you if you need it. Adolf will cover ya."

"Just take it and disappear when we get to Brazil, Carter, and don't do anything stupid." Carter's facial expression told

Alex that this man was as trustworthy as a wolverine. Perhaps not quite as bright as a wolverine, but equally cunning.

Before they got back to their compartment, Alex suggested they move forward to the lounge, where they would be more visible to the crew, in case Carter had any second thoughts.

Once they were seated in the lounge and satisfied that Carter would not leave the rear compartment and his newfound wealth, Alex told Rudi he thought it would be prudent for him to signal Canaris about Carter as soon as he got to Buenos Aires, or wherever he ended up in South America.

Rudi admitted that he had been thinking exactly the same thing. Alex said he would let Donovan know about the incident and Carter's plans as soon as he could when he got back to the states. And ask the man what he was thinking, sending that ape to tail them.

He was furious that Donovan had sent Carter to watch them. He wondered how much Donovan really knew about Carter, and the thought that Donovan knew what Carter was like – and that he had been behind the request to keep the man on the Clipper when it left Auckland – chilled him. The fact that the unstable man was armed chilled him even more.

But the man had referred to "that bastard in Washington," and what would be the point in his lying about that? And what other "bastard in Washington" would have had the knowledge of their going to Hawaii, the means to send Carter to watch them and the clout to get Pan American to keep Carter on the plane when it left Auckland? He planned to let Donovan know in the strongest words he knew how pissed off he was at having this thug sent to tail them. But, then, maybe he was not as stupid as he sometimes acted, Alex thought, and shuddered involuntarily.

In the Tirpitzufer, Major General Hans Oster was in the office of Admiral Wilhelm Canaris, briefing him on his plan for the repatriation of Rudi von Althorp. The Admiral was pleased with what he was hearing.

"Tell me again about our man who is meeting von Althorp in Brazil," he said.

"His name is Jorge Garcia, Herr Admiral," Oster said. "He is a Spaniard who was helpful to us during the Spanish Revolution and who emigrated to Buenos Aires in 1939. He assures me he has access to a small plane in Brazil, and he will meet von Althorp in Natal and fly him to Buenos Aires."

"And how is it that he has access to a plane, Hans?"

"He has an acquaintance in Brazil with whom he has worked before and who he trusts. The man is a German ex-patriot, as a matter of fact, according to Herr Garcia. I do not know the man's name."

"We don't know his name?" Canaris asked, suspicious. "What do your instincts tell you, Hans?"

"I have complete confidence in Garcia. As I said, he has been quite helpful to us many times in the past. Thus, I am inclined to trust his judgment. And I think we are better off using him for this mission than to ask our station chief in Buenos Aires because it gives us cover if something goes wrong. And it keeps the German community in Argentina at arm's length."

"That last point is important, Hans. Germany very much needs for Argentina to remain officially neutral, as you know, and ideally to maintain its pro-German leanings." Canaris stood and paced the room, as was his habit when thinking deeply about something.

"But one thing still bothers me, Hans. Does he have someplace safe – perhaps secure would be the better word –

where he can land the plane without suspicion?"

"Herr Garcia appears to have that covered, Herr Admiral. His man has access to a private airstrip not too far outside Natal. He will be watching in Natal when they land and he will devise a way somehow to make contact with von Althorp, using the same recognition code our man in Bahrain used. It worked in Bahrain and thus von Althorp will immediately recognize it."

"Where does this man Garcia get these men? Maybe I mean to ask, where does he get his resources? He is not one of our paid men, is he?"

"He is not on our payroll, but he has become a rather successful building contractor in Argentina, Uruguay and Brazil, Herr Admiral. Our people in Buenos Aires let it be known in the German communities of the three countries that he is a good man and loyal to us, and that has resulted in a good deal of business for him. He has his own resources, in other words, although we provide a stipend – a bonus for exemplary service, as it were - from time to time. His business provides him access to a workforce of men used to manual labor – men in good physical condition, in other words, if the Herr Admiral gets my meaning."

"How is it I have never come across him before this, Hans? Argentina, as you know, holds a special interest for me."

"Until now, in the time he has been in South America, he has not been involved in any major operation as the key man. His work has been in a support role, almost always working directly with Otto Gerlach." Gerlach was the Abwehr's Buenos Aires station chief and was hand-picked by Canaris for that assignment.

"I see. Thank you, Hans, for your usual excellent work. Please proceed." With a salute – not the Nazi salute – Hans left Canaris' office and walked directly to the signals section to confirm the operation. He knew Garcia and his men were already on station, since the aircraft in question was in the air.

.

CHAPTER 24

Natal, Brazil
January 3, 1941

Twenty-three and a half hours after the harrowing take-off and the anxiety of what Ford was certain was the longest overwater flight any Pan Am aircraft had ever attempted, he set the California Clipper down in the harbor at Natal, Brazil, a city of about 50,000 inhabitants and the easternmost harbor of any size in South America.

When they touched down it was just mid-day, local time, despite having to divert fairly severely from their intended course – twice – to avoid lines of thunderstorms.

Ford knew that Pan American had been using Natal Harbor's Rampa passenger terminal, which served both passenger ships and seaplanes, for several years. Thus, he was confident it had the facilities and staff to take care of his plane.

His recollection of the Natal facilities proved to be accurate, and they were met at a dock by the station manager. The station manager greeted Ford like an old acquaintance and offered his assistance for whatever they would need.

"I was hoping to go on to the Pan American station at Trinidad as soon as we can get the Clipper fueled," Ford said. "We all got quite a lot of rest on the flight, so I'd like to push on." He could see by their smiles that his crew all agreed.

The station manager told them that the Brazilians would have to have access to the plane for about an hour to spray it for mosquitoes. Yellow fever, he told them, was a threat in this part of the world, and one the Brazilian authorities took quite seriously. Then they would be able to fuel it.

Ford asked if the station manager could arrange for the crew bus to take them into town and get a good lunch while all that was going on. The station manager immediately called to one of his men, who scurried off to get the bus. He told Ford that they should dispose of any food still on the aircraft and take their personal luggage on the bus with them to avoid it being sprayed. The spray was quite toxic, he pointed out.

Alex and Rudi, of course, were delighted. They had not realized Ford intended to push on that afternoon and knew that doing so might have caused Rudi serious problems. Now he might have time to find out, if he could, how he was to break away from the crew and get to Argentina or wherever. And he would have his suitcase – and the gold coins - with him.

Carter was even more pleased. His disappearance could be accomplished while the men ate. He told Sawicki he wasn't hungry and would meet them back on the dock. Meantime, he told him, he wanted to take a walk around the harbor. Of course, he took his suitcase with him.

The restaurant they were taken to was in a hotel, which was not called the Grand but was quite nice nonetheless. The hotel had a cadre of bellmen, and one approached Rudi when he came out of the restroom, where he and Alex had stopped before joining the others in the dining room. When Alex had suggested the restroom stop, he had done so knowing that Rudi needed to be separated from the group if possible, even if for a brief time. He assumed Rudi's Abwehr contact – if there was one – would have his description, just as the Arab in Bahrain clearly had.

"I bring greetings from Mexico City and from your Uncle William," a bellhop said, smiling, when Rudi passed him.

Rudi's shock subsided quickly and when he shook his hand the man said his name was Antonio, just as his name tag indicated. He told Rudi they would leave immediately. Alex just smiled at Rudi and walked on.

Rudi went to the bus and retrieved his suitcase, waving to Alex as he hurried after Antonio. Alex watched him go, relieved but sorry to see him go. He wished he had had the chance to shake Rudi's hand and wish him luck, but that would have drawn unwanted attention. He might even have hugged him. They had been through a lot together in the last four months. *Has it just been four months? It seems like four years!*

They would drive about two hours southwest, Antonio told Rudi when they were in the car, where they would find a mostly-unused airfield and an airplane. The pilot of the plane, Antonio said, would take him – after two stops for fuel – to Buenos Aires. There, he would be met by a man who would have further instructions for him. He smiled and Rudi smiled back, somewhat warily. But with unmistakable relief. *So his suspicions had been right. Buenos Aires would be his destination.*

Alex waited in the hotel lobby for the others to finish their lunch. When they came out of the dining room, Alex waved Ford over to the couch on which he was sitting. Ford looked around, expecting to see Rudi, but instead, Alex advised him that they had received a couriered message from ONI – the officer courier had been watching the harbor in anticipation of their arrival - detaching Rudi immediately to work with Brazilian Naval Intelligence Office for "an undetermined period of time, not to exceed three months...."

He was glad they had rehearsed this story previously.

Rudi was now on his way to Rio de Janiero with two Brazilian Navy officers who were in a big hurry to get on their way, Alex said, concluding the story.

After Alex finished, the Captain's only comment was, "I wish he had stopped to say goodbye. He's a nice fellow and you guys have sure pulled your weight on our trip. When you see him next, please tell him that I said thanks and good luck." Alex assured him he would.

At the same time Alex was watching Rudi walk off with Antonio, Henry Carter, suitcase in hand, slipped around a corner at the far end of the harbor and disappeared.

After a hair-raising ride out of Natal – it seemed to Rudi that all the Brazilians they passed drove like maniacs - Rudi asked Antonio to pull over at a bend in the road. There Rudi burned his ONI credentials and all documents connected to them, scattering the ashes and melted plastic in the wind. Then he extracted his German diplomatic passport from the second false bottom of his suitcase, where it had been secreted with the gold coins. He kept the "Eugen Kraus" passport as well.

Just over two hours later, Antonio pointed ahead. "The airfield," he said simply, and when he got to the turn-off, skidded the car through a wild right turn and pulled up to a hanger that looked to be no more than even money to last the night without collapsing. Inside the dilapidated hangar was a very nice small plane of a type that Rudi immediately recognized. It was a Twin Beech, or Beechcraft 18, an American-made light transport aircraft, capable of carrying six passengers and two pilots.

The Beechcraft 18 was twin-engine, twin-tailed and used a tail wheel, so its pilots invariably referred to it as a "tail-dragger." It had a range of 1,200 miles at a cruising speed of about 215 miles per hour, faster by about 35 miles per hour than the California Clipper.

Rudi's first solo flight had been in a Fieseler Storch, a German-made aircraft designed as an artillery spotter plane which had two seats – one in back of the other – for the pilot and the artillery spotter, or in his case a student pilot and the instructor pilot, who rode in the rear seat.

However, during his stint in Washington, D.C. before the war, he had been taken up in a Twin Beech by a U.S. Army Air Corps captain he had met at a conference. The U.S. Army designated the aircraft the C-45.

The pilot was just finishing his walk-around and approached Antonio and Rudi when they walked into the hangar. Antonio introduced Rudi, in Spanish, by only his first name and the pilot said his name was Santos. Rudi did not know, nor care, whether Santos was his given name, his family name or an alias.

When Santos, who was obviously not a talkative man, motioned to the aircraft door, Rudi put his bag in the passenger compartment, then climbed into the co-pilot's seat and fastened his seat belts. Santos watched Rudi make himself at home in the co-pilot's seat with some measure of discomfort, then climbed in himself and Rudi, in Spanish, told him he had had "a little time" in this model and would be happy to help with the flying. Santos just nodded.

Santos engaged the ignition, and the Beech's engines fired immediately, one after the other. As Santos began to taxi out of the hangar, Rudi waved and saluted Antonio, whose job on this mission had now been successfully completed.

Santos taxied the Beech over the uneven and bumpy ground to a dirt runway that had probably been leveled most recently sometime in the 1920s. Still, the take-off roll did not seem very long to Rudi – especially after the seemingly endless time the Clipper took bouncing across the water before lifting off. Santos guided the plane effortlessly off the ground and fixed his heading to the south, following the coastline.

Back in Natal, Antonio reported his safe delivery of "the package" to Jorge Garcia and this information was passed up the chain to the Tirpitzufer.

Admiral Wilhelm Canaris smiled broadly when he heard the news from Oster. It was a good way to start the New Year.

Late that afternoon, Ford and the crew prepared to depart. As the men hurried aboard the California Clipper, Ford told them about "Dick Barnhardt's" reassignment and explained he would be staying in Brazil for a few months. He also asked where Carter was. Nobody had seen him since they had returned from lunch.

"Well, I told that son of a bitch I wasn't going to wait for him, so let's get going," Ford said. "I don't give a damn who in Washington wanted us to bring him with us."

When the lines had been cast off and the aircraft pushed away from the dock, Ford started the engines, warmed them up and quickly pushed the throttles forward. He did not want to see Carter running down the dock again at the last moment. After the predictable period of bumping over the water, Ford pulled back on the yoke, the plane got up on the step, and then once again rose into the air.

Alex wondered, somewhat fearfully, whether he had heard the last of Henry Carter. And more to the point, perhaps, whether Rudi had heard the last of him.

He wondered how Donovan would explain Carter. Donovan simply had to be the "bastard" in Washington to whom Carter had referred. Nobody else that he knew of, and who knew of their mission, could have pushed the right buttons to get Pan American to include him on the flight out of New Zealand. Of that he was now convinced. He had thought a lot about it and there were no other possibilities.

At least none that he had thought of.

Rudi and Santos settled in for a flight of about 2,500 miles that should take them a bit less than twelve hours in the air, perhaps fifteen or so when factoring in two refueling stops. Rudi marveled at how little engine noise the Beech generated compared to the California Clipper. At first, Santos said little and Rudi was alone with his thoughts.

Gradually, Santos began pointing out coastal villages and larger cities.

He told Rudi they would stop at a small airfield just short of Rio de Janiero for their first refueling stop.

After two and a half hours, Santos asked Rudi if he wanted to take the controls for a while and Rudi jumped at the chance to take his mind off the uncertainty ahead and to concentrate on something else. Santos had simply identified the Beech by its tail number when talking to air traffic control or to another aircraft when they twice found themselves sharing airspace with another small plane.

Rudi asked him who owned the plane and Santos gave him the name of a construction company that meant nothing to him. He assumed it was one of the cover operations that shielded many of Canaris' agents and assets from prying eyes. When he asked Santos where they would be landing in Argentina, however, the man just told him tersely that he would see when they got there.

The Beech, obviously well-maintained, performed flawlessly, the flight and the refueling stops went smoothly and at 9:00 the next morning Santos raised the tower at Jorge Newbery Airport in Buenos Aires and got landing instructions and clearance immediately. Santos landed the Beech with scarcely a bump, as he had at each of the refueling stops. Rudi had decided early in the flight that, while Santos was not a great conversationalist, he was most assuredly an excellent pilot. He had been confident enough, in fact, to take two naps of an hour or so each.

Santos turned off the active runway and taxied to what looked like a private hangar in a remote part of the airfield, which was less than two miles from the heart of Buenos Aires. When they deplaned, there were three men waiting to greet them. One was a uniformed officer of the Argentine customs and immigration service, who immediately took Rudi's and Santos' passports and went into the small office in the hangar to affix the proper entry stamps to them. Santos went with him.

Rudi looked at the other two, and the taller of the men extended his hand. "I am pleased to meet you, Herr von Althorp," he said in German. "I am Otto Gerlach, the Commercial Attaché of the Embassy of the German Reich in Argentina, and this gentleman is a good friend of mine, Herr Jorge Garcia." Garcia offered his hand.

"I am pleased to meet you, too, Herr Gerlach," Rudi responded in German, "and you as well, Herr Garcia."

Santos emerged from the hangar office, handed Rudi his passport and went to get the Beech refueled and ready for departure.

His part of this operation, like Antonio's, was now over.

As they strolled toward the hangar door, Garcia walked ahead and Rudi, in a low voice, said, "As you may know, Herr Gerlach, I am the Commercial Attaché in the Reich's Embassy in Tokyo. Perhaps I no longer am, since it has been several months since I left Tokyo. But I have not been notified that I have been replaced."

Rudi assumed that, by this time, Canaris may very well have sent someone else to Tokyo, but he could not know that.

"I am indeed aware of that fact, Herr von Althorp." Gerlach paused before continuing. "In fact, I am led to believe you have very much the same range of duties in Tokyo that I have here." And with that, he confirmed Rudi's suspicion that he was the Abwehr station chief in Argentina. That also meant he was operating on the direct orders, or at least with the support of, Admiral Canaris, and Rudi suddenly felt more on solid footing than he had since he had left Mexico City almost four months before.

"We will go to the Embassy now," Gerlach went on, "and in my office I will tell you what my instructions are. You will also be able to use the signals section to communicate with Berlin directly, if you wish. And my instructions include that, so far as the Ambassador – if you happen to meet him – or other Embassy personnel are concerned, you have just arrived from Mexico City, where, I understand, you were attending to your ill father. You left when Mexico broke diplomatic relations with the Reich after Germany declared war on the Americans. When that happened, the Embassy was closed and personnel evacuated."

Rudi said, "Indeed I was, Herr Gerlach. Thank you." Then he stopped. "Is that last part true, Herr Gerlach? The part about the Mexico City Embassy being closed?" Gerlach told him that, regrettably enough, it was true.

Suitcase in hand, Rudi followed Gerlach to a black Mercedes limousine, not wanting to ask any other questions with the others around. The uniformed driver opened the back door when he saw Gerlach walking toward him. Garcia had by that time got in his own car and departed.

The ride to the Embassy was quick.

CHAPTER 25

Natal, Brazil
January 3, 1942

Ford's plan was to simply follow the South American coast north, then northwest. His next destination, Trinidad, was just seven miles off the coast of Venezuela. To make sure of the headings Ford would need in the event they encountered a cloud bank that cut off visibility to the ground, Brown checked his maps. He looked around, a perplexed look on his face. Poindexter, noticing the look, asked him what he was looking for.

"What happened to the maps I got from that Military Attaché in Leopoldville?" he asked. They looked all over the various work stations on the flight deck level and could not find them. At about the same time, Sawicki came up to report that the storage locker in which the crew kept their personal papers, and in which Brown kept a lock box with what money they had left, was empty, the personal papers scattered around but the money gone.

"It must have been those fumigators," Sawicki said. "They were the only ones aboard the plane after we deplaned. I came out here and locked the hatches myself when they finished, and nobody got on before I did that."

"My God, Brazil is supposed to be an ally. I can't believe

the bastards treat an ally like that," Brown said with a lot of heat in his voice. "Can you imagine how they'd have treated a German or Italian crew?"

"It has nothing to do with allies or enemies," Ford said. "From everything I've heard, Brazilians steal things just because they can. Pan American hires its own security in Natal, at least for regular passenger flights. I hope Dick's careful while he's there."

"I'll send him a message and tell him what happened when we get home," Alex said, grateful for the opportunity to reinforce the cover story they had concocted to explain Rudi's disappearance. He hoped Rudi's escape to Argentina had gone well. *He's probably on his way to Buenos Aires by now,* he thought.

I wonder if he'll have the chance to let Canaris know about Carter.

Mack waved Alex forward and Ford asked him quietly if he had left his money in Brown's strongbox. Alex just smiled and patted his wallet pocket. He had been taking a few hundred dollars at a time from Rudi's suitcase throughout the journey, so Carter got by no means all the money they had left. Alex had about $300, more than enough to get to New York City now that they only had one more stop, and that at a Pan American base.

Alex was not actually carrying the money in his wallet, of course, but he knew it was locked safely in his luggage, which he had kept with him that morning. Brown was fuming over the loss of the maps more than any of the rest of it.

"Those were the only souvenirs I had of this damn trip," he said. "And they were damn good maps. What the hell are a bunch of fumigators going to do with them?"

"Sell them," Alex said simply. Soon, busy with the

normal business of flying the huge plane, the crew put the theft behind them. When they crossed the mouth of the Amazon River, all aboard marveled at the size of the mighty river. It was roughly 100 miles wide at the point at which it met the Atlantic and sediment from it turned the sea brown for a couple of miles out.

All aboard were increasingly excited to be getting so close to home. And while Trinidad was not a part of the United States, its position in the Caribbean and as a Pan American station made it seem like it to them. Curiously, that made the flight from Natal seem that much longer. The endless hours over the green jungle of the north coast of South America, became, in their minds, endless days. When Brown announced that they were approaching the Venezuelan border, excitement again gripped the men. Again, Alex wondered where Rudi was at that moment.

Finally, after over 13 hours in the air, the Trinidad archipelago became faintly visible, even at 2:30 a.m., and soon Ford put the California Clipper into a slow descent toward the northwest coast of the island of Trinidad, where the lights of Port-of-Spain were clearly visible.

The Gulf of Paria stretched in front of the capital city and provided a relatively – by Caribbean standards – protected waterfront. Ford could not try to raise the Pan American base, because of the radio silence they had been ordered to maintain, although at this point in their odyssey he did not think it was still necessary. But orders were orders.

Still, when the giant seaplane splashed onto the surface just offshore from the Port-of-Spain docks and made its way to its mooring, the entire Pan American Trinidad station contingent was there to meet it, even though it was 3:00 in the morning. They had heard the roar of the engines approaching and had rushed to the dock to see what it was. Although an active Pan American base for over ten years, none of the station personnel had ever seen a Boeing 314 there. Most of the Caribbean flights were operated using Martin 130 aircraft, nice enough planes but not like the Boeing.

The station manager, a tanned, fit 37-year-old man of medium height named Randolph Oakley, ushered Ford and the crew into the comfortable passenger lounge in the Pan American terminal. The lounge was deserted because the only flight scheduled that day, a flight to Miami, would not depart until much later that morning. In fact, all of the personnel had been at home sleeping but came back when alerted by the sound of the California Clipper inbound.

They had heard company scuttlebutt that it was being sent westbound back to the United States from New Zealand almost a month before, but nothing since – civilian radio silence about the plane was still being strictly enforced - and, of course, nobody knew what route the plane would take, or try to take, getting to New York. In other words, Trinidad being on the itinerary, while recognized by some as a possibility, still came as a bit of a surprise. But all of them knew that, if successful, the flight of the California Clipper would be history-making and, like human beings everywhere, they wanted to see part of that history being made.

Ford was now more relaxed than he had been since the California Clipper had left Noumea for Auckland, before the first Japanese bomb had fallen on Pearl Harbor. He decided that he and his men could use some serious rest after having been in the air for almost 40 hours continuously, less the rather brief stop in Natal. And he wanted them fully rested before they delivered themselves to New York, where, he suspected, they would be subject to endless questioning and debriefing by Pan American, probably the military and possibly the press.

He told Oakley he wanted his men taken to the crew hotel and asked him to put his mechanics and cleaning people to work checking and cleaning everything. As he told Oakley, "I want the plane to be as presentable as possible when it gets back to the states." He also asked him to get his mechanics to see if they could replace the exhaust stack on the number one engine. The rattle was driving everyone aboard nuts.

At the Embassy of the German Reich in Buenos Aires, Commercial Attaché Otto Gerlach offered Rudi von Althorp coffee when they walked through his reception area and into his private office. They had spoken in German from the time of their meeting at the airport, and continued to do so. Rudi felt quite at home, being able to return to his native tongue and the rather formal manner of speech used among members of the diplomatic corps.

He was also, he found, a bit relieved not to have to concentrate on spoken American English, which was so much more informal and colloquial than diplomatic German.

"You will find Argentine coffee to be excellent, Herr von Althorp," Gerlach said, then introduced him to his secretary, a very tall and very curvaceous woman with jet-black hair that hung to her shoulders, where it flipped outward. "Fraulein Guderian, this is Herr von Althorp. He is my counterpart in the Reich's Embassy in Tokyo. He will be working with me for a few days."

"It is a pleasure to meet you, Herr von Althorp," she said in German with a faint Argentine accent. "You may call me Ilse, if you wish. Please let me know if I can be of assistance in any way." With a slight curtsy, she turned and went to fetch the coffee. Rudi wondered whether "in any way" was meant on her part the way he took it, realizing it seemed like months, rather than weeks, since he had frolicked with a woman. Louise. Gerlach noticed the look on Rudi's face.

"Quite an attractive young woman, is she not?" Gerlach asked. Rudi nodded. "She is Argentine, of course," Gerlach went on. "The Foreign Ministry does not have the budget to send German citizens abroad to work as secretaries, except in the case of confidential secretaries to Ambassadors in some key countries."

"No, of course not," Rudi agreed. His mind flashed back to Meike Franzky in the Washington Embassy and wondered how that had come about.

"But we are fortunate here. As you probably know, Buenos Aires has a substantial population of Argentines of German ancestry, many of them fairly recent immigrants or first-generation Argentines who have maintained their loyalty to the Fatherland. Fraulein Guderian is one of the first-generation Argentines. And she is very loyal to Germany. She is actually related, somewhat distantly, to Generaloberst Heinz Guderian. I have found that she can be trusted to be completely discrete."

Heinz Guderian was a legendary German armor officer who many credited with developing and perfecting the doctrine of blitzkrieg, or lightning war, which had served Germany so well in Poland, France and North Africa. He was also known to be out of favor with Hitler much of the time, owing to his penchant for saying what was on his mind – what he believed to be the truth – rather than trying to anticipate what the Führer wanted to hear.

"That must be a great comfort to you, Herr Gerlach, especially considering your duties here," Rudi responded.

Fraulein Guderian just then reappeared with a very nice

silver coffee service and two cups with saucers.

When she had served the coffee and departed, closing the door quietly behind her, Rudi added, "My secretary in Tokyo was, I should perhaps say is, a woman of French ancestry who was married to a Japanese national who died three years ago. I have never really trusted her, and she does not have a key to either my office door or to my desk. And I keep all my papers in a safe to which only I am privy to the combination."

"Yes, I had that problem in my previous assignment in Spain," Gerlach said. "But even with Fraulein Guderian's obvious loyalty, in our line of work, one must always be careful. I have a safe here, as you can see. She has simply not received the, ah, training we have, Herr von Althorp. Who knows, after all, who she has dinner with and who her girlfriends – and maybe boyfriends – are?"

Rudi nodded, then said, "Herr Gerlach, perhaps if we are to be, what would you say – colleagues? – it would be easier if you were to call me Rudi."

Gerlach, who was in his mid-forties, Rudi guessed, smiled broadly and offered his hand. "Then we will reintroduce ourselves, Rudi. I am Otto. And now perhaps it is time to talk about what my instructions are." He gestured for Rudi to make himself comfortable. Rudi sat on a very fine cordovan-colored couch and Gerlach, after retrieving a file from his safe, took a matching chair.

Gerlach pulled a sheet of paper from the file and handed it to Rudi.

It was a decoded message from the Tirpitzufer, signed by Major General Hans Oster for Admiral Wilhelm Canaris.

In the message, Oster had informed the Station Chief in Buenos Aires – Gerlach – of Rudi's imminent arrival. The message said only that Rudolf von Althorp, Commercial

Attaché and Station Chief Tokyo, had been on an assignment in the South Pacific region when the Pacific war broke out, precluding his immediate return to Tokyo, and had managed to hitch a ride, so to speak, on a commercial aircraft – an American commercial aircraft, as it happened - that was similarly stranded in the South Pacific and would be landing shortly in Brazilian waters.

The message had also informed Gerlach that Berlin – read Oster and/or Canaris - had already arranged for Jorge Garcia, with whom Gerlach had had multiple dealings and who had a superb network in Brazil, to arrange for Herr von Althorp to be met in Brazil and transported to Buenos Aires, thence to be delivered into his – Gerlach's – hands.

Once delivered into his hands, von Althorp was to be transported to the Embassy, briefed on these instructions, then asked to signal the undersigned and await further instructions. The message instructed Gerlach to inform von Althorp that his father had arrived safely back in Berlin after hastily departing Mexico when it broke diplomatic relations with Germany and was on a 30-day leave pending reassignment. It also detailed the cover story that was to be used vis-à-vis von Althorp when he encountered the Ambassador or other Embassy personnel.

Obviously, Rudi thought as he read that part, Canaris had not decided what he could do, or what could be done, with Rudi, or with his father, for that matter. Of course, especially in the case of his father, von Ribbentrop would have the final word.

Gerlach told Rudi that he had then contacted Garcia to confirm that his plans were in place, but that Garcia had not specified what those plans were. "Herr Garcia and I had occasion to work together in Spain and I have had extensive contact with him since I have been in Argentina and he has never failed me," Gerlach said. "Moreover, he is a good man to work with. Loyal, always finds a way to get done what needs to be done. And never questions what he is asked to do. I wish I had a dozen like him."

"I was intrigued by his men, both the one who met me in Natal and the odd one – Santos was his name – who flew me down here," Rudi said.

"Santos has had occasion to fly me places a few times," Gerlach said. "He is indeed a quiet one, but in my experience he is a superb pilot and, like Garcia, asks no questions. He just does his job, and being quiet by nature is not a disadvantage for someone in our line of work, would you not say?"

Rudi smiled and nodded, conceding that Gerlach's point was excellent, and a bit chagrined that he had not recognized the advantage when he had been with Santos. He realized he was very tired after his trip, not thinking properly, and told Gerlach so.

"I would be fascinated to hear about your journey from the South Pacific, if you think you could tell me," Gerlach said.

Rudi paused, sipping his coffee, and said, "Perhaps I should first send a message to Berlin and find out what they have in mind for me, Otto. I will also ask specifically about briefing you on my mission, and if they have no objection, I will be happy to explain it all to you. It is a fascinating story indeed."

"Of course," Gerlach said. "That is a very good idea, Rudi. I will have Fraulein Guderian take you down to the signals section." He rose, reached across his desk, and pushing a button on his telephone, asked Ilse Guderian to come into his office. She appeared almost immediately.

"Please take Herr von Althorp down to the signals section, if you would be so kind, fraulein," Gerlach said. "You have his credentials ready, I assume?"

"Right here, Herr Gerlach," she said, handing an identification card in a very nice leather holder to Rudi. It had his photograph affixed already and he wondered how she had done that so quickly. He also noticed for the first time her blue eyes, which combined with the black hair and full mouth to give her a look that was both exotic and intoxicating. He had, he admitted to himself, not noticed the eyes earlier because his attention was drawn so strongly to her magnificent bust.

She was leading him down the stairs before Rudi registered the conscious thought that they had left Gerlach's office. He hoped he had remembered to say goodbye to him. As he watched the sway of Ilse's derriere descending the stairs, he thought, not for the first time, about Louise Wagner.

Louise was attractive and saucy and quite imaginative in bed, but Ilse Guderian's almost-aristocratic bearing, combined with her undeniable physical features, soon pushed Louise back out of his mind.

In the signals section, Ilse introduced Rudi to the chief clerk, a 60-year-old man named Dieter, who, she told him, was the longest-serving member of the Embassy staff, having been posted to Buenos Aires just after the end of the Great War. She told Rudi that when he was finished, Dieter would ring her and she would come back to escort him back to Herr Gerlach's office. She walked out the door and Rudi tried hard not to stare at her swaying rear end.

He was not quite successful.

It was quickly apparent to Rudi that Dieter was used to dealing with the difference between message traffic to and from the Foreign Ministry and that to and from the Tirpitzufer. They involved different codes and different security protocols. He handed Rudi a pad of paper and two pencils and showed him to a small anteroom with a desk where he could compose his message in private. Dieter told him he would personally encode, date and transmit it.

Less than fifteen minutes later, Rudi walked out of the small room and handed his message to Dieter. Dieter read it through to make certain he understood it all correctly before beginning his encoding process.

```
EYES ONLY
THE DIRECTOR
ABWEHR HEADQUARTERS
TIRPITZUFER
BERLIN
TODAY ARRIVED BA STOP MOST
ELEMENTS OF TRAVEL SUCCESSFUL STOP ONE
PASSENGER PROBLEMATIC STOP GERLACH
VERY HELPFUL STOP WILL AWAIT ORDERS
VIA EMBASSY BA STOP MEANTIME WILL
MAKE MYSELF AVAILABLE GERLACH STOP
HE IS CURIOUS ABOUT MY TRIP STOP WILL
AWAIT INSTRUCTIONS RE WHAT TO TELL HIM
STOP IF POSSIBLE WOULD ALSO PERSONALLY
APPRECIATE ANY WORD ON FROSCH THAT
COMES TO YOUR ATTENTION STOP WOULD
ALSO APPRECIATE LETTING FATHER KNOW OF
ARRIVAL OF UNDERSIGNED IF POSSIBLE STOP
STANDING BY STOP
     R VON ALTHORP
     EMBASSY OF THE GERMAN REICH
     BUENOS AIRES, ARGENTINA
     END MESSAGE
```

Three minutes after Dieter's call, Ilse Guderian hurried into the signals section. Rudi shook Dieter's hand formally and gestured for Ilse to lead the way. Climbing the stairs, he had a splendid opportunity to focus on the fraulein's legs, which, he noticed, were as nicely formed as was the rest of her. He wondered how old she was and whether she was "attached." She wore no rings, so he assumed she was not married. Why am I getting so far ahead of myself? I don't even know what Canaris is going to do with me or how long I'll be here.

In Gerlach's office, Rudi told the Abwehr station chief that he had asked for instructions – including as to briefing him on his South Pacific mission and subsequent arrival in Brazil – and that pending those instructions he was placing himself in the service of Gerlach. That pleased the man immensely.

"Well then, until we hear back from Berlin, you will need a place to stay," Gerlach said. "I regret that the apartment my wife and I share is not large enough to accommodate visitors. But there is a very nice hotel, which is only two blocks from here, that gives a very generous diplomatic rate and its rooms and service are quite satisfactory. I will have Fraulein Guderian contact them and make arrangements. Will you need a car, do you think?"

"If the hotel is just two blocks away, until we hear from Berlin I think assigning a car to me would be a waste of resources, Otto," Rudi said. "I can walk two blocks easily enough, especially in this beautiful weather." Being south of the equator, it was then summer in Argentina. It could be extremely hot and humid in the Argentine summer, but at the moment the temperatures were mild and the humidity not uncomfortable at all. Especially compared with Trincomalee and Leopoldville, he thought to himself. "But since I have my luggage here, I would appreciate a ride to the hotel, or perhaps it would be more convenient to call a taxi."

"Nonsense," Gerlach said. "I will take you there myself. And while the fraulein is calling the hotel, I will get you some Argentine currency." He got into his safe again and gave Rudi a thick wad of pesos, explaining the rough rate of exchange between the peso and the Reichsmark to give him an idea of relative value of anything he might be inclined to purchase. He told Rudi to sign everything he had in the way of food and beverage at the hotel to his room account, which would be forwarded directly to Ilse at the Embassy.

Ilse Guderian made the arrangements with the hotel and announced to Otto and Rudi that the room was available immediately. Rudi was happy to hear that, knowing he needed sleep very badly. Gerlach sensed the same thing and said, "Thank you, Fraulein Guderian. I will take Herr von Althorp immediately so he can rest from his journey. I will return in no more than 30 minutes."

Rudi's luggage was still in Gerlach's car, and by the time they walked out of the building, Ilse's call had resulted in the driver awaiting them.

By the time Gerlach got back to the embassy after getting Rudi checked in, Rudi was already sound asleep on the bed in his very nice room. He was still wearing his clothes, but had taken the time to remove his shoes.

In Trinidad, Ford passed the word, after consulting with Randy Oakley, that the cleaning and refurbishing of the plane should be completed by noon the next day - January 5 - and that he wished to arrive in New York at first light the following morning.

He told them that headquarters had also ordered that the Pan American markings be repainted on the aircraft and that it was to be renamed The Pacific Clipper. It was apparent that Pan American had big plans for their arrival. Therefore, he told his crew, he planned to depart Trinidad the next afternoon at 3:00. Oakley's people would repaint the Pan American markings, including its tail number and its new name.

They all went to their rooms and most slept for the better part of 24 hours. He and Brown had studied their maps and determined that New York was 2,400 miles away, give or take a few, as the crow flies. He wanted to fly a direct route to avoid any trigger-happy coastal defense batteries that may have been set up, or any coastal patrols.

He had been told by Oakley that both coasts of the United States were under black-out orders. The California Clipper had not failed him yet, except for the little problem taking off from Trincomalee, and he did not want to come all this way only to be shot down by some well-meaning American who did not know what a Boeing 314 was.

That meant a flight of about fifteen hours, depending on the winds and other weather conditions, which should put them overhead New York City at about 6:00 a.m. on the sixth. Nobody among the crew complained. They could hardly wait. But the anticipation caused no loss of sleep among them.

Ford used Oakley's office to send a coded message to Pan American headquarters informing them of his plan to service the aircraft and depart on the fifth with a New York arrival the morning of the sixth. Less than an hour later he got confirmation of receipt and congratulations on his planning. Pan American boss Juan Trippe, who was a visionary as well as an extremely astute businessman, had begun thinking of the public relations coup Pan American would enjoy - if the newly renamed Pacific Clipper made it home – as early as when the plane was still in Auckland and the decision was made to send it west.

Now, with only the Trinidad-to-New York leg standing between him and the certain news bonanza, Trippe was more than willing to wait an additional day to make sure the aircraft was spotless, repainted with the Pan American insignia and its engines refreshed with a check-up and a change of fluids. That would give him and his staff time to prepare and alert the press. This would be a dramatic demonstration of the safety and durability of Pan American's airplanes and a testament to the skill and ingenuity of its flight crews. It would also be a "good news" story for the American people amidst all the bad war news.

Trippe asked his radio operator to send a message in his name to the State Department advising it of the expected arrival – and the new name - of the Pacific Clipper, and in Washington, the message was received and acknowledged. Then the State Department duty officer dispatched runners with "eyes-only" copies to Colonel William Donovan and to Secretary of the Navy Frank Knox at the State, War and Navy Building.

Ford and Mack inspected and approved the painting that resulted in their aircraft once again looking like a Pan American Clipper.

It turned out none of them needed to have worried about the condition of the aircraft. The Trinidad ground crew could well imagine the punishment the airplane and its crew must had taken on this journey, and while most probably had no appreciation for the historic nature of the flight, they all wanted to do their part to make sure the Pacific Clipper reached New York safely, and looking good as well.

After Ford's message had been sent and acknowledged, Oakley turned his attention to seeing to the wants and needs of the crew. For lunch before their departure, as an example, the crew were taken to an open-air bayside restaurant and fed fresh pineapples and mangoes, conch soup and a variety of some of the best local fish that could be had. Although the crew had not exactly starved on the trip – in fact, because of the British and the Pan American people in Leopoldville, had been fed rather decently on several of the stops – they had experienced nothing like the Caribbean feast they enjoyed that day in Port-of-Spain.

More than one member of the crew fancifully wondered if they could get out of going to New York at all. Just sit out the war in this island paradise.

Trinidad would be a fine place indeed to wait out the war. But at the same time, all wanted to get back and do what they could for the war effort. They were aviators and Americans first, Pan American employees second.

Nobody had any idea how they would be called on to serve their country, and during lunch they talked among themselves about that. At the end of lunch, the consensus seemed to be that Pan American employees, along with the aircraft, would probably be placed in the service of the military and used to ferry men and materiel to where they were needed in the Caribbean, South America and perhaps Europe and the Pacific.

In fact, Ford knew, from the secret orders he had received in New Zealand, that when they arrived at the La Guardia Marine Terminal, the now-Pacific Clipper would be delivered into the hands of the government of the United States, most likely the United States Navy. He assumed that the same would go for the crews, but of course he said nothing to the others about the orders. That would be up to Pan American, or maybe to the government itself.

It was four hours later in the day in Berlin – mid-afternoon – when at about the same time Rudi was falling instantly asleep in Buenos Aires, Major General Hans Oster knocked softly on Admiral Wilhelm Canaris' door in the Tirpitzufer and, without waiting for a reply, walked in and handed Rudi's message to Canaris. Oster stood in front of the Admiral's desk while Canaris read the message through twice, a broad smile brightening his face when he first noted the sender.

"Sit down, Hans, and let us decide what to do with young Herr von Althorp." Oster sat. Canaris continued, "I do not see any reason to send him back to Tokyo. We have someone else there, at least temporarily, and I do not want to get into a long explanation with von Ribbentrop about why I want to send him back after all this time. He thinks von Althorp was still in Mexico City, attending to his father, when that Embassy was evacuated."

Shortly after the evacuation, Canaris had called von Ribbentrop to tell him that the younger von Althorp had been sent by his father to El Salvador to meet with members of that country's small but wealthy German ex-patriot community a day or two before Pearl Harbor, so was not in Mexico when the evacuation was ordered. Canaris had told the Foreign Minister that he had dispatched young von Althorp to Buenos Aires because, with Mexico now a nominal enemy, Argentina had become Germany's most important priority in Central and South America.

He had further told von Ribbentrop that transportation was spotty and that it would likely take some time for the young man to get to Buenos Aires, but that he would certainly notify the Herr Foreign Minister when he reported in to the Commercial Attaché down there. Von Ribbentrop had shown little interest. In fact, he had muttered something about leaving him in Argentina for the time being, and had probably by now forgotten him entirely.

"I was thinking the same thing, Herr Admiral," Oster now replied. "Perhaps it would be wise to send a signal to Gerlach asking if he has any suggestions about anything he is currently working on to which von Althorp could contribute. At least until the Herr Admiral decides on his next permanent assignment."

"That is a good thought, Hans. Send him a signal to that effect. And we had better send one to von Althorp as well, under the circumstances, detaching him from his Tokyo duty and placing him under Gerlach's orders for the time being." He paused in thought.

Then he continued, "And, unless you see some reason why it would not be a good idea, why don't we tell von Althorp he may brief Herr Gerlach on his mission and how he came to be in his care, so to speak? Tell him to share the reason for his mission as well as the adventure. That should give Otto some idea of young von Althorp's abilities and initiative."

"I think that is advisable, Herr Admiral. The Herr Admiral chose him for an assignment as important as Argentina because Otto is one of our best men."

"Very true, Hans. In fact, it may be to our advantage in the years ahead for Gerlach and von Althorp to get to know one another. We both know Gerlach shares our limited enthusiasm for the current leadership of our beloved Germany, as does von Althorp. That makes them both members of a network within a network, does it not?"

"I agree completely, Herr Admiral."

"Please send the signals as soon as you can find the time, Hans. Oh, in your signal to von Althorp, please ask him to elaborate, if he can, about the 'problematic' passenger on the plane. I wonder what he meant by that."

"I wondered about that myself, Herr Admiral. I'll send the signals immediately. Is there anything else at the moment?"

"No, Hans, but keep thinking about what else we could do with von Althorp. I will do the same, and I will notify our esteemed Foreign Minister that von Althorp has arrived in Buenos Aires and that I would like to take his advice and leave him there for the time being to assist Gerlach on a number of important matters. It will be up to him to notify the Ambassador of the new posting."

Oster nodded, rose from his chair and walked out of the office, headed for the signals section.

CHAPTER 26

Port of Spain, Trinidad
January 5, 1942

After lunch, the crew of the Pacific Clipper was looking forward to setting off on what everybody fervently hoped was the last leg of their journey and what they all expected would be a glorious homecoming.

It had been a fine lunch, but the crew was ready to go and at 2:00 began to move their luggage aboard the aircraft. Randy Oakley and most of his people were there to help in any way they could.

Just before 3:00, the lines were cast off and Ford started the first engine. Soon all four engines were roaring and Ford turned to the southwest to start his takeoff run.

When the Pacific Clipper rose slowly from the water and was flying, the crew cheered. They could not hear the louder cheering from the dock, where the Pan American people had been joined by over a hundred locals to see the huge plane off on its flight home. The chance to view history in the making was a powerful draw.

Ford wheeled the airplane to the right and climbed to the northwest, heading for a point east of Bermuda. The engines sounded as good as they had the whole trip as Ford cut them back from takeoff power to climb power. The crew at Trinidad had obviously been thorough with their maintenance work. The replaced exhaust stack on the number one engine returned the engine sound to the mighty roar which had become so familiar to them. Nobody missed the loud rattling sound the absence of the stack had caused.

Ford had considered leaving the barrel of oil they had loaded aboard at Noumea with the Trinidad crew, but in the end decided to take it. Who knew what might happen? It was still a 2,400-mile trip. And although he was not a superstitious man, he had made it this far with that trusty barrel in reserve, so why not keep it aboard? Pan American could have it back when they got to LaGuardia. Or maybe the Navy will take it.

Brown called to Ford that his heading was perfect, that they would next overfly Ciudad Trujillo, a large city on the island of La Hispaniola, then bear due north to New York.

Just after 6:30, the sun set far to the west and Mack, who was then in the left seat, thought he might begin to see the lights of the coastal areas in the distance. But there were none. He could see small clusters of lights beyond the coastal areas, but none along the coast. He was surprised. No matter the sensibility of the black-out order, he had expected that some people, who considered themselves special in some way, would ignore it in their own interests.

Then his mind wandered to other possibilities. Was there German naval activity – either submarines or surface vessels – this close to the U.S. East Coast? Why not? It was one more complicating consideration in a complicated journey.

In the galley, Alex was helping Sawicki and Edwards prepare sandwiches for the crew. Sawicki had tried – three times – to tell Alex that they could handle it, but with nothing else to do Alex was bored and badly in need of anything to take his mind off the monotony. And, to take his mind off of what might happen once they arrived at LaGuardia. Like his confrontation with Donovan on the subject of Henry Carter.

After they delivered the sandwiches, Alex stayed up on the flight deck, as curious as the others to be looking out at where they imagined they could see American cities and towns that were keeping themselves in the dark. All those aboard had had enough of jungles and deserts, of endless oceans, of searching for rivers and being surprised by Japanese submarines and Brazilian fumigators.

They were looking out the west-facing windows on the left side, at home, and, dammit, it felt good, even if the only things they could really make out were the outline of the coast, when it was illuminated by moonlight, and a few smaller towns which were several miles inland.

The mighty roar of the engines continued smoothly.

CHAPTER 27

Buenos Aires, Argentina
January 5, 1942

When Commercial Attaché Otto Gerlach and his counterpart from the Reich's Tokyo Embassy, Rudolf von Althorp, walked into the hotel dining room at 7:45 a.m., they were shown to a secluded table in a rear corner.

Gerlach had suggested to Rudi – he had called him at the hotel the night before to tell him about the arrival of the signals from Berlin – they meet at the hotel for breakfast, at which time they could review the signals.

As soon as they had both read and re-read their signals, they exchanged them and each read the other's. Then Gerlach motioned to the waiter that they were ready to order their breakfast.

"So, Rudi, it would seem we are to be colleagues after all, for a while, anyway," Gerlach said. His smile was quite genuine. They were both sitting with their backs to walls, giving them a full view of the dining room and making sure that nobody was at tables close enough to them to overhear their conversation.

"Perhaps we should start with my filling you in on my mission in the Pacific and how I came to be here in Argentina," Rudi suggested.

Gerlach nodded. "I would indeed be fascinated to hear

about that, Rudi. But first let us have our breakfast, then by the time we get back to my office it will have been swept." He might have been talking about the cleaning crew, but Rudi knew what he really meant. They enjoyed a nice breakfast consisting of soft-boiled eggs and a platter of croissants, served with a very fine selection of jams, jellies, sausages and cheeses.

On the short drive to the Embassy, Gerlach told Rudi that the technicians, who were German ex-patriots in the employ of the Argentine Federal Police, came to sweep the Abwehr spaces at 8:30 each morning. And, of course, the technicians had been thoroughly vetted by the Admiral's people.

After the Abwehr spaces, the men swept the Ambassador's office. The Ambassador's office was swept second because the Ambassador was almost never in attendance before 10:00 a.m.

They got to Gerlach's office just as the two technicians were finishing their work. The larger of the two, who had known Gerlach since Otto had arrived in Buenos Aires, smiled broadly and indicated "clean" with a hand gesture. The technicians departed for the Ambassador's office and Otto and Rudi sat down on the same couch and chair they had used the day before.

Otto said they would have more coffee as soon as Fraulein Guderian arrived, which should be soon. Just as Rudi started to speak, there was a soft knock on the door. Gerlach opened the door to the smiling face of Ilse, who was holding the silver coffee service.

"Ah, fraulein, reading my mind, as always," Gerlach said.

"Guten morgen, Herr Gerlach, and to you too, Herr von Althorp" she said with a dazzling smile. "I heard voices in here, and thought it must be the two of you rather than the security gentlemen, and that coffee might be in order. And I brought you some rolls and butter in case you were still hungry after breakfast."

"What would I do without you?" Gerlach asked in reply.

Rudi had several thoughts about how he might have responded. He kept them to himself. He was intrigued at how Gerlach kept his conversations with Ilse so formal and assumed that, given his marital status, it was at least partly a defense mechanism. He would ask more about her when he and Gerlach had become closer, perhaps over a beer. Ilse left, closing the door softly behind her.

As they sipped their excellent coffee, Rudi told Gerlach his story, starting with his seeing the Nakajimas practicing south of Kure, Japan. So long ago! "As you may know, Admiral Canaris was completely opposed to any action by Germany or her allies that would provoke the United States into entering the war," he said, a questioning look on his face.

"I shared the Admiral's views on that, Rudi," Gerlach responded in affirmation. "I have been an admirer of the Admiral for many years, and share most, if not all, of his military and political views, at least as I know them. He personally recruited me into the Abwehr. And I know that your father, Ambassador von Althorp, and the Admiral are great personal friends of long standing."

Thus reassured, Rudi continued his story. He told Gerlach of his orders to take his warning to the Americans, of his friendship – which became a working partnership - with an officer in the U.S. Office of Naval Intelligence, of the unheeded warnings in Washington, of their efforts to alert the admirals at Pearl Harbor and their attempt to get to Australia. Gerlach's eyebrows rose higher with each bit of information.

Then Rudi recounted, in some detail, the saga of the California Clipper and its unlikely journey, including the

Japanese submarine that fired on them off Ceylon, the engine failure leaving Trincomalee, the harrowing takeoff and climb-out from Leopoldville and the almost around-the-clock flight across the Atlantic. He even told Gerlach about "that disgusting little Arab bastard" in Bahrain who was working for the Abwehr. Gerlach nodded sympathetically at Rudi's disgust with the Arab.

When Rudi finished his saga by recounting the story of the trans-Atlantic flight and his contact with Antonio in Natal, Brazil, Gerlach sat staring at him, certain that he had never heard a tale to rival that one. He fervently wished he might have the chance to meet the captain of that aircraft someday. But with the Reich at war with the United States, that chance seemed, at best, remote.

And he wondered how Rudi – or any of the others on the aircraft, including the captain - had come through the journey without losing his mind.

As he told the story, Rudi consistently referred to Alex Jordan as Frosch, explaining the way the ONI officer had acquired that code name. But something kept him from giving Gerlach Alex's real name, and he knew Otto understood.

All agents in this line of business "ran" their own "assets," and the key to protecting those assets was to keep their identities compartmentalized and shared with others only on a need to know basis, and at this point, Otto did not have the need to know. Gerlach admired Rudi for his discretion, and told him so.

Then Gerlach asked about Canaris' reference in his signal to the problematic passenger and Rudi told him about Henry Carter, about the man accusing him of being a "Kraut spy," of demanding and getting money and planning to settle in South America so he could avoid the American military draft. He could not have known, of course, that avoiding the American draft was only a cover for the real reason Carter had no wish to return to the United States.

Especially to New York.

"Do you believe this man is a threat to continue this blackmail?" Gerlach asked, even though he already had concluded in his own mind he was probably enough of a threat that he needed to be dealt with.

"I know and respect the Herr Admiral's feeling about assassinations," Rudi said, "but I believe this man is cunning and greedy but seems not overly intelligent, which I think is a dangerous combination. Therefore, I believe we must deal with him before he does us great harm. I believe that if word were to reach the Reich – the SS-SD or Gestapo in particular - that an Abwehr man was on that Pan American flight, it would cause the Herr Admiral no end of grief. And, of course, the threat of continuing extortion exists as long as he breathes." Gerlach admitted that he had to agree with Rudi's logic.

"Perhaps we should send a signal advising the Herr Admiral of the threat this man Carter represents and suggesting that our conclusion is that the first order of business for the both of us should be to deal with it," Gerlach said, then added, "If we can find him. After all, Brazil is a vast country."

"I think that is indeed our first priority, Otto. But I think we must be circumspect in how we word our message, given the Herr Admiral's aversion to assassination." He paused. Then he continued. "I think he will know what we have in mind, but we should spare him the internal conflict that personally sanctioning an assassination would present to him."

"You do, indeed, know the Herr Admiral well, Rudi. Perhaps we can draft a message now, here in the office. It might be easier than downstairs."

The knock on Gerlach's door came just as he had put a note pad in front of them at the table. Gerlach called out the command to enter and Fraulein Guderian cracked the door a foot, stuck her head in, and asked Gerlach if she could refresh their coffee or get them anything else before she went to lunch. Both Rudi and Otto were astonished to notice that it was almost 1:00.

"Thank you, Fraulein, but we have just been chatting about various things," Gerlach said. "I think we will go to lunch ourselves. Enjoy yourself and we will see you this afternoon."

When she closed the door, Gerlach said, "My God, where did the time go? Did I ask that many questions?"

"I did not think so, Otto. Perhaps I went into unnecessary detail."

"Nonsense. That was one of the most incredible stories I have ever heard. In fact, I would like to hear it again. But for now, what about having lunch? The food in Argentina, you will find, is quite good, and the beef, in particular, is excellent, but then again, so is the lamb and the pork."

"A fine idea. Now that food has been mentioned, I find myself quite hungry."

"But before we do that, let me call Herr Garcia and have him get his extensive network on the alert for an American newcomer in east-central Brazil who is using American currency. He is quite thorough, and his network includes immigration officials, bankers and others who might get some early sighting of this man. We will refer to the man simply as your friend. That is absurd, I know, but it is best if nobody overhears us talking about the man by name. Then, after lunch, we can compose our message to Berlin."

Rudi thought that was a splendid idea.

The weather was again very nice, and the two men walked to a steakhouse that adjoined Rudi's hotel. Gerlach told Rudi that it was a favorite of his because of its food and atmosphere, and its proximity made it even more appealing. When they were shown to a table in the bar area, Rudi was surprised that many of the conversations he could overhear, including Otto's dealings with the maitre'd, were in German rather than Spanish, or sometimes in an odd mixture of the two languages.

He was also quite surprised when he noticed Ilse Guderian at another table with a blond woman who was almost – but not quite – as striking as she.

Ilse, noticing them at the same time, waved. Rudi waved back, but, he noticed, Otto just nodded.

"Pardon me for saying this, because it is really none of my business, and if I am out of line, please say so," Rudi said after they had ordered wine, "but this restaurant seems a bit expensive for a secretary to afford." Otto chuckled.

"Rudi, I do not think you need worry about Fraulein Guderian being able to afford to dine in this or any other restaurant in Buenos Aires." Seeing Rudi's questioning look, he went on. "The fraulein's father is a very successful rancher. Beef, primarily, but he also raises sheep and swine. He has a very large estancia – that is what they call a ranch here – in the northwest part of the country. He also owns two slaughterhouses where the animals are processed, and a wholesale meat distributorship.

"So you see, he makes money at every step in the process. And he has an interest in several restaurants that serve only meat from his processing plants. This is one of those restaurants, so like I said, I do not think the fraulein will have a problem paying her luncheon bill. In fact, I very seriously doubt she will be presented with one."

"Fascinating," Rudi said quietly. "If she, I mean to say her family, has that kind of money, why is she working at the Embassy? I would think she would have no reason to work at all, but if she wants to work, why not in the family business?"

Otto took a sip of his wine and studied the menu for 15 seconds before responding. "She answered an advertisement we placed in the German-language newspaper here. That was about 18 months ago. My previous secretary had become pregnant and her husband did not want her to work any longer. In Argentina, a woman stays home with her children. It was just as well. She was quite attractive but not nearly as efficient as Ilse. Nor was she as devout a German patriot as is our Fraulein Guderian.

"So when Ilse came for an interview and I saw her family history, I asked her the same questions you have put to me. She is quite a patriot – German patriot, as well as Argentine – and wanted to 'do her part,' as she phrased it. She didn't even ask what the job paid. Of course, we performed a background and security check on her, as well as on her father and everyone else in her family. We could find nothing inconsistent in her story, and they all seem to be loyal to Germany."

The waiter appeared and took their orders, now in Spanish, then Otto went on in German. "She is obviously well-bred. In fact, I have met both her parents. Lovely people. And I checked her references and school records. She is what she appears to be. I am lucky to have her."

Rudi asked, "Is she not married? With her looks and money, I would have thought she would have been pursued by Argentina's finest."

Otto laughed. "So now we come to the real reason for your questions, do we not, Rudi? I saw the look on your face. I don't blame you, of course. Were I not happily married to another beautiful German woman, I might be intrigued myself.

"But, to answer your question, no, she is not married. She is almost 26 years old, which in Latin America is quite old for a young lady to still be unmarried. I asked her about that in one of my interviews with her. She told me that she is very much afraid that she intimidates men. She has, of course, had a number of suitors, some of which she thought might become serious, but in each case the man has broken it off. She is taller than most women, and for that matter many of the men, and combined with her looks and family wealth, I think she is correct in her assessment. She could be very intimidating, especially to Latin men."

Rudi decided that it was time to change the subject, lest Otto suspect that all he was interested in was Ilse. The entrees arrived. Otto was having a small t-bone steak and Rudi had ordered schnitzel. It had been a very long time since he had seen schnitzel on a menu, and he was looking forward to one of his favorite dishes.

After two bites, Rudi looked at Otto. "So tell me about your work in Argentina." The tables were far enough away from each other that it was entirely possible to have a private conversation without fear of being overheard, if one was discretely quiet. The louder hum from the patrons seated at, or standing at, the bar also helped to mask table conversations.

"I love it here, Rudi. I truly do. The Argentine people are very friendly and they have a long history of comradeship with Germany, but they also have a long history with the United States, England and France. My most important mission here is to do what I can to keep Argentina officially neutral in the war. Joining the Axis is just not possible, I am afraid. They are very fearful that their standing in South America would be compromised by joining the Axis.

"They also have many important trading relationships with the United States and since the Americans have entered the war, they feel they are better off neutral. But, of course, the Americans, the British and others, such as the Dutch, pressure them constantly to join the Allies. With Brazil already siding with the Allies, Germany simply cannot allow Argentina to follow."

"How is the Ambassador? Is he helpful to you?"

"Let me ask you a question before I answer. When you were in Tokyo, was the Ambassador there helpful to you in your work?"

"He tolerated me, but I think it was only because he knows my father. He was quite concerned when he heard my father was ill," Rudi confessed. "But he actually told me once that he was offended that he was ordered to house a 'goddamn spy' in his embassy when he could have used another 'good diplomat.'"

Otto laughed. "My Ambassador has not said such a thing to me, but his actions say it. He told me I was to 'stay clean' – his words – and do nothing that might embarrass him or the Reich's Foreign Ministry. I have asked the Admiral if he can do anything about getting someone more attuned to the importance of intelligence appointed Ambassador in a country as important as this.

"But I know that von Ribbentrop, the aristocratic bastard, is barely able to be civil to Canaris, so I don't see anything like that happening. However, the Ambassador at least does not try to interfere with me. He assigned me the suite of offices and basically told me to stay away from the rest of the Embassy and 'his' personnel. Of course, that is not possible without announcing to the world that I am Abwehr, but I do my best. He does not ask me what I am doing, and I only tell him what

I think he needs to know."

"Is it the same all over the world?" Rudi asked.

"Anywhere one of the damned career diplomats is the Ambassador, I fear," Otto said sadly. "Those bastards think sitting and talking nice with someone will make them play nice, but we have to do our work in spite of them. The best we can hope is that they do not try to sabotage what we are doing."

On that note, Otto paid the bill and they got up to walk back to the Embassy. Only then did Rudi notice that Ilse Guderian and her friend had already departed.

"How did you like the food, Herr von Althorp?" Ilse asked when they walked past her desk toward Otto's office.

"It was excellent, Fraulein Guderian," Rudi said with a smile. "And yours?"

"It is always good there. My father is one of the owners." The pride on her pretty face was evident.

"Yes, Herr Gerlach was telling me about that. And that he raises the beef – and the lamb and pork – that are served there, I believe."

"Indeed he does, Herr von Althorp. He will be pleased when I tell him you liked it," she said with a dazzling smile.

Rudi and Otto went into Otto's office and Otto closed the door. He told Rudi that he trusted the fraulein completely, that in fact she had a top secret security clearance. But, he said, he always kept the door closed because he didn't want the SS-SD or one of the diplomats, especially the Ambassador, to overhear anything or to walk in on a conversation.

The men set to work composing their message to Canaris. Thirty minutes later, they were satisfied with the message and both went downstairs in search of Dieter. The signals officer, as usual, was at his desk and took the message and read through

it. Then he encoded it in the Abwehr's unique code and sent
the message.

```
EYES ONLY - URGENT
THE DIRECTOR
ABWEHR HEADQUARTERS
TIRPITZUFER
BERLIN
UNDERSIGNED ACKNOWLEDGE AND
UNDERSTAND PREVIOUS MESSAGE RE
ASSIGNMENTS IN ARGENTINA STOP
UNDERSIGNED BELIEVE PASSENGER ON
FLIGHT PREVIOUSLY REFERRED QUOTE
PROBLEMATIC UNQUOTE PRESENTS POSSIBLE
SECURITY RISK STOP SUBJECT ALLOWED TO
CONTINUE ON FLIGHT BELIEVED ORDERS US
GOVERNMENT BUT BELIEVE SUBJECT TO BE
MERCENARY NOT UNITED STATES AGENT  STOP
SUBJECT OVERHEARD PARTS OF CONVERSATION
WITH FROSCH STOP CONCLUDED UNDERSIGNED
QUOTE KRAUT SPY UNQUOTE STOP DEMANDED
MONEY STOP BELIEVE REMAINED IN BRAZIL
WHEN AIRCRAFT DEPARTED STOP BELIEVE
INTENT TO STAY IN SOUTH AMERICA TO
ESCAPE US MILITARY SERVICE STOP ALSO
BELIEVE SUBJECT A THREAT TO SELL
INFORMATION OR DEMAND ADDITIONAL MONEY
STOP HAVE TAKEN STEPS TO ATTEMPT LOCATE
SUBJECT STOP RECOMMEND UNDERSIGNED BE
AUTHORIZED FIND ASSESS AND DEAL WITH
THREAT STOP BELIEVE TIME OF ESSENCE STOP
AWAITING INSTRUCTIONS STOP
```

O GERLACH
R VON ALTHORP
EMBASSY OF THE GERMAN REICH
BUENOS AIRES, ARGENTINA
END MESSAGE

Dieter handed Gerlach a sheet of paper confirming that the message had been transmitted. They returned to Gerlach's office and settled in to await responses, both from Garcia and from Canaris, and hoped both would arrive quickly. Time, they knew, really was of the essence, that the more time that passed, the less likely they would be to locate Carter.

But they suspected that Canaris would recognize that, too.

Over the next two hours, Otto briefed Rudi on his current activities. Not all of them could accurately be called operations, but it was clear to Rudi that the man had his ear to the ground and little would happen in Argentina that could be harmful to Germany that he would not know about.

Although it was over two years in the past, Rudi was quite interested in Gerlach's account of the saga surrounding the German pocket battleship, Graf Spee, which in 1939 had been chased by British hunters into the Port of Montevideo, just across the River Plate from Buenos Aires. It had suffered serious battle damage before it had sought refuge in that neutral port.

After it had been in port 72 hours, the international time limit for a man-of-war in a neutral port, it had been ordered by the Uruguayan authorities to depart, even though necessary repairs had not been completed. The Uruguayans had been under great pressure from England and other countries to strictly enforce the 72-hour limit and in the end did so.

The captain of the ship, Hans Langsdorff, had put all but 40 of the men ashore – most had already been ashore – and he and the 40 remaining aboard had sailed out to the mouth of the Plate and scuttled the ship.

An Argentine tug had picked up Langsdorff and the 40 others and took them to Buenos Aires. The rest of the crew, wounded and healthy alike, had also been transported from Montevideo to Buenos Aires, where they were still interred.

Langsdorff, facing disgrace at home, had shot himself so that his body had fallen on the ship's battle ensign. Gerlach, who at the time had been relatively new to Buenos Aires, had worked with the Ambassador to get the crew moved to Argentina, rather than being held in the pro-British Uruguay, by appealing to the Uruguayan – and British – senses of fair play. After all, he had argued, one of the first things Langsdorff had done when he had steamed into Montevideo had been to release several hundred British sailors and assorted merchant mariners – many of them from neutral countries – who the Graf Spee had rescued from ships it had sunk.

It was one of the most widely-known stories of the war, so far at least. Not as widely-known as the bombing of Pearl Harbor, but a story a lot of people had heard. Both men knew that before the war was over, there would be a lot more stories.

Two hours after sending their message, Ilse knocked softly on Gerlach's door, entered and announced that Dieter was outside with a message addressed to Herr Gerlach and Herr von Althorp. Gerlach sprang to his feet and waved Dieter into his office, where he took the sealed envelope, signed for it and thanked the signals man for bringing it up personally.

When they were again alone, Gerlach slit the envelope open with a sharp knife and unfolded the yellow paper.

```
MOST URGENT - EYES ONLY
O GERLACH
R VON ALTHORP
OFFICE OF COMMERCIAL ATTACHE'
EMBASSY OF THE GERMAN REICH
BUENOS AIRES
IN RECEIPT OF MESSAGE THIS DAY
STOP SUGGESTED ACTION AUTHORIZED STOP
WILL LEAVE DISPOSITION OF THREAT TO
YOUR JUDGMENT STOP ADVISE PROGRESS AS
APPROPRIATE STOP GOOD LUCK STOP
    CANARIS
    ABWEHR
    BERLIN
    END MESSAGE
```

Otto and Rudi smiled at each other. They had their mission, and it had the blessing of the Admiral himself. They both realized it was well into the dinner hour in Germany, so the Admiral had surely been summoned back to the Tirpitzufer for their message and had made his decision quickly. They also realized that they had been authorized to kill Carter – if they could find him – and that meant the Admiral had great respect for the judgment of both of them. But their mood was tempered by the fact that they still had to find the man.

In his office in Washington, D.C., Colonel William J. Donovan read the message from Pan American for the third time and was fascinated with the complexity of the almost-complete journey undertaken by this Boeing 314 and its crew. Always the realist, he had nonetheless hoped, of course, for the safe return of the plane – and of the men he had sent off to Hawaii months before - but he had been far from confident they could pull it off.

Now, it appeared they were about to do just that.

Donovan wondered whether Alex and Rudi had figured out Carter and his mission. In truth, Carter was a thug and he was glad he had never used his name with the man. He was just a representative of senior officials of the government, as far as Carter was concerned. But the threat in Carter's telegram from Australia – and his reference to President Roosevelt – still worried him. He reminded himself to refer to Rudi as Dick or Lieutenant (j.g.) Barnhardt when others were around.

Donovan pressed the intercom button on his telephone and asked his secretary to see if she could get Secretary of the Navy Frank Knox on the phone. Knox was an old friend, who may not have been on this State Department distribution list, but who surely had seen the signal traffic between the Royal Navy and the U.S. Navy during the course of the California Clipper's odyssey and would be interested. He also had a favor to ask of the Navy Secretary.

Knox was on the line in short order. Few in Washington failed to take Donovan's calls immediately, given his far-flung sources of information, not to mention his well-known White House access and influence.

Knox was delighted with the news and, as a matter of fact, had been sent the same advisory by the State Department. Secretary of State Cordell Hull felt that Pan American's human and aircraft assets could be of particular value to the Navy, and in fact the transitional steps needed to convert some of the airline's assets to Navy use had already begun to take place.

Donovan had no problem getting his favor from Knox.

Donovan then called the White House switchboard using

a special telephone on his desk that required him only to pick up the handset to be connected. As usual, the President came on the line almost immediately. He was also delighted to hear the news about the now-Pacific Clipper. He chuckled at the renaming. Knowing Trippe as he did, he had no doubt the man would milk all the publicity possible out of this improbable adventure.

In addition, Roosevelt had been following the story, when he was able, and saw the safe return of the plane after such a journey as a morale booster for the American people, who were not getting much in the way of good news about the war. In fact, at this early stage, almost none of the news was good. The President also asked Donovan how his people in England were doing in the of sharing information – both ways – with MI6, the British foreign intelligence apparatus.

Donovan assured him that all was well on that front and that COI and the British had a number of operations – some joint and some simply requiring coordination - in the planning stages in France, the Netherlands, Norway and the Balkans, among others. Franklin D. Roosevelt voiced his relief at that news.

While British Prime Minister Winston Churchill had assured President Roosevelt that he would instruct the appropriate parties in his government to cooperate fully with the Americans, both men also knew that the British had been at "this spy thing" for hundreds of years while the Americans were painfully new at it.

This can lead to a feeling of superiority on the part of the experienced party – the Brits – so Churchill had asked Roosevelt to keep him apprised of any problems that resulted from his order to work as partners with the Americans, now that they were officially in the war. Roosevelt was glad he would not have to report problems of that sort to Churchill. There were enough problems related to cooperation – or more precisely, lack thereof - being reported by the Army and the Navy.

CHAPTER 28

Embassy of the German Reich
Buenos Aires, Argentina
January 6, 1942

Rudolf von Althorp was awakened by the telephone in his hotel room just after 7:00. It was Otto Gerlach calling from the lobby asking if he could have a minute of his time. In Rudi's room, Gerlach reported that he had been called to a meeting in Montevideo with his man in Uruguay and two Chileans who were, as Gerlach described them, "assets."

He would be leaving on a ferry within the hour, and thought the men he was meeting would be put off by a stranger joining them. He assured Rudi he would return that evening and would fill him in the next day.

Meanwhile, he said, Garcia would report to Ilse Guderian if his people spotted anyone who might be Carter and he asked the fraulein to let Rudi know immediately so he could begin considering their options.

When Rudi expressed surprise that Gerlach had a man in Montevideo, Gerlach explained that since they were adjacent to Argentina, Admiral Canaris had assigned Uruguay and Chile to Gerlach's overall area of interest and that he – Gerlach - had specifically recruited the man, who was shown on the books, so to speak, as an Assistant Commercial Attaché in the Embassy of the German Reich in Uruguay. Of course, Gerlach had also developed assets in Chile from among the German-Chilean community, and two of those would be in Montevideo.

He told Rudi to go ahead to the Embassy when he was ready, that the fraulein would provide him with several files for Rudi to review. He closed by saying, "I know you are still tired – perhaps exhausted would be a better word – from your travels, so do not feel you must stay at the Embassy all day. Leave when you wish and we will see each other tomorrow. And if fraulein Guderian hears anything from Senor Garcia, she will notify you immediately."

Rudi was passed through the Embassy gate at 9:25.

He went directly to Gerlach's office and was welcomed warmly by Ilse Guderian, who was wearing a white blouse with frills on the button line and a straight black skirt with black high heels. The skirt clung like a second skin from her waist to her buttocks, and the blouse clung similarly to her bosom.

She retrieved her keys from her purse and unlocked Gerlach's door, and when Rudi was seated at the small conference table piled with files, she departed to get coffee. She told Rudi she would speak with Herr Gerlach as soon as he returned about getting a key to the office for his use, or even better, perhaps appropriating a nearby office so that Rudi could have his own work area.

After all, she told him, he was now officially a member of the Embassy staff. The Ambassador had sent a memorandum to that effect to all Embassy personnel. Her copy had arrived just before closing time the evening before.

As she walked out, Rudi noticed for the second time – the first having been climbing up the stairs from the signals section two days before – that the seams of her nylon stockings were perfectly straight lines running up the back of her legs and he wondered how she managed that.

He thought the legs were perfect, straight seam lines or not.

When Ilse returned ten minutes later, Rudi was studying a file on a potentially-troublesome German-Argentine, a well-to-do rancher from the northwest corner of the country, near the Paraguayan border. The man was a German patriot and was determined to do his part for the war effort and had developed elaborate plans to sabotage Allied – mostly British, but a few American – cargo vessels in the harbors of Buenos Aires and Montevideo. He had recruited a significant, if not substantial, network of German-Argentines and ethnic Argentines who were simply German sympathizers.

"Here is your coffee, Herr von Althorp," she said as she set the silver service on the coffee table.

"When we first met, you told me to call you Ilse if I wished to. I realize we must show a certain propriety when Herr Gerlach or other staff are around, but when it is just you and me, do you think you could call me Rudi? That is what my friends call me."

"How very nice of you," Ilse said, her smile radiant. "Of course. Rudi it will be."

"Thanks you. Now, Ilse, would you care to join me for a coffee?"

"I would be delighted, Rudi," her emphasis on his name only a slight mocking of his. She moved to close the door. "Perhaps I can help you with your research. Herr Gerlach has been quite generous with his trust in me and I have some knowledge of many of the files you have before you. It is better that others not be able to overhear our conversation in that case."

"Herr Gerlach told me that he always closes the door.

Thank you."

Ilse poured them both coffee and returned to the table. She sat quite deliberately and ladylike, then asked, "Which file have you been reading?" He turned the file to her and she said, "Ah, Senor Ausberger, yes, a very interesting matter, is it not?" Rudi noted that, even though they were speaking in German, when she referred to an Argentine citizen, she used the Spanish, "Senor," rather than the corresponding German term, "Herr," just as had Otto when referring to Senor Garcia. He filed that away.

"Fascinating," Rudi said. "A rich man, a German patriot who wishes to assist the Reich and poor Herr Gerlach must rein him in like an over-tired polo pony. But not so easy to do, is it? Those who are most consumed by a cause are usually those who are most difficult to control." Clearly but subtly, he was referring to Hitler and those who surrounded him, and watched carefully for Ilse's response.

"It is, indeed," she responded with a knowing smile that told Rudi that she got his meaning and did not disagree with it. "Herr Ausberger is a very stubborn man and is well known in the German-Argentine community. He and my father are friends, and I have been to his estancia a few times when I was younger. It is not far to the north from my father's estancia. In fact, he and my father have had something of a falling out over his activities. He tried to recruit my father to help finance what he wishes to do and my father would have none of it."

"That is good to know."

"My father is a good man, Rudi, and a realistic one. He knows that if Argentina is drawn into this war – on either side – our way of life is in peril. As you know, Argentina is in quite a strategic location, and my father feels that it would become a war zone as soon as it takes a side. I must say that, especially after working with Herr Gerlach for the last year and a half, I agree with my father."

"So do I, Ilse. There is little chance, I'm afraid, that Argentina would declare itself part of the Axis, and siding with the Allies would be devastating to the Argentines of German descent – and devastating as well to the Reich.

"And if it joined the Axis, as remote as that possibility might be, the Allies would surely try to destroy Buenos Aires to secure the Plate estuary. As you know better than I, Buenos Aires and Montevideo share what amounts to an enormous harbor from which either side could control the entire South Atlantic."

Rudi sipped his coffee and digested what Ilse had said, which was not only true, but was succinctly and thoughtfully stated. As taken as he was with her beauty, he increasingly realized she was an extremely intelligent and articulate woman. He wondered whether Otto Gerlach had plans to make her an analyst – even a field operative. She was too bright to remain "just" a secretary, but, then, it was quite possible that Otto, cunning devil that he seemed to be, was already using her, de facto, as an analyst.

She certainly had his full confidence as a confidential secretary and gatekeeper, and she seemed to be functioning as the Abwehr's second-in-command in Argentina.

They finished the Ausberger file and went through four more – none as interesting or potentially disastrous - and at 12:45, Ilse said, "Perhaps we should get some lunch. If you enjoyed the food at the restaurant as much as you said, we could walk there."

Rudi was immediately on his feet, helping with Ilse's chair. "You are so kind," she said when she was standing.

"Argentine men seem not to have the kind of manners with women that most European and American men have. But all of Latin America, of course, is quite a male-dominant culture." Rudi wondered how many European and American men Ilse had known, and how well. Was that a pang of jealousy? For what reason? I hardly know this woman!

A little more than ten minutes later, they were seated at a very private corner table by a very deferential host.

An equally attentive and deferential waiter – motivated, no doubt both by Ilse's looks and by the fact that her father owned part of the restaurant – brought menus and took their drink orders. Both ordered a local red wine, which Ilse recommended without the waiter's help. It was excellent.

The waiter checked back with them periodically, but it was over an hour – and two more glasses of wine each – before they broke from their conversation and realized with a start how long they had been there. They ordered, again based entirely on Ilse's recommendations.

They had spent the hour talking about growing up in Argentina and in Germany, and Rudi had told her a quick version – leaving out the part about him being on a mission to get Japanese intel into the hands of the Americans - of his having been on the California Clipper. She had been transfixed by the story, her eyes wide and staring.

Rudi knew he was in the early stages of intoxication and, mixed with an advanced stage of lust, fought the urge to inquire whether Ilse might be willing to spend the afternoon next door in his hotel room rather than back at the Embassy. This woman, he knew with certainty, was a well-bred beauty and he was equally certain that pushing too fast would be the worst thing he could do. And he still did not have any real idea of how long he was to be left in Argentina by the Admiral.

The waiter served their lunch but never reappeared with the check, and when they were finished, Ilse said, "If you are ready, Rudi?"

"What about the check?" Rudi asked.

Ilse laughed. "Please do not worry about that. They will send it to my father." She laughed again.

"I am afraid that I've had a bit more wine than I am used to."

"And I am sure you are still quite tired from your travels. Why do you not just take a nap and we can finish reviewing the files tomorrow?"

Rudi conceded that would be a very good idea.

"If anything comes in from Senor Garcia, I will call you at the hotel," she added as they rose from their seats.

He thought that was the second best suggestion she could have offered.

Otto Gerlach returned to Buenos Aires at 4:30 that afternoon, a bit earlier than he had expected and when he stopped at the Embassy, Ilse told him Rudi was at the hotel resting. She did not mention the wine, and Otto called the hotel.

Rudi answered the phone in his room on the first ring. He had napped for about ninety minutes and felt surprisingly refreshed. He readily agreed to meet Gerlach in the hotel bar at 7:30.

When Gerlach walked into the bar at 7:40, Rudi was surprised to find himself somewhat disappointed that he had not brought Ilse with him. Despite his desire to see Ilse, he knew he and Gerlach had much to discuss, and not in the company of Ilse Guderian or anyone else.

"How was your trip, Otto?" Rudi said, extending his hand.

"It was quite productive," he responded with a broad

smile. "Thank you for asking." They ordered German beer – Bitburger - at the bar, then took the bottles with them to a table in the corner. The Bitburger was served ice cold in the American fashion, Rudi noted with great satisfaction.

"Fraulein Guderian tells me we have received no word from Senor Garcia," Otto said. "I had hoped we could find your friend soon."

"Brazil is a very big country," Rudi said unnecessarily, "and it has some big cities. It may take time, I'm afraid."

"Yes, unfortunately. But have you been able to give the matter any thought?"

Rudi looked somber. "I have. I think our only alternative – assuming we can find him – is to simply make him disappear. I do not know who he was really working for, but I do not think he is a man who can be bargained with. Frosch and I paid him once, and I believe he will continue to demand payments of one sort of another as long as he thinks that what he has is valuable." He paused, thinking, before going on.

"He knows that I planned to leave the plane in Natal, as he did. He does not know what my plans were from Natal, but I do not think it would be a stretch for him to assume I came to Argentina. Frosch and I talked about Argentina during the conversation he partly overheard. And if he is convinced that I am, as he said, 'a kraut spy,' I think our Embassy would be the first place he would look."

Rudi paused, thinking, then added, "And if he cannot find me, or does not come to Argentina, he may simply go to another German embassy or consulate and try to sell them the story of a German operative on that Pan American flight. Or to the Americans, or even to the press. Any way he plays it, it will be disastrous for the Herr Admiral."

"I have had time to think the matter through as well," Otto

said quietly. "And I agree with your conclusions. All of them, in fact. The problem will be for my people – Senor Garcia's people to be exact – to establish a positive identification. So far, we are looking for an American who is new to the area and seems to have a lot of American currency. There is probably more than one person who fits that description in South America." He paused, his brow creased.

"We also know he is of medium height, stocky and is unremarkable in appearance," Otto went on thoughtfully. "But again, there is quite likely more than one man in South America who fits that description. Unfortunately, we do not have a photograph of the man."

"I agree on all counts," Rudi said. "How can Garcia's men positively identify him?"

Otto sat in silence and took a sip of his beer. "Have you ever been in the field, Rudi?" Rudi studied the man before answering.

"Not in the sense that I think you are meaning," he said cautiously. "Why?"

Otto laughed. "Rudi, I am not suggesting you be sent out to find Carter and deal with him. But perhaps the best way to approach this is to have you ready to go, when and if Garcia's people locate a suspect. After all, only you could make the positive identification. Then people who are trained in, let us say, the darker arts would do what it takes to remove the threat that he poses. To, as you say, make him disappear."

Rudi sat back, considering what Otto had said. In the end, he realized it was the only way to do the job and be certain. And some experience in the field – other than in offices and hotel rooms in Tokyo, Washington and Honolulu – would no doubt make him more rounded as an Abwehr agent. He told Otto this and the man nodded, smiling.

"Then that is how we will approach this," Otto said. "Now all we await is some word from Garcia."

They had another beer in the bar, then went into the dining room and had dinner. They talked about Rudi's time in Washington as a junior diplomat and Abwehr man, his time in Tokyo, and more about Otto's operations in Argentina. Rudi was quite interested in the dilemma posed by Max Ausberger and his group.

After dinner, Otto got in his car to be driven home and Rudi went up to his room.

The next morning, Rudi von Althorp and Otto Gerlach were discussing Max Ausberger and various approaches to thwart his over-zealous patriotism when Ilse Guderian knocked and entered the office rather hastily.

"Herr Gerlach, I have Senor Garcia on the telephone," she said. "He wishes to speak with you." Gerlach sprung to his feet, heading for his desk.

"Thank you, fraulein. Please put him through."

The telephone on Gerlach's desk buzzed and he snatched up the receiver. "Senor Garcia," he said in Spanish. "Do you have news for me?"

"I may have good news for you, Senor Gerlach," Garcia responded, also in Spanish. Rudi found that interesting. He had seen them conversing in German at Jorge Newbery Airport and knew they both spoke English as well. Perhaps it was an effort to stay as fluent as possible in all three languages, or perhaps Gerlach did not remember that Rudi was fluent in Spanish and was, for whatever reason, trying to keep the conversation with Garcia private.

"One of my men has seen a man matching the description you gave me," Garcia said to Gerlach. "He is in a small hotel in a small village just north of Recife. That is the first large city south of Natal. My man checked with the hotel and this man checked in only yesterday and paid with United States currency.

"He had travelled from the north, and told the hotel desk clerk that the driver of a small jitney bus service had recommended the place. He said the driver had told him that by mentioning the bus company he would receive a discount. He paid for one month in advance. In that hotel, he receives a further discount from the daily rate by doing that."

"That sounds promising indeed," Gerlach responded. "Can your man keep an eye on the gentleman for a day or two while I organize things at this end?"

"We are at your service, Senor Gerlach," Garcia said. "I will, of course, keep you advised. If the gentleman appears to be leaving the area, do you wish for my man to detain him?"

"No, Jorge, until we positively identify him just stay with him and keep me advised as to where he goes."

"Muy bien. It will be done." Gerlach hung up and filled Rudi in on the conversation, making it clear that his use of Spanish was apparently not for the purpose of keeping Rudi in the dark. He suggested that Rudi go back to the hotel and prepare to depart, possibly the next day. Gerlach, meanwhile would arrange for an airplane and get together with Garcia to work out the plan to be put in motion once Rudi could provide the positive identification.

Rudi walked out of Gerlach's office, barely pausing at Ilse's desk to say goodbye. His mind was racing. Ilse watched him walk out of the office, a smile curling the corners of her mouth.

Rudi had purchased a small canvas valise at a shop in the hotel before going up to his room, and now it was packed. He had also picked up an extra razor, comb, toothbrush and other toiletries. He did not want it to appear to the maids or other hotel staff that he had left the room. He would keep the room and if anyone at the front desk inquired about the unused bed when he got back – unlikely, he thought, but better to be prepared – he would look embarrassed and say he'd had the opportunity to spend the night, or nights, with a woman he had met. Any Argentine male would understand – and admire – that.

More likely, they would call the Embassy and Ilse would tell them that Senor von Althorp was on a short business trip and did, indeed, wish to keep the room.

At 8:30 that evening, the phone in Rudi's room rang. It was Otto, asking if it would be convenient to meet him and Jorge Garcia at a small tavern two blocks south of the hotel. They were already there, so the sooner, the better.

Rudi had no trouble finding the place and walked into it nine minutes after replacing the receiver. Gerlach and Garcia were standing alone at the far end of the bar, nothing but wall behind and to the side of them. The tavern had no tables, chairs or barstools. It was simply a long, narrow space with just the long bar at which patrons stood.

There were only two other patrons and they were near the entry and far out of earshot of the two men Rudi was meeting. Still, Rudi wondered about the wisdom of talking in a tavern. He assumed they were here to talk about the Carter matter. He asked Gerlach about that. Gerlach laughed.

"Rudi, our friend, Jorge here, owns this place and it is probably safer than speaking in your hotel room or in my office," he said. "And his bartender, Guillermo there, knows to keep his distance when Jorge gives him a certain signal. Is that not right, Jorge?" Still, Rudi noticed, they were now speaking in English, rather than Spanish. Undoubtedly an additional precaution, he assumed.

"It is so," Garcia answered. "Guillermo knows that when I come here with others, especially with my friend, Otto, I do not wish to be disturbed except when we need a drink. Guillermo is a friend as well as an employee, and he is quite discrete. He will keep those two occupied and out of our hair." He nodded toward the two men at the other end of the bar, who were talking loudly with Guillermo in Spanish.

"So let us get to our business," Otto said, still in English. He turned to Rudi. "Jorge has arranged for your old friend, Santos, to meet the two of you at Jose Newbery tomorrow afternoon at 2:00. He will fly you to a small airport just north and west of Recife, where you will be met by two of Jorge's best men in Brazil."

Rudi stared at Garcia. "You are quite efficient, Senor Garcia."

"Please, among friends I am called Jorge," he responded.

"Excuse me, Jorge," Rudi said with a smile.

Gerlach was nursing a schnapps, but Garcia and Rudi were drinking a good Argentine beer from the bottle. Neither relished the idea of a hangover the next day. It would be another long flight in the Twin Beech. Probably almost the same, time-wise, as the flight from Natal.

"Here is my basic plan," Garcia said after checking again that no other customers had entered the tavern. "We will be driven from the airfield to the vicinity of the hotel where this man is registered. We should arrive there early in the morning, the day after tomorrow. I am told that, so far, he has stayed close to the hotel, but found a local bar less than two blocks from the hotel and seemed to enjoy passing his afternoon – and part of his evening – there. We think he may become attached to the place, one reason being that there are not that many other places in the town to choose from.

"He took his meals there as well on the day he arrived in the town. So we will go and wait until you can get a good look at him, to see if he is your friend. My men will have some items of disguise – a stick-on mustache, hair coloring, a floppy wide-brimmed hat, that kind of thing – for you to wear if it becomes necessary to go into the bar or the hotel to get a good look at him.

"Once you are certain that this man is your friend, we will drive back to the airfield and be flown back here. My people will handle matters from that point."

"What do you think, Rudi?" Gerlach asked.

"What do you mean by 'handle matters,' Jorge?" Rudi asked.

Gerlach answered for Garcia. "Rudi, to my way of thinking, you and I are better off having no direct knowledge of those 'matters,' if you know what I mean. Our only concern is that your friend be unable to cause any harm to us or to the Reich. That he simply disappear, as you so eloquently phrased it."

"You are quite right, of course, Otto. I fear my naiveté is once again showing."

"And, Rudi," Garcia put in, "another point I would make in that regard is that the fewer people with direct knowledge of a matter such as this, the safer my men are."

"Another excellent point, Jorge," Rudi said.

CHAPTER 29

LaGuardia Marine Terminal
New York City
January 6, 1942

As they passed what they were sure was Philadelphia on their left, the crew of the Pacific Clipper could see the faint outline of New York City and Long Island through the moonlight on the horizon, and in the east they saw the first faint glow of the approaching dawn.

For a moment, even the always steady Captain Robert Ford thought he was hallucinating. It had been a long ordeal, there had been so many places and circumstances where something could have gone tragically wrong. It had been such a mental and physical strain.

It was hard to believe that now, thirty days after it had started, they could actually see their destination. He called back to Jack Poindexter and told him to turn on the radio. The crew exhaled as one, and Poindexter grinned widely.

Just before six o'clock, the Pacific Clipper roared toward the southern shore of Long Island and before he began his bank to the left to line up over Long Island Sound for the East River landing area, Ford keyed his radio and made the call he had dreamed of for so long.

"LaGuardia approach control," he said in a remarkably

even tone. "This is the Pan American Pacific Clipper, inbound from Auckland, New Zealand. Request approach and landing at Pan American Marine Terminal. Estimate five minutes your station." The entire flight deck crew smiled but showed little other emotion. They still had work to do.

The response was immediate.

"Pacific Clipper, LaGuardia approach. Sorry to report that no marine landings are permitted until sunrise. You are clear to circle the field at 5,000 feet."

"LaGuardia, Pacific Clipper. Do you have an estimate for us?"

"Estimate five-five minutes from now, Clipper."

"Copy. Pacific Clipper is holding overhead for five-five minutes."

Ford descended to 5,000 feet and put the Pacific Clipper into a racetrack-shaped holding pattern.

Every man on the crew was frustrated. After all the takeoffs and landings they had made in total darkness on this trip, a landing in the waters of the LaGuardia Marine Terminal, with the pre-dawn glow and some ambient light from surrounding buildings, would have been a piece of cake. But every man on the crew was equally determined not to let his frustration show. They would take it like professionals and show Pan American in its best possible light.

Sawicki and Edwards, knowing the hoopla that awaited them when they landed, made fried egg sandwiches for the crew as they waited. Who knew when they would have their next chance to eat? The bread and eggs they had taken aboard in Trinidad were fresh.

Finally, at 6:45, LaGuardia approach control came on the radio with instructions to break out of their holding pattern and turn for the Marine Terminal. Just before seven o'clock, Ford splashed the Pacific Clipper perfectly onto the water and when he had bled off enough speed, turned for the docking buoy.

Pan American ground crewmen, who had been alerted by LaGuardia Approach Control fifty minutes earlier, immediately moved the launches from the dock to the aircraft, and one man jumped aboard as soon as the cabin door opened.

He was carrying a small bundle which anyone watching from shore would have assumed was cleaning supplies.

After identifying Alex, he handed him the package. Inside was a set of Pan American overalls identical to the ones the ground crewmen were wearing. He told them a Mr. Donovan wished him to put them on and did not wish to publicize his having been on the flight from the beginning. Ford had briefed Pan American from Trinidad on the fact that Mr. Barnhardt had been reassigned by the Navy in Brazil and that Mr. Carter had missed the flight. Donovan had been made aware of that by Trippe the night before.

Thus, when Alex got off the plane, he was helping to offload the crew's luggage, along with several other similarly-dressed and anonymous men. But before he got off the plane, Alex made the rounds of the crew, shaking each man's hand and thanking them for allowing him to tag along with them.

In the last thirty days, they had become friends and he would miss them. They all wished him well in the war and when he stepped off with the luggage, he wondered if he would ever see any of them again.

As expected, Juan Trippe and a delegation of Pan American personnel were at the terminal to meet the crew. Trippe was beaming but continuously whispered instructions and suggestions to the press relations aide who was with him.

A horde of reporters, photographers and radio correspondents waited impatiently behind a rope.

Eventually, the press would be given a more close-up look at the Pacific Clipper but first they would hear Juan Trippe introduce Captain Ford and tell them about the enormity of the journey from which this plane and this crew had just returned.

When the crew arrived on the dock and lined up behind him, as instructed by the handlers, Trippe stepped to a bank of microphones, one of which was hooked to a make-shift set of speakers so that the press and the crowd of onlookers who had gathered could hear.

"Ladies and gentlemen," Trippe said. "My name is Juan Trippe, and it is my honor to serve as President of Pan American Airways, the greatest air transportation company on earth.

"I am proud to stand before you to welcome home the Pacific Clipper and its heroic crew. This aircraft was in the air, bound from Noumea, New Caledonia, to Auckland, New Zealand, about to complete its scheduled flight from San Francisco, when Pearl Harbor was attacked. With no way to return to its base in California, we had no choice but to send it westbound, virtually around the world. Before I say anything more, I would like to introduce the commander of the Pacific Clipper, Captain Robert Ford, and ask him to introduce his crew. Captain Ford?"

Trippe stepped aside and Ford stepped to the microphones. He introduced himself, and then one by one introduced each member of the crew and described his primary role on the aircraft. Ford stepped back to a loud round of applause and Trippe again stepped to the microphones.

"Pan American will have more details about the specifics of the flight of the Pacific Clipper," he said, "after our operations people are able to talk with Captain Ford and his crew. We will do that as soon as possible and should have additional details for you later today or tomorrow at the latest.

"For now, let me give you a few facts that we already know about the flight. And to be clear, here I am talking about the entire flight, from San Francisco all the way to New York. First, it was the first-ever around-the-world flight by a commercial airliner.

"Second, Captain Ford and his crew crossed the Equator four times and were on all but two of the seven continents on our planet.

"Third, our staff estimates – and we will pin this down more precisely as we talk with the crew – that the Pacific Clipper flew more than 31,000 miles in something just over 200 flight hours.

"Fourth, we estimate they made 18 stops and visited 12 different nations, plus a number of territories. Again, we will be more precise about this as soon as we can.

"And fifth, by our current estimates, the Pacific Clipper completed the longest single non-stop flight in our company's history when it crossed the Atlantic from the Belgian Congo to Brazil. We estimate that leg was at least 3,500 miles."

Trippe stopped, allowing the reporters to catch up in their note-taking.

"Thank you for coming out today, ladies and gentlemen," Trippe began his wrap-up. "I am going to let these men get some well-deserved rest and then we'll be working with them to reconstruct the details of the flight, and we will let you in on those details when we have them."

Trippe and the crew walked to the terminal building, where Pan American had a large passenger lounge and where they would eat and wait until the crowd dispersed before going into Manhattan, where hotel rooms awaited.

The public relations types stayed with the reporters until they got a signal from the maintenance staff that the Pacific Clipper had been cleaned so the reporters could get a close-up view of the aircraft. However, the reporters were told, no photographs would be permitted of the aircraft's interior, nor would they be able to describe details of the interior, for reasons of national security.

Outside the terminal, where the ground crewmen were stacking the crew's luggage, Alex was startled to see Colonel William J. Donovan, the Coordinator of Information, walking toward him. He asked Alex if they might have a private word. Donovan gestured toward a doorway labeled "Administration," behind which, Alex assumed, were the offices of the management of the LaGuardia Marine Terminal. Inside, Donovan led Alex to another door on which was stenciled, "Conference." There was another man in the room, his back to him, looking out the far window.

The man turned around and smiled and Alex felt his knees get rubbery. He almost collapsed, so great was the shock.

Lieutenant Commander Wallace Hammond of the Office of Naval Intelligence smiled at him. He was not in uniform. Hammond walked quickly around the table and extended his hand to Alex, grinning broadly.

"You look like you've seen a ghost, Alex."

"I thought you were dead," Alex blurted as he shook Hammond's hand vigorously.

"Appearances can be deceiving, can't they?"

Donovan sat down at the table and gestured for Alex and Hammond to do the same. "Perhaps I can clear the air a bit," he said. "For a variety of reasons, I thought that staging Wally's death was the best way to make him disappear suddenly from ONI, and to impress on you the sensitivity of what your mission was. We have cleared that up with ONI – we arranged for the Washington police to later discover the true identity of the body that was discovered, a transient who had died from natural causes – and at some point in the future, Wally will be free to resume his Navy career."

"Why did he need to disappear from ONI?" Alex asked.

"Because I wanted him for COI," Donovan responded simply. "I was impressed with him when the two of you first came to see me. And I must say that I was right. He has been a great addition to my office. And now, I would like to know what happened to the two other gentlemen who were on the flight with you."

Alex told them about the Abwehr contact with Rudi in Bahrain and the plan Canaris had apparently put in motion to pick up Rudi on the Brazil stop and take him to Argentina. At least, he thought it was Argentina, he hedged, still not certain of Donovan's agenda. He told Donovan how he had explained "Dick Barnhardt's" disappearance to Captain Ford and the crew in Natal.

"And you did nothing to stop him from leaving?" Donovan asked with an arched eyebrow.

"I did not," Alex said firmly. "For several reasons. Rudi is a German and, although he is not a Nazi, would have no part of being a deserter or a traitor. He and I talked at length about that, many times. He wanted to return to work for Canaris, for whom he has the utmost respect, as well as a lot of family history.

"Also, I was afraid that if we kept him with us – with or without his consent – you would determine you had no choice but to imprison him until the end of the war, because the risk of his mission being exposed would be too great. And if it got out, it would cause great embarrassment to you, not to mention that Hitler would inevitably hear of it and probably kill Canaris. At the least, he would imprison him.

"And maybe I'm out of my league here, but I thought having a friend in the Abwehr might prove helpful to us later in the war."

"And Henry Carter?" Donovan asked. His face had not changed expression.

"That miserable son of a bitch overheard Rudi and me talking on the leg from Africa to Brazil and accused Rudi of being a 'kraut spy' – those were his words – and shook us down for money so he could get off the plane in Brazil. He wanted to stay down there because he thought he'd get drafted if he came back here." He paused and pointed an accusatory finger at Donovan.

"He was working for you, wasn't he? How could you use someone like that?"

"Unfortunately," Donovan said with a perfectly neutral voice, "in my line of work, 'someone like that' sometimes have their uses. His use, in this case, was nothing more than to watch your back in Hawaii. I knew neither of you were trained field agents and I wanted to make sure that you didn't run into anything you couldn't handle in Hawaii. I arranged for him to join you on the plane to New Zealand because I had no idea what you were doing or where you were going. I thought you might try to go to Manila, but I could not imagine why you were going to New Zealand. Then, when Pearl Harbor was attacked, I asked Pan American to bring him back with you. That, I now realize, was a mistake. But an honest one, and I really hope you believe that."

"I guess it really doesn't make much of a difference, one way or the other, whether I believe you or not, does it?"

Alex was clearly tired and feeling it.

"Oh, but there you're wrong, Alex, very wrong," Donovan said. "It will complicate our working relationship greatly if you do not believe the things I tell you." He reached into his inside coat pocket and produced an envelope. "Please read this."

Alex tore open the envelope and extracted the single page. It was from the Department of the Navy, detaching Lieutenant Alex Jordan from the Office of Naval Intelligence and assigning him on Temporary Duty to the Coordinator of Information, such duty to be until further notice.

It was the favor Secretary of the Navy Frank Knox had promised Donovan.

"Welcome aboard, Alex," Wally Hammond said as he extended his hand again to Alex. Alex was stunned. What would that do to his naval career? Like all Annapolis graduates, he longed for a command at sea, and hopefully a flag rank before he retired. Would this assignment while the world was at war, when promotions often came fast and furious, derail his chances at a future command? Almost certainly!

But down deep, he could feel the excitement already building.

Donovan excused himself. He would spend the night at his New York home. Alex and Wally Hammond had reservations, courtesy of COI, at the Plaza Hotel in Manhattan that night and would join Donovan on the train to Washington the next morning.

As soon as he walked into his room in the Plaza that afternoon, Alex picked up the telephone and asked the hotel operator to put in a call, person-to-person, to Ann Lassiter in San Francisco.

EPILOGUE

North of Recife, Brazil
January 8, 1942

Rudolf von Althorp and Jorge Garcia sat in a beat-up car of indeterminate manufacture across the street and half a block from a small hotel that would, in most of the cities of the world, be condemned as an eyesore. Or, at best, it would have been nothing more than a place that provided sagging beds on which low-priced prostitutes could ply their trade. Of course, this village would hardly fit anyone's definition of a city.

They had been there since early that morning and both were quite bored, as well as very tired from the all-night flight. Rudi was having trouble keeping his eyes open, while Jorge, who had accompanied him from Argentina, seemed unfazed. At 2:30, he nudged Rudi in the arm and pointed. A stocky man of medium height had emerged from the hotel, squinting against the bright sunlight.

"That could be him," Rudi said. "I just can't tell for sure with the sun in my eyes."

Jorge waited until the man had turned to his left, toward the bar he was reported to frequent, and started the engine. It coughed to life, billowing smoke. Rudi put the floppy-brimmed hat on his head as they started forward. When they passed the man, Rudi clearly saw that it was Henry Carter. There was no doubt. The bastard's image was embedded in Rudi's brain for all time. As soon as he had confirmed this, Jorge accelerated and turned right.

A few minutes later, on the road out of town, Jorge pulled to the side of the road, behind another car. In it, Antonio, who had met Rudi in Natal, Brazil, and taken him to Santos and the flight to Argentina, waited. Jorge told Antonio that Rudi had identified their man, then returned to his car and drove on, toward the airfield and their return flight to Jorge Newbery Airport in Buenos Aires.

On the drive, Jorge and Rudi marveled at their luck, first that Jorge's men had spotted Carter so soon and second that Rudi had been able to verify his identity the first day they were in town. Jorge said that was because Carter was stupid. He had made three mistakes. He had stopped in too small a town, he had stopped too soon and he had quickly developed a routine which was predictable.

"If he had just gone on to Recife, we may never have found him," Jorge said. "But in Recife, everything would cost him more. He would have been even smarter to go farther south. He was trying to save his money. That was his biggest mistake. He won't need the money now."

"Why didn't he go inland?" Rudi asked. "In the interior of Brazil he would have easily gotten lost, would he not?"

"He had to stay to the coastal areas," Jorge said matter-of-factly. "The tourists and foreign business people are mostly concentrated on the coast. In the interior, the people are natives, most still tribal, and he would have stood out too much. Not to mention that he would have been robbed, probably killed, by the natives." Rudi wondered how Carter would have known that. Maybe he's not as stupid as we think he is. Maybe he had been thinking of fleeing the United States even before this all started. Maybe he had already checked out Brazil and the flight just gave him an earlier opportunity than he had been planning.

The next afternoon, Henry Carter sat at the nearly-empty bar and was on his third beer when a woman walked in and sat down at the bar three stools from him. She was tall and very attractive, with the shiny black hair so common in South America. Carter congratulated himself on his decision to get off the plane. The broads in this country beat the shit out of the ones in New York, he thought to himself.

He envisioned Emily in Hawaii and felt a stirring. She had shiny black hair, too. He had really liked that Jap. Maybe, he thought, after things settled down, or maybe after the war, he would try to get back to Hawaii and look her up. He heard a voice in the back of his consciousness and realized the black-haired woman was talking to him. He did not know what she was saying.

"English?" he asked.

"Un poco," she said. "A little." She pronounced the word, "leetle." She was holding a cigarette in her left hand. It was not lit.

"You need a light?" Carter asked as he pulled his Zippo out of his pocket.

She smiled and nodded. "Si, gracias," she said. "Thank you."

The woman leaned toward him as he extended the light. He moved over two stools to he could reach her. When her cigarette was lit, he moved his beer and his own pack of cigarettes down to where he was now sitting. He was still one stool away from her, but he did not want to appear too forward. He figured if he played this fish right, he would sure as hell get her in the sack.

He lit a cigarette of his own. She had ordered what looked like some exotic local drink. Carter ordered another beer, and the bartender winked at him when he delivered it, collecting the equivalent of less than five cents.

Carter had gone to the only bank in town and gotten a fistful of Brazilian currency for $200 in U.S. dollars, which the banker had seemed quite excited to get. The banker, whose English was passable, had given him a small card with exchange rate equivalencies, and Carter had been very pleased with what he quickly computed to be his cost of living here. He had told the banker he was in the village because he heard the fishing was good and the cost of living was cheap. The banker had welcomed him to the village and told him he was always welcome at the bank if he had any more U.S. currency to change. Then the banker had called Jorge Garcia's man in Recife.

"Americano?" the woman asked in her broken, barely passable English.

"Yeah. I'm on vacation. You? You from around here?"

She didn't seem to understand at first, then caught on. "No. I live Recife. But born here. Come to see mama. Why you pick this place?"

"A friend told me about it. It's quiet, peaceful."

She looked perplexed, like she was trying to digest what he had said. Then she smiled. She really was a good-looking dame, Carter noted.

They made what passed for conversation for another half hour, while she finished her second drink.

"You go down to water?" she asked. "You know, beach? Muy, uh, peaceful? You like this?"

"No, I haven't been to the water," he said. "It's nice?"

She paused, translating in her mind, then smiled

and nodded. "Si, muy, uh, nice." She watched him for a few heartbeats, then asked, "You want go see? The water?"

Carter told her he thought that was a fine idea, but unfortunately he did not have a car.

"We walk. Is close," she said in a tone that was at once shy and bold.

She produced an old thermos bottle from the bag she had been carrying when she came into the bar and asked the bartender in a mixture of Spanish and Portuguese to mix her enough of her drink to fill it up. Carter asked for six bottles of beer and a bottle opener. He was charged the equivalent of 80 cents for his beers, the opener and her full thermos. He was growing to love this place.

He had given little thought to what he would do when the $6,700 ran out. He figured he could last three or four years on that much money, anyway, especially combined with the $2,000 or so he still had left from "Oscar's" money.

And he had the dough in the bank in New York he could send for if he needed to. Then again, maybe he would make his way to Argentina – he had heard that Kraut spy talking about going there – and tell the bastard he wanted some more money. If he could find him down there, and he was betting he could if he decided to.

As soon as Carter and the woman walked out of the bar and toward the beach, such as it was, two men slipped into the old hotel and up to Henry Carter's room, which was easy to open. There, they quickly accessed his suitcase and extracted a substantial sum of money – they did not stop to count it - and a mysterious envelope they found at the bottom.

Eight minutes later, after walking down a dusty dirt road Carter and the woman came to an outcropping above a small cove that looked absolutely deserted.

Carter was feeling very good about what lay ahead this afternoon.

The woman took a thin blanket from her bag and spread it carefully on the beach, which was only a few yards wide but, because it was a very narrow and protected cove, got little wave action. They had both taken off their shoes and Carter ventured down to the water, which he found too cold for his taste even though it was summer and the air was quite warm.

He walked back to where the woman had sat on the blanket.

They sat together and sipped their drinks and smoked and admired the view out to sea. She seemed to get a little more comfortable with English as they talked. Carter had never been one for small talk and was having more trouble than the Brazilian woman in keeping up with the conversation. By the time he had finished the second of his six beers, Carter could think of no new questions to ask or subjects to raise.

But she was a toucher and often laid her hand lightly on Carter's arm – and once or twice brushed his leg – as she talked. At each touch, a jolt of electricity passed through him and he found it more difficult to focus on what she was saying, or what he should say in response.

Soon, the light began to fade as the sun dipped behind the mountains at their backs. Finally, overcome with attraction and beer, Carter leaned over to her and kissed her on the lips. Somewhat to his surprise, she did not immediately pull away. Her blouse was very thin, white, typical summer attire for Brazilian women and Carter could see plenty of cleavage. He wanted more.

He lay back and tried to pull her down with him.

The woman reached a hand into her bag, which was lying next to her, and when it came back up into his sight, Carter got a different kind of jolt. She was holding a small revolver. His practiced eye immediately identified it as a .38 Colt, or maybe a South American copy of one. He instinctively twisted his arm behind his back, frantic to get his own pistol in his hand.

It was to be his last conscious thought.

She pulled the trigger and a hole appeared neatly in Henry Carter's forehead. The back of his skull and much of his brain was now splattered over the blanket, his eyes wide in an eternal stare of shocked disbelief, his arm still twisted uselessly behind his back. The woman quickly began rolling up Henry Carter's body in the blanket.

Two men appeared, signaled by the sound of the shot. They picked up the blanket encasing Carter's body and carried it around a large rock, behind which they had secreted a small boat with a 75 horsepower outboard motor.

In the boat were two old anchors attached to lengths of a heavy chain. They wrapped the body inside the blanket with the lengths of chain and secured them both with stout wire.

The woman handed one man her gun. In turn, he handed her a bag full of money and an envelope, mysteriously marked OPEN ONLY WHEN INSTRUCTED.

The two men pushed the boat, with its cargo, away from the beach and one pulled on the cord and the outboard motor started immediately. They headed out to sea at high speed. Two miles out, they throttled back and sent Henry Carter to the bottom of the Atlantic Ocean. The woman's revolver followed his body to the bottom.

On the beach, Ilse Guderian tossed her bag, which now contained a smaller bag of money and the mysterious envelope, into a waiting car. Once she jumped into the front seat, the car turned in the direction of the airport in Recife and her commercial flight back to Buenos Aires.

Authors' Note

This is a work of fiction, but a central theme of the book, the flight of the California/Pacific Clipper, is real and was one of least-known but most compelling stories in the early days of the United States' involvement in World War II.

Captain Robert Ford was real and was the pilot on that historic flight. Likewise, we have used the real names, and, as far as we know, the real duties aboard the aircraft, of Mack, Brown, Rothe, Parrish, Poindexter, Sawicki and the rest of the crew. They were true heroes and their story has been too seldom told and too little heard.

We follow the actual route of the flight as we know it, although we took a few liberties with some of the details for the sake of the story. On the real flight, there were no passengers, other than the Pan American mechanics who were being ferried to Karachi and Bahrain, once they off-loaded the Noumea personnel in Gladstone, Australia. There was no Mormon couple. Many of the flight details actually occurred: staying in a former whorehouse in Darwin, the minefield at Surabaya, the Japanese submarine off Ceylon, the engine problem in Ceylon, the rapids in Leopoldville, the thieving fumigators in Natal, the delayed landing in New York and others.

Some details of the flight are either unknown or subject to dispute. In cases where details are disputed from one account to another, we have chosen to use as the basis of our timeline, as well as the names and duties of the crew members, Ed Dover's well-done 1999 book, The Long Way Home, which was based on interviews with Captain Ford and the radio technician they picked up in Noumea, Eugene Leach. Leach provided him a copy of the actual flight log, which was maintained by Fourth Officer John D. Steers. We also use Mr. Dover's book as our source in quoting from Pan American's Plan A, the instructions Ford opens in case of hostilities.

The Japanese man the fictional Henry Carter met in the Honolulu teahouse was real. In Hawaii, he used the assumed name of Tadashi Morimura. His real name was Takeo Yoshikawa, and he was a Japanese spy sent to provide information on ship movements in Pearl Harbor to assist in the planning of the attack. One segment in Walter Cronkite's magnificent CBS Video Library of World War II features an interview with Yoshikawa, filmed in 1961, 20 years after the attack.

Juan Trippe, of course, was the legendary founder and CEO of Pan American Airways whose vision made that great airline America's ambassador to the world. Its demise in the 1990s was a tragedy to aviation enthusiasts and travelers alike.

Colonel William Donovan and other government officials who were brought into the story were also real men who had historic impacts of one sort or another on the America of the early 40s and throughout the war.

Admiral Wilhelm Canaris was real and a historic, heroic and tragic figure in his own right. His anti-Nazi and anti-Hitler feelings as described in this book were real and led ultimately to his being executed, at Hitler's orders, shortly before the end of the war by the ignoble means of being hanged with piano wire while naked. Hitler would not allow him to die as an officer. Canaris' World War I actions on the Dresden, his escape from Chile and return to Germany were also real, but Ernst von

Althorp is fictional.

Major General Hans Oster was also real and served as Canaris' faithful deputy and confidante throughout the war, until he, too, was hanged, naked and in disgrace, along with Canaris and the famous German theologian Dietrich Bonhöffer.

Military historians have long debated whether President Franklin D. Roosevelt had advance knowledge of Japanese plans to attack Pearl Harbor and allowed it to happen to jar the United States out of its isolationism and into the war. While we allowed that question into our story, we offer no opinions, nor do we draw any conclusions on this. It is simply beyond our level of knowledge or expertise.

On the USS Arizona, Admiral Isaac Campbell Kidd, Captain Franklin Van Valkenburgh, Lieutenant Commander Samuel Fuqua, Quartermaster 2nd Curt Haynes (no relation to the authors), Seaman 1st Adolphus Abercrombie (who was related, very distantly, to the authors), and Quartermaster 3rd Louis A. Conter (whom the authors met at the annual Pearl Harbor ceremony on December 7, 2010) were real and all but Fuqua and Conter went down with the ship. Their names appear on the wall of honor on the USS Arizona Memorial. Lt. Commander Fuqua, the damage control officer (and highest-ranking officer to survive), was awarded the Congressional Medal of Honor for his actions on December 7, as did Admiral Kidd and Captain Van Valkenburgh, posthumously. Commander Curt Vinson is fictional.

Navy Lieutenant Commander Alvin Kramer and Army Colonel Rufus Bratton were real and were tireless is their efforts to alert the powers that be to the threat of imminent attack by the Japanese. Their roles are accurately portrayed, we believe, in the classic Pearl Harbor movie, Tora! Tora! Tora!

Alex, Rudi, Wally Hammond, Henry Carter, Otto

Gerlach, Ilse Guderian and most of the other characters in this book are fictional but are portrayed, we hope, as people in their respective situations would have acted in the early years of the Second World War.

About the Authors

James Earl Haynes Jr. was born in Bakersfield, California at the height of World War II shortly after his father was shipped overseas with the U.S. Army prior to the invasion of Europe. The eldest of four siblings, he played baseball at Bakersfield College and Los Angeles State University, graduating with a degree in Journalism. Always an avid reader of history and adventure and a writer, he has written for the *Arizona Republic* as a columnist, and co-written several books. <u>A Desperate Journey</u> is his first book co-written with his son. He lives in Phoenix, Arizona, and is the grandfather of three.

Andrew Jordan Haynes was born in Fort Worth, Texas and raised in Phoenix, Arizona, where he graduated from Arizona State University with a degree in history and was a proud member of Kappa Alpha Order. An avid World War II historian, Andrew has traveled the world to see many of the locations mentioned in this book, and has been a member of numerous living history groups, in an effort to explore what the men and women experienced in the Second World War. He flies 747s as an international airline pilot. Married with three children, Andrew and his family split their time between Ettlingen, Germany and Fort Worth, Texas.